Dear reader,

This book is all about leaving behind your cage. In *Glint*, the world of Orea slowly starts opening up, and we see what's outside of Sixth Kingdom through Auren's eyes. And what better way to do that than with an enemy army?

Enter the notorious Commander Rip.

The tension between the commander and Auren was one of my favorite things to write. *Glint* is all about the tension, about facing truths, and about ruining long-standing beliefs.

Because, sometimes, things need first to be ruined in order to then be remade.

Happy reading!

GLINT

RAVEN KENNEDY

Bloom books

Sourcebooks and the colophon are registered trademarks of
Sourcebooks. Bloom Books is a trademark of Sourcebooks.

Published by Bloom Books, an imprint of Sourcebooks
P.O. Box 4410, Naperville, Illinois 60567-4410
(630) 961-3900
sourcebooks.com

Originally self-published in 2021 by Raven Kennedy.

Cataloging-in-Publication data is on file with the Library of Congress.

Printed and bound in the United States of America.
VP 10 9 8 7 6 5 4 3 2 1

ABOUT THE BOOK

THE MYTH OF
KING MIDAS REIMAGINED.

This compelling and dark adult fantasy series is as addictive as it is unexpected. With romance, fae, and intrigue, the gilded world of Orea will grip you from the very first page. Be immersed in this journey of greed, love, and finding inner strength.

Please Note: This series will contain explicit content and dark elements that may be triggering to some. It will include explicit romance, mature language, violence, nonconsensual sex, emotional manipulation and abuse, sex trafficking and on-page sexual assault, and other dark and potentially triggering content. It is not intended for anyone under 18 years of age. This is book two in a series.

Dedicated to those who see no bars but still feel caged.
Fly.

CHAPTER 1

QUEEN MALINA

old, as far as the eye can see.

Every inch of Highbell Castle carries the telltale shine. In the past decade, people have traveled far and wide across all of Orea just to look upon it. It is heralded for its magnificence, the people always impressed with its overwhelming splendor.

But I remember how it used to be. I remember the slate of the parapets and the iron doors of the gate. I remember when I had gowns in every color and the dishes on the tables were white to match the Colier hair. I remember when the bell in the tower was copper, its chime light and clear.

Things that were once feather-light now take several men to pick up. Parts that once carried the colors of age and history now glisten as if new. Even the roses in the atrium have been gold-touched, never again to sprout a new bud or fill the air with their perfume.

I grew up in Highbell Castle. I knew every rough rock and speckled stairway. I knew the dark grains of wood on the window frames. I can still recall the way my father's throne felt, melded together with stone and diamonds cut from the mountains to the east.

Sometimes, I wake in the middle of the night, trapped in the tangles of my golden sheets, and I can't tell where I am. I don't recognize this place at all, not anymore.

Most days, I don't even recognize myself.

The dignitaries who visit revel in the gloss and glamour. They stand awed by the precision of every surface's change and celebrate Midas's power.

But I miss the way Highbell used to look.

Every gray nook, every raw chair, even the ugly blue tapestries that used to hang in my old bedroom. It's surprising, the things you come to miss once they're stripped away from you.

I knew I was going to pine over the loss of control over Sixth Kingdom when I agreed to marry. I knew I'd mourn my father when he died. I even knew that I'd miss being addressed by my old name and title, Princess Malina Colier.

But I never anticipated that I'd feel the loss of the palace itself. It wasn't something I could've predicted would happen. Yet room by room, item by item, everything was changed before my eyes, down to each pillow and wine glass.

It was exciting at first, I can't deny that. A gold castle

in the frozen mountains was something out of a fairy tale, and I had a king to make me a queen. I had a marriage that would ensure I could stay here, in my home, to carry on my royal bloodline.

But here I sit, in my gilded drawing room, my naivety long since ripped away. I have no heirs, no family, no magic, no partnership with my husband, and no recognition of the very place I grew up in.

I'm surrounded by wealth that holds no value to me.

This castle, the place where my mother birthed me, where my father and grandfather ruled, where all of my fondest memories reside, has become foreign. It holds no comfort, no excitement, and certainly no fairy tale.

People are dazzled by it, whereas my eyes see every single scratch in the golden surfaces of the floors and walls. I notice every inch where the soft metal has worn down, distorting the shapes. I catch the corners where the servants haven't polished, I note each fragment that's gone dull.

Gold may gleam, but it doesn't stand the test of time. It wears down, loses its luster, becomes nothing but a needy, malleable surface with no durability.

I loathe it. Just as I've come to loathe *him*.

My renowned husband. The people fall to their knees for him instead of me. I might not have magic, but resentment is a powerful thing.

Tyndall will be sorry. For every time he pushed me aside, for always underestimating me, for taking away my kingdom.

I'll make him pay for all of it—just not with gold.

"Would you like me to sing for you, Your Majesty?"

My gaze cuts over to the courtier sitting across from me. He's young, probably only around twenty, pretty on the eyes and easy on the ears. Traits that *all* my courtiers have.

I loathe them as well.

They buzz like pests, consuming pretty dishes of food, taking up air with their mindless chatter. No matter how many times I try to swat them away, they always swarm around me again.

"Do you *want* to sing?" I retort, though it's honestly a moot point, because...

His smile broadens. "I want to do whatever will please my queen."

A fake answer from a fake companion.

That's all these courtiers are. Pretenders. Gossipers. Sent to my side to distract and entertain me. As if I'm a simpering, foolish female in need of mindless recreation all hours of the day.

But Tyndall is gone—swept off to Fifth Kingdom where the people will no doubt bow at the Golden King's feet. Midas will like that immensely, and that's just fine with me.

Because while he's there, I'm *here*. For the first time, I'm in Highbell without his flashy presence.

It's as if it's a sign from the great Divine. No husband to defer to. No king to bow to. No golden puppet at his side, greed incarnate, glossing over the ugliness of lies.

It's my chance.

With Tyndall away, distracted by putting Fifth Kingdom beneath his thumb, I have an opportunity, and I won't squander it.

I may not recognize the walls of this castle anymore, but it's still *mine*.

I still have the same ambition I did when I was a little girl, before it became clear that I have no magic, before my father gave me to Tyndall, blinded by the gleam of his gold.

The gold doesn't dazzle me, though. Not anymore.

Because my dream, my role, my *due*, it was always to rule Highbell.

No submitting to a husband, no being shoved aside or treated like a coddled pushover. Tyndall Midas has put his hands on everything, glazing over my entire life.

And I let him. My father let him. This whole damn kingdom let him.

But I'm done.

I'm done sitting in a cushioned chair, embroidering silly handkerchiefs, eating sickly sweet cakes while the courtiers talk about which dress so-and-so wore, simply because they like hearing the sound of their own voices.

I'm done being the silent cold queen frozen in place.

Tyndall is gone, and for the first time since I've become queen, I can actually *be* a queen.

And I intend to.

I've worn a crown my entire life, but I'm finally going to wield it.

CHAPTER 2

AUREN

T*he wooden wheels of the* carriage churn as much as my stomach.

Every rotation expels another memory to the forefront of my mind's eye, an endless cycle that keeps circling and unloading, like vultures dropping forgotten carrion from the sky.

Death clings to me.

I wanted so badly to leave my cage. To be able to roam freely in Midas's castle. My boredom and loneliness was a gaping yawn that I couldn't speak past, couldn't swallow down, couldn't close off. My mouth kept widening, tongue flat, chest open, wishing and hoping for that deep breath to come into my lungs and set me free from the growing suffocation of my bars.

But now…

There's blood on my hands, though no red stains my skin. But I feel it there, with every graze of my fingertip, like the truth is ingrained in the fortune lines across my palms.

My fault. Sail's death, Rissa's pain, Digby's absence, all of them my fault.

I flick my gaze toward the cloud-covered sky, though I don't really see the haze of white and gray. Instead, those relentless spinning memories keep falling behind my temples, landing at the backs of my eyes.

I see Digby riding off, his retreating form pressed between a sky of black and a ground of white. I see red flames crackling from the paws of the fire claws, the powder of snow flying up beneath the pirates' ships like waves in a frozen sea. I see Rissa crying, Captain Fane poised over her, a belt in hand.

But mostly, I see Sail. I see his heart being pricked with the blade of the captain's dagger like a finger on a spindle, his blood dripping out in threads of red, tied to the puddle on the ground.

I can still feel the scream that came out of me when his body slumped down, caught by my hands and the bitter arms of Death.

My throat is raw and sore, abused from the night that seemed to never end. First it wailed in shocked misery, and then it squeezed, closing out any hope of breath.

My throat clogged when the Red Raids strung up Sail's body to the mast at the front of the ship, making an evil mockery of his name, suspending him up on a sail-less ship.

I'll never forget the way his rigid body hung there, his unblinking blue eyes being pelted with wind and snow.

Just like I'll never forget the way I used every ounce of my strength to push his body overboard so the pirates couldn't continue to abuse and disrespect him.

My aching ribbons throb with the memory of slicing the ropes that held him, of dragging his cold corpse across coarse wooden planks.

He was the first friend I've had in ten years, and I only got to have him for such a short time before I had to watch him be brutally murdered right in front of me.

He didn't deserve his end. He didn't deserve an unmarked grave in the emptiness of the Barrens, his body entombed by an ocean of snow.

It's okay, it's okay, it's okay.

I squeeze my eyes shut, his voice echoing in my ears and piercing right through my heart. He tried to reassure me, tried to hold my spirit and courage up, but we both knew the truth. As soon as my carriage toppled over and the Red Raids captured us, it wasn't going to be okay.

He knew, but he still tried to defend me, to guard me, until his last breath.

A painful sob rips up my throat, snagging against the soreness like string caught on a hangnail. My golden eyes burn as another droplet of salt slips down my windblown cheek.

Maybe I'm being punished by the great Divine—the entity that makes up all of the gods and goddesses of this world. Maybe what's happened is a warning that I was overreaching, that I need to remember the terrors of the outside world.

I was safe. At the top of a frozen mountain, up in the highest point in a golden castle, I was safe inside my gilded cage. But I got restless. Greedy. Ungrateful.

This is what I get. This is my fault. For having those far-reaching thoughts, for wanting more than I already had.

I feel my wilted ribbons quiver, like they want to rise up and brush against my swollen cheek, like they want to offer me comfort.

But I deserve none. Sail won't get comfort from his mother ever again. Rissa won't get comfort in the arms of the men she's paid to bed. Midas won't have comfort with an army marching toward him.

Outside, the soldiers of Fourth Kingdom travel through the snow, a dark force moving across the empty landscape. They're a river of black leather and sleek obsidian horses, cutting across the land of perpetual cold.

I can see why all of Orea fears the army of King Ravinger—of King Rot. His magic aside, these soldiers, even without being clad in their battle armor, are an intimidating sight.

But none so much as the commander leading them.

From time to time, I glimpse him riding his horse outside, the line of vicious spikes along his spine curving down like cruel frowns. Black eyes like bottomless pits, waiting to ensnare anyone who looks into them.

Fae.

A full-blooded fae right here. Not in hiding, but leading an army for a cruel king.

Our earlier conversation replays in my head, making my palms go clammy, making my hands shake.

I know what you are.

Funny, I was about to say the same thing to you.

My mind stuttered when he said those words, mouth opening like a gaping fish. He merely smirked, flashing a glimpse of his wicked fangs, before jerking his head to this carriage and locking me inside.

But I'm used to being locked away.

I've been in here for hours now. Worrying, thinking, letting tears and ragged breaths fill the space, letting my mind catch up on everything that's happened.

Mostly, I've just allowed myself to react while no one's here to see.

I know better than to show weakness to the soldiers outside, especially the commander.

So I let myself feel it all now behind the privacy of the wooden walls, let my emotions roil, let the anxious "what nows" run through my head.

Because once the carriage stops for the night, I know I can't afford to let any of this vulnerability out for anyone to see.

So I sit.

I sit and I look out the window, my mind spinning, body aching, tears falling, all while I gently pull out the knots on my poor abused ribbons.

The gold satiny strands that grow from the sides of my spine feel broken. They ache and sting from where Captain Fane tied them in brutal tangles. Every touch makes them flinch and has me grinding my teeth.

It takes me hours of sweating and shaking in grimacing pain, but I manage to get the knots undone.

"Finally," I mutter as I set the last one down.

I roll my shoulders back, the skin along the length of my spine twinging where each ribbon is attached, twelve on each side, from between my shoulder blades to just above the curve of my bottom.

I spread all twenty-four strands out as much as I can in this cramped space, smoothing them with a soft touch, hoping it will help ease the hurt running through them.

They look wrinkled and limp where they lie on the carriage floor and bench. Even their golden color is slightly muted from their usual luster, like tarnished gold in need of polishing.

I let out a shaky sigh, my fingers sore from how long it's taken me to tug out every knot. My ribbons have never hurt so badly before. I'm so used to hiding them, to keeping them a secret, that I've never used them like I did on that pirate ship, and it's obvious.

While I let my ribbons rest, I use the last shards of the gray daylight to check over the rest of my body. My shoulder and head hurt from my carriage toppling over and from being dragged out of it when the Red Raids captured me.

I also have a small split on my bottom lip, but I barely notice it. The sharper pains come from my cheek where Captain Fane struck me, and my side where he kicked me in the ribs. I don't think anything is broken, but each movement has me sucking in a breath through clenched teeth.

A gnawing in my stomach reminds me that it's hollow and angry, while my mouth is dry with thirst. But my most demanding feeling is how incredibly depleted I am.

Exhaustion is a chain locked around my ankles, cuffed over my wrists, draped around my shoulders. My strength and energy are gone, like someone pulled a plug from my back and let it all drain out.

Bright side? At least I'm alive. At least I got away from the Red Raids. I won't be subjected to whatever Quarter wanted to do with me once he discovered his captain was missing. Quarter isn't the kind of man you want for a captor.

Although my new *escorts* are far from ideal, at least I'm heading toward Midas, even if I don't know what will happen once we get there.

Glancing out the carriage window, I watch dark

hooves mottle the snow, their riders sitting proud on their saddles as they march on.

I have to be strong now.

I'm the captive of Fourth's army, and there will be no room for fragility. I don't know if the bones in my body are as gold as the rest of me, but for my sake, I hope they are. I hope my spine is gilded, because I'm going to need a strong backbone if I want to survive.

Closing my eyes, I reach up and press my fingertips against my lids, trying to rub away the sting. Though as tired as I am, I don't sleep. I don't relax. I can't. Not with the enemy marching outside and those terrible memories hovering over my head.

Was it really just yesterday morning that Sail was alive? That Digby was barking out gruff orders to his men? It seems like weeks, months, years ago.

Time changes with torment. It stretches on, lengthening seconds, extending minutes. I've learned that pain and fear have a way of prolonging. And as if that weren't cruel enough, our minds make sure we relive those moments again and again and again, long after they've passed.

What a bastard, time is.

I know that I've left a part of me behind on that pirate ship. I've been through enough tragic moments to recognize the feeling of rawness left to ache.

Every heartbreak I've endured in my life, every harrowing pain, it's ripped a part of me away. I've felt every piece of myself that's been torn off, seen each bit where it fell behind me in the path of my past like breadcrumbs, only to be snapped up by vicious birds of prey.

In Highbell, people sometimes traveled for weeks just to look at me. Midas would let me stand beside him in the throne room as they gawked.

But no matter how long I stood there on the pedestal for them to look, no one really *saw* me. If they did, they'd know I'm just a girl with jagged rips and pitted holes inside of her, with golden skin hiding a broken heart.

My eyes burn, telling me that I'd be crying again if I had any tears left to fall, but I guess that's drained out of me too.

I have no idea where the other saddles or guards are, and I have no idea what the commander intends to do with me, but I'm not a fool. King Rot sent the might of his army to Fifth Kingdom to confront Midas, and I fear for my king as much as I fear for myself.

I shiver when the last sliver of sunlight finally drops down to be tucked beneath the blanket of the horizon. Day has officially ended, and with it, I force myself to lock away my emotions.

Now that dusk is turning into the promise of night, the carriage comes to a lurching halt. When you're on this side of the world of Orea, night descends swiftly and brutally, so it's no surprise that Fourth's army begins to make camp.

I'm left inside the motionless carriage while I listen to the sounds of the soldiers. Horses on either side block me from being able to see much out the windows, shadowed figures moving swiftly to do one job or another.

After nearly a half hour of waiting, I'm squirming, the need to relieve myself urgent. My body is pitching a fit, my thirst and hunger refusing to be ignored, exhaustion lapping at my limbs like a turmoiled sea that wants to drag me underwater.

I just want to sleep. Fall asleep and not wake up until everything stops hurting—physically and emotionally.

Not yet, I remind myself. I can't rest yet.

I pinch myself on the arm, forcing my senses to stay alert, my ears trying to filter through the many sounds outside as the last of the light dims, the press of night draping over me like a chilled blanket.

Resting my head back against the carriage wall, I close my eyes for a moment. Just a moment, I tell myself. Just to relieve the fire burning in my swollen eyes, just to help ease my many aches.

Just for a moment...

I lurch, my eyes springing open at the sound of a key shoved into a lock.

The carriage door suddenly swings open as swiftly as the gasp of my breath, and then there he is, standing menacingly under the cover of dark, a pair of cavernous eyes staring me down.

Commander Rip.

CHAPTER 3

AUREN

I *hold my breath, watching* the commander without blinking, my body tense and alert. In this moment, I'm going to find out what it truly means to be his prisoner.

My mind whirls. Endless possibilities flit through my thoughts one after another as I attempt to brace myself.

Will he snatch me by my hair and drag me out? Will he threaten me, manhandle me? Will he force me to strip so he can see the gilt on every inch of my skin? Will he pass me around to his soldiers? Will I be forced to wear chains?

I don't dare let my thoughts show on my face. I can't give any indication of the what-ifs pounding against my skull.

All the grief, all the worry, I wrap it up like old yarn

on a spool, tucking away every frayed strand. Because if I show him my fear, if I reveal my weaknesses to this male, he'll latch onto those threads and yank them all, unraveling me completely.

Shove down weakness, and strength will rise...

Those old, nearly forgotten words float up from out of nowhere, as if my mind saved them for me, ready to pluck them out when I needed them most.

I remember suddenly how that was hummed against my ear, spoken softly, but carrying an edge of steel.

They echo through me now, and it helps me to pull my shoulders back, helps me to tip my chin up to face the commander head-on.

He has a helmet tucked beneath his arm and his black hair is slightly rumpled from the long hours of wearing it. I take in his pale face, the short and blunted row of tiny spikes above each dark eyebrow. His pressing aura saturates the air, coating my tongue like icing sugar, clogging every taste bud.

It tastes like power.

I wonder how people would react if they knew what he truly was. Not a man with residual magic running in his veins from distant fae ancestors. Not someone whose body was corrupted and morphed by King Rot. Not just an army commander with a bloodthirsty rage who enjoys ripping the heads off his enemies.

No, he's something deadlier. More fearful. A full-blooded fae, hiding in plain sight.

If they knew the truth, would they run in fear? Or

would they rise up against him like Oreans did hundreds of years ago, killing him, like they killed all the rest?

Some fae fought back during that dark time, but they were outnumbered, and even with their superior magic, it wasn't enough. For some fae, they simply didn't *want* to fight. They didn't want to kill the people who they considered friends, lovers, family.

But one look at him, and I know that Commander Rip would fight. He would fight, and Orea would lose.

It may have been hundreds of years since Orea and Annwyn—the realm of the fae—were cleaved apart, but even still, I'm shocked that no one knows, that no one *sees* what he truly is, when it's so incredibly obvious to me.

Based on the intensity of Rip's gaze, I know that I'm not the only one whose mind is turning as we study each other in silence, judging, analyzing, considering.

Curiosity tumbles through me like a windswept plant with no roots. I wonder how Commander Rip got here, what his purpose is. Is he simply King Ravinger's hired guard dog, put out on a leash to snap and snarl at enemies? Or does he have another agenda?

He assesses every inch of me while I sit, trapped in the confines of the carriage, and I can see him mentally taking notes. It takes everything in me not to fidget, not to cringe beneath his stare.

His eyes catch on my swollen cheek and split lip before dropping down to my crumpled ribbons sprawled throughout the space. I don't like his interest in them. Every time he looks at them, I want to hide them away. I would've wrapped them around my torso to keep them out of sight if they weren't so sore.

When he's finally done with his appraisal, he lifts his black eyes to look into mine. I tense, waiting for him to haul me out, bark orders, or issue threats, but he just continues to look at me, as if he's waiting for something.

If he wants me to break or cry or plead, I refuse. I won't fold under the pressure of his scrutiny or shatter beneath his piercing silence. I'll sit here all damned night if I have to.

Unfortunately, my stomach doesn't seem to have the same stubborn will as I do, because right then, it lets out an obnoxiously loud growl.

The commander's eyes narrow at the sound, as if it personally offends him. "You're hungry."

If I wasn't so terrified, I'd roll my eyes. "Of course I'm hungry. I've been in this carriage all day, and it's not as if the Red Raids gave us a lavish meal after they captured us."

If the disrespect in my tone surprises him, he doesn't show it.

"Goldfinch has some bite to her beak," he murmurs, his eyes flicking over the feathers on my coat's sleeve.

I bristle at the nickname, my jaw going tight.

There's something about him. Or maybe it's something about *me* after the hell I've faced. Whatever the reason, be it circumstances or a clash of natures, anger begins to dominate my emotions. I try to clamp down on the response like a spring in a mouse trap, but it doesn't want to settle.

I should stay impassive, untouchable. I need to be a stone in the middle of his rushing current. I'm in the thick of it now, more vulnerable than ever, and I can't afford to get swept away.

The commander tips his head. "You'll stay in the tent right there," he says, his hand motioning to his left. "Food and water will be brought to you. The latrine is at the outskirts of the camp to the west."

I wait for more instructions, or threats, or violence, but none come. "That's it?" I ask with distrust.

He cocks his head, the move so very fae-like, and I catch a glimpse of the highest spike between his shoulder blades. "What were you expecting?"

I narrow my eyes. "You're the most feared army commander in all of Orea. I don't expect you to behave any other way but to reflect your reputation."

As soon as the words are out of my mouth, he leans in, arms braced against the frame of the carriage, the wicked spikes along his forearms on display. The faint gray iridescent scales along his cheekbones glint like the flash of a silver blade, a warning all its own.

The breath I was inhaling stops in its tracks, sticking in my chest like syrup, clogging my throat.

"Since you seem to already know the character of

the person whose custody you're in, I won't waste your time on explaining anything to you," Rip says, his voice low, a chilling edge slicing the tip of each word. "You seem to be an intelligent female, so I shouldn't need to tell you that you can't leave. You'd freeze to death out here on your own, and I'd find you anyway."

My heart gallops in my chest, his promise teetering on a threat.

I'd find you.

Not *his soldiers* would find me, but him personally. I have no doubt he'd search all over the Barrens and hunt me down if I tried to get away. He really would find me, too. That's just the kind of luck I have.

"King Midas will kill you for taking me," I say in response, even though my entire body wants to cringe back from his nearness, from his overwhelming presence that fills up the interior of the carriage.

The corner of his mouth curves as much as his bowing spikes. "I look forward to the attempt."

His arrogance turns my stomach, but the problem is, I know his cockiness is warranted. Even without the powerful, ancient fae magic I can sense in him, he's a warrior through and through. With muscles boasting of strength and a demeanor that confesses his deadliness, he's not someone I want anywhere near Midas. Some of my thoughts must slip through the cracks of my stoicism, because he straightens up, expression melting into condescension. "Ah, I see now."

"See what?"

"You *care* for your King Captor." He practically spits the words, accusation as sharp as his fangs.

I blink at him, at the hatred dripping off his lips like a slow, cold rain. If I confirm it, what will he do to use it against me? If I deny it, would he believe me?

He makes a derisive noise at the look on my face. "The goldfinch likes her cage. What a shame."

My hands curl in anger. I don't need his judgment, his scorn, his complete assumption that he knows me and my circumstances or has any right to criticize my relationship with Midas. "You don't know me."

"Don't I?" he fires back, his voice grating against my ears. "Everyone in Orea knows about Midas's favored as much as they know about his golden touch."

My eyes flash. "Just as everyone knows about King Rot sending out his leashed monster to do his dirty work," I say, giving the spikes on his forearm a pointed look.

A dark reverberation in the air around him coils, making the hairs on the back of my neck rise. "Oh, Goldfinch. You think I'm a monster now, but you haven't seen *anything* yet."

The implied threat sweeps in like an arid wind, making my mouth go dry.

I need to be very careful with this male. I need to avoid him at all costs, skirt around his viciousness, and try to come out unscathed. But I can't plan ahead if I don't know what to expect.

"What are you going to do with me?" I ask, risking the vulnerable question in hopes it will give me a hint of what's to come.

A dark, threatening smile forms on his lips. "Didn't I tell you? I'm bringing you back to the captor you miss so much. What a reunion *that* will be."

Without another word, the commander turns on his heel and leaves me there to stare after him, my pulse pounding in tune with his footsteps.

I'm not sure what he has planned for my king, but I know it's nothing good. Midas is expecting his saddles and his favored to arrive, not an enemy army marching up to his doorstep.

Forcing myself to get out of the carriage, my ribbons dragging behind me in the snow, a knowing resignation fills me. I know what I have to do. I need to figure out a way to warn my king.

I just hope it doesn't cost me my life.

CHAPTER 4

AUREN

You'd think that after weeks of traveling, I'd be used to using a latrine dug in the ground to relieve myself. But nope. There's something about having to lift your skirts and squat in the snow that really drags a girl down.

I do my business as quickly as I can. Bright side, I manage to do it without splashing on my own boots or falling ass-first into the snow. It's all about the small victories right now.

Luckily, I get done before anyone else walks up to use the latrine, so I don't have to worry about being watched. Scooping up some powdery snow, I use it to rinse my hands before I straighten and run my palms over my wrinkled skirts.

Now that my most pressing need is out of the way, I

cross my arms around myself to ward off the chill that's easily cutting through my wool dress and the pirate captain's feather coat.

I take a moment to look around and get my bearings, but all I can see is the same landscape more or less that I've seen for days. Snow and ice and nothing.

The flat expanse of the Barrens seems to go on forever, the dark outline of the mountains far in the distance, the gentle sloping snow drifts never ending.

Commander Rip is right. I could run right now, and maybe I could even evade him and his soldiers for a while, but then what? I have no provisions of my own, no shelter, no true sense of direction. I would freeze to death out there.

Still, the empty horizon taunts me, a bitter temptress that mocks me with her open freedom. It's a lie, one that would wrap me in its freeze and shatter my brittle body like ice.

With a hardened jaw, I turn and walk away, heading back into camp. The soldiers made quick work of setting it up. It's nothing fancy, just crude leather tents speckled every few feet and campfires peppered throughout, but even so, this army doesn't seem to shirk from the cold, doesn't seem to be breaking down from the harsh elements.

As I breach the first of the tents, I glance around warily, keeping a look out for the commander or any of his soldiers who might slink out of the shadows and try to hurt me or force me into my tent.

But no one comes.

I don't trust this fake freedom, not for a second.

Completely on my own, I wander the grounds, my eyes peeled. I don't see any of the saddles or Midas's guards, but the sheer numbers in this army make it hard to spot much of anything.

Even though I'm tired and aching, I force myself to push past it for a little while longer, to take advantage of this time alone while I have it, because I might not get this opportunity again.

Back on the pirate ship, a messenger hawk was sent to Captain Fane, alerting him of Commander Rip's impending arrival. Which means that the commander has at least one hawk, if not more. I need to find them.

As I skirt tents and groups of soldiers eating around their fires, I stay quiet, keeping my head down but my eyes up, searching and watching, my ribbons dragging in the snow behind me, leaving feather-light tracks in my wake.

The scent of food makes my angry stomach pitch a petulant fit, but I can't succumb to my hunger or my dragging body. *Not yet.*

I don't think messenger hawks would be kept in a tent, so I ignore those. If I had to guess, I'd say the animals are being transported in covered carts, so that's what I look for, though I try to seem like I'm just walking around aimlessly. It's not difficult, considering I am aimless, unsure where to go.

The sounds of the army surround me. Soldiers

talking, campfires burning, horses whinnying. Every gruff laugh or cracking spark from the wet logs makes me jump, my entire body anticipating someone grabbing me at any moment.

Soldiers watch me as I go. My body stays tense, but aside from their distrustful eyes following me, no one approaches me. It's disconcerting, unexpected, and I don't know what to think of it.

What is Commander Rip's game?

Finally, when my boots are soaked from trudging through the slush and I'm shivering with cold, I spot several wooden carts covered in leather tarps across the way, on the outskirts of the camp.

My stomach leaps, and I get a sense of urgency, but I don't dare head straight for them. I don't dare rush.

Instead, I circle around, forcing my shaky steps to go unhurried, making sure to keep my face timid, my eyes desultory.

After being as careful as I can possibly be, I make it to the carts, the full dark of night helping to hide me in the shadows.

There's a campfire thirty feet away, but only four men are sitting there, and they're in deep discussion about something, though I can't hear what they're saying.

I carefully walk down the line of carts, peeking beneath tarps as I go, trying to be quick because I don't want to be caught.

The first four carts aren't covered, and they're empty

and smelling of leather, probably where the tents were stored. The next several are filled with bales of hay and barrels of oats for the horses, and after that, I come upon cart after cart of provisions for the soldiers. I'm running out of hope.

When I get to the last one, I see the square shape of some kind of crates—*animal crates?*

I duck behind it, praying to the great Divines that this is it. With a deep breath, I glance around before flipping the tarp back to check it, but as soon as I do, my hope drops straight through my sodden boots. Not crates. Just a cart full of tightly folded furs.

I stare at it in defeat, though I try to keep my emotions in check. I know I'm exhausted and emotionally bombarded, but this failure makes my shoulders slump and my eyes prick with panic.

Where the Divine hell are they? If I can't warn Midas…

"You lost?"

I jerk at the voice, my hand dropping the tarp as I whirl around. I look up and up and *up*, finding a bear of a man towering over me.

I recognize him immediately, based on the mass of his body alone. Back on the pirate ship, Rip was flanked by two soldiers, and even though they had their helmets on at the time, I just *know* that this huge man was one of them, that he led Rissa and me off the ship.

Now, without his armor or his helmet, I see his

round face, bottom lip pierced through with a short, twisted piece of wood resembling the sigil of Fourth Kingdom's gnarled tree. He has brown leather straps wrapped around his thick biceps and black leather covering the rest of him.

Somehow, he seems even larger than before—a good three heads taller than me, legs as thick as tree trunks and fists as big as my face.

Great. I had to be discovered by *this* big bastard?

Honestly, I don't know what I did to piss off the goddesses so much.

I tilt my chin up at the brown-haired brute, suddenly very glad that I visited the latrine, because he's scary enough to make someone pee their frozen pants.

I clear my throat. "No."

He lifts a bushy brow, brown eyes filled with a scowling suspicion, long hair hanging around his face and flattened at the top from its time in a helmet. "No? Then what are you doing over here, so far away from your tent?"

He knows where my tent is? That's disturbing...

I turn and snatch a fur from the cart behind me, draping it over my shoulders. "I was cold."

He gives me a look that tells me he doesn't believe a single word out of my mouth. "Cold? Then maybe Midas's golden pet should have gone *to her tent*."

I tug the sleek black fur tighter around my shoulders. I've known men like this, they're nothing but bullies. The worst thing to do is to let him walk all over me and make myself an even easier target.

I raise my chin. "Am I not allowed to walk around? Am I going to be forced in there against my will?" I challenge, because it's what I expect, and I want to beat him to the chase.

The scowl on his face deepens, and my heart pounds in my chest like it wants to get out and go hide. I don't really blame it. If this man wanted to, he could take my neck between his meaty hands and snap it in half.

Instead, he crosses his arms in front of him, his intimidating posture bearing down on me. "Rumor is, that's exactly the way you like it, *pet*."

Anger surges through me. That's the second time tonight I've been looked at so scathingly, judged for the cage I live in.

"Better to be safe with the Golden King than to serve in the army of your rotten monarch who's nothing but a scourge to the land," I spit.

As soon as my words hit his ears, he goes preternaturally still.

I know I've made a mistake. I've way overstepped. I let him get to me, and I allowed my mouth to run away with my anger and fear instead of being that unmovable stone I need to be.

I went from standing up to a bully to bullying him back. Considering his heft, that probably wasn't the smartest move.

I wasn't paying attention to the murmuring voices at the campfire, but I do when I hear the soldiers go quiet. There's a tinge of tense excitement in the air, as if they can't wait to see what he'll do to me.

My heart gallops with the need to flee, trapped in the thrumming of my pulse.

With deadly enmity, the man leans down until his face is just an inch from mine. Furious eyes glare bright, burning up any hope of air for me to breathe.

His voice goes as low as a warning growl from a wolf, and it makes my blood run cold. "Insult my king again, and I don't care what color your fucking skin is, I'll whip the flesh from your back until an apology sobs out of your throat."

I swallow hard.

He means every word. Of that, I have no doubt, because I can see it in his face. He'll toss me down in the snow, right here and make pain my only reality.

He nods as he looks me in the eyes. "Good. I can see you're taking things more seriously now." He's still standing entirely too close, still stealing all my space, my air, an invisible bubble bursting with his invasive presence. "You're not with that gilt prick Midas anymore. You're here now, with us, so if I were you, I'd be respectful, and I'd make myself *very* useful."

My eyes widen at the dark things his words imply, but he cuts off my train of thought.

"Not *that*. None of us are interested in having

Midas's gold-plated leftovers," he sneers, and I immediately exhale in relief. But I shouldn't. "You want to make your life easier? Then be the caged bird that you are and *sing*."

Comprehension dawns on me like a jaundiced sun. "You think I'll give you information? You think I'll betray my king?"

He lifts a shoulder. "If you're smart."

Loathing hammers inside of me in a fierce melody. Whatever he sees in my eyes makes the cruel giant lean away, straightening up to his full height with a sigh. "Hmm. Maybe not. What a shame."

My hands curl into fists. "I will *never* betray King Midas to you."

A wicked grin splits his mouth. "We'll see."

The hammering melody skips, thumps, crashes into my gut. I don't know whether I should be more offended that he thinks I'm so weak, or fearful that I'll turn out to be.

"Where are the other saddles?" I ask suddenly, wanting to take the reins of the conversation and steer it in my favor. "The other guards?"

He says nothing, arrogance rising off him like steam.

I dig in my heels. "If any of you hurt them—"

He lifts his palm up to cut me off, and I notice an old scar there, a straight slice cut all the way across. "Careful, there," he growls. "Fourth's soldiers don't take kindly to threats."

My eyes dart to the left. Still sitting around the camp-fire, still quietly watching, the other soldiers within ear-shot are staring right at me, forearms leaned over knees, knuckles cracking, eyes glaring. Hatred glows over their faces alongside the orange flickering flames.

Whatever I was about to say on behalf of my travel-ing party dies beneath the smoking threat. Maybe this is the game. Maybe Commander Rip left me to wander on my own so that his soldiers would punish me however they wanted.

The man in front of me makes a noise of amusement, and I tear my eyes away from the others. "Run along now. Your tent is back that way. I assume Midas's pet knows how to find her kennel?"

I give him a scathing look as the man turns and stomps away, settling his body at the campfire, joining the glaring men.

Holding the fur close to my chest, I turn away, feel-ing their sharp gazes on my back like the edge of a blade scratching down my spine. I walk away as quickly as I can without running, their mocking laughter tossed at my retreating form, making my cheeks burn.

I stick to the paths of footsteps that have made crude tracks in the snow, trying to keep my boots from sink-ing into the thicker patches as I take a more direct route to where my carriage and tent—my apparent *kennel*—is located.

It could be my imagination, but every soldier I pass

by eyes me with a gaze that feels heavier, more malignant. Without a word spoken to me, with only their exuding energy as a declaration, I'm put in my place.

I'm the enemy, one they expect will break. I may not have a guard at my heels, but they're watching me. Ready to pounce. And still, none of them do.

I ignore them all, not looking at anyone, not faltering when their conversations immediately die down upon my passing. I keep my eyes forward as I walk, though my entire body is trembling, my skin tight, heart galloping.

I don't care what they think, I won't betray Midas. I *won't.*

With every step in my cold, wet boots, I inwardly curse myself. I didn't find where the messenger hawks are kept, and I was obvious enough to warrant that soldier approaching me. If I'm going to survive Fourth Kingdom's army, I need to be better, smarter, stealthier.

And stronger. I need to be strong in the days to come.

Determined anger rises up in my chest, making me fist my hands inside the pockets of my coat. Tomorrow. I'll try again tomorrow. And the next day. And the day after that. And the day after *that*.

I won't give up until I've searched every inch of this damned army and found a way to warn Midas. And through it all, I won't break. I won't give them anything they could use against my king.

The commander thinks so little of me that he doesn't

even keep a guard on me, so I'll repay him tenfold. I'll use his cockiness to tear away their element of surprise, and I'll do it with a smile on my golden lips.

They think I'll buckle, but they'll soon realize I'm not that kind of saddle.

CHAPTER 5

AUREN

I get lost on my way back trying to find my tent. At one point, I take a wrong turn and walk in a circle, passing by the same set of soldiers twice. They chuckle, sharing knowing looks, but not one of them offers to point me in the right direction, and I refuse to ask. They wouldn't help me even if I did.

By the time I spot the black carriage I rode in all day, I sigh in relief, my teeth chattering, face cold despite the hood pulled over my head.

Heading to the carriage, I note that the tent Commander Rip told me to use is much farther off than the rest of the camp's set up. Instead of clumped together with the others, it's set off on the outskirts.

I pause in front of it, looking around. The nearest tent to mine is several yards away. It seems like it would be a good thing, more privacy allowed, but dread shifts through me.

There can only be one reason why my tent is so far away. It offers more chances for someone to sneak in, for them to hurt me without anyone hearing or seeing a thing. Easier for everyone to turn a blind eye and claim obliviousness.

With a lump forming in my throat, I step forward, only to frown down at the ground. Someone has shoveled a path straight to the tent flaps, clearing the way so my boots don't sink into the deep snow.

I look around again, but no one is watching me. The nearest campfire is a good distance away, the soldiers bathed in shadow, not looking at me.

Why would someone shovel a path to make it easier for a prisoner to go to her jail? A quick glance around shows that the other tents don't have the same treatment, trails made through the thick snow only by their booted steps.

Unable to shake off my uneasiness, I turn back to the tent and duck beneath the black leather flaps. Inside, I'm immediately greeted by a soft glow and a blanket of warmth that has my shaking body sagging in relief.

Kicking my boots off at the entry, I brush away as much of the snow as I can before straightening up and looking around.

The lantern is sitting on an upturned bucket next to me, but the delicious warmth and more of the glowing light is coming from a carefully arranged pile of smoldering coals in the middle of the floor. Circled with blackened stones, they give off enough warmth to make me whimper.

There's a pile of sleek black furs in one corner and a pallet making up a bed on the other. Just as the commander promised, there's a wooden tray with my dinner waiting for me, and there's even a pitcher of water next to a bowl, a tiny square of soap, and a cleaning cloth.

I check the tent flaps, but there's no way to secure it. Honestly, what would a leather tie do anyway? If someone wants to come in here, they will.

I bite my lip, considering, but I can't just stand here too afraid to move. So I pull off the fur from around my shoulders and set it on the ground, though there's already furs laid out on the floor, keeping the snow at bay. I sit down on it, my feet curling beneath me as I tug the tray onto my lap.

There's a hunk of bread and a piece of salted meat, plus a bowl of some kind of broth. Even though it's a modest soldier's ration, my mouth waters and my stomach growls as if it's the most delicious meal I've ever laid eyes on.

I immediately devour it, eating every bit and sucking down the lukewarm broth without coming up for air. The food hits my empty stomach, appeasing its angry hunger, and I feel instantly better.

When it's all gone, I lick my fingers and lips, wishing

I had more but knowing I'm lucky to have gotten this much. Everyone in this regime will be rationing as they march, and I doubt they'll look kindly on their prisoner asking for more food.

I gulp down the pouch of ice-cold drinking water, no doubt collected from melted snowfall. I don't care that it's cold enough to make my teeth ache, it eases my cloying thirst in an instant.

Now that I'm fed and watered, the tempting furs are calling to me, but I know I need to wash first. Maybe it's only in my head, but I swear I can still smell Captain Fane, and I want to scrub my skin clean of him, as if I can rinse away the memory of his hands on me, of my time with him on the ship.

It probably doesn't help that I'm wearing the coat I stole from his room, but I can't abandon it. It's not like I have anything else to wear, and I gave Polly my other coat.

Careful not to bend the brown feathers out of place, I lay the coat on the floor and then quickly strip out of my heavy wool gown. Getting undressed without the help of my ribbons almost feels like I'm short a limb...or twenty-four.

I let my gown pool at my feet before lifting my legs up and peeling off my thick stockings. Left in only my golden chemise, I shiver despite the heat coming off the simmering coals. I need to be quick, because I don't trust this privacy, not for a second. I quickly strip the rest of the way, hands trembling in both cold and anxiety.

Naked, I'm able to see my injuries for the first time. Just like I assumed, there's a large bruise marked over my ribs where Captain Fane kicked me.

I brush my fingers over the tarnished spot, and even that slight touch makes me hiss in pain. It looks worse than I imagined, my entire left side black and mottled, like soot rubbed into the glint of my skin.

Dropping my hand away, I walk over to the pitcher and pour out the water into the shallow bowl. I dip the cloth into it, braced for icy water to wash with, but I'm pleasantly surprised that the coals have made it almost lukewarm.

All these furs, this private tent, steaming coals, food rations, water that's not frozen, no guards trailing me, no chains to bind me... It seems like a bribe, some kind of play that the commander has planned.

That male doesn't do anything that isn't calculated. Maybe he's giving me a false sense of security, tricking me into relaxing, softening me up, but I won't fall for it. I will take advantage of it, though.

With a frown on my face, I quickly dampen my skin, stroking soapy water all over my body and then wiping down every inch of myself, including my ribbons.

I swipe the cloth over my arm, only to pause when I see a streak of red stained into the cloth. I stare at it, knowing it's blood, knowing that it's Sail's.

I don't know why I'm so shocked to see it. Even

though I washed up on the ship, there was bound to still be some blood on me. I caught him as he was dying, held him as he took his last breath.

Seeing it makes my eyes water. This is the last of him. The only thing I have. It may seem strange, but it's his *life*. And I just washed it away, erasing him completely.

A sob shakes my lip, forcing me to tuck it between my teeth and hold it there. He's gone. I'll never see that smile in his blue eyes again, but I'll always hear the last *it's okay* on his lips.

My fault.

I wash the rest of my body in a haze of grief, vision clouded over like I'm walking through mist. I wish I knew where Digby was. It was easier to sleep knowing he was near, watching over me.

I feel so alone.

I finish up with my body, but I don't attempt to wash my hair. Tackling the long golden strands and their countless tangles without the help of my ribbons is too daunting in my current state. Tomorrow. I'll deal with that mess tomorrow.

By the time I dry myself off, my skin has pebbled from my calves to my chest, and I'm standing as close to the coals as I can without getting burned.

I bend down to pick up my chemise, but at that exact moment, the tent flap opens.

A burst of cold air flies in, provoking the chills

already covering my body, but I freeze in an entirely different way, for an entirely different reason as Commander Rip steps inside.

CHAPTER 6

AUREN

I shouldn't be startled by his sudden presence, but fear locks my knees and traps the breath in my throat, and for a second, I can't move.

The commander stops short upon his entry, his black eyes widening when he sees my nakedness.

My momentary shock-stillness snaps, and I yank up the chemise to hold it in front of me. "What do you want?" I demand with a shrill voice, but I know. Of course I know, because it's what all men want, and why should he be any different just because he's fae?

The commander's eyes snap up to my face, irritation showing with a tic in his jaw that makes the muscle jump. Without saying a word, he turns and walks out, the curved spike between his shoulder blades nearly catching on the flap as he goes.

I stand there in shock, gaping at the place he just was, emotions filtering in one after the other like scents in a garden. I'm embarrassed, baffled, angry, and vulnerable. Entirely too vulnerable.

Why did he just walk out?

With trembling fingers, I quickly snap into action, pulling the chemise on over my head. He left, but he could be back.

I hear footsteps outside, and I curse as I yank up the dropped fur and clutch it against my chest. Even with my chemise on, I feel naked, terror coursing through me as I look around for a weapon.

"Coming in."

I frown at the voice, because I know for certain that it's *not* the commander. It's too high-pitched, too...friendly.

A man I don't recognize steps inside, instantly straightening up as soon as the flap drops behind him. The first thing I notice about him is how slight he is.

The second thing I notice is that the left side of his face looks deformed, as if it were burned many years ago, healing badly with creases of skin and marks of ruin. He has no eyebrow on that side, his eyelid droops, and the corner of his lips doesn't quite split correctly.

He's probably in his forties, with thin brown hair and olive skin, and instead of the leathers that all the soldiers wear, he has on a thick black coat that goes all the way down to his knees, secured by a belt at his waist.

"I am Hojat," he says, voice thick with a south Orean accent that I haven't heard in years. "I am here to see you."

My eyebrows pull together, mind leaping as the man watches me. The commander catches a glimpse of me naked, and now he's sending in his men to have a peek too?

My face hardens, fingers tightening on my fur, my throat clamping with a readied scream. "Get out."

Hojat blinks, head rearing back at the vitriol sparking from my tongue. "Pardon? The commander gave me leave to have a look at you."

Terrified fury makes my body go rigid. "Did he? Well *I* don't give you leave to *look at me*, no matter what the commander said. So you can turn around and leave. Now."

Hojat blinks. "But I... No. My lady, I am a *mender*."

Now it's my turn to look confused. My eyes sweep over him again, noticing for the first time that he's carrying a satchel and has red bands stitched on both of his sleeves around his biceps. The customary mark of an Orean army healer.

"Oh," I say, anger immediately deflating. "I'm sorry. I thought... Never mind. Why did the commander send you?"

He nods at my split lip and what I can only imagine is a very bruised cheek. "I think I can see why, my lady."

I'm surprised at the formality he's using. I would've

expected an army's healer to be gruffer, especially given which army he serves.

"I'm fine. It'll heal."

He doesn't let my dismissive tone faze him. "All the same, I still need to look you over."

My lips press together. "Let me guess. Because the commander ordered it."

One side of his mouth tips up in a smile, the scarred side left behind. "You catch on quick, my lady."

"It's mostly just aches and pains, and you can call me Auren."

He nods and sets his satchel down. "Let's take a look anyway, lady Auren."

I huff a breath out, half in humor at the title he insists on using, and half in exasperation. "Honestly, I've had worse."

"Not something a mender likes to hear, I don't think," Hojat mutters before he walks over, eyes scanning me as he steps in close. Fortunately, his gaze is clinical, nothing leering or intimidating about it. "How did you get this?" he asks, motioning to my cheek.

My eyes flick away. "I was struck."

"Hmm. And any pain when you speak or chew?"

"No."

"Good." Brown eyes move down to my swollen lip, though I can feel that the split is scabbed over.

"And this here, any aching or loose teeth?"

"Thankfully, no."

"Good, good, good," he says. "Any other injuries?"

I fidget on my feet. "I fell and landed on a rock. I think it pierced me on my shoulder, but I can't see it to know for sure."

He hums in his throat and moves to my side, but I hesitate. "Umm, only look. Don't touch it."

He pauses, but nods and stays where he is. Keeping one eye on him, I pull the collar of my chemise down to expose the back of my shoulder. He leans in close but, thankfully, doesn't try to touch. "Yes, there's a small wound here. Let me get something for it."

He goes over to his satchel and digs around, pulling out some kind of tincture. I watch, standing awkwardly as he tips the glass vial over onto the corner of a cloth, grabs another vial, and then walks back over.

Hojat reaches up to put the cloth against my skin, but I instinctively jerk back. He stops with wide eyes. "Sorry, my lady. I forgot."

I clear my throat. "It's fine. I'll do it."

He passes it over, and I take the cloth, pressing the damp material against the wound. It stings instantly, and Hojat tips his head at my hiss. "It hurts a bit, but it'll get it clean."

"Thanks for the warning," I say dryly.

I finish dabbing it, and with a nod from Hojat, I hand the cloth back to him. "Let it dry a bit before you cover it again," he instructs.

"Okay."

Hojat turns to put the cloth away, but he accidentally steps on my ribbons. I suck in a breath as he unin-
tentionally pulls them taut, sore lengths crushed under
his heel.

At the grimace on my face, he immediately jumps back.
"Oh, apologies, lady, I—" Eyes dropping, he notices what
he stepped on, and his words cut off. "What... What's this?"

I grab my ribbons and push them behind me.
"They're just the ties to my chemise."

His expression tells me that he doesn't believe me at
all, and honestly, he shouldn't, because they're obviously
too thick and long.

A shift of his eyes has me stiffening, as he no doubt
notices that the ribbons are poking out from *beneath* my
chemise, not over. I quickly wrap the fur around my body
to cover my back, but I know it's too late.

"Is that all?" I ask, hoping that I can get him to leave.

Hojat clears his throat and jerks his eyes away. "Ah,
no. The commander mentioned an injury on your ribs."

I shake my head. "It's fine, they're—"

"I'm afraid I must insist. Commander's orders."

I clench my teeth. "And I'm afraid *I* must insist. I
said it's fine, and it's my body."

In order to see my ribs, I'd have to lift up my chemise way higher than I'm comfortable doing, or I'd have
to take it off completely, and I'd be even more vulnerable than I am now. He'd be able to see my body and my
ribbons, and that's not something I'm willing to allow,

mender or not.

Having the commander walk in on me was enough.

Hojat's face softens. "You have nothing to fear from me, lady Auren. Just disrobe, lie down on the pallet, and I'll be quick—"

My chest constricts. "No."

Just lie down on the pallet, girl. This will be quick.

The voice that springs up from my memory is hoarse, bristly. I recall it with perfect clarity, and it makes me break out into a sweat. I can almost catch the scent of a wet wheat field, manure sodden in its soil. My stomach churns.

I've let myself wallow for too long today, left too many wounds open. My mind is vulnerable, letting things slip out that I buried long ago.

With a shaky breath, I shove away the jagged memory as hard as I can. "I'd like to rest now, Hojat."

The mender looks like he wants to argue some more, but instead, he simply shakes his head with a resigned sigh.

Will the commander punish him? Will he punish me?

"Very well," Hojat says.

My tense shoulders relax slightly as he turns away. I watch him fiddle around in his satchel again, then kneel at the flaps of the tent, scooping up some snow from outside and dumping it in a small rag that he ties at the corners.

I'm about to ask what he's doing when he walks over

with the tied bundle and another vial that he holds out to me. "Cold compress and some Ruxroot. It will help with the pain and sleep."

I nod, taking them both. I pop open the cork of the small vial, pouring the contents in my mouth. As soon as it hits my tongue, I cough, nearly gagging, the heat and bitter taste so odious that tears flood my eyes. I barely manage to swallow it down.

"Great Divine, what *is* that?" I choke out. "I've taken Ruxroot plenty of times, and it never tasted like that."

Hojat gives me a sheepish look as he takes back the empty vial. "Sorry, my lady, I forgot to warn you. I mix all of my remedies with henade."

My eyes widen incredulously, my throat bobbing like it's still trying to get rid of the burn. "You spike your medicinal brews with the strongest alcohol in all of Orea?" I ask.

He shrugs with a smile. "What did you expect? I'm an army mender. I mostly treat pissed-off soldiers fresh off the battlefield. Believe me, the more alcohol, the better in those cases. It helps deaden the pain for even the most brutal of wounds, and it improves their foul moods," he says with a wink from his good eye.

I wipe my mouth on the fur hanging over my shoulder. "Ugh. I prefer wine."

He chuckles and motions to the pack of snow I'm holding in the other hand. "Ice your cheek and lip tonight.

The swelling will go down."

I nod. "Thank you."

"Good rest, my lady." Hojat gathers his satchel and walks out, leaving me alone once again.

While I wait for the liquid on my shoulder to dry completely, I clean up my tray of food, and then I take the time to check over my dress and scrub out as much of the blood as I can before hanging it up on one of the poles of the tent to quasi-dry.

I swig down the last drops of my water to try and clean out the taste of the horrible tincture, but it doesn't do much of anything. I hope that henade was the only extra ingredient mixed in there.

I probably shouldn't have trusted Hojat so easily, but I was too relieved to be offered a pain suppressant that I didn't even think. The mender doesn't seem the type to slip me poison, but I really shouldn't dismiss *anyone* in Fourth's army.

Feeling like I'm nearly ready to collapse, I fold back some of the furs on the pallet and practically fall into the makeshift bed, carefully arranging my ribbons so they won't tangle with my legs during the night.

I cover myself from cheeks to toes with the heavy furs, rolling up another to stuff under my head. Once I'm settled, I take the cold compress and hold it against my cheek.

My body soon warms beneath the thick layers, and I sigh, feeling the effects of Ruxroot begin to work itself through me.

But just when I start to close my heavy eyes, the tent flap lifts again, blowing in fresh snow. My eyes snap over to the commander as he ducks inside, the flaps falling closed behind him.

I have a feeling that this time, he won't be walking back out.

CHAPTER 7

AUREN

M *y entire body stiffens. I* should've known that I didn't really get off the hook. Maybe he sent his mender to me so that I could be tended to so I could be well enough for him to have his way with me.

Bile rises in my throat, burning the back of my tongue, my body locked in place. "What are you doing?" I ask, acidic fear coating my voice.

But the commander doesn't answer me. Instead, he stalks over to the other side of the tent where the extra pile of furs is located.

I hold my breath, fingers curled tightly on my coverings, clutching them for dear life as he leans down and starts to undo his boots. Breath gets caught in my throat as I watch him take off one, then the other. They land with a thump that matches the heavy beat in my chest.

I can't help but think of the way he walked in on me, at what parts of my naked flesh he probably saw.

His fingers go up to his chest plate next, the black metal slipping off with a few rough tugs of the belted loops at either side. He sets it aside, and then begins to loosen the brown leather straps that crisscross over his chest to remove his black leather jerkin.

I'm just beginning to question how he's going to take that off when the spikes along his arms and down his spine retract. Slowly, they sink beneath his skin, disappearing from view one by one, and as soon as they're gone, he pulls off the jerkin, hanging it up on the tent pole above.

You'd think that in only a simple long-sleeved tunic and pants that he'd be less intimidating, but he's not. The circular holes in his sleeves remind me of what lies beneath.

My entire body begins to tremble when he yanks the hem of his tunic out of his pants.

I bite my bottom lip so hard that I nearly tear the split open even more. *No. This can't happen. No, no, no.*

I'm so stupid. Why did I let my guard down? Why did I ever consider that this wouldn't happen?

Maybe the tincture Hojat gave me was spiked with something to knock me out. It probably wasn't Ruxroot at all. Why would the mender of Fourth's army care if I was in pain, anyway? I'm only being kept so I can serve as a taunt, a ransom, a threat to Midas.

I'm at my weakest. After the night and day I endured, I'm injured, exhausted, now drugged, and I'm left alone at the mercy of the most feared army commander in the world.

Anger kicks my stomach with a painful lurch. I'm angry at the commander for being such a vile person. I'm angry at Hojat for tricking me into a sense of calm. Angry at the Red Raids for attacking and capturing me in the first place.

But more than anything, I'm angry at myself, for always finding myself in situations like this one.

When Commander Rip moves toward me, I jerk upright and scrabble as far back on the pallet as I can without tearing straight through the material of the tent behind me. "Stay right there! Don't come any closer."

Rip pauses, the hint of scales on his cheeks shining in the miniscule light. Taking in my posture and my expression, a scowl darkens his face.

A scream is on the back of my curling tongue, ready to unleash, though I doubt it will do me any good. But I won't be silent.

The commander moves again, and my scream is ready to rent in the air...but he doesn't cross over to me.

Instead, he grabs a metal covering I hadn't noticed before and places it over the coals.

I watch, not daring to breathe, as he then picks up his boots and armor, propping everything up neatly beside the rocks. He moves to the lantern, turning down the flame until it extinguishes, bathing us in flickering darkness. The only light comes from the slits in the vented lid, the red-hot coals still brimming with heat beneath.

My tense body is ready to spring up, my teeth clamped so tightly that my jaw hurts, but he doesn't come toward me.

I squint in the darkness, my body trembling all over, but instead of making his way over to me, he turns and goes to the other pile of furs in the corner of the tent.

When he pulls them back and slips under them, stretching out to lie down, I realize that they aren't just an extra pile of furs, it's another sleeping pallet.

My mind stutters.

What? *What?*

A flinch back, my heart beating wildly in my chest, like I'm a fish who was just released back into water, off the hook and back into safety.

I blink in shock, staring at his shadowed form. He's not forcing himself on me. He's not coming near.

He's just...lying on the second pallet. A pallet, I notice, which is extra long to accommodate his height.

"Is this a trick?" I find myself asking, my voice shaky with uneven breath. I'm still clutching the bundle of snow in my hand, my grip so hard that my fingernails are nearly piercing the cloth. I immediately let go and drop it to the floor.

He says nothing as he straightens the furs around him

to his liking, and I realize something I should have before.

Why the tent has so many comforts, why it's set apart from the others, why there are so many furs, even the whole floor lined with them. No one would do that for a damn prisoner's tent. But they would if the prisoner has to share with the commander.

My breath hitches. "This is *your* tent."

He's lying on his back, telling me that his spikes are still tucked away. "Of course it's my tent," he answers.

"Why? Why did you put me in *your* tent?" I demand, still sitting up, knees bent in front of me as I huddle inside my furs.

Black eyes cut over to me across the space. "You'd prefer sleeping in the snow?"

"Shouldn't I be with the other prisoners? The other saddles and guards?"

"I'd rather keep an eye on you."

Wariness floods me. "Why?"

When he doesn't answer, I narrow my eyes, glaring at his shadowed silhouette. "Are you keeping me in here so that your disgusting men won't abuse me in the middle of the night without your permission?"

I see him tense. I see it, but I *feel* it even more. His irritation presses into the air and threatens to bruise.

He slowly sits up on one bent elbow, staring hard at me with an anger I want no part of. "I trust my soldiers implicitly," he bites out. "They wouldn't touch you. It's *you* I don't trust. That's why you sleep here, in my tent.

Your loyalty to the Golden King speaks of your character, and I won't allow my soldiers to bear any brunt of your plots."

My mouth drops open in shock.

He's keeping me in here so that *I* don't do anything to *them*? The idea is so ludicrous it's nearly laughable. Yet the way he degraded my character…

I shouldn't care, not in the least. But I do. This male, who lies about what he is, who commands a vicious, barbaric army, dares to look down on *me*? He's known as Commander Rip, for Divine's sake. He rips foes' heads off and leaves them to bleed on the ground while his king leaves rotten corpses of fallen soldiers in his wake.

"I don't want to be in here with you," I grit out.

He lies back down, seeming not to care in the slightest. "Captives don't get to choose where they sleep. Be grateful that you have it as good as you do."

That sets my hackles rising again as I try to decipher the underlying message. "What's that supposed to mean? Where are the other saddles? The guards?"

He doesn't answer me. The bastard just slings an arm over his eyes, like he's ready to tuck in.

"I asked you a question, Commander."

"And I chose not to answer," he replies without moving his arm. "Now be quiet and rest. Unless you need a gag to help suppress the urge to speak?"

My lips press together tightly. He's awful enough to follow through, so instead of being forced to sleep around a gag all night, I make myself lie back down.

Despite the tincture trying to drag me under, I keep my back against the tent and my eyes on him for over an hour, just in case this is all a trick, just in case he's waiting to attack when I'm at my most vulnerable during sleep.

But the longer I try to stay awake, the heavier my eyes become.

Every blink stings, like my lids are trying to hold onto each other, scraping against my eyes when I force them open again and again.

Losing the battle, sleep starts to drag me under with the aid of the alcohol and pain suppressant. I finally succumb to the exhaustion that's been riding me, and I fall asleep, dreaming in the tent of the enemy.

CHAPTER 8

AUREN

"Come, Auren."

I look back at Midas, at his outstretched hand. Such a simple gesture to many, but for me, it's a big deal.

It took me a while to willingly place my palm in his. Every time he did it before, I'd flinch.

But he's been so patient with me, so kind. I've never known kindness before, not since I was a little girl still safe at home with my parents.

I slip my hand into his before I glance longingly back at the fire several yards away, at the group of nomads gathered around it on the grass, the pond glittering behind them.

Midas and I are normally alone on the road, but we're going to cross out of Second Kingdom soon, and there are always more travelers near the borders. The nomads have been keeping pace with us for a few days now, and I'm curious about them.

"Can't we share their fire?" I ask as Midas starts to tug me away. The night is balmy with a hint of a breeze, an inky sky dipped with a dusting of stars.

"No, Precious."

Every time he calls me that, I still get butterflies in my stomach. The fact that anyone would consider me precious, let alone someone as handsome as him, makes me surge with newfound happiness.

I keep thinking that this happiness is going to be torn away—that he's going to leave, but Midas tells me I don't ever have to worry about that.

He pulls me to our own small campfire, and I settle myself close to his side. I keep my thigh pressed against his because I crave the contact. Now that I'm getting touches that aren't meant to hurt, I can't get enough.

"Why not?" I ask curiously. Midas is so friendly and charismatic. I'm surprised that he doesn't seem to care for the company of others.

He releases my hand so he can grab the meat he's been roasting, and he splits off the bigger piece for me. I smile as I take it, biting into the tender meal with relish.

"Because it's best that we keep to ourselves," Midas patiently explains while he eats, stripping the meat of the bone. "You can't trust people, Auren."

I look across at him, wondering if he's learned that

the hard way, as I have. Neither of us likes to talk about our past, though, and I'm glad he doesn't needle me. We're both happier in the here and now.

"I thought it would be nice to have other company," I admit quietly, slurping the juices from my fingers as I finish up the last of the meat. "We've been traveling, just the two of us, for a couple months now. Thought you might be getting bored of me," I tease, but there's always a hint of question there, always an edge of self-doubt.

I still don't understand why someone like him bothers with someone like me.

Midas turns to look at my face, the orange glow of the flames blending with his eyes, making them crackle with warmth. He reaches over and strokes a thumb over my cheek. "I will never get bored of you, Auren. You're perfect."

My breath catches in my throat. "You think I'm perfect?"

He leans in and kisses me, and I don't even mind that our lips are greased with food or that the smoke of the fire clings to my hair. He thinks I'm perfect. He saved me, and he'll never tire of me, and he thinks I'm perfect enough to kiss.

I didn't know happiness could ever feel like this.

When he pulls back, his flame-filled eyes caress my face, an adoring look in his expression. "Don't ever think that I'll get bored of you or that you aren't precious to me. You're my gold-touched girl, right?"

I nod shyly, my tongue darting out to lick my lips,

tasting the sweetness of his kiss. This still feels so new, so fragile. My heart is full enough to burst, and I'm always afraid that it will.

"Why me, Midas?" I ask quietly, my question slipping out to float in the air.

It's one that's been tumbling silently in my head for weeks, months, ever since he lifted me up from my lonely squalor, stuck in an alleyway with nowhere to go, no one to care.

Maybe I'm finally letting the words out because he breathed some of his unending confidence into me. Or maybe I feel bolder when I'm shadowed by night.

I think some questions can't bear to face the light. It's easier for hesitant words and feared answers to be given in the dark. At least then, we can hide them in the shadows—hide ourselves from them.

I wait for him to answer, my fingers curling in the grass, plucking at the blades just so I have something to do with my hands.

Midas taps my chin so I'll look up at him. "What do you mean?"

I shrug self-consciously. "You could've taken anyone else at that village after you got rid of the raiders. There were plenty of others scared and crying," I say, my eyes dropping down to the top of his gold tunic where the laces have come undone, showing his tanned skin beneath. "Why me? Why did you come into that alleyway and decide to take me with you?"

Midas reaches over and pulls me onto his lap. My

stomach leaps at the contact, an automatic reaction caught between having fear of a person's touch and surprise at liking it. As soon as the initial tension is gone, I settle against him, my head resting on his chest.

"It was always going to be you," he says quietly. "As soon as I saw your face, I was already lost to you, Auren." He picks up my hand and places it over his chest. I feel the beat of his life thrum against my fingers, like it's singing a song just for me. "Hear that? You have my heart, Precious. Always."

A smile stretches my lips, and I bury my face into his neck, nuzzle against the staccato of his pulse. I feel so light and happy that I'm surprised I don't float into the air and sparkle with the stars.

He places a kiss on my hair. "Let's get to bed," he murmurs before tapping me on the nose. "We can't oversleep."

I nod against him, but instead of putting me down, he carries me to the tent, ducking inside. He lays me down on our blanket roll gently, and I fall asleep in his arms, snuggled up against him.

I'm not sure what exactly wakes me up.

Maybe it was a sound. Maybe it was intuition.

I sit up in the dark, noting that there's no more orange glow floating through our tent, which means the fire has gone out, probably hours ago.

Beside me, Midas is sleeping, soft snores coming from his parted mouth. I smile because those cooed rumbles make him so endearing for some reason, like a secret only I know about him, an innocent vulnerability.

I look around with my head tilted, listening to the quiet night, wondering what could have pulled me out of such a deep sleep.

But I hear nothing. Dawn is probably not too far away though, so I decide to slip quietly out of the tent and go wash up a bit before it's time to leave.

Outside, I pass the charred and ashen pit of our old fire, and I stretch my arms over my head, looking around at the moonlit surroundings. All is still, nothing out of place, the soft chirping of crickets sounding off near the pond.

I head that way, wanting to take advantage of the empty water while I can. My bare feet sink into the plush grass with every step as I pick my way toward the water. The open plain is dusted with a few trees here and there, and I can see the shadows of the nomads' tents in the distance, their camp quiet enough that I can tell everyone is still sleeping.

When I get to the pond, I start to undress, toe dipping into the water to get a feel. It's cold, but not too bad. I'll just take a quick dip to wash before the sun dawns.

I start to loosen the gold ties at my collar when a hand suddenly slams over my mouth.

Startled, a yelp flies out of me, uselessly caught in the palm of someone's hand. The person's other arm comes around me, bending around my throat, making me choke.

"Get her clothes," the man's voice barks out against

my ear.

My eyes are as wide as saucers as my tunic is tugged, the material pinching my skin painfully.

In my panic, my frenzied senses tell me that there are three of them—two women and the man holding me from behind.

No, not two women, I realize. One of them is just a girl, about my age. I recognize her. This family belongs to the traveling nomads.

I struggle, trying to kick, but the man holds me tighter, making it hard to breathe. "Hold still and this will go better for you," he says low in my ear.

The woman trying to tear off my shirt looks over her shoulder. "Pass me the knife," she hisses at her daughter.

The girl is apparently the lookout, but she rushes forward, a glint of metal shining as she passes a pocket-knife to her mother. I try to look at her, pleading with my eyes, but she doesn't even look at me.

I try to buck the man away and tear his arm away from my neck. I attempt to scream past the man's fingers, teeth gnashing, trying to bite, but he just shoves his fingers in my mouth and presses on my tongue, making me gag.

In the next moment, I hear a slicing sound, and then a bite of pain slashes across my stomach. I scream as the shirt is cut from my body, my long skirt and leggings following directly after.

"Quick! Give me the knife!" the man hisses.

I'm going to die. He's about to slit my throat, and all I can think is—Midas was right.

You can't trust people.

The man fists my hair in his hand, blessedly letting go of my neck and my mouth, but I'm too busy gulping in the much-needed air that I don't have the breath to scream. My throat is so battered, I'm not even sure if I can.

My neck is wrenched to the side as he pulls my hair with an agonizing tug, and then there's a horrible sawing as he begins to cut through my thick golden tresses.

I'm shoved down onto the ground, naked, scalp screaming, throat bruised.

When the last of my hair is cut, there's no more grip on my body, so I drop uselessly to the ground like soiled laundry dumped on the floor. I can't get up, I'm too stuck in shock, too focused on taking in one ragged inhale after another.

If they say anything to me, I don't hear it. All I know is their footsteps run away, taking their menacing shadows with them, and then I'm alone, crumpled in a heap at the edge of the pond. One foot is lying ankle-deep in the cold water while the rest of me is sunken into the grass, but I don't feel it.

I'm not sure how long I lie there, but I'm too afraid to move. Too afraid to get up and find Midas. Too afraid of everything.

But Midas finds me. Just like before, in that alleyway, he finds me broken on the ground, beneath a watching moon.

I hear him call my name, hear him curse. Then he's gathering me into his arms, and my tears fall down as he lifts me up.

I cry into his golden tunic, my tears soaking through to his chest—that chest that's still beating, still singing to me.

I feel the scratchy, crooked ends of my shorn hair scrape against my cheeks. I feel the slice on my stomach where the sloppy blade cut into my skin. But mostly, I just feel fear.

Midas takes care of me, and even though I know I must look ugly now, and that he must be angry that I left the tent without him, he doesn't say anything. He simply washes the green stains off my skin, cleans the cut on my belly, and kisses my wet cheeks.

All the while, his earlier declaration becomes my mantra, one that makes my heart harden, makes my fear solidify, makes me want to hide away from the world forever.

You can't trust people.

The only person I can trust is him.

I promise myself right then and there, that from now on, that's what I'll do. I will always trust him, in all things, because he knows what's best. He's always right.

I'm done with the ugliness of this world, and I want him to keep me safe from it.

All of it.

CHAPTER 9

AUREN

The brush of silken tendrils across my swollen cheek wakes me up.

As my eyes peel open, I see my ribbons stretching, curling, moving slowly around me, as if testing for tenderness. I smile at the soft golden glow of them, immediately noting how much better they look and feel. I can actually move them without wincing.

I sit up, careful to keep the furs from falling off, because the pre-dawn morning chill is stark. The coals have long since turned cold with ash, and the tent is dark. I can see the shadowed silhouette of the commander's body stretched out on his furs, his breaths steady and quiet.

It's not too surprising that he's still asleep, since the sun hasn't risen yet. But seeing him asleep like this, without the pressing demand of his power, without the harsh scowl...it makes him seem different. Less threatening.

I find myself watching him, studying the smooth lines of his face. I'm curious what the silvery scales along his cheekbones would feel like if I touched them. I wonder if it hurts to have his spikes retracted beneath his skin for so long or if he doesn't even feel it.

But mostly, I wonder what kind of power he carries in his veins. Whatever he's capable of, it's vast and ruthless. I can sense it.

His power must be the reason why King Ravinger wields him like a hammerhead. But how did the king even find him? How does he keep the truth from the masses?

Are people so content in ignorance that they'll believe every lie fed to them, despite what they see right in front of their eyes? Then again, perhaps it isn't ignorance. Maybe it's just...fear. They don't want to even consider the alternative. It would make people uneasy, make it hard to sleep at night.

Maybe ignorance isn't a vice, but a reprieve. And a reprieve into ignorance is something I've done myself, many times.

Commander Rip makes a noise in his sleep, low and rumbling, like a faraway quake of the earth, shifting plates that I can almost feel beneath unsteady feet.

He didn't touch me last night.

Even in my exhausted sleep, he never once tried to

take advantage, never even got up from his pallet. I wasn't chained or watched or hurt. He wasn't even worried that *I'd* do something to *him* while he slept.

Being his captive...it isn't what I expected. It's mind games rather than physical harassment. It's pointed questions instead of vague threats.

I don't trust it one bit.

One of my ribbons curls in front of my face, moving in a clear order to get going. I bat it away playfully, carefully peeling away from the furs as I quietly get to my feet.

My body is sore, my bruised side twinging as soon as I stand, but at least my shoulder feels better, so whatever ointment Hojat used on me must've helped. The tonic clearly helped too, because while I'm still aching, it's not nearly as bad as it was yesterday.

I'm immediately cold without the covers, goose bumps rising along my skin. I wish I could dive back beneath the warmth of my pallet, but instead, I grab my dress from where it's hung and yank it over my head.

With the aid of my ribbons, I get dressed quickly and quietly. I'm so relieved at how much better they feel after only a night's rest. With one eye on the commander, I slip into my leggings and boots before snatching up the gloves and pulling them on nearly to my elbows, and then I tug on my coat.

I plait my hair in a simple braid down my back that I quickly stuff into the hood of the coat before pulling it over my head. Finished, my ribbons slip beneath the coat and wrap around my torso in loose yet secure loops, adding another layer of insulation.

I creep to the entrance of the tent and duck out, casting one last glance back at the commander. I doubt he's much of a heavy sleeper, and I don't want to be caught sneaking out before dawn.

As soon as I'm outside, my breath hitches with the lonely cold that greets me like the empty bedside of an absent lover.

With boots crunching over packed snow, I head toward the latrine so I can get it over with, while the hint of morning begins to cast a gray pallor over the sky.

It seems even colder today than it was last night. My teeth are chattering loudly by the time I leave the latrine, just in time for it to start snowing. I walk back to camp briskly, trying to get my blood moving so I don't feel so frozen, and I'm greeted by the sounds of the army waking up.

The scent of food drifts over, and I turn to follow it, letting my nose lead me. I pick my way past tents and grumbling men, some yawning, some coughing up phlegm, past more who are breaking down their tents to ready for another day of travel.

I make it to a low burning fire, finding a man presiding over a tripod of sticks with a large iron pot cooking on the flames. He has black skin and long spun hair, pieces of wood dangling from the lengths in tribute to his kingdom's sigil.

In front of him stands a line of already-dressed soldiers, each of them holding an iron cup. One by one, the man plops a spoonful of whatever it is he's serving into the cups. As I get closer, I can hear him jabbering to the men he's serving.

"Don't give me that look, or you'll get my foot up your arse. This is what I've got to serve."

Plop.

"Next! Yeah, yeah, walk a little slower, why don't you?"

Plop.

"You're sick of porridge? We're *all* sick of porridge, you bandy-legged prick," he says, making the soldier stomp off.

The next one who comes up looks down at the slop with a frown. "Can't you put some spices in it or something, Keg?"

The man—Keg—tips his head back and laughs, the movement making the wooden pieces in his hair strike together, tinkling hollowly. "*Spices?* Look around," he says, swinging his dripping spoon to point at the frozen wasteland. "Does it look like there's any spices to be had out here in this Divine-forsaken place?"

The soldier walks off with a sigh, but when the next one comes up for his turn, Keg shakes his head and taps his spoon against the huge bowl. "Uh-uh. You know you already got your ration for the day. Get out of my line unless you want my foot up your arse."

Keg seems to like that threat.

I hesitate behind the soldiers, my stomach grumbling, gaze flicking over to the horizon. There's a good fifty soldiers in front of me. Maybe I should see if I can find food somewhere else. If I hurry, I might be able to make it to those carts again and—

"Ho there!"

I snap my head over and find Keg looking right at me, but I glance around just in case. All the other soldiers are turning around to peer at me too.

I tug my hood tighter over my face before pointing a finger at my chest. "Me?"

Keg rolls his eyes. "Yes, you. Come on up here."

The soldiers begin to mutter quietly to one another, noticing me for the first time.

"That's her."

"She's Midas's gilded woman?"

"She don't look like much."

"Eh, I gotta couple of coins more golden than her."

I sink my chin down until it nearly hits my chest. Their undivided attention makes me want to bolt. Keg must see it in my expression, because he smacks the spoon against the bowl like he's hitting a gong, the noise clanging loudly enough to put a wince on several soldiers' faces.

"Come on, girl. Up front," Keg calls.

Steeling myself, I walk forward, trying to ignore the attention of the others as I approach. I stop a couple feet away from him, and his dark brown eyes sweep over me. "Ho boy. You're the Sixth King's gilded saddle?"

My ribbons tighten around for a moment before I answer. "Yes."

He nods his head, making the winding lengths of his long hair fall in front of one eye. "I thought you'd be shinier. Stiff. Like I could rap my knuckles against you, and it'd clang like a statue."

I blink. "What?"

A dripping spoon moves up and down the length of me. "You know, more metallic. Reflective. Cold. But you're all flesh and warmth, aren't you? All womanly curves and soft flesh, but just..." He tips his head as if searching for the right word. "Gilded."

My cheeks are hot beneath the shadow of my hood, and I shift on my feet, undecided if I should spin around and walk away or if it's worth it to stay so that I can eat. Though, I realize that his words weren't spoken with any cruelty or lewdness, just with pure surprise instead.

"That's why she's called the gilded pet, you idiot," one of the soldiers gripes behind me, making me tense. "Now can you stop yapping and serve us? We're hungry, and your slop doesn't get any better when it's cold."

Keg's attention shifts over my head, and he points his spoon again, making a particularly lumpy bit fall to the ground an inch away from my skirts. "You can fuck off and wait in line, or I'll dump this here *slop* on the ground and then plant my foot up your arse, how about that, soldier?"

I can't help it. I smile.

Keg sees, his smug eyes moving back to me, same as his still outstretched spoon. "See? The gilded one gets me. That means she gets to be served before the rest of you ungrateful lot."

The men in line groan, but my smile drops off my face, and I shake my head adamantly. "Oh, no. No, that's okay. I'll wait," I insist. The last thing I need is the men behind me taking offense and making me pay for it.

"What the fuck, Keg? She's a Divine-damned *prisoner*!" One of them directly behind me growls, which only proves that this is a bad idea.

Keg doesn't look nearly as worried as I do. "Yeah, well, I like *her* more than I like your annoying ass voice right now, and seeing as how *I'm* the cook here, I decide who gets served. So you can take your hairy arses to one of the other cooks' fires if you don't like it."

Keg turns away from the men and grabs a tin cup from a pile on the ground. He dips his spoon into the bowl and plops a serving of porridge in it before holding it out to me. "Here you go, Gild."

I look over, waiting for more objections, but Keg practically shoves it in my face. "Take it, girl."

Blowing out a breath and hoping I won't regret this, I take the cup. "Thanks," I say quietly.

I grasp the iron cup between my gloved hands, the warmth soaking into my cold palms.

"So...your name is Keg."

The army's cook grins at me. "My family owns a brewery back in Fourth. But I got off easy. My older brother is named Distill." His brown eyes gleam with mirth as he shakes his head. "Unlucky, that. But we're both a bit jealous of our sister, Barley. She's got the best name of the lot."

A surprised chuckle sneaks out of my mouth before I can tuck it back in. Despite my reservations and doubts, Keg is way too easy to like.

I lift the cup to my mouth, the rough metal scraping against my lips as I tip the contents into my mouth. I swallow it all down without really tasting it, which is probably for the best based on the way the men complained about it.

The sludge has the consistency of watery porridge with a few clumpy bits, but it's hot and it's edible, so I'm grateful for it. As soon as I swallow every bit, I turn and deposit the empty cup on the ground with the rest of the dirty ones.

Keg bangs his spoon against the bowl with a grin as he looks at me. "Ha! See how fast she ate that? Couldn't get enough. You all would do well to take some lessons from her."

"The only lesson anyone could take from the saddle is how to spread her legs."

My shoulders stiffen, and all of my previous ease leaves me as several of the soldiers bark out laughter.

"I'll volunteer for that lesson!" someone else calls out. More snickering.

"Aye, me too. Let's see it!"

My spine goes rigid. Keg frowns.

Then, a dark, foreboding voice answers from across the campfire. "What 'it' would you like to see, *exactly*?"

CHAPTER 10

AUREN

*M*y heart leaps into my throat. The soldiers all go still, the mood gone from mocking to uneasy in a single second.

I find the source of the voice, gaze jumping to the figure on the other side of the fire. Commander Rip is standing there, arms loose at his sides, spikes jutting from the middle of his forearms like curved fangs in a wolf's mouth.

For all his easy, relaxed posture he seems to import, there's menace rising off him like steam.

He looks so different from when I left the tent this morning. All traces of the mellowed, softened look that he had while he slept is gone. Right now, that recollection is so foreign, so ill-fitting, that I doubt whether he really looked like that to begin with. How could I think for a single second that this male was anything but sinister?

In the dappled gray lighting of an almost-dawn, Rip is formidable. The last remnants of night cling to his jet-black hair, to his depthless eyes, the shadows of other-worldliness splashed across his cheeks.

His is a presence meant to chill, to frighten. To take one look and want to run the other way, and I must not be the only one who thinks that, because the soldiers go tense, as if they want to flee.

He's wearing the same black leather outfit as before, the same contorted branch sword hilt hanging at the belt on his waist. Simple soldier's clothes that do nothing to hide the threat beneath. A hush weighs over everyone—even Keg falls quiet.

I'm so focused on Rip that I don't even notice the soldier with him until they both begin walking forward. A foot taller than the commander, bulky chest, mean eyes, pierced lip, long brown hair. *The soldier who approached me when I was snooping around the carts.*

Great.

No wonder he's such an observant asshole. It looks like he's Rip's right-hand man.

The two of them stop in front of the line of soldiers, homing in on a pair in particular. "Osrik," Commander Rip says, his tone gruff. "I think these men said something about wanting lessons."

"I heard that too, Commander," Osrik replies, a wicked smirk tugging at his lips.

The two soldiers shift on their feet. One of them seems to have gone pale.

Rip stares at them without a hint of emotion. The edge in his eyes is sharp enough to cut glass. "Go ahead and teach them one, Captain Osrik."

Osrik's smile is not a nice one. "Gladly."

Both soldiers blanch, one of them swallowing hard enough that I can hear it from where I stand. "Let's go." Osrik turns and the soldiers follow after him, everyone watching them go, including me.

Well, everyone except...

"Come, Auren."

I startle, Commander Rip suddenly right beside me.

"Where?" I ask warily.

"The carriage," he answers. I don't know which I'm more surprised by, the destination, or the fact that he actually answered me.

"Ho, Commander, you want a cup?" Keg asks, breaking the stare-off I didn't realize I was having with Rip.

The commander shakes his head. "Not right now." Black eyes flick back to me, and he lifts his hand, motioning for me to walk.

I start forward, and Rip matches my stride. Instead of leading me, he walks on my left, not going faster or slower, our steps in sync. I'm all too cognizant of the sharp tips of his spikes on his arms, careful not to get too close. Every time his arm swings, I tuck mine in a little bit closer to my body.

Rip notices, and a black brow arches up at me. "Nervous?"

"Careful," I correct, looking straight ahead.

As we walk, I note that the camp is roused now, nearly all of the tents already broken down, horses fed and packed, the army readying to get back into formation for another long day of marching.

The other soldiers, no matter their age or bulk, seem to scatter out of our way when they see Rip coming. Every single one of them tilts their head in respect.

I dart a look at him out of the corner of my eye. "What will you and Osrik do to them?"

"Who?"

"Those two soldiers."

He shrugs, shoulder lifting. "Don't be concerned about them."

My teeth grind ever so slightly. "Their comments were directed at me, so I *am* concerned. Besides, you told me that you trust your soldiers implicitly."

"I do."

I shake my head with a frustrated sigh. "You can't claim to trust your soldiers and then turn around and punish or kill them for a few passing comments spoken to a prisoner."

Rip stops walking suddenly, making me draw up

short. We turn at the same time, facing each other amidst the busy camp. The snow has turned to slosh at our feet, the air cloying with newly doused fires and a heavy, wet chill that sticks to my lungs.

The commander studies me with an unreadable expression. "You're defending them?"

I bristle at his tone. I don't like that it's incredulous, that he thinks me so petty.

"I'm not defending their crude remarks. But *you're* the self-proclaimed monster, not me. I don't want their punishment on my conscience," I say, because I have enough blood on my hands. I don't need to add more. "If you need to flex your authority or prove me right about your earlier 'implicit trust' statement, leave me out of it. You can hardly blame your soldiers for speaking ill of me. I'm the enemy. Your *prisoner*," I remind him.

For the life of me, I can't think of *why* I'm reminding him of that. Seems like a bad idea, to be honest. And yet, there's just something about this male that stokes my anger.

For so long, I've swallowed my own tongue. I've tamped down every emotion, careful to ride every tide in the hopes that I don't become submerged. So these reactions, these unbridled retorts, surprise even me. I have no idea where it's coming from, but it leaves me feeling flustered.

"Allow me to set some things straight," Rip says, cutting off my train of thought. "I'm not having those soldiers punished, least of all killed. Osrik will be doing exactly what was stated—he'll be teaching them a lesson."

"And what does this *lesson* include?"

"Latrine duty, mostly. Until they remember how to behave as befitting of a royal soldier serving in King Ravinger's army."

I blink at him. "Oh." That's not what I was expecting.

Our little chat is going uninterrupted, but not unobserved. All of the passing soldiers give us a wide berth, but I feel them darting glances our way, though no one gets too close. We're in an untouchable circle, like one of the old fairy rings that used to dot across Orea long ago.

"Let me make one last thing clear," Rip says, taking a step toward me. I've noticed that this is a tactic of his. To unnerve me, intimidate me with his nearness. I want to back up, but I also don't want to give him the satisfaction. So instead, I plant my feet and tip up my chin.

"Just because those men acted crude and discordant, does not mean I don't trust them. What I said before is still true. They would not touch a single hair on your head, unless I ordered them to. You are safe from every single soldier here." He pauses, making sure I take in what he's saying. "Unfortunately, basic manners are not included in that. Fortunately, Osrik is well-versed in setting untoward behavior straight."

I think of the man's scowl and massive size. "I'll bet he is."

Rip cuts me a look. "Now that we have *that* out of

the way and your conscience has been spared of guilt, would you like to tell me why Osrik reported to me this morning that you were acting suspicious last night?"

Shit.

"I was not acting *suspicious*," I deny. "I was simply walking around the camp. Something *you* allowed me to do, since I have no guard or chains. I'm surrounded by these soldiers you trust so much in a frozen wasteland that you promised to track me down in if I should be stupid enough to try to leave."

"Hmm," he says, not commenting on my snide tone. His eyes flick down to my coat. "And your ribs? My mender reported that you did not allow him to examine you."

"I'm fine."

"If you insist on lying, at least be better at it."

He's got it wrong there. I *am* fine, and I'm also excellent at lying. After all, I've been lying to myself for years. Pretty lies cover up a lot of ugly truths.

"My ribs are fine, but why would you care either way?" I snap.

Maybe I speak to him like this because it's my way of feeling like I hold some power between us. My attitude is a brick façade over crumbling plaster vulnerabilities.

"Since you don't like lies, let's speak honestly, Commander Rip," I say with a challenging taunt. "I know what you are, and I also know what I am: a pawn to hold for ransom. Something to dangle in front of King Midas."

"True," Rip replies coldly, making my lips press

together in a hard line. "Still, it would be rude of me to return Midas's pet in poor condition."

A tic jumps in my jaw.

Pet. Saddle. Whore. I am so incredibly tired of the brands people attach to me.

"I'm not his pet. I'm his favored."

Commander Rip makes a derisive noise in the back of his throat. "A different word for the same connotation."

I open my mouth in a retort, but Rip holds up a hand to stop me. "This talk of Midas bores me."

"Good. I don't want to talk to you anyway," I retort.

He releases a biting smile, sure to show a hint of fang. "I have a feeling you'll be changing your mind *very* soon, Goldfinch."

My spine stiffens. There's an underlying threat in those words, but I can't for the life of me guess what he means.

"Get to the carriage," he says, his demeanor rigid, settling into his commander role seamlessly. "We move out in ten, and we won't be stopping until dusk. I suggest you visit the latrine before we depart, or it's sure to be a very uncomfortable day for you."

"I want to see the saddles and the guards," I reply, completely ignoring his order.

He rests a hand on the wooden hilt of his sword and leans in to my face, so close that I nearly swallow my tongue. I lean back, feeling like a rabbit being held by the scruff of its neck.

"If you want something, you're going to have to earn it."

Rip turns on his boots and leaves, soldiers moving out of his path as he stalks away, while I'm left to stare after him.

I don't know what *earning* consists of, but I have a feeling I'm not going to like it.

CHAPTER 11

QUEEN MALINA

My handmaidens are uneasy.

I keep catching them sharing looks with one another, but I pretend not to see, not to care. One of them is so nervous that she seems close to fainting. If I weren't so well-trained at keeping my expression as flat as a stone, my mouth might've lifted in a sly smile.

The dressmaker I hired from the city sits back on her knees, a deep V creased between her brows as she peers at the hem of my dress with assessing, aged eyes. She has sharp needles stuck in the pincushion that's sewn into the belt around her waist, like a metal cactus jutting from her stomach.

"All finished, Your Majesty."

"Good."

I step down from the wooden stair she brought and walk over to the full length mirror that sits against the wall in my dressing room. The sight of my reflection fills me with a quiet sort of vindication, the kind that simmers just on the surface of still waters.

I turn to glance at the back of the new gown with pointed assessment before facing front again, running my hands down the skirts. "This will do."

My handmaidens share another look.

"You may go," I say to the dressmaker.

She bites her lip, getting to her feet, old knees cracking as she straightens. She's the oldest dressmaker in Highbell, but her age is a boon rather than a downfall, because she worked for my mother when I was just a girl. She's the only tailor left who remembers the clothes of my old court.

"Your Majesty, if I may... The king decreed that all clothes in his court be *gold*," the old crone says, as if this rule somehow slipped my mind. As if it ever *could* when the gaudy color is everywhere.

"I'm quite aware of all the king has decreed," I say coolly, fingering the velvet buttons at my chest. The entire ensemble is perfect. Just the way I remember my mother's gowns looking. White with a trim of fur at the sleeves and collar, ice-blue threading embellished in rosettes that perfectly match my eyes.

It suits me far better than any of the golden dresses I've worn these last ten years.

"You'll have the rest of the gowns and coats finished

by the end of the fortnight?" I confirm.

"I will, Your Majesty," she answers.

"Good. You are dismissed."

The woman quickly gathers her things, knobby hands flipping the wooden stair over to use like a bucket as she dumps her measuring chain, spare needles, fabric strips, and shears inside before bowing low and retreating out the door.

"My queen, shall I do your hair?"

I look over at my handmaiden, the apples of her cheeks rouged with glimmering gold powder. It's a fashion statement for all the women—and some of the men— who reside in Highbell. But on her, the yellow of the gold dusting just makes her look sickly. Another thing I need to change.

After all, appearance makes up more than half of an opinion.

"Yes," I answer before walking over to the vanity and sitting down.

When I see the girl reach for the box of gold glitter to dust over my white hair, I shake my head. "No. Nothing gold. Not anymore."

Her hand freezes in surprise, but by now, my intentions must be more than clear. She recovers quickly, grabbing the comb, brushing out my tresses with a gentle touch.

I scrutinize everything she does, directing her every move as she fashions my hair. She plaits a single braid starting at my right temple, no bigger than the width of my finger, and curves it around to end below my left ear. A waterfall effect of my sleek white hair, as if rapids froze on the way to their plummet.

Instead of having her finish with golden pins or ribbons, I say, "Just the crown."

She nods, turning to head for the case where I keep my royal jewels and crowns at the back of the room, but I stop her. "Nothing from there. I'll wear this."

She hesitates, unable to keep the confused frown from appearing on her face. "Your Majesty?"

I reach for the silver box that I'd set out on my vanity earlier. It's heavy, the metal dull, but my fingers trace the delicate filigree adorning the case, my touch nothing less than reverent.

"This was my mother's," I say quietly, my eyes following the direction of my finger as I trail along the outline of the bell, an icicle hanging from its hollow middle. I can almost hear the sound it would make, a cold, clear call to echo through the frozen mountains.

My handmaiden approaches as I open the box, revealing the crown inside. It's made entirely of white opal, sculpted from a single gemstone. It must have been the size of five hand spans, a glistening stone pulled from a roughshod mine.

The weak gray sunlight coming in through the window reveals only the barest hint of the delicate prism of colors held within the crown's depths. It's sturdy, but not nearly as heavy as the gold crown Tyndall has me wear. Just another thing to weigh me down.

The design itself is simple, carved to look like icicles jutting up from the top—dainty, yet sharp. I place it on my head, centering it perfectly, and for the first time in years, I finally feel like myself.

I am Queen Malina Colier Midas, and I was born to rule.

White gown, white hair, white crown—and not a hint of gold anywhere. This is how it should've been. This is how it *will* be.

I stand, and my handmaiden rushes forward to slip shoes over my feet. I cast my reflection one last look before I sweep out of the room, each step surer than the one before.

Guards coalesce around me like smoke, trailing me while I descend the stairwell. I enter the throne room through the back door, the chatter of occupants an indistinct hum that fills my ears.

The moment I enter the room, the nobles and courtiers inside bow and curtsy to fulfill their customary deference to their queen.

It's not until they straighten up that I feel the ripple of surprise pass over the gold-clothed congregation in a widespread arc.

Keeping my eyes poised on the dais, shoulders back in perfect posture, I walk determinedly forward. At the press of weighted silence that's fallen over the crowd, a seed of nervousness tries to settle in my stomach, burrowing deeper to set roots, but I yank it out like a weed.

I am Queen Malina Colier Midas, and I was born to rule.

I stop at the pair of thrones on the dais. Both gilded, one larger, one smaller. Tyndall's throne has a tall back, spires jutting out on either end, six glittering diamonds set into the back to depict Sixth Kingdom.

In comparison, the queen's throne is much smaller and less imposing. A pretty accompaniment and nothing more. The true power is in the king's throne, and everyone here knows it.

Including me.

Which is why I walk straight past the queen's seat and sit in the throne meant for the true ruler of Highbell.

An audible gasp rolls over the congregation, like apples down a hill, too many to catch.

My hands come down on the armrests as I settle onto the throne, fingertips digging into a notch in the gilt where Tyndall often tapped his fingers in boredom.

He was never good at open forums like this. Even holding them only once a month was enough to make his temper flare. He loathed sitting here, listening to the people of his kingdom raise concerns and beg for pardon.

He flourishes at balls, meeting with other royalty, charming guests at dinners. But then, Tyndall has always thrived under attention, adoration, and the secret manipulation that goes on behind closed doors.

But when it comes to *this*, the grit that collects on the

day-to-day wheels of the kingdom's cogs...it bores him.

Yet this room, this monthly forum, it's where power in a kingdom can be won. If you can snap the reins over the nobles and courtiers gathered here, you can steer a kingdom.

I stare out at the gathered crowd with an impassive face, letting them look, letting them whisper. They take in every single meticulously planned part of me, notice the complete lack of gold, the old royal colors of Highbell now reborn.

I give them another moment for my silent statement to sink in. I let them take the time to truly realize what I'm saying before I even open my mouth to speak. And I give *myself* a moment to relish in this, to hold my head up and be who I was raised to be.

I let out a calm breath, gaze skating over the room as the people wait with bated breath to hear me speak. *Me.* Not Tyndall.

"People of Highbell, your queen will hear your concerns now."

For a moment, everyone is quiet, like they don't know whether or not they should take me seriously. I'm sure most of them thought that Tyndall's advisors would appear and tell them all to state their concerns. But those written accounts would only gather dust in Tyndall's meeting room, if he even requested them at all.

Finally, one nobleman, Sir Dorrie, comes forward. He bows once he reaches the bottom steps of the dais.

"Your Majesty," he begins, face red with birthmarks, like a handful of raspberries smashed against his cheeks. "My pardon, but I feel I must point out that you are sitting in the *king's* throne."

My fingers curl around the edge of the armrest. I can see they're going to need a more direct response.

"On the contrary, Sir Dorrie. I am sitting in the throne of Highbell's *ruler*, which is exactly where I belong."

Whispers hiss like agitated snakes slithering along the golden marble, but I hold my gaze.

"My queen... King Midas—"

"Is not here to rule," I say, cutting him off. "*I* am. So speak your concerns, or my guards shall escort you out so that someone else more worthy of my time may come forward."

My warning travels throughout the entire throne room. A message for them to hear loud and clear. I wait. Small rises of my chest, impassive face, the cold indifference of a monarch who knows how to put her people in their place.

They're either going to fall in line, or I'll make them.

Sir Dorrie hesitates. He looks back, but no one in the congregation says a word. Not a single one of these simpering nobles joins him to defend Tyndall's position and my blatant move for control.

"Ah, I beg your forgiveness, Your Majesty. I would be honored if you would hear my concerns," Sir Dorrie finally says.

And just like that, I've collared them. Victory, not boredom, is what has me tapping my finger against the armrest. I'll make my own divots now.

The crowd doesn't raise a word of argument. Not even the guards behind me shift on the feet of uncertainty. Because when you've been raised your entire life to be royal, that's what you are. It doesn't matter that I have no magic flowing in my veins, because I have a different power, one passed down from generations.

Ruling Sixth Kingdom is in my blood.

After today, news will spread like snow across the white plains of our wintry land, drifting and covering every inch. I can almost hear the gossip, the whispers, the news drenching the kingdom like sleet.

Accounts of my opal crown will be explained as a beacon amidst the tawdry room, the bell of the castle will ring out the start of a new monarch, and the genuflection for the Golden King will end.

I'm going to freeze him out, ice him over. I'm going to make Tyndall regret ever marrying me.

A rare smile curves the pale edges of my lips.

I am Queen Malina Colier Midas, and I was born to rule.

CHAPTER 12

AUREN

Being made to ride alone in a carriage all day might be some kind of punishment—a silent reminder of my outsider status. But I guess there's something to be said for solitude.

There's safety in loneliness, but there's a lurking danger too. One that doesn't come from anything other than yourself.

The danger for me, of course, is the memories.

The long hours offer me a lot of time to think. Without anyone else around, no distractions, no words besides my inner voice. There's nowhere for those memories to be shoved away while I'm exposed, stagnant in my own festering company.

And so, I remember. Even though I don't really want to.

"How many coins, girl?"

My six-year-old hands are sweaty, hidden behind my back, fingers curled tight.

The man looks me over, impatient, tired, a pipe stuck in the corner of his mouth that breathes out smoke of blue.

He snaps his fingers. Zakir doesn't like to linger with me beneath the red striped overhang in the market square. If he's caught peddling beggar kids, he'd be in a world of trouble.

Rain drips off the awning cloth like strings of drool hanging from snarling lips of the wild dogs that run rampant through the city. The sky hasn't let up from its drizzle all day.

My hair is wet, making it look darker than it is, no shine to hide the matted knots. At least the burlap fabric of my dress helps sluice some of the water off, though I still feel like a drowned rat.

When Zakir's glare grows dark, I quickly pull my hand out from behind my back, begrudgingly unfurling my fingers.

He looks down at the offering in my palm, pipe bitten between his back teeth. "Two coppers? All you've gotten all day is two bloody coppers?" he growls.

I tremble at his tone. I don't like making him mad.

He snatches the coins and shoves them into his pocket. Taking the pipe out of his mouth, he spits at my feet, though I'm used to it enough that I don't grimace anymore.

"All you gotta do is stand there," he snaps, shaking

his head as he looks down on me in disappointment.

His accent is harsh to my ears still, even after all these months I've been with him. Some of the other kids call him Toad behind his back, because he's always making this croaking sound when he first gets up in the morning to clear his throat.

"Stand at your corner and smile, and these numps will practically toss money at ya!" he says, spitting the words like an accusation, like I'm not doing everything he's told me to do.

I bite my lip, looking down at the ground, pinching my arm as a reminder not to cry. "It—it's raining, Sir Zakir. I don't get as much when it's raining," I explain shakily.

"Bah!" Zakir waves a hand dismissively. He digs through the front pocket of his checkered vest to pull out his box of matches, relighting the end of his pipe where the leaves got soggy from the rain. "Get back out there."

My bottom lip wobbles. I'm hungry, cold, tired. Inara is a bad sleeper, and I got stuck next to her all night, crammed between her flailing legs and the corner of the room, so I'm dragging even more than normal. I've been looking forward to getting out of the rain, to being allowed to eat and rest.

"But—"

"You got rain in your ears, girl? I didn't ask for argument." Zakir flicks the used match at the ground. I watch it land in a puddle, flame smothered in an instant. "Six

more coins, or else you won't be sleeping inside tonight."

Collar pulled up against his neck, hat placed on head, Zakir leaves, probably to go meet with the other kids, while I slink back to my designated corner in the market square, knowing full well I won't earn six more coins.

I can usually get people interested enough to stop instead of walk by like I'm invisible, but under the shadow of dripping clouds, I'm just a wet beggar child, far beneath notice.

Still, I stand at my muddy corner between a hat-maker and an egg stall, and I smile. I wave. I make eye contact with everyone who passes by, stuck in the heart of a foreign city that smells of fish and iron.

The shoppers don't stop, the merchants ignore me.

No one can tell the difference between tears and raindrops on your cheeks. No one sees your watery smile when you've got the clouds to compete with. Even if they could, they wouldn't do anything, anyway.

So I beg all day and well into the night, with wet hands cupped out in a plea. If anyone really looked at me, they'd know I'm not begging for money. Not really.

But no one looks, and I don't earn those six coins.

When I finally drag my pitiful self to Zakir's house much later, I curl up in a puddle on the front doorstep—me and one other kid who didn't meet his quota. Even though we could offer each other warmth and comfort on this dreary night, the boy shuns me too, deciding to climb up the dilapidated eaves and sleep on the roof instead. None of the kids like me much.

That night, I promise the goddesses to never complain about Inara's sleep-flailing ever again, because getting kicked is a whole lot better than sleeping outside alone.

My chest aches as that memory fades. I sniff, like I'm getting rid of the scent of the sopping village, the saltwater fish, and Zakir's pipe smoke. I was with him for a long time. Too long. I spent many nights where the only blanket I had was the cover of darkness.

From five years old to fifteen, I never truly had a good night's sleep—not until Midas rescued me.

"You're safe now. Let me help you."

It's so strange to think about—how I went from that girl begging on a muddy corner, to a woman adorned in a gilded castle. Life takes you on paths you don't have a map for.

I turn my face to the carriage window, seeing the snow flurries drifting by, fog clouding up the glass. What I wouldn't give for Midas to ride in right now with torch and sword in hand to rescue me.

But he doesn't know where I am, doesn't even know that I'm in trouble. Which is why it's more important than ever that I get a message to him. Not just for myself, but because the last thing I want is for this army to sneak up on Fifth Kingdom and slaughter them all.

If I don't do everything in my power to warn Midas

of what's coming, then the fate of Fifth Kingdom will be my fault.

I can't fail.

A warning is all I have to offer. It's not much, but hopefully it's enough to help Midas meet the threat on a more even footing.

Once he finds out that I've been taken, I know there's nothing he won't do to get me back. *Nothing.*

When the gloom of a gray dusk descends, my carriage lurches to a stop, and I feel the jostle of my driver jumping down from his seat. I swipe my sleeve against the window, leaving a clear streak to peek out.

Outside, there's a singular rise in the ground, a hill that slopes gently up like a dune of snow. At its center, the hill is hollow and shockingly blue. It's so bright, even in the dark, that it almost seems unnatural, like a giant who's fallen asleep on the ground, a blanket of snow covering all of him except for that dazzling blue iris peeking out.

The soldiers make their main camp right at the center of the short, yet wide length of cave. Soon, they have a large fire built right at its pupil, a glittering wink of flame that sheds light on the deeper part of the cavern.

The click of my lock sounds, and the carriage door swings open, revealing Osrik. I step down, the ground slightly slippery beneath my shoes. All around me, tents are being put up, horses gathered, fires lit, a latrine being shoveled.

"Commander wants to see you."

I look up at him. "Why?"

His tongue moves the wooden piercing in his bottom lip in an absentminded gesture.

"I'm tasked to fetch you. Not to answer stupid questions."

I sigh. "Great. Lead the way."

I follow him as he cuts a path through the camp, but it's not easy. I have to dodge soldiers, veer around exposed stakes in the ground, and slog through snow that hasn't been packed down by footsteps yet.

When I nearly trip over a pile of wood that's been dumped to make a campfire, I curse, barely catching myself before I end up face-first in the snow. Osrik looks back at me with a smirk.

My blood boils. "You're purposely leading me on the shittiest path you can find, aren't you?"

"You catch on a little slow, but I'm glad to see you've arrived at the realization," he replies, the bastard.

I step over the rest of the disarrayed woodpile, catching up to him. "You really don't like me, do you?"

He grunts, as if my blunt question surprises him. "I don't like Midas, and you're his symbol."

I falter, footsteps stopping for a moment before I snap myself back into movement. "What do you mean I'm his *symbol*?" I've never heard anyone refer to me that way before.

Osrik leads me past a circle of horses huddling around bales of hay, making me step around the manure peppered over the ground.

"You're his trophy, sure, but you're also his mirror," Osrik tells me. "When everyone looks at you, all they see is *him*. All they think about is his gold-touch power and what it would be like to have magic like that, that endless wealth. You represent his reign—not just over his kingdom, but over all the greed in Orea, *and he fucking loves it*."

I'm stunned, too surprised by his words to form a response.

"So yeah, when I look at you—his little golden pet that he shows off—it pisses me off."

"Then don't look at me," I retort, my voice carrying a hard edge.

Osrik snorts. "I try not to."

I don't know why shame crawls up my neck and into my cheeks, leaving me with a rusty blush, but it does.

"For the record, I get pissed off when I look at you, too," I reply.

A rough, quick bark of a laugh escapes him, so loud and sudden that it makes me jump.

"I guess neither of us should look at one another then."

I dart a look at him. "I guess not."

We walk the rest of the way in silence, but I notice that this time, Osrik chooses an easier path.

CHAPTER 13

AUREN

srik leads me to a large tent, one that's different from the others. It's clearly a meeting space, based on its size and shape—rounded, like a tent in a royal tournament.

I follow him inside, finding furs on the floor and a circular table in the middle of the space. Three soldiers are sitting there on stools, speaking with the commander, who sits directly across from the doorway. When they see us enter, everyone's head turns, their attention landing on me.

Rip's eyes shift to his men. "We'll reconvene later."

The soldiers nod and stand up, shooting me assessing looks as they leave.

When it's just the three of us, I hesitate near the entry. Commander Rip is studying me in that unnerving way of his, looking no different than he did this morning, except the spikes on his arms seem to be shorter than usual, like he's retracted them partially.

"Have a seat," he finally says.

I skirt the table, choosing the spot farthest from his. He smirks as I pull out the stool, as if he knew I would choose to sit here. I glare at him. His smirk widens.

Osrik gathers the papers laid out on the table, and I silently kick myself for not taking the time to try and study them while I had the chance. I see a hint of a map and some written missives before Osrik removes them, letting them roll up to prop against a wall of the tent.

With the tabletop now clear except for a couple of lanterns, I glance around nervously. For some reason, the emptiness of the space makes the commander's attention more daunting.

There's nothing else for me to focus on, nothing else to distract me. Maybe he planned it that way.

Osrik pulls out the stool beside the commander and sits down, though I'm not sure how he fits on it. It's got to be a half-ass kind of situation.

I look across the table at them both, and although my hands are wringing together in my lap, I make sure that the movement is hidden from their view.

They're intimidating when they're apart, but together? It's like being stuck in the middle of a pack of ravenous wolves.

Rip sits at ease, back straight, forearms braced on

the table, spikes reflecting the light. He scrutinizes me, making my chilled skin crawl.

It takes great effort not to openly squirm, but I force my body to be still, only letting my nerves show themselves in the hidden squeezes of my hands.

"So, you've been King Midas's favored for ten years."

I glance between him and Osrik. "Yes…" I answer tentatively.

"Do you enjoy it?"

I blink at his question. "Do I enjoy it?" I echo, my confusion showing on the frown that pulls at my lips. What kind of question is that?

He nods once, and I feel my defenses build up around me like a wall being bricked.

"Just so you're aware, I won't betray Midas by feeding you information."

"Yes, Osrik informed me you said as much," Rip replies, a hint of mirth on his lips. "But I'm not asking about Midas. I'm asking about *you*."

My fingers curl against each other, nails digging into the fabric of my gloves. "Why?"

Commander Rip cocks his head. "Has no one ever talked openly with you, Auren?"

I scoff bitterly before I can stop myself. "No."

Osrik glances at Rip, and heat pinches my cheeks at my uncensored words.

"Not even Midas?" the commander asks.

"I thought we weren't talking about Midas," I counter snidely.

Rip tips his head down. "You're right. We're getting off-topic." A hand comes up to run over the black scruff of his jaw. "Was the gilded cage a rumor? Or is that truly where you were kept in Highbell?"

My golden eyes shine with a glare that has nothing to do with the lantern light. "I know what you're doing."

The sides of his mouth curl up in a wicked smirk. "Oh, I doubt that."

His condescending tone has two of my bottom ribbons unwinding from my waist, slipping between my tense hands like they're trying to hold me back from doing something foolish, like launching across the table and smashing a lantern into his smug face.

"So distrustful," he says, clicking his tongue. "I'm simply making conversation." The lie falls easily off his tongue, rolling to a stop at my feet. "After all, I have King Midas's famous favored in my company. I'm intensely curious about you."

I nearly roll my eyes. *Right.*

I feel a change in the air behind me, but when I tense and whip my head around, there's only a young boy coming from outside. He's dressed in the same leathers as the rest of the soldiers, except instead of black, his are solid brown.

He hurries inside carrying a tray, a few flakes of snow gathered on his chestnut hair. "Commander," he says, tipping his head respectfully.

"Thank you, Twig. You can leave it here."

"Yes, sir." The boy quickly places the tray down before hurrying out.

I look between them. "Your king forces boys that young to serve in his army?" I ask hotly. Twig looked barely ten years old.

Commander Rip reaches for the items on the tray, seeming unbothered by my tone. "He's grateful to serve Fourth Kingdom."

"He's a child," I snap.

"Watch your tone, pet," Osrik growls, but the commander shakes his head.

"It's alright, Os. She's probably just hungry."

My eyes flash with irritation. The last thing I ate was the slop for breakfast. *Of course* I'm hungry. But I'm not about to admit it, and it's definitely not the reason why I'm pissed. Children shouldn't be used.

"I'm not hungry," I lie.

"No?" Rip replies mockingly. "Shame."

He reaches for the tray and begins doling out three portions of dinner. I can smell rich, hearty soup, see curls of steam wicking up from each bowl. A large loaf of bread sits off to the side, with three iron cups that I *really* hope are filled with wine.

I could really use some damn wine.

Together, he and Osrik begin to eat, tin spoons dragging, the sound scraping against my nerves. I watch in agonized silence, and even though I try not to, my eyes follow every dip of his spoon, every bob of Rip's throat.

Stupid. Why did I have to go and open my stupid mouth? I should've only opened it to shove food in.

"So, the cage is true then."

My gaze snaps up from where I was watching his mouth, a sheen of broth covering his plush lips.

"Makes me wonder what's in it for you." Rip speaks conversationally, though his intense attention belies the easygoing tone.

My hunger tangles with my nerves, and knots together with my growing anger. The ribbons in my hand wind around my fingers, squeezing. "You don't need to wonder anything about me," I reply hotly.

"I disagree."

Every time one of them lifts the spoons to their mouths and drinks down more soup, I seethe. When Osrik tips the whole bowl back and gulps it down, my anger snaps. "It kept me safe. *That's* what was in it for me."

Rip angles his head. "Safe from whom?"

"Everyone."

Silence breeches the wall between us, slipping between the cracks. I don't understand this game he's playing. I don't know the ramifications of my responses.

Rip reaches for the third bowl and begins to slowly push it toward me, iron scraping over rough wood in a loaded path. My mouth waters.

When it stops directly in front of me, my eyes flick up to him.

"Eat, Auren."

I narrow my eyes. "Is that an order, Commander?"

Instead of rising to the bait of my taunt, he slowly shakes his head and lifts up his soup, dark eyes watching me over the rim of the bowl. "I think you've had enough orders, Goldfinch," he murmurs with a silken tone that makes me fidget in my seat.

His reply causes my eyes to lower with a weight I don't know how to measure. I don't know why his answer bothers me so much, but it does.

How is it that this male can strip me down to my thinnest layers, no matter how thick I try to build my walls?

I haven't forgotten who I'm dealing with. He's arguably the most cunning strategist in the world, which is probably why I always feel so off-center when I'm around him. He never behaves the way I expect him to.

But I bet that's calculated too.

To make myself busy, I lift the bowl to my lips and take a long gulp, bypassing the spoon completely. The salty broth hits my tastebuds, the hot liquid a balm to my timidity.

"Did you often dine with Midas?"

I lower the bowl from my lips so I can look across the table at him.

Another question. A seemingly innocent one. One poised about *me* but having everything to do with my king.

When I don't reply, Commander Rip drags the loaf of bread in front of him and lifts the knife from the tray. With meticulous precision, he begins to cut three even portions, the scent of rosemary immediately wafting out as the blade scrapes against the crust.

Once all three pieces are cut, he hands one to me. I almost turn it down out of spite, but I'm too hungry to refuse food twice, so I pluck it from his fingers instead.

His black eyes skim over my hands. "Wouldn't you rather take your gloves off to eat?"

I stiffen. "No. I'm cold."

Rip watches me—they *both* watch me—and even though I'm hungry, my stomach begins to churn with unease.

He raises the slice to his mouth as I do, both of us taking a bite at the same time. Osrik, on the other hand, shoves the whole piece into his mouth, chewing obnoxiously, crumbs falling on his jerkin that he dusts off absently.

"Are you going to ignore and deflect all of my questions?" Rip asks after swallowing his bite.

Dipping the bread into my last inch of soup, I soak up as much of the broth as I can, mostly so I don't have to soak in his gaze. "Why do you want to know if I dined with Midas?"

He rests an arm on the table, eyes unreadable. "I have my reasons."

I finish the remaining bread, though I'm unable to

enjoy the taste. "Right. And I'm sure those reasons are to find weaknesses, right? You're probably trying to determine how important I am to him. What you can get in exchange for me." I level him with a look. "Let me make this easy on you, Commander Rip. My king loves me."

"Indeed. Loves you so much he keeps you in a cage," he says with dark derision.

My temper flares, and I slam the bowl against the table as I set it down. "I *wanted* to be in there!" I say with a snarl.

Rip leans forward in his seat, as if my anger draws him in, as if it's his goal—to make me mad, to see me snap. "You want to know what I think?"

"No."

He ignores me. "I think it's a lie."

My glare is so hot, I'm surprised my ears aren't smoking. "Oh? That's funny, coming from you."

Finally, *finally*, Rip's impassive demeanor cracks. His black eyes narrow on me.

"Since you seem to want to talk about lies, tell me, Commander, does your right-hand man here know what you are? Does your king know?" I challenge.

Both he and Osrik go utterly still.

I stare at Rip with vindication, celebrating the fact that I've turned this around, that I've put *him* on the spot.

His spikes seem to flex—maybe in anger or threat, I don't know.

Rip's voice goes low. Coarse. Like jagged rocks

along a shore. "If you'd like to talk about *that*, then by all means," he says, lifting a hand. "You first, Goldfinch."

Shit.

My gaze darts to Osrik for a second, but the man is stony. I can't get a read on the behemoth at all. No surprise there.

In my lap, my ribbons swivel from the adrenaline sweeping through me. There's no possible way he can see them, and yet, Rip's eyes fall to the edge of the table before lifting back to my face.

The soup sours in my stomach, acid crawling up the back of my throat.

"Keep a lie for a lie, or tell a truth for a truth. What's it going to be, Auren?" he asks, voice like dark honey, wicked and tempting.

My breath breaks apart. Like it froze in my chest, a brittle, sharp thing with nowhere to go.

The truth… Such a complicated thing.

The problem with truths is that they're like spices. Add a little, and it can enrich things, let you experience more layers. But if you pour out too much, it becomes unpalatable.

My truths seem to always ruin the meal.

And yet, I *almost* want to blurt it out. To say what I haven't said. To shrug off the weight of my secrets. Just to surprise him—to put *him* on his back foot and catch him off guard.

It's tempting, like the way firelight must tempt the

moth. The promise of light draws me in, but I know that if I open my mouth, the truth will burn me up.

I clamp my lips shut.

Rip smirks and leans back, a victorious opponent sitting smugly across from me. I hate him, and yet somehow, I hate myself just a little bit more.

"Thank you for dinner," I say evenly as I get to my feet, all emotion drained out of my voice.

I'm suddenly exhausted and bent. A blade of grass trampled beneath stomping feet.

Osrik moves to get up, the silent observer of the room, but I look at him dismissively. "Don't worry, I'll find my own way back to my kennel. That's what a good pet does, right?" I taunt.

I turn and walk out without waiting for the commander to dismiss me, without even getting his permission. But thankfully, he doesn't stop me, and Osrik doesn't follow.

For now, my unpalatable truths are still sitting safely on the back of my tongue, everlasting with their bittersweet bite.

CHAPTER 14

AUREN

*H*ood up, *hands tucked into* pockets, I observe the soldiers from the nook I found—a shallow notch in the blue iced cave, just big enough for me to sit in.

The spot is perfect for me to keep isolated, while close enough that I can see the bonfire built into the middle of the hollow hill.

The icicles on the ceiling are dripping from the heat of the flames. Puddles have collected on the ground, but no one seems to mind. They're too happy to be out of the snow.

The savory smell coming from the spit turning over the fire tells me that somehow, they managed to find fresh meat out in this frozen wasteland. My mouth waters at the scent, but that won't tempt me to go closer. I'll have to be satisfied with the soup and bread I got.

Bright side, at least I ate before I stormed out. Next

time, I'll make sure to stay until I've had the wine too.

I stay pressed against the sleek ice wall as I watch everyone. I can't help but be curious about them, to look for their faults, to study their interactions. For all Rip's bluster about trusting his soldiers, I like to see them for myself. I also like to do it from afar.

I suppose it's not unusual, after being kept mostly isolated for so many years. For the most part, I still crave interaction with people, despite my unfortunate history. But sometimes, being around so many without the protection of my cage lights me up with sparking nerves. You can't trust people.

Especially a crowd of them. And this crowd? They're supposed to be the evilest, the deadliest.

But the more I watch them, the more I realize that they simply don't fit that narrative. They aren't a blood-thirsty group with rotted hearts and corrupted morals. They're just people. They're an enemy army, yes, but they aren't monstrous. Not that I've seen, at least.

And Rip…

I close my eyes, hugging my knees against my chest. I wish I could say that I do it to keep myself warm, but the real reason is that I'm clutching onto me, trying to keep myself together.

The moment Commander Rip stepped onto that pirate ship and into my life, my world tilted on its axis. Every time we interact, that axis dips just a little bit more.

Rip is smart. These little talks between us are meant

to throw me off. He's manipulating me, trying to turn me against Midas.

I know what he's doing, and yet, I can't stop the doubt he's casting. Like shadows over the ground, it will spread and grow unless I block it out.

Right now, I'm jumbled. Torn. A mess of thoughts and emotions, of doubts and complications. This is probably exactly what Rip wants, and I'm playing right into his hands by letting my mind spin in agonizing circles.

I sit for a few minutes more, just until I can finally inhale without my breath shaking. Just until I can give myself a pep talk to remind myself to stay on guard and not let my walls drop.

Above me, the snow begins to fall harder, the flakes as thick as fingernails scratching across a starless sky.

Casting one more look across the gathered soldiers, I crawl out of my hideaway spot. I tug my coat close around me, burying my hands under my arms. My ribs ache a little, and my cheek still feels a bit swollen, but the cold is good for one thing at least, because for the most part, I'm numb.

But then again, maybe that has nothing to do with the cold.

I walk away from the bonfire, knowing the general direction of where the carriage is, knowing the tent won't be far off. All I want to do is crawl into my pallet and sleep, but I can't. Not yet.

I need to always remember who I'm with. I need to

stay on track and not let Rip get under my skin.

I let my feet follow my eyes as a new determination fills me.

The tents I pass by are like a patchwork of leather sewn into the snow, every footstep a stitch. I walk past the gathered horses, their breaths huffing out like smoke, noses nuzzling into bales of hay. There's a launder tent not far off, where soldiers are scrubbing soiled clothes and brushing black wax over scuffed boots.

No one bothers me aside from a few lingering glances, but I keep my eyes averted. My face is cold even with my hood pulled up, the snow already beginning to pile onto the top of the tents, soaking into the fabric and making the scent of wet leather fill the air.

I've found that some smells are strings tied around memories. When you catch certain scents, those strings pull taut. Like a boat being brought to dock, forced to float in the sentiment. Unfortunately for me, wet leather does not moor me with a nice memory.

Wet leather. Not dampened by snow, but by the saliva on my tongue, soaking up my taste and voice. Strips torn from Divine knows what. I was too afraid to spit it out.

Is that memory going to merge with what's happening now? Wet leather changing from the gag to the cloying scent of Fourth's tents saturated with snow?

My thoughts swirl and fall.

My king loves me.

Indeed. Loves you so much he keeps you in a cage.

A deep frown pulls my eyebrows together, but I banish Rip's echoing words.

His aim is to drive a wedge between Midas and me, so I can't for a second believe he truly just wants to talk. He's a strategist. An *enemy* strategist, trying to trick me into switching sides, trying to loosen my tongue.

Which is why I need to find that messenger hawk. I need to find it, send a warning to Midas, and then Rip will know how solid my loyalty is. No matter how respectful and conversational he pretends to be, I have to remember the truth.

"He's an arrogant, devious bastard," I mutter beneath my breath.

"Sure hope you're not talking about me, my lady."

I whip my head to the left, finding Hojat turned in profile. He's looking down, stirring a pot of something over a small campfire. The scarred part of his face looks a deeper pink tonight, like the cold is bothering the contorted skin.

No one else is around to share his fire, but as soon as I get a whiff of whatever he's cooking, I understand why.

I hold my hand over my nose and mouth before I start gagging. "Great Divine, what is *that*?"

He doesn't even look up from mixing. "Wormwood, bishopwort, cattle cartilage, and a few other odds and ends."

My nose wrinkles. "It smells…" I stop short when he looks over at me. "Umm…it smells pungent," I finish, barely stopping myself from saying what I really mean. Awful. Disgusting. Completely rancid.

I honestly have no idea how he's leaning over it so closely, letting that foul steam waft in his face like that. "Does it? That's probably the bit of boiled intestines. It can be quite strong."

This time, I can't stop the gag that presses on the back of my tongue and cinches my throat. I gulp some air, keeping my eyes averted from the pot. "Why are you making that, exactly?"

"It's a new mixture I'm trying out to treat aches and pains." He suddenly straightens up and faces me, a gleam in his drooping eye. "Would you like to be my test subject?"

My mouth pops open. "You want someone to *drink* that?" I can't keep the horrified tone out of my voice.

"Course not, my lady. I'm going to cook it down to be a topical ointment."

I can't blink, because my mind is too busy picturing him rubbing around boiled cartilage and intestines. If my skin wasn't gold, it would be turning green right about now.

Hojat is still looking at me expectantly, and I realize he's actually waiting for my answer.

"Oh, umm, maybe next time?"

A look of disappointment flashes over his expression, but he nods. "Of course, my lady. I see your lip has improved."

I lift a hand, fingers skimming over the healing split. I haven't seen my reflection in a long while, and I'd rather it stay that way.

"The cheek could be better," he muses, the accent pulling at his *t*'s like his tongue wants to drag them under. "You didn't ice it like I told you, did you?"

"Yes..." I say, trying to keep the guilt out of my tone. "For a couple minutes."

He sighs and shakes his head, the corner of his lips looking like they want to fuse in a frown. "They always ignore the order to ice it," he grumbles under his breath.

"I'll do it tonight," I assure him quickly.

"Sure you will," he says, brown eyes rolling, like he doesn't believe me at all. "If you like, I can make you another tonic for the pain? If you let me check your ribs, that is..."

I quickly stiffen. "No thanks."

Hojat sighs. "You Midas lot are a distrusting bunch, aren't you?"

My body goes still.

Midas lot. He's seen the others.

It takes a lot of effort not to jump in eagerness. "Can you blame us? We're captives in Fourth's army."

"We're all captives of something, even things we don't want to admit to."

I frown at his words, but I don't have time to linger on them. "I'm actually headed over to visit them right now. I could help you talk them into whatever treatments they need if you want to walk with me?"

It's a bad lie. I know it, and based on the way he

looks at me, he knows it too.

"You are allowed to do this?" he asks doubtfully.

"Yes," I answer quickly.

Apparently, he's not buying my lies, because he shakes his head. "If you want to see the others, you'll have to get permission from the commander first."

A breath of frustration slides between my teeth like a hiss.

"Please," I say, my tone begging. "I'm not going to cause any trouble. I just want to make sure they're all okay. Surely, as a mender, you can understand that?" It's a cheap shot, but sometimes, cheap shots have a way of paying off.

A hesitant yet sympathetic look crosses Hojat's face, and for a moment, I think I've got him. But then he shakes his head. "I can't, my lady. I'm sorry."

"I'll take her."

We both flinch as a soldier suddenly appears beside us, like she materialized out of the shadows.

For a second, I'm so stunned to see a woman soldier that all I can do is openly gape at her. She's dressed in black and brown leathers, a sword at her hip, and a cock-sure expression.

She has beautiful, smooth dark skin like umber, warm undertones that bloom at the apples of her cheeks. Her black hair is cut short against her scalp, and it's been shaved in intricate designs. At first, I think the designs are pointed petals, but when I look closer, I see that they're actually sharp daggers shorn around her head like a crown, tips pointing up.

"Who are you?" I ask, my gaze lured to the small piercing above her upper lip. The shard of wood fits perfectly into the middle of her cupid's bow, topped with a tiny, gleaming red gemstone.

She doesn't answer me, her attention on Hojat. "You should go get your supper before all the assholes finish off the last of it, Mender."

The left side of his mouth tugs down roughly, a frown that's more apt as a grimace. "Soon. I've got to stir for at least five more minutes before I can leave this to cool." He looks from her to me and then back again. "You sure you'll be alright with the lady?"

He still addresses me as *lady*, never anything crude, not even setting me apart as a captive. It's hard not to like Hojat when he does things like that.

The woman smirks. "I can handle escorting our plated prisoner."

Hojat hesitates. "The commander—"

"It's fine." She claps him on the shoulder, successfully cutting him off. "Good luck with your stirring, Mender."

Hojat shoots me an unreadable look, but then he turns back to his pot, stirring and looking into the mixture like it's the most interesting thing he's ever seen. Uneasiness crawls over me like an insect in my sheets.

The woman looks me up and down. "Let's go see your saddles, shall we?"

I shoot one more look at Hojat, but he's pointedly

ignoring us.

I clear my throat. "Lead the way."

Warily, I fall into step with her. My need to see the others is outweighing all of my reservations. Besides, Hojat would've warned me if she was bad news...

Right?

CHAPTER 15

AUREN

The woman beside me moves like a bird.

Light on her feet, she doesn't stalk, or stomp, or even do what I'd describe as a walk. She flits, moving over packed snow with a swooping grace I didn't know was possible, while all I can do is try not to slip.

She takes me in the opposite direction I was heading, keeping away from the crowded bonfire at the cave, and even though I don't *see* her eyes on me, I can feel them. The prickle on the side of my face tells me that she's taking my measure.

My shoulders are tight under the silent observation, my lips pressed together to keep from speaking. It's not until we're well away from Hojat that she talks to me.

"So, *you're* the famous gilded woman that everyone's been talking about."

"Unless you have another one stashed somewhere."

She huffs, though I can't tell if it's in irritation or amusement. I hope it's the latter.

We approach a smaller campfire with a group of thirty or so soldiers gathered around it, but she abruptly veers to the left, behind a stack of firewood. I nearly trip from her sudden change in direction.

On the next aisle, there are a few soldiers walking around, and once again, she cuts a corner, making us squeeze between tightly-packed tents as she leads us to another pathway.

A sense of foreboding crawls over my skin as I look around the empty aisle. "You *are* taking me to see the saddles...right?"

"I said I was, didn't I?"

Well, that's not an answer at all.

Every time we see another soldier, she changes direction, until I'm so turned around and worried about her clandestine efforts that I don't know which one is making me more nauseated. Either the commander really wouldn't give me permission to see the saddles and she's breaking the rules, or...

Oh, great Divine. She's going to murder me.

Every sharp turn and ducking maneuver she performs to avoid nearby soldiers makes me more certain it's the latter option.

Thanks a lot, Hojat. I'd really started to like the intestine-stirring army mender, too.

My ribbons trill nervously beneath my coat, but just as I'm about to turn and try to make a break for it, the woman claps her hands. "Yes!"

I stop in my tracks, watching as she hurries over to one of the tents and crouches down beside a large wooden barrel sitting right at the front of it.

When she sees me still standing a few paces away, she gives me an impatient look. "What are you doing over there? Hurry up and come help me with this."

I blink in bewilderment before lurching forward at her glare, stopping in front of the barrel. "What do you want me to do?"

She rolls her eyes. "What do you think? Grab the end of this." Without warning, she shoves the barrel over, giving me only a split-second warning to catch it.

The weight of it crashes into my arms, and I let out a yelp of surprise. I nearly drop it when she grabs the bottom and heaves it up, forcing me to follow suit.

I straighten on my legs, the barrel lifted between the two of us on its side, liquid splashing around inside.

"Come on, Gildy Locks. Pick up those feet," she tells me, and then we're slogging through the narrow path again, but this time, carrying a heavy ass barrel.

"What is in this damn thing?" I ask through gritted teeth, trying not to fall.

"It's mine," she replies loftily.

"*Okay*...and why are we carrying it?"

"Because these left flank bastards stole it from the right flank. So I'm stealing it back."

The liquid inside sloshes against my ear as we carry it, the rough wood catching into the fingers of my gloves. "And you're the right flank?" I guess.

"Yep. Now pick up your side more. Don't make me do all the work."

I try to glare at her over the barrel, but I nearly trip, so I'm forced to watch my feet instead. My escort is forcing me into thiefdom. Probably not the best circumstance for me, considering I'm already their prisoner.

Bright side? At least she's not murdering me. I'm just an accomplice to a crime.

The woman adjusts her grip. "So, was it painful?"

I frown, shooting her a confused look as I do my best not to pant. "Was what painful?"

She turns sideways, leading me between a pair of tents in a ridiculously tight squeeze. "Everyone in Orea has heard about you. But now that I see you're real, not painted or just some bullshit rumor, I want to know if it hurt when King Midas gold-touched you and turned you into...*this*," she says, brown eyes flicking over my body.

My mind stutters at her question, surprise nearly making me forget that I'm holding a hundred-pound barrel. She wants to know if being gold-touched *hurt me*?

No one has ever asked me that before.

They've asked other things, sure. Crude things.

Words that would never pass their lips if they actually saw me as a regular person deserving of common decency.

Yet because Midas has made me a *symbol*, they can say whatever they want to assuage their curiosity. They believe my notoriety gives them the right to ask whatever obnoxious question piques their interest.

But this is different. It's not about what my gold body means to *her*. It's what it meant for *me*.

I realize that she's still waiting for an answer, that a long pause of silence has stretched between us, spreading like a shadow.

I clear my throat. "No. No, it didn't hurt."

She hums in thought, the hilt of her sword lightly tapping against the wood every time she takes a step. "Do you hate it? To be stared at all the time?"

Another thing I've never been asked. But this time, I don't have to pause before answering.

"Yes." The word comes out like a rush—involuntary, immediate.

Whenever Midas brought me around others— whether it was a throne room full of revelers, or an intimate breakfast meant to impress—it was always the same result. People stare. They talk. They judge.

That's why befriending Sail was such a breath of fresh air. He didn't ask me questions about being gold. He didn't gawk or treat me like a novelty.

He just...saw me as a person, treated me like a friend. Such a simple thing, but for me, it was everything.

But Sail is gone, and I'm here. With a woman I know nothing about, other than the fact that Hojat seemed a little scared of her and she likes to steal barrels in her free time.

Noting the shape of muscles visible beneath the black sleeves of her leathers and the confident way she touches her hilt, to me, she looks like a warrior.

I study her curiously, but my hands are strained, my arms burning and shaky. "I can't hold this thing much longer," I warn.

A click of her tongue. "Need to build up that arm strength, Gildy," she says before she nods toward a circle of tents. "Right up here."

She leads me to one of them, and we carefully set the barrel down. As soon as it's on the ground, her face splits with a smug smile, while mine pulls into a grimace as I shake out my sore hands and arms.

She ducks inside the tent and comes out with a pile of furs, throwing them over the barrel haphazardly. "There."

I look down at the sloppy covering with an arched brow. "It's not exactly hidden."

Her leather jerkin moves with the shrug of her shoulders. "Eh, good enough. Here." She reaches into the tent again, pulling out an iron goblet. Kneeling in the snow, she slips her hand beneath the furs at the bottom of the barrel, and with a twist of her arm, I hear liquid pour out.

Standing up, she takes a hearty drink, draining half the cup before she hands it to me.

I stare at the red liquid, eyes wide. "Is that…"

"Wine. Made from the vineyards in Fourth Kingdom."

I've snatched the cup from her hand before she even finished explaining, downing it all in a few gluttonous gulps. It's sweet yet spiced, thick, rich, yet refreshing. Maybe this is the withdrawals talking, but I think it might be the best wine I've ever tasted.

An appreciative groan leaves my lips as I swipe my sleeve against my lips. "Great Divine, that's delicious."

She smirks. "I know."

I try not to pout when she takes the cup back and chucks it into her tent. I missed wine so, so much.

"Alright, I'll take you to your saddles now. But this wine barrel thing? Never happened," she tells me sternly, pointing at my face. "I'm not joking."

"I never joke about wine," I reply.

"Good. Let's go."

Maybe it's because my tongue is now coated in alcohol, but I feel much calmer now with this strange woman. "So...you're a soldier."

"What gave me away?" she says dryly.

"Has King Ravinger always allowed women to serve in his army?"

Her head snaps over as she pins me with a glare, eyes flashing in the dark, lip curled back. "*Allowed*? Like he's doing us women a favor?"

"No, I just—"

"He's lucky to have women in his army," she interrupts. "*All* the kingdoms in Orea would be smart to utilize their women, but they don't. Which is why Fourth will always be superior."

Going off the impassioned vehemence of her voice, I'd say she's had this argument with people before.

"Sorry," I say quickly, hoping to assuage her. "I was just surprised. I've never heard of women in other kingdoms being accepted to serve as soldiers."

She gives a terse nod as we sidestep a row of buckets on the ground. "Like I said, Fourth's army is superior."

I slip my hands into my coat pockets. "Do the men... Are they cruel to you and the other women serving?"

"You mean you want to know if they fuck with us."

"Yes."

She shrugs. "There's always a few pricks who like to think that they're better than us," she tells me. "But it's not what you think. No soldier in this entire army would abuse one of the women."

"Really?" I ask dubiously.

"Of course," she says with unrivaled confidence. "For one, the commander would rip their heads clear off their necks if they did anything so disgraceful. But secondly, this army is a clan. We might have caught some shit in training, but everyone here has earned their place, whether they have a cock or a cunt. Being in Fourth's army under the commander is an honor none of us take lightly."

She speaks about Rip like serving under him is an immense honor, sounds almost fanatic in her respect for him.

I never imagined that Rip nor King Ravinger would ever hold such stock in equality of women. Midas wouldn't dream of allowing females to serve in his army.

As if she's reading my mind, she glances over at me with a knowing look, hand running over her shaved head to dust the collecting snow off. "I'm not surprised that the idea seems so foreign to you. Your Golden King wants women to *be* saddles, not sit on top of one to ride into battle."

I don't respond, because there's nothing to say in defense. She's right.

"What's your name?" I say instead. I should know it, now that we've stolen a wine barrel together.

"Lu," she answers.

"Just Lu?"

"Talula Gallerin, but if you call me Talula, I'll knock you on your golden ass, Gildy Locks."

My lips twitch. "Thanks for the warning. And it's Auren."

"*Just* Auren?" she retorts with a wry look. "No family name?"

I shrug. "No family."

Lu goes quiet at that. Whatever family I once had is gone forever. I wish I'd known that night was the last time

I'd ever see them. I would've hugged my father a little bit tighter. I would've buried my nose in my mother's hair as she held me and tried to memorize her scent.

It's funny how I forgot that smell, but I vividly remember the taste of the honeyed candy she slipped to me that night, because they were my favorite, and she was bribing me to be brave.

I remember the way it felt in the pocket of my nightgown, how it softened inside my shaking, sweaty palm. I recall how it tasted too, a burst of chewy warmth that melted against my tongue, the flavor mixing with the salt of my tears.

A small, sweet candy for a dark, bitter night.

I shove the memory away, crumpling it like I did the paper wrapper I buried deep into my pocket that night.

Lu brings me to a large tent, coming to a stop in front of it where two soldiers are outside, both of them sitting on stools beside a small campfire, the flames casting an orange glow across their faces. They're playing some kind of game, tossing down dice made of wood, the worn edges rolling with the shake of their hands.

Turning at the sound of our footsteps, their eyes widen on me. "What…" The man's question cuts off when he tears his gaze away from me and notices Lu.

The other soldier lets out a curse as they both immediately jump up to stand at attention.

"Captain," the man on the left says with a wary nod, while the one on the right spits out the rolled cigarette in his mouth, leaving it to hiss in the snow like an angry serpent.

"Evening, gentlemen," she says cheerfully. "Gildy Locks here would like to see the saddles."

The soldiers share a look. "Erm…"

Just like she did with Hojat, Lu grins and claps the soldier on the back, cutting off his hesitation. "Won't be but five minutes."

She moves and sits down on one of the stools they were just occupying before plucking up the used cigarette from the ground. It's still smoking a little as she sticks it in the fire to relight it.

She perches it between her lips before looking up at them with a cock of her brow. "Well? You assholes just going to stand there, or are you going to teach me how to play this dice game?"

The men pause, fidgeting on their feet with uncertainty, but when she snaps her fingers, they rush forward to accommodate her.

First Hojat is a little skittish around her, and now these soldiers called her Captain. Clearly, she's not just a soldier, but she has status too.

Interesting.

Lu smirks at them and gives me a conspiratorial wink. "Five minutes, Gildy. And don't even think about trying anything stupid. You do, and it won't be just you who gets in trouble, you get me?"

I nod slowly. "I get you."

"Good. Because if you do anything to undermine

their capture, there will be a price to pay," she says.

I have no doubt there will be. Just like I have no doubt that I won't want to pay it.

CHAPTER 16

AUREN

I *don't let myself hesitate* too long in front of the tent, because if I do, I'm worried I'll chicken out. I'll turn around and tell Lu I'd rather play dice with them than to actually face the saddles.

The problem is, I don't know what to expect, but I'm going to go out on a frozen limb and say they still don't like me.

Pinching the corner of the leather flap, I lift it up and duck inside.

As soon as my eyes adjust, I'm already doing a mental count. When I confirm that all twelve of them are accounted for, I let out a breath of relief.

Even though I stand at the entrance awkwardly with the chill of night at my back, none of the saddles see me at first. They're too busy arguing with each other to notice.

There are fur piles everywhere, flickering lanterns hanging on the poles that hold up the fabric of the tent, and food trays shoved aside, forgotten. The tent is big, but it seems tiny with all of them inside, the energy thick with irritation as they bicker with each other.

My gaze flicks to the loudest voice, and I find black-haired Mist arguing with a small, pixie-looking female named Gia. They're standing face-to-face, arms crossed, anger flashing in their eyes.

"You ripped my Divine-damned dress!" Gia growls, the sleeve of her bodice clearly torn, making it sag slightly.

Mist shrugs. "I warned you not to stretch your gangly ass limbs on my side."

"I'll stretch wherever I damn well please, Mist. You're not in charge, and this tent barely fits all of us, in case you haven't noticed. Not that *you're* helping any, since you're about two of me put together."

Mist bares her teeth like she's about to tear the girl's throat out, but a saddle with long red hair cuts in. "You think you have it bad, Gia? Isis stinks so bad that even the goddesses in the high heavens are pinching their noses."

Isis, the statuesque saddle on the other end of the tent, whips her head in the redhead's direction. "Excuse me? You think *you* smell like roses, bitch?" she demands, angry red patches appearing on her cheeks. "You're bathing with melted snow rags and shitting in holes just like the rest of us, so don't try to pretend you're any better!"

she screeches.

"I don't care who stinks," Mist cuts in, still glaring daggers at Gia. "If you touch me again while I'm trying to sleep, it won't be your dress next time. I'll rip out your stupid hair."

Gia fists her hands. "Try it, you whore!"

Several other saddles jump in to defend whichever side they're on, tossing insults vicious enough that I worry they're about to physically tackle each other.

Okay, so, the saddles aren't doing great.

Bright side? All twelve of them are alive.

I clear my throat, trying to cut through the multiple spats that seem to be going on. "Umm...hi." Not my best opening, but at least everyone stops arguing.

Immediately, two blondes who had their backs to me whip around at the sound of my voice. "What are *you* doing here?" Polly asks, looking me up and down. She's still wearing my old golden coat, and her sneer for me seems to have returned.

Mist rounds on me, all of the vitriol she'd been using on Gia now directed at me. "Oh, look, it's the *favored*," she says, practically spitting.

I ignore her. "I just came to make sure you're all okay," I say, glancing around.

Mist lets out a dry, ugly laugh as she sits down, propping herself up on a pile of furs and snatching one to drape over her. "You hear that? The *favored* came down from her pedestal to check on us lowly saddles. How kind."

My ribbons tug against my back, like they're envisioning coming out and shoving her again the way they did on the pirate ship.

I pointedly ignore her. "Is everyone okay?" I ask, glancing to Rissa for an answer.

She hasn't said a word since I came in, and she, more than the others, makes me nervous. I truly did want to make sure the saddles were alright, but I'd be lying to myself if I didn't admit that I specifically came to see her.

My life depends on it.

Rissa shrugs a shoulder, her hands braiding small sections of her hair while her shrewd blue eyes watch me. "As well as can be expected."

My head bobs. "I saw the army mender. He mentioned some of you wouldn't accept his help?"

Another girl, Noel, rolls her eyes. "Trust one of *them*? Are you really that daft?"

"He won't hurt you."

Several of the saddles laugh, shaking their heads. "Guess she *is* that daft," Noel mutters.

"Shouldn't come as a surprise. We all knew King Midas wasn't keeping her for her mind, just her gilded cunt," someone snickers under their breath.

I feel my face go hot, embarrassment clawing at my cheeks and leaving scratches of color behind. Once again, I'm put in my place. An outsider, always. They might have been arguing when I walked in here, but it seems like they can all agree on one thing.

They hate me.

Taking a breath to keep myself calm, I force their words to run off me like rain over oil. "If any of you are injured or feeling sick, you should let the mender tend to you. He hasn't hurt me, and I don't believe he holds any ill will."

"Why bother?" Mist asks.

My eyes cut over to her. "What do you mean?"

Behind the hatred in her face, I see the tiredness, the worry. Her black hair is tangled, heavy shadows hanging black crescents beneath her eyes. "Pretty soon, the soldiers will get bored, and they'll start to have their fun with us. Even if that mender really does do his job, we're just going to end up worse off anyway."

My nerves knot with worry. "You've heard the soldiers say they're going to do that?"

"We don't need to hear them," Polly interjects as she leans her head against the male saddle, Rosh's shoulder. "Look around, Auren. We're captives in the middle of an army full of lonely soldiers. They're going to take advantage sooner or later. Men are all the same." She looks up at Rosh and pats him on the cheek. "Except for you, Roshy."

He snorts and shakes his head at her, but even he seems uneasy at her words. As I look at the others, I can see it in *all* of their faces—the troubled resignation.

Every single one of them truly believes that this reprieve in captivity will be over soon, that the soldiers will use them however they like. And really, why wouldn't they believe that? It would be naive to think otherwise.

Just as I'm seen as a statue on a pedestal to be gawked at, they've always been treated as saddles to be ridden.

A sick feeling drenches me, an agitated wave crashing against the pit of my stomach, soaking me in worry.

What if they're right? What if Fourth's soldiers do start using them?

It's no secret the saddles are here, and who knows how long the soldiers have been traveling day in and day out?

Rip says he trusts his army, and even Lu said no one would hurt her fellow female soldiers, but what about hurting the saddles? After all, they belong to the enemy.

"This is the real world, Auren," Polly tells me haughtily. "We aren't Midas's *favored*. We don't have that title to protect us like you do. That's why we're in here and you're out there."

The saddles all nod, their gazes stuck on me like pins, every envious, hateful glare another prick to sting my skin and hold me in place.

I wish I could tell them they're wrong, that no one will hurt them. But the fact is, I don't know. I can't shovel them a pile of false promises and hope it doesn't collapse.

"Do you know where they're keeping our guards?" I ask, my voice quieter. What little confidence I had before I walked in this tent is long gone.

"No idea," Gia answers, legs curled beneath her

small body as she now sits, tugging at the torn hem of her dirty dress. "They keep us apart, probably so that we don't try something suicidal, like escape."

I nod distractedly, cataloging their tired, rumpled, and worried faces. No wonder they're at each other's throats. They're taking their emotions out on one another, and I can't blame them.

They're scared, they're crammed together like ants in a hole, walking over each other and ready to pinch. They've been captured by Orea's most fearful army, and they're living in fear that at any moment, they could be abused. I'd probably be fighting about leg space and body odor too.

My eyes skim back to Rissa. Unsaid words thicken my tongue, making me feel clumsy. "Rissa, can I talk to you for a moment?"

She looks at me steadily, a knowing glint in her blue eyes. My palms start sweating inside my gloves, while one question thrums in my head like a drum.

We're both still wearing our same dresses, the ones we had on when we were with the captain. I wonder if it makes her skin crawl, knowing that the fabric holds his touch? I wonder if she scrubbed it as madly as I did, if she found any blood stained into the threads.

While the two of us stare at each other, the other saddles look between us, picking up on the tension. My hands wring in front of me, my stomach twisting the same way.

One question keeps running through my head as I

look at her, the unknown circling me like a vulture ready to dive.

Did she tell?

CHAPTER 17

AUREN

B lue eyes watch me, pretty face revealing nothing. I'm not surprised. Rissa isn't one to break character and give anything away.

I can't judge the feel of the other saddles either. They're too good at pretending, too practiced in courtly words of tricks and riddles.

"Can I please talk to you?" I ask again when the silence becomes too much. She's making me squirm, every second worse than the last.

Rissa's attention flicks down, catching me nibbling on my bottom lip before I can stop myself. She knows my most important, most guarded secret, and I have no idea if she's told anyone. I have no idea what she's thinking, and that worries me.

Finally, she gets to her feet. "Sure, we can talk."

An audible breath of relief leaves my chest, but I look around, heart sinking. There's nowhere in this space that we wouldn't be overheard.

Rissa's one step ahead. "Come. The guards let us step outside a few times a day to stretch our legs."

I follow behind her out of the tent, and Lu's head snaps in my direction as soon as I'm outside. Rissa looks at the guards. "Just stretching my legs, boys," she says with a practiced smile, blonde braids prettily woven through her hair. Even though she's been wearing that same dress for days and has no hairbrush, she somehow still looks beautiful.

The closest guard narrows his eyes on us. "You know the rules. Only one at a time."

"It's alright," Lu intervenes, looking at me steadily. "Gildy Locks will stick close. Won't you?"

"Yes," I answer quickly.

The soldier's mouth turns down in displeasure, but he relents. "Circle the tent only."

"Of course," Rissa purrs before turning, and I follow beside her as we begin a slow circle around the saddles' tent, the shadow of night giving us a pretense of privacy.

I'm brimming with worry, practically shaking with it while we walk in the snow side by side, her finger trailing lightly over the leather tent as she goes. I can hear the muffled voices of the saddles inside, already picking up on another argument.

"You know what I'm going to ask," I say, breaking

the silence.

"Do I?" Rissa replies coyly.

A breath of frustration winds out of me, a tight spiral that springs up in my throat. She's not going to make this easy on me. I knew that as soon as she made me wait.

We may have gone through a traumatic moment with Captain Fane, but that doesn't mean she's my ally now.

I pitch my voice low, our slow, meandering footsteps matching in pace. "Did you tell anyone?"

The only light we have is a milky moon amidst ashen clouds, like cream poured over slate.

"Did I tell anyone what?" she says breezily.

My jaw tightens. "Did you tell anyone about what I did to the pirate captain?"

My question falls slowly, like the snowflakes drifting down around us. Once again, she's silent, letting me squirm as we walk, her blonde hair going ginger as we pass by a lantern hanging on a nearby tent.

She finally answers me. "I didn't tell anyone."

I sag, hand over my thumping chest. "Thank Divine," I breathe, condensation puffing out of my lips like smoke.

She turns to me and stops, cutting me off. "*Yet.*"

My short-lived relief stutters and stumbles, a newborn calf falling on the ground.

I watch her face, her eyes. Sparkling blue to distract from the darker depths within. "You promised not to tell," I remind her.

"I have to make a lot of promises. Doesn't mean I

keep them." Her tone is a bite, frothing in warning. "How does it work, anyway?"

An incredulous frown drops my brow. "You just admitted that you might be going back on your promise to me, and yet you think I'm going to tell you anything?"

She shrugs a dainty shoulder, flicking snow off her hair. "I want to know how it works."

"How *what* works?"

Rissa smiles, like me doing the same thing—purposely being difficult—amuses her. "Never mind. It's obvious that King Midas transferred some of his powers to you when he gold-touched you, and he doesn't want anyone to know," she says quietly, making my heart stop.

She studies my face, and I don't know what she sees on my expression, but it makes her lips tilt up in victory.

"That's why he refuses to gold-touch anyone else. Not because you're his one and only favored, but because he doesn't want to accidentally give anyone else his magic too."

She's speaking more to herself than to me, a confirmation that she reads from the lines on my face.

I glance around to make sure no one is around, terrified despite her hushed words. A hard lump has lodged in my throat, a graveled pebble that won't move.

If Midas ever caught wind of this conversation...

"How often can you tap into his power?" she asks

thoughtfully.

"You need to stop asking those kinds of questions, Rissa. You can't tell anyone what happened with Captain Fane. It needs to stay a secret," I say in a rushed, desperate whisper, eyes darting left and right.

She tilts her head, wheels churning, mind working. "You want my silence?"

"*Yes*," I say emphatically.

Something flashes in her eyes—like the glint a fish sees right before they swallow the hook.

"Fine. But I want gold."

My heart drops, because I both knew this was coming—and hoped that it wouldn't. "Rissa..."

She looks back at me without remorse. "Secrets have a price in this world, and we all have to pay. Even the girl made of gold."

I want to laugh humorlessly, not because she's wrong, but because I know exactly how right she is.

I have spent *everything* on secrets. Coin. Time. Heartache. Precious moments. I've had to give up my childhood, my freedom, any scrap of happiness I've ever had.

Secrets, I've learned, cost far too much.

"I have to survive, same as you," Rissa says steadily, voice holding no remorse. "You need my silence? I need gold. That's my price."

Seconds pass between us like breaths, one after another, no break between. She holds her chin up and her back straight, but I know the mark on her back where Captain Fane struck her with his belt will still be there, just like his kick to my ribs is still healing.

Yet it's the hurts without marks that worry me the most.

I sag a little where I stand, a dejected breath passing my lips. "I'm sorry Captain Fane touched you," I say quietly. "I'm sorry I let it get that far."

She scoffs. "I'm not doing this because he touched me, and I don't need your pity. I've been touched by far worse for far longer. Besides, it's my job as a saddle to be ridden."

I shake my head. "Don't do that. You don't have to make the offense seem like nothing. Not with me," I tell her. "You may be a saddle, but you're a royal saddle, only meant to be with the king. But more than that, you're a woman who deserves to be treated with love and respect."

She outright laughs at me this time—head tilted back, creased eyes pointed at flakes that fall from the sky. She lets the sharp coldness land on her face, snow dropping into her open mouth and salting her blonde hair.

I cross my arms in front of me, gloved fingers holding on like I can contain my roiling emotions. "What's so funny?"

Rissa shakes her head and starts walking again, forcing me to match her steps. "After all this time, you still think those things are real?" she asks.

We pass by the guards and Lu just then, which is good, because it gives me an excuse to hesitate before answering.

Do I? Do I think those things are real?

If Rissa had asked me this question a couple of months ago, I would have answered straight away that Midas loves me. He always has, since the moment he rescued me.

And yet…

My king loves me.

Indeed. Loves you so much he keeps you in a cage.

That crack in the glass is back—the one that formed when I thought Midas was giving me to King Fulke.

The splintering crack is creeping out, like the web of a spider, silk-thin strands spreading, imperfections in the clear love I've always had for him. It's getting hard to see through it. But is that my fault? Am I letting Commander Rip get to me?

"Love and respect exist," I say quietly, just as we round the side of the tent again.

I might be a confused mess right now when it comes to Midas, but my parents loved each other. I don't remember much, but I know that.

"Maybe it does for some," she concedes, her voice also softer now, sadder. "But it doesn't exist for women like us."

Her confession is spoken to the horizon, words for

the clouds to soak in and rain down.

"We're beautiful and pleasing to the eye, meant to fuel a person's lust, meant to play a part. But we don't get true love, Auren. And the only women in Orea who have respect are the ones who sit on a throne. Even then, they'll *always* be secondary to their male counterparts. You should know that by now."

"King Midas—"

Rissa cuts me off. "King Midas is just that, a *king*. And kings love one thing above all else. Power."

The pessimism seeping from her tongue is a strong poison without any antidote.

"Gold, Auren," she reiterates quietly, barely taking a step. "If you want me to keep your secret, I want gold."

"I can't make you gold." I rub at my eyes, watching the hems of our skirts brush through the thick snow.

Her shrewd attention refuses to leave me. "So you can tap into his power but not very often? That makes sense. You clearly exhausted yourself the other night. I thought you were going to pass out after you gilded the captain with his pants stuck around his ankles."

"I very nearly did." Only pure adrenaline and fear kept me going.

She thinks quietly for a moment as we do another lap, passing Lu and the guards. My escort gives me a pointed look, letting me know my time is dwindling.

"Can King Midas tell when you've used his power?"

Rissa asks.

"Shh!" I say hurriedly, looking back to make sure they didn't hear. None of them are looking our way. Lu is too busy gloating that she won the round, while the other two are grumbling about beginner's luck.

I relax slightly as we round the corner, though her lack of discretion is unsettling. "You should've carved a piece out from Highbell Castle if you wanted gold so badly," I mutter.

"Do you have any idea how often the guards inspected every inch of that place?" Rissa scoffs and looks at me like I'm an idiot. "I'm not a fool. The few saddles who ever dared to take a single, tiny piece were always caught. *Always*. And believe me, their fate wasn't worth it."

I swallow hard, my mind conjuring up all sorts of punishments. I never considered what inspections Midas must have put into place to ensure no one stole anything from inside the castle, or even pieces of the structure itself.

"The gold you get me has to be new, completely sep-arate from anything the king owns or touches. Turn the damned spoons gold, I don't care. Just get me enough."

The idea of smuggling gold to her fills my stomach with unease. "Enough for what? What will you do with it?"

"Buy out my employment."

She answers so quickly and succinctly, it's clear that she's been thinking of this for a while. "But...the royal saddle contract is incredibly high. You'd need—"

"*A lot* of gold to buy it," she finishes for me with a nod. "I'm aware. That's where you come in."

I shake my head vehemently. "There's no way you could have that much gold without raising suspicion. The king would find out."

"He won't if I do it right, which I will. Believe me, I have no intention of getting caught and having my head on a golden spike."

"This is ludicrous, Rissa."

"It's not completely unheard of for saddles to be given extra coin if they've pleased the rider enough," she says. "And I've been tipped before."

"But—"

She waves me off. "It's simple. Whatever golden bits you give me, I'll trade for coin. I'll buy out my contract when I have enough. If the king makes inquiries, I'll explain that I've been saving every extra bit of coin I've earned over the last seven years. I'll even say that Captain Fane himself was so pleased with my performance that he gave me a hefty sum," she smirks. "The king will believe it. I'm his best saddle."

I can't argue with her confidence, because it's true. She's been with Midas for years, and she's the best, most poised, most seductive saddle I've ever seen.

"I'll finally be my own master," she whispers, stopping at the back of the tent. Her voice rings with the clarity of deep-seated want. I can tell right then that there's no hope of trying to talk her out of this.

Rissa's eyes glitter. "*Freedom*, Auren. I'll finally have freedom, and you're going to help me get it." She takes a deep breath in through her mouth, like she can already taste it. "You help me buy myself out of the royal contract and ensure I have enough coin left over to start fresh somewhere new, and I'll keep your secret. Forever."

"That's a hefty price."

"It's a fair price," Rissa counters.

"Some would say that you should keep my secret out of loyalty."

"I'm only loyal to myself." Her tone holds no guilt, no shame. But can I really blame her? In this world, giving loyalty to anyone other than yourself is dangerous.

"I don't want to have to tell your secret, Auren. But I will do whatever it takes to gain my own freedom."

With the look of unrelenting determination on her face, I have no doubt in my mind that she means it. She will do whatever it takes, and despite the fact that it puts me in a horrible position, I find that I'm not angry at her. I *want* to help her.

I just hope it doesn't come back to bite me.

"Fine," I finally relent, and Rissa's sharp inhale reveals just how much she was hanging on my answer. "Don't breathe a word of this, to *anyone*, and I'll get you your gold. One payment. Enough to buy your freedom and start fresh. Nothing more."

"When?" she asks, eyes alight with impatience.

My mind whirls, trying to think of what I can do, how to do it. *No one* can know. Especially not Midas.

"I can't turn anything gold now. When we're back with King Midas, I can do it then."

"Why? You need to touch him to recharge?" she asks with a coy tilt of her head, fishing for more information.

I give her a flat look. "When we get to Fifth Kingdom, Rissa. That's the best I can do. Take it or leave it."

Two beats pass between us, and then she nods. "Deal."

We walk back to the front of the tent in silence, passing the guards one last time.

"Time's up," Lu tells me.

"We're done," Rissa assures her with a friendly smile.

But that smile fades when she stops quickly in front of the flaps, nearly causing me to run into her. I jerk to a halt, blinking at her in surprise.

Her voice drops quieter again, and she pins me with a fierce look. "As soon as we get to Fifth."

I nod warily.

I can tell she's reading my expression, my body language, weighing my words, double checking that my promise is sincere. She's close enough that I can feel her breath on my cheek, her own face lit up from the campfire beside us.

"Don't go back on your word, Auren," she murmurs

to me, a dangerous fire in her voice—one that I helped to spark. "If you do, I'll make a better deal with someone else."

She turns and slips into the tent without another word, leaving me in the snow, stuck to sweat in the middle of her promised threat, wondering which of us will end up burned.

CHAPTER 18

QUEEN MALINA

The atrium is my least favorite room in the entire castle.

I liked it here once. When it was full of the plants that my mother tended, when the air was brimming with soil and flowers and *life*.

Now, it's a tomb.

Hundreds of plants, all dead, all stuck inside their gilded caskets. With the open dome ceiling made entirely of glass windows, there's no escape from the gleam as the gray, cloudy daylight filters in.

Every plant I walk by is a memory.

My mother's fingernails lined with soil, her smile when she placed shears in my hand. The way she hummed as she walked, aisle by aisle, watering every rosebush and sprout.

I loved it then. Now, it makes my skin crawl.

Of course, as the ruling queen, I'm forced to come here more often. As luck would have it, it's always the one room that visiting nobles want to see.

Lady Helayna stops, skirts brushing against the perfectly arranged tulips, some of them still drooping slightly from the weight of their petals.

Eyes gleaming, black hair perfectly shiny and swept up into a loose bun, this pristine countess belongs to one of the wealthiest families in Sixth Kingdom, and now, she's the head of it. A rare position of power for a woman in a strong family.

"This is extraordinary," she says, her eyes holding wonder as she looks up at the solid gold fountain.

I try to see it from her viewpoint, her fingertip dragging across the stagnant ripples. The water's descent is frozen in time, the continuous stream like golden curtains.

At the bottom well of the fountain, there's a splash that will never settle, water that will never again be clear and cool, or pure enough to cup your fingers in and drink. Water that once spewed from the top is now caught in a graceful arc, solid gold rivulets as thick as my arm.

"So perfect, Queen Malina. So utterly captivating."

"I'm glad you enjoy it, Lady Helayna. I should have invited you to Highbell ages ago."

"Yes, well, I'm so glad for the time to do such things now." She smooths the front of her black dress, my eyes following the movement.

"How are you faring?" I ask as I purposely start leading her away. The wind has begun to howl outside, snow battering against the window panes like the angry fists of ghosts. Further proof that this room haunts me.

Lady Helayna fidgets with the gauzy fabric that's tucked into the high collar of her dress. The mourning veil will be worn over her face for a month, only to be taken off in the confines of her home or in the presence of royalty.

"Oh, I've been managing, Your Majesty."

Our heeled footsteps echo in the large space, and even though all I want to do is run out, I manage to lead her away at a respectable pace. Although, when she stops at the vines draping down the wall, I clench my teeth.

"I imagine it's been very difficult since your late husband's passing," I say gently, cupping her elbow in a show of remorse, when really, I do it to pry her away, to keep her walking.

The golden vines may be tempting to look at, but I've learned that everything in this castle is insidious. Every tangled trail and curling bloom is nothing but a baited trap.

Lady Helayna digs into her pocket and pulls out a handkerchief, wiping at her watery eyes as we head for the door. "Yes, I miss my Ike. He was a good man."

He was a cheater like all the rest, though I keep that thought to myself.

My head dips. "I was very sorry to have missed his burial."

"Oh, I didn't presume to expect your attendance, Your Majesty. You're so busy managing the kingdom," she assures me, tucking her handkerchief away.

She pauses before we can make our escape to the door, noting the cage built on the other end of the room, the bars stretching all the way to the hidden hallway at the back.

"Strange," she murmurs, gaze pausing on the pile of silken pillows still lying on the ground, as if Tyndall's pet is still around to laze on them day and night.

When my husband told me he'd be expanding Auren's cages to allow her entry to the atrium, I was livid. This room, even though I detest it now for what he's turned it into, it's still *mine*.

My mother cared for these plants that were so carelessly killed, choked inside metallic coffins. This was the room where she died, her bed brought up so she could be amongst all the green, thriving growth, breathing in the perfumed blossoms on her dying breath.

Tyndall threw it all in my face by bringing *her* in here. By letting her look up at the windows my mother lived and died beneath.

Perhaps that was when I truly started to hate him.

"Your Majesty?"

I blink over at Lady Helayna in surprise. I hadn't even realized I was still stopped, staring at the cage.

Shaking my head, I give her another practiced smile. "Pardon. I was just watching the storm begin to break," I lie, purposely flicking my gaze past the cage to the windows instead.

She nods knowingly, her gaze moving up to watch the thickening snow as it begins to pile over the dome, casting us in hues of gray—a somber sky. "I should go before the storm gets worse."

"Let me walk you down."

We pass by four of my guards on either side of the atrium's doorway, their sure footsteps following behind us as we begin the long journey down the stairs.

"Thank you for inviting me to tea and for the tour of your atrium, Your Majesty."

"Of course. I do hope you'll come again," I reply.

I wait, hoping for her to bring up the one topic we've both been dancing around all afternoon, but she says nothing. My teeth start clenching together again.

By the time we reach the first floor, Lady Helayna's handmaidens are already there, waiting with her coat and hat. She draws her mourning veil back up, hooking it to the hat that her lady places on her head, features going muddled behind the sheer black fabric that drapes over her face.

Once she's helped into her coat, she turns to me. I keep the pleasant smile on my face, though beneath it, I'm fuming, going over everything I could have done or said differently, wondering if another tactic would've worked. Calculating which of the nobles might still be swayed even without her.

Lady Helayna curtsies, her dress sweeping across the worn golden floors. "My queen."

I give her my hand, though my smile is tight. An entire day. I wasted an *entire* day on her and—

Her grip tightens on mine in a friendly squeeze, face slightly obscured as she leans in conspiratorially. "You have my full support of ruling Sixth in your husband's stead."

I pause, the cool, smooth victory spreading through me like fresh ice. The cold is a balm to my spirit, a win that brings me that much closer to keeping control.

I may not have been born with magic, but I'm going to prove to Tyndall, to my court, to my *entire kingdom*, that I hold my own kind of power. With it, Sixth Kingdom will become stronger than ever. *I* will become stronger than ever.

"The fact that any of the other noble houses are hesitant is beyond me," she says, and I can almost feel the roll of her eyes. "A Colier has ruled Sixth for generations and will continue to do so. You can rule here, while the king continues to aid Fifth Kingdom and secure our borders."

This time, the smile that curls my lips is genuine. Having a female head of house is a rare thing, and I knew it was the perfect opportunity to gain a foothold inside the noble circles. A simple afternoon of pandering, and I've got her.

Having the countess in my corner will make it easier to gain the trust of the other noblewomen. I know for a fact that they all speak to one another, and Lady Helayna is the one they look to as a leader amongst them. If I can get all of the women on my side, it'll be a major victory.

The women might not all be the heads of their houses, but they speak into the ears of the men who are. If done right, those whispered encouragements can become the subconscious thoughts of ignorant men.

"You have my thanks, Lady Helayna. The crown is ever grateful for your support."

"We women have to stick together," she says, a coy smile barely visible behind her veil. "Have a pleasant day, Your Majesty."

"And you," I reply with a conspiratorial tilt of my head.

The moment Lady Helayna is gone, my advisors come in, like birds of prey dropping in a swoop. "Your Majesty."

"I've got Lady Helayna's backing," I say smugly, looking at the three of them. Barthal, Wilcox, and Uwen—advisors to my husband who were left behind to run Highbell. Now, they answer to me.

"You do?" Wilcox asks, clear disbelief on his aged face.

I nod. "As I told you before, gentleman, there is nothing wrong with me ruling in my husband's absence."

"Of course, my queen," Uwen says, hand holding the belt at his hip to keep his stomach from overflowing over the top of it. "Our concern was simply that King Midas gave us *very* clear instructions. We were to continue business as usual and send a hawk for any concerns as well as regular updates. He was to make the decisions, and—"

"*I* will be making the decisions."

I've been working nonstop to tighten my tentative hold on the kingdom, and the three of them are my most vocal doubters. Which is why I've been doing everything in my power to prove them wrong, to put them in their place.

"As I told you before, we have no need for hawks. Any updates and concerns will come to me," I tell them.

I turn and begin to walk up the stairs, though I get immense pleasure from the fact that they start hurrying after me, like trained dogs come to heel.

"But the nobles..." Barthal begins.

"The nobles, as I have shown you all week, are loyal to the Colier family," I say firmly, my steps silent on the golden carpet.

"You have met with many nobles this week, that is true," Barthal admits.

"Yes, and not one of them has any doubt that Sixth Kingdom is in good hands," I point out.

"Yet, I fear that the shift in power you are enacting in the kingdom will worry some of these noble families, and we can't afford any dissent," Uwen puts in.

I stop, whirling on the three of them at the second floor landing, my guards halting a pace behind. "Look around you. Highbell can *afford* anything." My tone is harsh, my eyes cold. "If there is any dissent in the future, I will handle it, but for now, continue setting up meetings. I want to see a member of *every single* strong-standing noble family in Highbell."

They look amongst themselves, burning with the question that they don't dare ask. They know better than to directly inquire about what my intentions are with gaining personal support from the nobles.

But they know. They at least *suspect* that I plan to make these changes permanent. To make the people answer to me instead of him.

My husband might have the golden touch and the silver tongue, but I have the blood and the history. It was my ancestors who ruled this kingdom.

As a Colier, I know everything there is to know about this land and the families of Highbell, and I know how to manipulate their loyalty.

"Yes, Your Majesty," Uwen replies with a bow.

I look down at them coolly. "Now, unless you plan on following me to my personal chambers, I think we're finished today. I'm tired, and you still have to answer those inquiries I drew up. I'm waiting for those findings."

Wilcox scratches the whiskers on his chin. "About that, Your Majesty. The questions about our forces..."

"I want them all answered, Wilcox."

"Yes, but..." He hesitates, sharing another look with the other two, but they leave him high and dry. Uwen suddenly finds the floor fascinating, while Barthal is busy fixing his lapel.

Wilcox sighs and looks back at me. "Forgive me if I'm speaking out of turn, but those inquiries...it sounds as if you plan to prepare for war."

I flash him a benign smile and take a decisive step down. One stair, then two, until I'm directly in front of him. He freezes, blue eyes wide as I reach up to straighten the Sixth Kingdom insignia on his tunic, the metal brooch pinned through the middle of his collar. I close my fingers around it tight enough that he flinches.

I suppress a smile while I move to tighten his collar, fix the position of the gleaming gold bell at his throat. "Do you recall what King Colier, my late father, said?"

Wilcox swallows audibly, his throat moving with a nervous bob as he shakes his head.

"He said, 'Foolish is the king who does not prepare for attack. From outsiders, as well as those *within*.'" I drop my hand, eyes lifting up to his face that's gone pale. "Don't you agree that's good advice, Wilcox?"

A shaky, nervous breath comes from between thin lips, but he manages a nod. "Yes, Your Majesty."

Casting a casual glance at the other two, I note their shock—the sweat on Uwen's bushy brows, the paled face of Barthal.

One carefully worded statement, and I've issued my warnings. I consider every ally as a potential threat, and I won't hesitate to end anyone who goes against me.

"I expect an answer to my inquiries soon. That will be all, gentlemen," I say in clear dismissal, enjoying every part of their discomfort as my guards follow me, moving past my dumbstruck advisors.

I turn at the second floor railing, hand curving over the banister as I look down on them. "Oh, and all hawks have been suspended from use as of today. No messages will be allowed in or out without my direct approval."

The sight of their slack-jawed faces nearly makes me smile. I turn, satisfaction brewing through me as I stride for my chambers, knowing that every day I spend, every maneuver I make, I'm that much closer to tightening my grasp over Highbell.

By the time Tyndall tries to return to Sixth Kingdom, it will be far too late.

CHAPTER 19

AUREN

I *'m sick.*

I don't know if I caught something from the horde of soldiers or if it's the stress or if it's simply that my body just can't take being out in the endless cold anymore. Whatever it is, my brain feels like it's ready to thump out of my skull.

I haven't felt sick like this in a long time, but it brings back bad memories of Zakir. I was sick a lot back then—all the children were.

His business of buying us to run his beggar scheme was good for his bottom line, but apparently, not good enough to want to take proper care of us. We just had to suffer through it, because he certainly didn't give us a day off. He said people were more likely to feel sorry for sick children, anyway.

There were a lot of us, tightly packed together in

the cold and sometimes even wet sleeping arrangements, never with enough food, hygiene less than stellar.

I don't even like to think about the times I had to dig for tossed out leftovers. Garbage. I ate garbage sometimes.

Even then, kids would steal it from you if you tried to stash it away; it didn't matter how much gunk was gathered on it. No wonder sickness ran rampant.

Still, I hate feeling weaker than I already am. All I can do is sleep it off and hope no one notices that I'm even more vulnerable than before.

I nearly snort. If there's one thing the commander is aware of, it's my vulnerabilities. The saddles too, for that matter.

It's been three days since Rissa set the price for her silence. But in those three days, I haven't seen Commander Rip once, except for his sleeping silhouette when I sneak out of the tent every morning before dawn.

I've tried to go visit the saddles again every night once we stop traveling. Twice I was turned away. Last night, the guards who saw me with Lu were on duty, so they allowed me a short visit, but that was almost worse.

The girls wouldn't even look at me except to spew their frustrations about my freedom to walk around versus their inability to leave their crowded tent.

At least I was able to confirm that no soldier has tried to use them yet.

I want to keep trying, to break through to them and let them see that I'm not their enemy, but the effort is always so disheartening because it never gets me anywhere.

If anything, they've just started hating me *more*.

Yet they're not the only reason why I've been making it a point to visit. It's also so that I can continue my search for the messenger hawks.

I make sure to go a different way every time, to continue to map the camp. They set it up nearly the same every single night. It would be easy if this army weren't so damn big.

But the thought of trekking around in the snow right now and then dealing with the saddles makes me groan in exhaustion.

I'll give myself the night off and pick back up tomorrow, when it doesn't feel like the commander's spikes are stabbing through my head.

Speak of the devil...

The carriage door opens, and I squint over at Rip, his silhouette dusted with the light of dusk.

No armor today, leather coat frosted at the edges, his black hair windswept and his spikes nowhere to be seen.

"Does it hurt when you keep those in?" I blurt.

Rip glances down at the arm I'm looking at, like he's surprised his spikes aren't out—or maybe that I asked about them. "No."

"Hmm." I lick my dry lips and swallow with a twinge of pain but then remember what I really wanted to talk to him about. I pick my head up straighter when I realize I've slumped a bit. "I want to know where Midas's guards are."

"Do you?" he asks in a gravelly voice, shoulder leaning against the doorframe. "Well, I'd like to know who your closest friends were in Sixth Kingdom."

I blink at him through stinging eyes, my mind a little slower than normal at processing his words. Even when I do, I'm still confused. "Why do you always ask the strangest questions about me? Why do you want to know that?" My tone is both bewildered and defensive.

"Is it the saddles you've been visiting?"

So he knows I've visited them. I guess I shouldn't be surprised at that, though I am that he's allowed it to go on.

A chuff escapes me as I tilt my head down, fingers coming up to rub my burning eyes. "Oh, yeah. They *adore* me. We braid each other's hair while trading stories about Midas in bed."

Great Divine, did I just say that? I must be sicker than I thought.

I hear a rasp of a chuckle. "Interesting."

My hand drops away, the scraping talons against my skull making my eyes sensitive even in the dim light. "What's interesting?"

"Interesting that you should attempt to visit them every night when you wouldn't consider them your friends. Makes one wonder why."

I bristle, suddenly wishing that we could've made it to day four without interacting. I'm just not that lucky,

I guess.

"Are you going to block me in this carriage all night, or can I get out? I'm tired."

Rip's head tilts to the side, the short spikes along his brow line more pronounced. "Tired? You're usually chomping at the bit to go eat and visit the saddles."

"Yeah, well, as you pointed out, they're not my friends, so I'll just save myself the trip," I snap.

This male makes my headache so much worse.

Black eyes narrow as he studies me closely, gaze smoothing over my body from head to toe. "Are you ill?"

"I'm fine. Now, if you don't mind..." I look point-edly where he's still blocking the doorway.

I'm surprised when he actually steps aside to let me out. Dusk is still the victor against night, the last of the graying light quickly fading. I take in a deep breath, the fresh air making me feel so much better after being stuck in the stagnant carriage all day.

My teeth begin to chatter, and I band my arms around myself like a shield, trying to hold in a shiver, trying to create a layer of armor against this male. He has a way of making me feel like he's peeling away my layers, seeing what I want to hide. And right now, I don't feel well enough to fend him off, to keep up with his battle-minded tactics.

Thankfully, the tent is already set up, erected right beside the carriage. I want to collapse on the pallet under a pile of furs and not come out until my head stops pounding.

I take one step toward it, but my vision suddenly swims, pain lancing through my forehead. I squeeze my eyes shut and stumble, my legs like jelly.

Rip's hand lashes out lightning-quick, fingers curling around my arm. His catch steadies me, freezes me in place. The disorienting feeling is swept away from my head, like his touch is a chain to an anchor I thought had broken away. I teeter, a boat in the water, reeling as that anchoring grip holds steady, keeping me upright.

A split second later, I realize my mistake—dependent on his hold as I am. Eyes springing open, I whirl, yanking my arm from his grasp.

"Don't touch me!" I hiss, looking around wildly, my heart nearly beating right out of my chest as I glance at the sky.

A dizzying feeling comes over me again, but I lift my hands in front of me to ward him off.

Rip's eyes harden like inky steel, his spikes erupting from his sleeves and down his back. They seem to breathe, each sharp curve expanding like ribs.

He glares down at me. "You can barely stand. You *are* ill."

"I said I'm fine."

He takes a step forward, coming into my space, forcing my head to tilt back. "And *I* said don't lie until you can do it better," he replies quietly, his voice an even rumble, a saw dragging through wood. "Go to the tent. I'll send for the mender."

I grit my teeth at his order, since that's obviously what I was doing in the first place. My head hurts too much to think of a retort though, and I can't breathe correctly with him so close.

Cursing him under my breath, I turn and walk off, keeping my attention on my feet, feeling his eyes on my back until I duck into the tent.

There's a slight chill in the space since the burning coals haven't had enough time to heat it up, but I kick my snowy boots off and strip out of my coat before I collapse onto the pallet on the right, burying myself beneath layers of blessed fur.

I feel like I've just barely closed my eyes when I feel a hand pressing against my brow. My head swims, and for a moment, I think it's my mother's hand, her comforting touch come to say goodnight.

But then I notice the calluses on the palm, the rough grit sliding against my forehead like sandpaper smoothing wood.

It can't be her—her hands were soft, dainty. Hers was a mother's caressing touch, not this clinical, unfamiliar graze.

I startle awake, blinking blearily as Hojat comes into focus above me. It takes a second, but once I realize that it's his hand touching my forehead, blind panic comes roaring up.

In a rush of alarmed horror, I jerk upright, my ribbons

straightening out, acting on pure instinct. They shove him away hard, curled edges of satin slamming into his chest with a furor.

With wide, surprised eyes and a grunt from the force of my push, Hojat's body goes flying back. It happens almost in slow motion, while I watch in horrified shock.

A strangled yelp chokes out of me as his body barely misses hitting the burning hot coals. His momentum keeps him going, my hit far too hard, and I suck in a breath as I watch his trajectory head for the poles of the tent.

A second before he would've crashed into them, Rip is there, taking the brunt of the mender's fall.

The commander manages to catch him, hands on shoulders, where Hojat regains his feet instead of colliding into the tent and taking the whole thing down, probably cracking his head open in the process.

An exhale whooshes out of me.

For a moment, none of us move, none of us speak. With my ribbons flared out on either side of me, the only sound that can be heard are my heaving breaths.

When I manage to calm myself enough to breathe normally, my eyes flick to the tent flaps, where I can see the blackness of night bleeding through the cracks. I must've only dozed off for a little while.

But in my panicked overreaction, I just showed my hand—or more accurately, my ribbons.

Hojat steps away from the commander to straighten himself. "Well, you're a strong one," he jokes with a nervous laugh that tugs the left side of his scarred mouth in a grimace.

Blearily, my ribbons drop as I lower myself back onto the pallet, shaky legs curled beneath me. "I'm sorry. I didn't mean to," I say, shoving sweaty strands of hair off my face. "I just...I don't like to be touched. No one is allowed to touch me."

Pity crosses his face. "I didn't mean to scare you."

I find the courage to flick my eyes to Rip. I don't know what he's thinking. His expression is far too unreadable, his stare too still. It sets my already racing heart on edge.

Sweat gathers across my brow and back, and I suddenly regret falling asleep beneath all those furs, because I'm no longer cold. I'm *sweltering*.

And it has everything to do with the way that Rip's gaze is burning into me.

CHAPTER 20

AUREN

Rip and Hojat continue to stand there, staring. I feel like a little girl caught red-handed with stolen food.

Hojat looks nervous and embarrassed, though I don't miss the curious edge of his brown eyes as his attention flickers to the satiny strips that just launched him across the room.

"So you *can* move them," Rip says, voice cutting through the air like shears.

His tone is thoughtful, as though he's talking mostly to himself. He rubs the black scruff of his chin, his gaze running over the long length of ribbons now lying motionless on the floor.

I don't know what to say. I'm stuck between a lie and a truth. Squeezed from both sides, trapped between two unyielding walls. Neither of them is the right choice. Neither will protect me.

It's why I've always chosen silence when I can, because silence is sometimes all you have. Like the Deify—the pious people who reside in the Mirrored Sahara of Second Kingdom. Once they go through those doors to take their vow of silence, there's no going back. Tongues cut from their mouths, they never have to choose between uttering truths or lies again.

I envy them sometimes, that they've learned to cheat those crushing walls.

Eyes dropping down, I dig my trembling fingers into the skirts of my dress, faded from its golden glory, wrinkled, slightly damp, baggy, and overworn. I feel every inch of the fabric hanging over me, as heavy as Rip's stare.

"I knew I saw you use them to break your fall when you descended the Red Raids' ship."

I maintain my silence. It's not like I can deny it. But I don't have to admit it, either.

"Why do you hide them?" he asks curiously, no mention of the fact that I just almost took out poor Hojat, like he isn't concerned that I could be considered a threat. I guess to Rip, even with my ribbons, I'm not. Not compared to him, anyway.

I flick my hand against the ribbons, urging them to move behind me on the pallet, where they wind themselves up in tight curls. "Why do you *think* I hide them?" I ask, my voice cracking, snapping words in half like brittle branches. "Should I keep them out all the time like you show off your spikes?"

An arrogant shrug. "That's exactly what you should do."

I scoff. "Easy for you to say, *Commander*. No one would dare touch you. But these?" I ask, picking up a clump of them in my sweaty palm. "I don't need another reason for people to gawk and pluck at me. Hiding is the only thing I can do."

"Is that why you don't like to be touched?"

I feel the blood drain from my face.

"Did people...*pluck* at you because of those?" Rip asks, gesturing to my ribbons.

A breath sucks in through my teeth, but I'm saved from answering because a dry, scratchy cough tears out of my throat and splits the seams of his question.

Hojat, still frozen on the other side of the tent, suddenly comes alive at the sound. "Pardon, Commander," he mumbles before coming over to me.

He kneels down at my pallet and pulls off his satchel, digging through the contents inside. "I know you have a fever and a cough. Is that all that ails you, my lady? Is it your ribs?"

I let out a breath and press a thumb against my aching temple. "My throat is a little scratchy, and my head hurts," I admit. "But my ribs feel healed."

His eyes quickly skate over my face. "Your cheek

and lip healed, too."

My fingers rub over the areas. "Yes, all better."

"Okay, let's get the rest of you right as rain." He brings out three vials along with a cloth that has some herbs wrapped inside it. He wisely places everything on the furs beside me, careful not to touch me.

I eye the glass bottles. "None of those happen to have boiled intestines in them, do they?"

Hojat shakes his head, and some of the lingering trepidation eases off his face. "No intestines this time, my lady."

"Bright side," I mumble under my breath before coughing again.

He taps on the vial nearest me, the liquid green and oily. "Drink half of this now to help that cough. We don't want it settling into your chest."

I dutifully pick up the vial and pop the cork off, downing half of it with a grimace on my face, expecting the taste to be awful. However, it's surprisingly sweet. "That wasn't as bad as I thought it would be," I admit, sealing it again before handing it back.

"There's some honey in there to cover the taste of the—"

I quickly toss up my hand. "Don't tell me."

His lips seal, though his brown eyes twinkle with amusement. It's a relief that he's no longer looking at me with skittish unease.

"This one can be rubbed on your chest if the cough

gets worse," he instructs, tapping on the second vial. "And this third one can be soaked into the cloth, mixed with some snow to hold over your eyes and forehead for the headache. The snow will also help ease the fever."

I nod, glancing at the dried herbs wrapped in the cloth. "And those?"

"They're to put under your pillow."

My brows pull together. "Why?"

He picks up the cloth and unwraps it. They're not herbs like I thought, but dried flowers. "Where I come from, it is good luck to place peonies beneath your pillow when you are ill, my lady. You'll have to settle for putting it beneath the furs, though," he says, winking with his good eye.

"You're giving me these?" I whisper in touched surprise.

The tops of his cheeks redden slightly, his accent thicker with his sudden shyness. "Here." He holds them out for me to take.

They're delicate, three blooms on dried stems, parts of their leaves cracked off and crumbled. I turn them around in my hand, the pink color of the flowers gone dusty, the edges of their petals browned like the crust of bread.

"Thank you," I murmur, tears springing to the backs of my eyes.

Peonies for good health. A willow branch for luck. Cotton stems for prosperity. The fleshy leaf of a jade to bring harmony.

Hojat hesitates, maybe noting the way the flowers are affecting me. I take a steadying breath and set them aside, blinking away the watery blur.

"Keep snow on your head, but send for me if you start to feel worse," he tells me.

"You're a very well-prepared army mender," I say with a smile, gently setting the flowers aside. I'm still pointedly ignoring Rip, wishing that he'd leave, wishing that he hadn't seen what he did. It's only a matter of time before he starts asking questions and demanding answers.

"I have to be," Hojat replies with a shrug as he settles things inside his satchel, arranging them just so. "Oh, I also wanted to thank you, my lady."

"For what?"

"For speaking with the saddles. Because of you, a few of them allowed me to treat them," he says cheerfully, all previous awkwardness gone.

"Really?" I reply, surprised. I didn't think the girls would listen to me about Hojat, but I'm glad to hear that they have. Who knows what sort of injuries they sustained when we got captured from the Red Raids?

"Yes. It's a good thing, too, considering the condition of the one woman," he goes on while he places the other vials for me on the ground near my pallet. "She'll need to be careful, especially considering our current whereabouts. It won't do for her to get too cold, and the travel rations haven't been too kind on her stomach."

I watch him walk to the tent flaps and gather some snow, piling it into the cloth. He then pours some of the liquid from the other vial into it before tying it off.

"Is she going to be alright?"

"Yes," he answers, handing me the snowpack. "She's progressing nicely. No signs that she's in any danger of miscarriage."

My heart slams to a stop.

"Wait. *What*?"

Hojat turns, his expression changing because of whatever he sees on my face. He looks over at Rip, who's still standing across from us, silent as a stone gargoyle, spikes gone, arms crossed in front of him.

"Apologies," Hojat mumbles. "I just assumed. Well, with you visiting them… Never mind."

"Which one?" I breathe, and I don't move my eyes off the scarred lines of his face, don't miss how the misshapen skin creases with contrition.

Hojat spares another look at Rip, and the commander gives a tiny nod, though he never takes his eyes off me.

The mender shuffles on his feet, the hesitation of truth caught in the harsh slash of his mouth. "Straight black hair, a bit standoffish. I think her name started with an M…"

A snap in my chest—like a frozen pine needle crushed beneath a hard boot. "Mist."

He nods slowly. "That's the one."

The last of whatever air I'd had in my chest whooshes out of me as my mind begins to spin and churn, my thoughts spiraling like a whirlpool in a river, spinning my head, yanking me down.

"*Pregnant*," I say, staring off, not seeing anything. "She's pregnant." My voice is nothing but a hoarse whisper.

It's Midas's baby. It has to be.

The sound of a crunch makes my head tilt down, and my eyes fall to the stems of peonies I've accidentally crushed inside the curl of my fist. I didn't even feel that I'd grabbed them again.

I quickly drop them, but pieces of broken green are stuck to my glove, the stems snapped in half.

Mist is pregnant with Midas's baby.

Mist, who's been the most vocal, the most vehement in her hate for me. She's *pregnant* with Midas's illegitimate heir.

Tears slip down my face, but I can't feel the heat of them against my fevered cheeks.

A baby. *Midas's baby.*

Something he warned me, again and again, that I could never have. He couldn't afford to have a bastard with me. Not when Queen Malina never fell pregnant. I'm his Precious, not his breeder. He said it wouldn't be right to his wife.

A sob scrapes up my throat, jagged edges of frozen rock making me bleed. I want to hide beneath the furs again, block out every revealing light, every raw chill. I want Hojat to take it all back, for this to be an elaborate lie.

But I know it's not. I can see the truth of it in the mender's twisted face.

Whenever we were intimate, Midas never finished inside me. He never wanted to risk it. With his saddles, he was always more careless. I tried not to let it bother me, because I knew they all took something to prevent pregnancy. But me, he never wanted to give me that herb, said he wouldn't risk me taking it after one of the saddles got really sick and died from it.

From my peripheral, I notice Hojat trade a look with the commander and say something quietly, but I'm too devastated to listen.

He slings the strap of his satchel over his shoulder and walks out of the tent, and as soon as the flaps close out the night air, I drop my head into my hands. My palms curl over my eyes, tears dropping into them like they're slowly filling cups.

Cracks. So many cracks in the glass.

How did that happen? How did I get here, when I thought I'd never have to look through broken things again? So long as my reflection was with Midas, I thought it would always be whole and good and clear. And yet, these cracks keep appearing, keep splintering.

I know Midas has sex with all of his saddles. Hell, he shows it off. Having me watch, having me there like a silent bystander behind gilded bars. Maybe he thought of it as his way to include me, as warped as that seems.

I managed to quell the grieving hurt of it over the years, but this… Mist's stomach is going to swell with a child she made with the man I love. How can I quell *that*?

The truth of it sinks in, lower and lower, like rough sediment at the bottom of a pond, sharp against bare feet, muddying up the water.

I always preferred to ignore it. To shove away all the bad and look at the good. But Mist being pregnant changes things from lustful, meaningless liaisons to something else. Something *more*.

All of Mist's hate makes so much more sense now.

In her eyes, I'm the woman he puts on a pedestal. She doesn't just have to worry about the queen, but me too. And here she is, carrying his child.

Great Divine, what a mess.

I pick my head up, lashes stuck together with wet hurt, throat cinched tight. Rip is sitting on his pallet now, the low lighting of the coals and lantern pitching him in shadow and flame. A villain to spectate my stumbles.

Whatever was in that vial has already helped the itchiness in my throat, but the tightness in my chest, the feeling of the tent closing in on me, that isn't going away, though it has nothing to do with my being sick.

"Go ahead," I say, tone numb, eyes flat. "Go ahead and gloat. Drive your wedge between Midas and me. Make me question everything. Make me doubt and rage and flounder."

I want to slap him. I want to let my ribbons come out and send *him* flying backwards. I want to fight and storm, just so I don't have to feel this crushing grief.

The harsh planes of Rip's cheekbones look even sharper right now, the pointed tips of his ears a stark reminder of what he is. My opponent. My enemy. A fae renowned for his cruelty. And right now, that's exactly what I want.

"Do it," I hiss, anger drowning out the urge to vomit.

Something flickers in his gaze, something I can't quite place. "I don't think I need to do any of that right now, Goldfinch," he says quietly.

Fury rears up in me like a leviathan, its massive presence breaking the surface. "Fuck you," I spit, acid spewing off my tongue that's hot enough to burn away the chill on my soul. "You planned all of this, didn't you? You're manipulating me, every step of the way, making me question everything!"

My furious words end in a cough, but it doesn't choke off my ire.

Rip shows no remorse on his face, no change in the black void of his eyes. "I find it funny that you so easily accuse *me* of manipulating you, when you seem to have turned a blind eye to *your beloved king* doing it for years."

Before I even know what I'm doing, I've picked up the vial at my feet and chucked it at him.

His hand comes up, catching it with a smack against

his palm.

"That's not true!" I yell, hands going up to thread through my hair, pulling, like I can pluck out the vicious words from my skull.

"Stop lying to yourself," he counters with infuriating calm.

I hate him in this moment more than all the rest combined.

"I bet it's not even true," I spit. "You made Hojat tell me that, didn't you?"

"Powerful as I am, I don't have enough bribes in the world to make Hojat lie. My mender is infuriatingly honest at times."

Fire burns in my chest, steaming my eyes. "I hate you."

Rip tilts his head. "Your anger is misplaced, but *I like it*," he says with a feral grin, sharp canines gleaming. "Every time you let it leak out just a little bit more, I can see you better, Goldfinch."

The muscle in my jaw jumps. "You see *nothing*."

"Oh, I do," he counters, voice low, rough, like two stones clashing together, trying to ignite. "I can't wait to see the rest of you. When you let it go, when you finally let that *out*, your fury is going to light up the spirit you've shadowed." He looks like someone who's won, boasting in superiority. "I hope you burn so bright that you scorch your Golden King down to ash."

My vision flares. "Get out."

He smirks at me, the bastard.

Smoothly, he gets to his feet, spikes unfurling from his spine and arms like a dragon stretching its wings.

He looks at me, but the tears that run out of my eyes extinguish my glare. For a split second, his face softens, his merciless eyes reflecting something other than arrogance.

"You want to know what I think?" he asks quietly.

"No."

"Well, I'm going to tell you anyway."

I sneer. "Goody."

His lips flicker with amusement for a brief moment. "You may not be behind bars anymore, but you're still in that cage. And I think part of you wants to stay in there because you're afraid."

My mouth goes hard, ribbons tightening like fists.

"But..." he goes on, taking a single step forward, pressing into my space, his invisible aura licking off my skin like a testing taste before the bite. "I think another part of you, the part you repress, is ready to be free."

The pulse in my veins feels like thunder, a crash of lightning with every blink. "You'd like that, wouldn't you? To ruin me?"

He looks at me with something close to pity. "Not ruin. You forget, I know what you are. You're so much more than what you let yourself be."

I try not to flinch, try not to let it show just how much his words are affecting me, just how hard they're hitting.

My chin tilts up, faking whatever confidence I can. "I'm not going to change sides. I'm *always* going to choose him."

Rip tsks, a rueful, disappointed click of his venomous tongue. "Oh, Goldfinch. For your sake, I hope that's not true."

He walks out of the tent, his retreat making all my adrenaline flee, leaving me tired and weak.

For a moment, all I can do is stare.

Then I pick up the snowpack from the ground where I dropped it, and strip out of my dress, socks, and gloves. I take the broken peonies and slip them beneath the furs at my head, then lay my heavy body down on the pallet.

Rip's words repeat cruelly in my head while I envision Mist's stomach growing, Midas's cracked reflection, my ribbons hurting Hojat.

I hold the cold cloth over my eyes and tell myself that the wetness there is from the melting snow, that the ache in my head is worse than the ache in my heart.

I guess the commander is right. I should be better at lying, because I don't believe myself at all.

CHAPTER 21

AUREN

I look around the formal dining room, at the tapestries hanging over windows that stretch from floor to ceiling, the paneled walls adorned with ornamental embellishments. A chandelier hangs like icicles above us, its crystals glittering like the sparkle of a lover's eye.

Even after months of being here, I'm still not over all the lavishness, the sheer size of the palace. It's all incredibly elaborate, making me feel so out of place, so small.

The amount of wealth in Highbell Castle is enough to make my head spin, and that was even before Midas decided he wanted everything to be turned gold.

"You alright, Precious?"

At Midas's query, I glance over, a smile already turning up my lips. "Yes," I reply. "It looks good like this, don't you think?"

We both stand alone in the room, and it's still strange to think that this is where we live now. I haven't gotten used to it. I also haven't gotten used to us, either. Midas used to wear cheaply made trousers and scuffed boots. Now, he's always in silk tunics and perfectly tailored pants. The strangest of all is when a crown rests on his copper-blond head.

Even so, it fits him. It's like he was made for it—all of this finery doesn't leave him feeling awkward or make him seem out of place. If anything, he's flourished in Highbell despite having to take up the mantle of king so quickly.

I'm proud of him. So proud of the way he hasn't faltered, hasn't backed down. For a man who was raised on a farm with no family left, he's taken on the role of king with ease.

His eyes, the color reminding me of the pod on a carob tree, look over the room with meticulous assessment.

I've been all over the castle with him today, parts of it transforming before our eyes. A windowsill here, a rug there, teacups and chair cushions, wall sconces and doorknobs.

Night fell a few minutes ago, taking away the last of the day's watery light. Servants have already come in to feed the fireplace, the flames a hungry, wakeful beast that growls and spits, casting the room in its orange glow.

Dozens of candles adorn the dining table, place

settings waiting perfectly arranged over the newly shimmering surface. I can still see the grains of the wood, but the polished timber is now remade—gold, to match the rug and curtains and dishes.

"It does look good," Midas hums, his eyes catching on the spots that haven't been turned yet—the white marble floors, the paneled walls, the ceiling, and the backs of the chairs. "But it will look even better when it's all golden in here," he finishes with a smile in my direction. "You must be hungry. Let's eat."

With a hand on my back, he leads me toward the table, two servants already there with our chairs pulled out. Before I've even finished sitting down, my ears prickle with the noise of a door opening, of heels clicking against the floor.

I freeze, unable to help the servant to push in my seat. I shoot Midas a wide-eyed look, but he's looking at the doorway where she just walked in. His wife, his queen.

I hear her skirts swish against the floor as she comes closer. She rounds the table, sitting at Midas's right, directly across from me.

The dining room is filled with sudden tension, and Queen Malina knows it. A gentle nudge behind me unsticks my hesitation, and I murmur a thanks to the servant as they finish pushing in my chair.

"Wife, you've joined me for dinner," Midas says, the cool blanket of his tone covering up whatever other *emotions he might be feeling.*

The queen never dines with him for supper unless they have guests. They share breakfast or sometimes tea, but not dinner.

Dinner is supposed to be mine.

The servants come up, placing a plate and bowl in front of each of us, wine poured in our glasses. If they've picked up on the discomfort, they don't let it show.

"I was out all afternoon in the city, and I've only just gotten back. I skipped lunch, so I thought I'd dine with you tonight," Malina says with unruffled ease.

Her snow-white hair is parted on the side, front strands swept over loosely, all of it gathered into a knot at the nape of her neck. She's wearing a gold dress, just like me, but hers is far more elaborate, the skirts full, the bodice bedecked with lace and frills and layers.

Compared to her, I feel like my satin slip of a dress is barely a step above a nightgown. The only garnishments are the gold rings at my shoulders that hold the fabric in place.

"I'm glad to have your company," Midas replies.

My gaze burrows into the bowl of soup in front of me, wishing that I could be anywhere but here. I'm angry that she's here taking away my one meal with him. It's all I get anymore, and sometimes, I don't even get that.

I can feel the queen's eyes on my downturned head, my scalp tingling with cold, like her wintry blue gaze carries the chill of winter itself.

At the sound of Midas starting to eat, I lift my hand

woodenly, forcing myself to do the same. I can't let myself look at him, since that would only enrage her. The last thing I want to do is gain attention. I don't dare slurp or drop my spoon as I eat. In fact, I try not to make any noise at all.

All three of us eat in uncomfortable silence for a few minutes, throats swallowing, broth sipped. I'm sure it's delicious—everything here always is—but I can't taste it around the bitterness I feel.

Malina sits straight and proud across from me, no hair or thread out of place, her very essence regal and overwhelming. Looking at her, there's no doubt she's royal.

"Hmm," she hums, stirring her soup before lifting her gaze up to me. "It seems your gilded orphan girl has learned better table manners since last time."

I freeze, the spoon halfway to my mouth.

A quiet sigh comes from Midas. "Malina, don't start."

She manages an elegant, uncaring shrug, except I can see the hardening ice of her gaze. "It was meant as a compliment, Tyndall. The last time I saw her eat, I thought we were going to have to sop up the stew from her lap."

My fingers tighten as I lower the spoon, my eyes flicking up to her. Our gazes collide, blue and gold, ice and metal. I can see it, there in her eyes—the jealousy, the anger.

And she can see it too, in mine.

Beneath the table, Midas's foot brushes against my leg. It's a small, hidden touch of comfort that helps me loosen my breath, but it's also a reminder.

Malina can provoke me all she wants, because her status allows it. But I'm just the favored saddle *that she tolerates. I'm the other woman, and I can't openly do anything to show disrespect.*

Subtly put in my place, the stirring fire inside of me goes out, like a snuff over a lit wick. My eyes drop from hers.

"How do you like the room?" Midas asks Malina, diverting her attention, changing the subject. I'm grateful for his attempt at moving the conversation away from her verbal criticism of me, but for once, I wish he'd stand up for me instead.

He can't, though. That's his ring on her finger. She's the one who sits beside him on a throne, the one on his arm when they visit town. I can't be that with him.

He's a king, and I'm no queen.

Malina looks around, noting all the changes in the room, all the places that have been gold-touched. I wonder what she thinks of it, all the things tinged new.

Ever since her father passed away, Midas has been dubbed the Golden King. He's certainly living up to the title, too. Room by room, the castle is being transformed. Every day, a little bit more gold shines on its surfaces.

Sometimes, Midas wants things to go solid because he likes the way it looks—like the plants in the atrium, now ageless and unchanging. A bold statement of wealth that requires no words.

But that wouldn't do for everything. It certainly wouldn't be comfortable to sleep on solid gold beds. So for the most part, the material itself is morphed, glass cups tinted, supple thread spun golden, wooden frames gone gilt, all of it done with a single touch.

"It looks fine," Malina finally answers, voice gone stiff.

"Fine?" Midas repeats with a frown marring his tanned, handsome face. "Highbell has never looked better. By the time I'm finished, it will be so superior no one will even remember what it was before."

If I wasn't looking at her already, I'd have missed the flinch of pain that crosses her face. It's a split second, there one moment and gone the next, but I saw it.

It surprises me, because the cold queen never shows any emotion other than superiority.

Malina swallows, delicate throat bobbing, before placing her spoon down on the napkin in front of her. "The soup seems to be disagreeing with me," she states. "I think I'll head up to my rooms, after all."

"Would you like me to escort you?" Midas asks.

"No, thank you."

I can't help it—a sigh of relief passes my lips, and my eyes lighten with the weight of her presence lifting.

But I should've hidden it, shouldn't have reacted, because she notices. Her eyes narrow, an acrimonious chill meant to freeze me out.

I immediately install my cordial, careful expression

again, but it's too late. The damage is done.

A servant rushes forward to pull out her chair as Malina rises to her feet. She pauses beside Midas, her ghostly pale hand coming down to rest on his shoulder. I can see the blue veins beneath the cream of her porcelain skin as her fingers toy with the short ends of his hair.

"Coming up tonight?" she asks him, voice dropped low.

Midas's leg moves away from mine before he nods at her. "Yes, of course."

She beams, but her attention is on me, stealing every bit of that relief and replacing it with something that makes my stomach churn.

"Wonderful," Malina purrs before bending forward to place a kiss on his cheek. "Have a good supper with your pet, Midas. I'll see you soon in bed."

The ice from her gaze goes right through my heart.

I don't know what she sees in my expression, but it makes the grin of smug vindication spread on her face. Satisfied, Malina straightens up and turns away, walking with the click, click of her heels, while I'm left stuck in grim jealousy that I can't let show.

Don't cry. Don't you dare cry.

When the dining room door closes, Midas immediately reaches over, his bent finger tapping the bottom of my chin. "Auren."

My eyes lift to his, his expression apologetic yet stern, soft lips pressed together.

"You can't react to her," he tells me.

A well in my eyes fills up, like water in a bucket, threatening to spill over. "I know."

"Oh, Precious," he murmurs, gaze caressing my face. "You know you have my heart. I need an heir, that's all."

I may not be a queen, I may not be his wife, but I have his heart.

It's enough. It has to be. Yet this keeps happening, this gutted feeling, over and over again.

I liked it better when Malina ignored me. I think she thought he'd tire of me at first. Maybe now, she's come to realize that he never will.

When a tear slips down my cheek, Midas brushes it away with his thumb, and I lean into his touch.

"Come here." He scoots back, and that's all the invitation I need. I slip into his lap, and his arms come around to hold me as the servants scurry away. "You're still adjusting," he says, his hand brushing my braided hair off my shoulder.

"I guess so."

"It'll get easier with time," he assures me.

I sniff, pulling myself together. "Yeah."

His chin rests securely on the top of my head, his thighs beneath me, holding me up. "We both knew what was going to happen when we decided to come here to Highbell."

"I just...I didn't know it was going to be this hard," I admit in a soft voice. I didn't know it was going to hurt this much.

A comforting stroke skims down my back. "Marrying

Malina was necessary. Not only because it secured the future of Sixth Kingdom, but also because it's secured a future for you," he says, the timbre of his voice rumbling evenly against my ear pressed to his chest.

He's right, of course.

His hand moves, again tapping my chin so I'll look at him. "You're safe and protected here, Auren, and that's what matters the most to me. You know that, right? I won't ever let the world hurt you again."

I nod, my eyes dropping to his lips. I want to kiss his cheek, to replace the one his wife left there, but that feels juvenile, so I don't.

"I am safe, thanks to you," I tell him with a small smile.

The skin of his eyes crinkles in the corners as he smiles back. I love that smile. It makes my heart squeeze inside my chest, like the feel of someone taking your hand. "And you always will be, here with me," he promises. "Are you still hungry?"

I shake my head in answer. What little I managed to eat has gone sour in my stomach.

"Alright, how about I walk you upstairs and I'll send for some food to be brought up a little bit later?"

"Yes, please."

He places a kiss on my forehead and helps me stand, his hand going to my back again as he walks me out of the dining room.

I'm quiet while he leads me up floor after floor of the

castle. I've grown used to taking the trek by now, so my legs don't ache as much from all the steps, yet my spirit seems to drag its feet.

When we get to the top level, Midas nods at the guards standing watch in the hall. We go through the doorway together, stopping in the middle of the room. Not just any room—my bedroom. Complete with an attached dressing room and bathroom.

"Ready?" he asks, and I nod, though a small sigh escapes my lips as I look at the gilded bars.

Midas had a renowned blacksmith come to the castle to build this for me. It took weeks, but now there's an elegant birdcage built into the room, except it's big enough to house a person, its size easily accommodating all the furniture inside.

Its domed structure is elaborate, swirling metal that coils at the bottom and top, pretty vines engraved into the golden band that circles around the roof.

It's intricate and beautiful and strong. No man could break the bars, no body could squeeze between them. When Midas promised to keep me safe, I asked him to prove it.

This is him proving it.

He strides toward the cage door, and the hinge doesn't make a single squeak when he opens it. Midas comes inside with me, both of us passing the bed and chair as I head for the window. The glass panes are rimmed with snow, like powdered sugar clinging to the edges. I don't have the best view from it, but I still love looking outside.

His fingers come up to play with my ribbons tied into bows at my back. I know the caress is meant to make me feel better. Not just because of the confrontation with Malina, but because as much as I'm comforted by the safety of my cage, I still get lonely inside. Bored. Sometimes, when I sleep, I wake up panicked at the feeling of being trapped.

"Eat more food tonight," he tells me.

"I will."

"And play your harp. You're so good at it."

I laugh, turning away from the view of the window to look at the golden harp he gifted me a couple of months ago. "You're just saying that. I'm awful at it."

His lips twitch. "You'll get better with practice."

"I have lots of time for that," I tease. Though I'd much rather be bored sometimes than be back on the streets with someone like Zakir. If all I have to complain of is a little boredom here and there, then my life is really good. Something I need to remember.

"I have a surprise for you," Midas says suddenly.

My eyebrows lift, and I bounce on my feet. "What is it?"

His lips tilt up at my brimming excitement. I can't help it—I love gifts.

"I'm going to have your cage expanded."

My eyes widen. "What...?"

"It's going to take a bit of work, and it won't happen overnight," he quickly explains. "The carpenters will have to cut out a few walls and build a private hallway to connect to your cage, but when they're done, you'll be able to visit the library and atrium whenever you like and be safe in your own space."

Lips parting in shock, all I can do is stare at him for a moment, like I'm checking to see if he's actually serious. "Really?" I breathe.

His grin dazzles me. "Really."

Before he's even finished answering, I'm launching myself at him, my arms wrapped around his neck as I pepper his face with kisses. "Thank you, thank you, thank you!"

He laughs, the carefree sound warming me up from the inside, my heart swelling. "I know how much you like the atrium and reading," he tells me, leaning back to look at me as I pull away. "And you know I like to make you happy."

"Thank you," I say again, my face stretched wide with a smile. Once I'm able to go into the atrium whenever I like, I won't feel so trapped all the time. I'll have the best view of the castle.

"Happy?" he asks.

I nod through my grin. "I'm happy."

"Good." Midas taps me on the nose.

The giant bell in the castle's tower begins to chime, the sound marking the hour of the night. It *trills loud enough to be heard all the way down the mountain and into Highbell city proper, its resonance like rippled air.*

When the noise stops, Midas brushes his hand over my cheek. "I'll see you in the morning. Make sure you get plenty of rest tonight. We have a lot to do tomorrow."

"I will."

I walk him to the cage door, and he goes out, turning to shut it behind him, locking it securely. He slips the key into his pocket and lightly pats it. A reminder that no one can get to me, that he and he alone can open my cage.

"Good night, Precious."

My hands come up to curl around the bars. "Good night."

With a nod, Midas walks out, the bedroom door closing behind him.

As soon as he's gone, the happy smile slips off my face, like water that drips from slow-melting snow. I try not to think of where he's going, what he'll do. She's his wife, and I'm the gilded pet she tolerates.

I turn, my back leaning against the bars, my gaze skimming over the chair, the table, the pillows piled on my four poster bed, the blankets in a fluffed tangle. I have everything I could ever need here, every comfort I never thought I'd have.

Midas has never let me down. I'm no longer in danger. I no longer have to worry *every moment of every day. He's kept his promise, kept it the moment he found me.*

So why, when that cage door shuts, do I still feel lost?

CHAPTER 22

AUREN

H o there, Gild, that you?"

I stiffen at Keg's loud voice and stop in my tracks. All of the soldiers standing in line for their ration of dinner look over at me.

I'm surprised Keg picked me out in the crowd. I thought I'd been doing a pretty good job of being covert. But I guess even at night, I'm like a beacon. Glowing gold in the light of the fires, while everyone else is shrouded in black.

"I know you hear me, girl. Get your arse over here!"

With a sigh of defeat, I turn and make my way toward the fire. As I walk, the soldiers move out of my way, giving me a wide berth. Maybe talk of Osrik teaching a lesson to those two soldiers has spread throughout the camp.

Keg slops out spoonfuls of food to waiting soldiers as I

stop in front of him. Just like at breakfast, he's stirring something in a massive pot, except it's soup instead of porridge.

"Where have you been? I haven't seen you at my fire the last two mornings," he says with a frown.

"I was a little under the weather." Despite the fact that I tossed Hojat like a wad of paper, the mender has been very attentive, making sure I'm loaded up with medicines and food and extra furs.

Keg impatiently snaps his finger for another soldier to hold his bowl out, so he can dole out another serving. "Sorry to hear that," he tells me. "You know what's good for being under the weather?"

"What?"

Brown eyes flick over to me. "Eating *my* hot food that I serve at *my* fire."

A snort escapes me. "Sorry. I'll be sure to remember that for next time."

"See that you do," he says with an imperious nod. "You feeling better now?"

"Much." And it's true. My headache is gone, my throat no longer sore. I don't even have a cough. Even my ribs, shoulder, and face are all healed up.

"Alright then, no reason not to be eating now." He holds a hand up at the people in line to stop them from coming forward and then picks up an iron cup from the pile before shoving it at me. "You'll get an extra portion tonight since you missed this morning."

"Hey, your breakfast gave me the runs earlier. Can I

get an extra serving too?" one of the men guffaws.

"No," Keg snaps. "And you got the runs 'cause your uniform squeezes your fat ass belly all day," he retorts, making some of the others bark out laughter.

"Here," Keg says, knocking his spoon against my cup and filling it to the brim. "That'll stick to your ribs."

"Thanks, Keg."

I tilt the cup back and drink the slop that vaguely resembles some kind of fishy chowder. Keg is right—it really does feel like it's sticking to my insides, but not in a good way.

Yet I drink every drop, because despite the fact that I've lived and dined in a palace for the past ten years, I'm no food snob. I can thank my formative years for that, always hungry, never getting enough to eat.

I hand the cup back to him as soon as I finish. "Thanks. It was...good." Ish. It was good*ish*.

Keg puffs up his chest in pride. He really loves feeding me for some reason. "You're still my quickest eater, Gildy Locks."

I pause, my eyes narrowing. "You've been talking to Lu, haven't you?"

Keg grins. "I think the nickname she made for you is a good one."

"Great," I say dryly, though my lips twitch in amusement. It's so strange, though, to have *this*—this sense of camaraderie with him. Not once has Keg made me feel like an enemy. The opposite has been true, in fact.

Maybe that's another reason I've avoided him. Every time I talk to Lu, or Keg, or Hojat, I feel a little bit like a traitor.

"Hey, asshole, how long do I have to wait for dinner?" a soldier hollers.

Keg rolls his eyes. "Bunch of whiners in this army."

I smile. "See you later, Keg."

"Tomorrow," he counters. "For *breakfast.*"

"Tomorrow," I promise before edging away from the fire.

I stretch my legs as I walk around camp, fires dotting the ground and voices a constant low roar like the sea. It's not snowing tonight, and the air is feeling crisp and clean, the way that only wintry temperatures can. I should take the time to go visit the saddles since I'm no longer sick, but...

The thought of facing Mist makes me nauseated.

Plus, Rissa watches me now with an almost hungry expression on her face, like I'm the answer to her prayers. Though I suppose that's better than the loathing looks from the others.

No, I'm definitely not up to visiting the saddles tonight.

Instead, I wander around aimlessly, half-heartedly looking for signs of where the commander keeps his hawks, the other half feeling guilty.

Despite my reservations and prejudgments, I *like*

Keg, and Lu, and Hojat. And that...that complicates things. It makes everything not so cut and dry.

It would be so much easier on my conscience if they were cruel to me. If this whole damn army was cruel and horrible. I expected that, expected to steam beneath the pile of their stark wickedness, hissing beneath crushing punishment.

Except that's not what's happened at all. Fourth army is no longer just a faceless enemy that I can blanket with hate.

So where do I stand, if not securely on the opposing side?

My troubled thoughts get yanked away when I hear a sudden shouting in the distance.

With a frown, I change direction and head toward the noise, my steps quickening. A collective cheer rises up just as I reach a short slope. I dig in my heels and scale the thick snow, footsteps sliding to a stop on the top of the embankment.

Below, there's maybe two hundred soldiers gathered, lit up by a blazing fire on the flat terrain. There's a large, crude circle drawn into the snow, and inside of it are a group of soldiers fighting.

Four-on-four, the bare chested men go at each other with a brutality that makes my breath catch. Some of them are riddled with bruises, blood splattering the snow at their feet. They circle each other, attacking with practiced moves, getting a hit in wherever and whenever they can.

Some fight with swords, some with fists, but with every strike, missed or struck, the spectators' voices rise up in cheers or curses, faces alight with eager fervor. Every time a hit lands, they stomp their feet in the snow, a bloodthirsty drum that reverberates through the ground and travels up my spine.

When one of the fighters manages to slash a red line across the belly of another, the spray of blood makes me flinch.

A second later, someone else gets tossed on their back, snow flying up around his body. His opponent straddles him, fists pummeling his face, one after another. Even from up here, I swear I can *hear* bones crack. I can smell the sharp iron of blood as it bursts from his split cheek and splatters onto the snow.

Up until now, the soldiers have seemed relatively docile. Marching day after day in perfect formation and setting up camp every night.

But this is like peeking behind the curtain to witness their viciousness, as if I'm seeing what lurks behind the glass. These men are trained fighters, and the excitement of the crowd shows how strong their bloodlust and penchant for violence really is.

A sharp whistle cuts through the din, immediately ceasing the fighting. My gaze finds the source for the noise, zeroing in on Osrik.

He's standing at the front of the crowd, just outside

of the fighting circle. Legs spread wide, massive arms crossed in front of him, his face is stony and authoritative. I know instantly that he's running this show.

He says something to the fighters, making all eight of them walk out of the circle, some limping, others bleeding. Their bare chests are riddled with the marks they've sustained, cheeks pink from the cold, lips swollen from punches. But they grin. Actually *grin,* like tearing each other apart is fun for them.

I think this army needs a new hobby.

Hojat is down there, flitting around with his satchel, eyeing the injuries. He starts applying ointments and bandages to the wounds while the men clap each other on the backs and trade insults, the crowd tossing over taunts and applause.

I'm about to turn away, since I have no desire to watch people get hurt for entertainment, but right as my foot lifts, I see Osrik point to the crowd, picking new fighters.

My mouth drops open when the young serving boy, Twig, gets picked. Floppy brown hair, brown leathers that don't quite fit him, he looks lanky and small, a stick amidst all the rough and gruff men. That's probably how he earned his moniker.

Twig walks into the fighting circle and strips off his leather coat and shirt, tossing them in the snow. His bare, skinny chest makes him stand out even more than before. My hands curl into fists as the crowd cheers, while Twig shifts nervously on his feet.

Osrik seems to debate for a moment, and then chooses another fighter from the crowd. The man has blond hair that's as yellow as a mustard plant and sticks out like a sore thumb. Nothing that bright and colorful belongs in this barbaric display.

His body is lithe and tall, but his slim build doesn't matter. He's still a grown ass man with muscles, age, and experience. He has no business fighting a child.

Before I know it, my legs are carrying me down the slope of the snowy bank. Then I'm slipping past tightly packed bodies, shoving, ducking, using my smaller stature to my advantage in order to squeeze through the crowd.

I reach the front just in time to see the yellow-haired man toss an elbow into the boy's belly. The force of it takes the breath out of Twig, making him bend in half like...well, like a snapped twig.

Anger floods my vision until I'm submerged in a sea of red.

Twig brings his arms up to protect his head, trying to block a set of sharp, quick jabs. The mustard-haired man grins, like this amuses him. The air is tight with thrill from the crowd as they shout, their voices indistinguishable.

My ears burn with every violent encouragement.

Before Mustard can land another hit, I stalk forward and enter the fighting circle. Without hesitation, I implant myself in front of Twig, facing down the soldier with a furious glare.

CHAPTER 23

AUREN

The mustard-haired man jolts to a stop right before he would've struck me. His eyes widen as he drops his fists and looks around, like he's searching for a reason for my sudden appearance.

The crowd jeers in confusion and irritation, their hoarse heckles flinging at me like slaps against my back.

Up close, I can see that Mustard is older than I first thought—his clean shaven jaw giving him a boyish look. But in his eyes, you can see the truth of a hardened warrior.

"Leave the boy alone," I demand, and I'm impressed at how strong I manage to keep my voice, that it doesn't crack under the pressure.

"Erm… What?" Mustard says, mouth gaping.

A sharp whistle sounds, and then Osrik is striding up. His damn body is so big I can practically feel the ground tremble every time he takes a step. Or maybe that's just me shaking in my boots.

"What the fuck are you doing?" he demands, stopping in front of me.

I lift my chin. "Stopping this. I won't let you have a boy pummeled for your soldiers' entertainment."

Osrik's mouth opens, the wooden piercing in his bottom lip shifting, the vein at his temple pulsing with irritation. "Excuse me? Who the *fuck* do you think you are?"

Behind me, Twig's small voice sounds. "Miss, you shouldn't have come in the circle."

I glance at him over my shoulder. "Don't worry about it, Twig. I can handle this."

Osrik barks out a cruel laugh. "No, you really can't. And the kid is right. You shouldn't have crossed into the fight circle."

"Nope," Mustard chimes in, rocking back on his heels with amusement as he crosses his arms over his strong, tanned chest. "Tell her what the rules are, Os."

Osrik looks steadily back at me. "If someone crosses into the fight circle, they have to fight."

"And take off their shirts. Don't forget that important bit," Mustard grins. "Wouldn't do to get blood on our clothes," he adds with a wink.

My stomach churns.

"Shut up, Judd," Osrik snaps.

"Miss, it's *really* okay," Twig tries to intervene again.

My heart hurts at how *he's* trying to protect *me*.

I stand my ground, even as the crowd of onlookers becomes antsier, louder. Even though they aren't crossing into the circle, it seems like they've packed more tightly together, like they're closing in on me. The tension is thick and clinging, oily air that makes it hard to breathe, coating my skin with grime.

Osrik looks past me. "Get back into formation, kid."

Twig moves obediently out from behind me, but I move with him, shaking my head. "No."

I don't care how big Osrik is, how strong, or how mean. There are some things that give you the courage to face a giant.

Osrik tips his head back and lets out a sigh, like he's trying to find some patience that he can pluck out of the smoky air. When that doesn't seem to work, he takes a step toward me. If he does it on purpose to intimidate me, then it works. He could snap me and Twig in half without even trying.

But still, I don't back down. Because at one point, that was *me*, forced to fight on the streets, kids pitted against each other while my owner Zakir traded bets with the other men. Nobody ever intervened on my behalf, no matter how hard I wished someone would.

I lock my knees into place. "Do what you want to me, but I'm not going to stand by and let Twig get beaten."

Beside me, Judd whistles low under his breath.

Osrik rolls his brown eyes, his beard looking even

wilder than usual. "This may come as a surprise, since you're used to being coddled in your castle," he begins. "But guess what? There is no coddling in the real world, and there sure as hell isn't any going on in Fourth's army either. Everyone has to earn their place here. Including Twig."

My hands fist at my sides. "He's a *child*."

"Yep, and he's gotta learn how to defend himself. So that he can be a good soldier one day, so that he can have a future. Earn coin. Have honor. He *chose* to be here." Osrik waves a hand around the circle. "This isn't cheap entertainment, and I'm not having him *beaten*. This is fucking training."

My lips part in surprise, all of my righteous indignation deflating. I look at Twig, who's glancing back at me sheepishly, with visible embarrassment tinging his cheeks. "You...you *want* to do this?"

Twig nods slowly, like he's worried about hurting my feelings. "Yes, Miss. Sir Os and Sir Judd always let me train a little during fight circles."

Great Divine, where's a hole in the ground when you need it?

"Oh. Well…" I clear my throat, try to muster up some dignity. "Carry on then. I'll just...be on my way."

Osrik sidesteps in front of me, eyes dancing, scruffy face pulled into a shit-eating grin. "Not so fast. You heard the rule. If you step into the fight circle, you have to fight."

I glare at him. "I will knee you in your balls if you

don't move."

Judd barks out a laugh. "Now *that* would be entertainment."

Osrik just continues to smirk at me. "Come on, then. I'd *love* to see you try."

The joined voices of the crowd go berserk, a roar from the jaws of a beast.

Osrik looks like he thoroughly enjoys cornering me like this in front of everyone. "You're not in Sixth Kingdom anymore, little pet. If you want to toss around accusations and orders, then you better back up your shit. And rules *are* rules. *You* stepped into the circle."

I shake my head, feeling strands of my hair come loose from my braid, sweat gathering at the nape of my neck.

He leans in, getting closer to my face, making me flinch back. "Aww, come on, show me your golden claws, pet. Let's see what you got."

The shouts of the crowd crash against my ears, yelling at me to fight. The sound, the very *energy* beats against my skin, against my resolve, pushing me from every direction. I can taste violence from their every exhale until it feels like I might burst from it.

I'm surrounded by noise and pressure, pressure and noise, and I just want it to stop.

"Stop," I say, but my hands are shaking now, the bloodthirsty onlookers making my own mouth go dry.

"You walked in here, what did you think was going

to happen?" he demands.

"I hadn't thought that far ahead, to be honest," I mumble. Judd tips his head back and laughs.

Osrik would *love* if I tried to attack him, because we both know I wouldn't stand a chance. And if I attacked him, he'd have free reign to attack *me*. No thanks.

"Come on, Midas's pet. Where's your fight?" Osrik goads, the taunt beating against my chest.

My entire body is tense, everything so loud that I can't discern between my pulse and the stomping feet of the crowd.

I back up a step, two, three.

He eats up the space in a single stride. "What's wrong? You're not *scared*, are you?"

I am scared. But it's not just of him. Not, really.

I'm here, but I'm also there. Cornered against a building, rough brick at my back, while men peck at me, plucking at my ribbons, ripping at my hair, tugging at my dress.

The crowd back then, even though it was only half a dozen or so, still sounded the same. That familiar clamor, with me caught in the swell of its crash.

I don't want to get swept away again.

"Enough, Os."

Somehow, that single steady voice pierces through all the noise. The sound makes everyone go quiet, the bubble of pressure suddenly popping.

I turn my head and see Rip standing there, and the shock of his presence is like a bucket of cold water dumped over my head.

Osrik, the bastard, has the audacity to chuckle. "Aww, but it was just starting to get interesting. I think I almost got her."

Rip's face is unreadable as his black eyes skate away to the soldiers standing around. "Everyone back to camp." His command strikes down like lightning, and everyone scatters, trying to outrun a storm.

It's shocking just how quickly they follow orders. No grumbling, no hesitation. In a split second, they go from a riled horde to a compliant regiment. Absolute obedience to their commander.

Osrik looks at Twig. "Go on, boy. We'll train tomorrow."

Twig nods and scoops up his clothes. He hesitates, turning to me. "Umm, Miss?"

"Yeah?" I ask.

"Thanks for thinking you were protecting me...but can you not do that again? They're gonna give me shit for this for *weeks*."

"Umm, yes. Sorry."

Osrik and Judd snicker.

"Language, Twig."

The boy's head swivels toward Rip, who's somehow made it all the way over to us without me seeing him move. "Sorry, sir," the boy replies with immediate contrition.

Rip nods at him. "Go on."

Twig doesn't need more encouragement. He turns

and sprints off like he can't get away fast enough.

I turn and start to walk away too, but of course, I don't even make it three steps.

"Not you."

With a sigh, I turn around, but I keep my attention stubbornly off of Rip. Instead, I choose to watch the retreating soldiers as they make their way back into camp.

Soon, the only people left are Rip, Osrik, Judd, and me.

Their intense scrutiny makes my skin crawl. It was foolish for me to step in and make assumptions, but the fact that Rip saw it somehow makes it so much worse.

I feel vulnerable. Beaten. Like I was one of those soldiers who got bloodied in the snow.

My eyes settle on the commander, my body braced with tension. "Alright, out with it."

Rip arches a black brow, those tiny, stubbed spikes lifting with it. "Out with what?"

I wave a hand at the three of them. "Mock me for stepping in. Get pissed for my assumptions. Make fun of me. Whatever you're going to do, just get it over with." My voice warbles at the end, and I hate myself for it.

"Maybe later," he replies with a tinge of amusement. "For now, we're going to be busy with something else."

Alarm pulses through me like a drum. "With what?"

I can't read the expression on Rip's face, but I'm sure it's nothing good. "You heard Os. You stepped into the fight circle. You'll have to fight before you can leave it."

My mouth drops open. "You can't be serious."

"The commander is always serious, love," Judd cuts in. "It's one of his worst qualities."

Rip lets out a long-suffering sigh and says, "Os."

Without missing a beat, Osrik reaches over and smacks Judd on the back of the head. The mustard-haired man just laughs.

I shake my head, bewildered at the sight as realization clicks.

They're...friends.

I knew Osrik was something of a right-hand man to Rip, but now, I can see the camaraderie between them, the trust. The fact that the notorious killer is actually *friends* with these two men somehow changes things. It leaves me reeling, like my mind is trying to look at every interaction and reanalyze it.

"Nothing to say?" Rip asks me, tearing my attention back to his question.

I shake my head. "Yeah, can I go? I'm cold."

"Sure you can. As soon as you fight," he replies with a smirk, making the other two snicker.

Irritation bubbles up. "I don't know how to fight," I grit out.

"No better place to learn," Rip counters.

My eyes flick between the three of them, waiting for the punchline, but I realize that he's entirely serious. Not only that, he looks excited at the idea. No wonder his soldiers are so damn bloodthirsty. They get it from him.

I cross my arms in front of me. "I'm not going to fight."

"Well, then you're going to be very uncomfortable staying out here in the circle all night," Rip replies smoothly.

I feel the tic in my jaw twitch. I don't doubt for a second that he really will leave me out here if I refuse. He's that much of a prick.

"Yeah, her feet will probably go numb at some point, Commander," Judd puts in unhelpfully.

"No nice fur pallet to sleep in," Osrik adds with a nod.

My hands curl into fists. I suppose this is my punishment for interrupting their stupid fight circle, or maybe it's for being loyal to Midas.

"I hate you," I glare at them.

"Hate can be a very powerful emotion when fighting. Just make sure to use it to your advantage," Rip tells me. Arrogant ass.

"Great Divine, I'm not fighting!" I shout, irritated, cold, and more than a little intimidated.

He looks down at me levelly, without remorse, without budging an inch. "Then you'll stay here in this circle until you do."

An honest-to-goddess growl comes out of my throat. "Why are you such an ass?"

"Ha! I've been asking him that for years."

My attention snaps to Lu, who's flitting toward us,

steps barely making indentations in the snow. Her hand holds the hilt of her sword as she walks, eyes alight as she looks between us.

"What did I miss?" she asks, coming up to stop beside Rip and Judd with familiarity. Another piece of the little friendship circle snaps into place.

Judd tosses an arm over her shoulder, still bare chested and clearly not minding it even though the temperature is well below freezing. "She thought we were putting on some sort of show to beat Twig up for sport, so Gildy Locks here intervened."

A puff of air passes through my lips as I look at Lu. "Did you tell *everyone* that damn nickname?"

She beams, the piercing at her cupid's bow gleaming red. "It caught on quick," she says cheerfully. "But back to the point. You stepped into the fight circle?"

If they mention that stupid rule one more time…

"Who's she gonna fight?" Lu asks, practically bouncing on her feet.

I answer, "No one," at the same time that Rip answers, "Me."

My eyes snap to him, my heart skipping a beat. Fight *him*? Is he insane? Osrik was bad enough. I couldn't possibly fight the damn commander and live to talk about it.

"Absolutely not," I say, taking a step back like the distance will help.

A hint of fang shows through his smirk. "Scared?" he challenges, and there's a croon in his voice that sets me on edge.

"Of course I'm scared. You're the commander of Fourth's army." I retort. "Your damn nickname is *Rip* because you rip your opponents' heads off!"

The four of them go still at my words. And then, like a burst dam, they all lose it, laughter pouring out of them in rushing rivulets.

I stand in stunned uneasiness. "What the hell is so funny?"

Osrik's entire chest is rumbling, Judd is bent over clutching his stomach, and Lu has to wipe tears from her eyes. "Yeah, *Rip*," she says through her laughs. "Why don't you tell Gildy what's so funny."

He's the first one to stop chuckling, but his dry amusement stays on his face. "Which one of you was it who spread that particular rumor?" he asks.

"Me," Judd says proudly, running a hand through his floppy mustard hair. "Good to know it spread all the way to Sixth Kingdom."

My brows draw together tight as I try to keep up. "Wait...what?"

Osrik is the one to answer me this time. "We gave him that nickname," he explains with a lopsided grin. A smiling Osrik is a little freaky. "But it's not for ripping people's heads off. Nice touch, though, Judd."

Mustard looks thoroughly pleased with himself. "I thought so."

My thoughts stutter. "So Rip isn't for...ripping off

heads?" I repeat lamely.

Lu shakes her head. "No, but that's funny as shit. Does everyone in Sixth think that?"

I shrug. "I don't know. I just heard it somewhere."

"Divine, no wonder Midas's guards nearly piss themselves every time you come around," she laughs to Rip.

My shoulders stiffen as I round on him. "The guards? *My* guards?"

Black eyes flick over to me. "Midas's guards, yes."

I ignore his pointed correction. "I want to see them," I say, taking a step forward as new desperation fills me.

He doesn't even blink. "No."

Anger makes my ribbons tighten. "Why not? You let me visit the saddles."

"That's different."

"*How*?" I press.

"Because those soldiers were meant to serve as your protection, and they failed," he says evenly, all amusement gone from his expression, the shadows seeming suddenly darker over his face. "They don't deserve for you to visit them."

My head jerks back. "Don't talk about them that way. There was *nothing* they could've done against the Red Raids. I want to see them," I demand, my glare daring him to deny me.

The other three grow quiet, and I can practically feel their gazes bouncing between Rip and me.

The commander takes a step forward, and I instantly

back up a step. I tell myself it's an automatic reaction because he has all those sharp spikes out, but really, he's plenty intimidating even without them.

"Fine," he says, surprising me.

I should've known better, though. Should've seen where this was going by the arrogant tilt of his mouth.

He leans in dangerously close. "If you want to see them that badly, then I guess you'd better get started," he tells me, black eyes glinting. "Because like I said, you're not leaving the circle until you fight."

CHAPTER 24

AUREN

ip circles me.

The highest spike between his shoulder blades juts up like the fin of a shark breaking the surface of the water.

The other three have squared off against each other, every man and woman for herself, fighting like it's their favorite game as they trade insults and goad one another.

But I can only pay attention to them for the barest of moments in my peripheral vision, because I know better than to take my eye off the male stalking me.

The bonfire is to my left, draping a blanket of orange over the snowy ground, casting everything in fiery light.

"You still look scared," Rip says as he comes to a stop in front of me.

"I'd be stupid not to be."

I don't care if he really doesn't rip people's heads off. He's still a killer. Still capable of cutting down armies and slaying kingdoms. His entire body sings with strength. I can almost hear the vibrato of violence as it hums through his veins.

"You're right." He shrugs off his fitted leather coat and drops it to the ground. My heart starts to pound.

His eyes stroke over the length of my body, probably to set me even more on edge. "Do you want to take off your feathers, Goldfinch?"

I clutch my own coat to my chest. "No, thanks."

With lips twitching, his hands come up, deft fingers unlacing the brown straps across his jerkin. The spikes along his forearms and back recede beneath his skin before he slips the leather off and tosses it away.

He watches me as he reaches behind him, pulling the black cotton tunic off and dropping it on the pile. Then he's standing there bare-chested in front of me, and time freezes, like suspended sand in an hourglass, grains paused in their plummet.

I shiver from the intimidation of seeing him like this, because he *is* intimidating. But he's also beautiful. Rip has otherworldly allure and unmistakable magnetism.

I suddenly understand the insects that fly willingly into carnivorous plants. The draw is too strong, the pull too bewitching, that you forget about the danger until you're already trapped inside.

Why is it that *he* can undress, and yet, it makes *me*

feel vulnerable?

Bright side? At least the view is nice.

My eyes drift of their own accord as I take in just how strong Rip really is. His body is a vessel for battle. Every single muscle has been worked to perfection, and the sight makes my mouth go dry.

His pale skin isn't ghostly or sickly like Malina's. It's chiseled, with a light dusting of hair on his chest, but my eyes move to the row of black dots that go up his forearms.

It should look odd, or freakish, or scary, but it's none of those things.

He's so entirely *fae*.

He stands in front of me, not hiding, but letting me see, letting me assess, and I can tell from his stance that he's proud of who he is. Of *what* he is.

It makes something in me ache. I can't look away from the fierce refinement of him, the predatory grace. My heartbeat pounds in my ears, my lips parting with a shaken breath.

Before I can stop myself, I've stepped forward, so close that my skirts brush against his pants. Rip goes still. I don't think he's breathing.

I stare at the four spots from wrist to elbow where the spikes have sunken in. There's just the slightest peek of them beneath the separation of his skin, like a notch in his arm. There's no strange bulging or odd angles with them retracted. It's as if they've melded into his bones.

"Incredible..." My whisper passes unbidden.

Unable to help myself, I lift my hand, my fingertips brushing against the black indentations in his ashen-white skin. I hiss out a surprised breath when I feel the spike catch on the fabric of my glove, the sharp tip of a talon ready to pierce.

Rip clears his throat, and the noise yanks me out of my reverie.

Mortified that I'd touched him so boldly, I snatch my hand back. "I'm sorry," I blurt. "I don't know what came over me."

The blacks of Rip's eyes, indistinguishable between iris and pupil, look larger right now, like the color is taking over. "*You* don't like to be touched. I don't seem to mind so much."

My cheeks go hot. There's something there in his voice. A caress that smoothed over its harsh edges and slid over my skin. It scares me, even as it draws me in.

My already heated face burns hotter, but I don't look away, don't back up. I'm that beguiled insect, caught in his carnivorous clutches, ready to be devoured.

All this time, I've been cautious of him. Cautious because of his rumored viciousness, of the danger he poses to my secrets, of his threat to Midas.

But right now, I realize that there's an entirely different reason I need to stay guarded against him. And it has everything to do with the way warmth is spreading through my chest, with the way chills have scattered over my skin from the purr of his voice.

Warning bells peal through my head, but they sound like the best sort of song.

He dips his chin. "Did you know, the color of your cheeks grows darker when you blush? Like warm umber," Rip says, words pitched low, a sound that seems to dig beneath my skin and burrow in the deepest parts of me.

I shiver, as if a phantom drew a finger down my back. I can't even hear the others fighting anymore. It's just him and me, me and him.

"Why do they really call you Rip?" I ask. I barely recognize the whisper as mine.

He shakes his head once. "You remember the rules, Auren. Keep a lie for a lie, or tell a truth for a truth. That's the only way I'll play."

I swallow thickly. "Then I don't want to know the answer."

"You will." He lets a lazy smile crawl up his face. He takes a step back, arms hanging loosely at his sides. "Now, we fight."

Just like that, the moment between us is doused, old fire beneath a toss of water. I blink quickly and shake my head, as if I'm waking up from a dream.

"If you want to see your guards, this is the only way," he reminds me.

All of those confusing emotions roiling through me

get shoved beneath the mask of his smug arrogance. I'm a puppet being made to jump through hoops. I just need to get this over with.

"Fine," I say. "What do you want me to do?"

"For one, we'll start with your stance. It's all wrong."

I look down at my body. "What's wrong with it?"

"You're too tense. If I were to come at you right now, you'd be too locked up to react smoothly," he explains, circling me again. "You need to be ready to move, not have such a stranglehold on your muscles."

I have to force myself to let out a steadying breath, and only then does my body relax a fraction.

"Better," he says.

And then he comes at me.

No warning, no change of expression, *nothing*.

He flashes forward quicker than I can blink, and then I'm on my back, staring up at the sky in shock, while the air is knocked out of my lungs and puffed out in a cloud that hovers above my lips.

Rip stands over me with his arms crossed, looking entirely too pleased with himself.

I manage to get up, choking on breath, shoving snow off my ass as I stand. "You prick!"

He grins. Actually *grins* at me, teeth and all. I forget all about his otherworldly beauty, about the strange moment that was just between us. Right now, I just want to smack him.

"What the hell was that?" My words spark with

anger, a fire wanting to catch.

"We're fighting," he reminds me, still amused as hell.

"I wasn't ready!"

"Your opponent isn't going to do a countdown, Auren," he explains, like I'm an idiot.

"I can't fight you," I snap. He's too strong, too experienced, and I don't want to turn into that little girl grappling in the street, getting my ass handed to me every time I'm shoved forward.

"No? That's unfortunate for you," Rip replies.

He spins—I don't even know how he does it so fast—and then he's suddenly behind me. He hooks one arm beneath both mine and pulls them against my back, wrenching a grunt of pain from my lips. His other hand presses between my shoulder blades as he tips me forward, completely at his mercy with my ass jutting into his thigh.

"Try to break away," he says calmly, like he doesn't have me bent to his will, sputtering like a hissing cat.

I struggle, but I realize very quickly that I can't straighten up because he's too strong, holding me too firmly. I can't lean forward either, because I'd just land on my face. I can't even get my arms out of his hold with the way he's gripping me. My ribbons tense and swivel at my spine like snakes provoked, wanting to lunge and bite. I grit my teeth, hold them back, keep them wrapped.

"I can't."

Rip clicks his tongue in disapproval.

A second later, I'm released. My steps stumble, barely keeping me upright with his sudden departure. When I look up, he's already in front of me again, ready and cocky. I glare at him, shoving hair out of my face, while he stands there with brooding cockiness. The ends of my ribbons trill.

"Try and hit me," he says.

He certainly doesn't have to talk me into it.

I rush forward with balled fists. I don't even know what I'm going to try to hit, but I suppose smacking the smug look off his face would be a good place to start.

Before I can even raise my hand, I'm spun around, legs knocked out from under me, cheek shoved against the ground. "You know you won't hit me like that," he says with mirth.

Spitting mad, I try to roll, but his knee lands against my spine, pinning me in place. White-hot anger courses through me, because not only is this humiliating, but that also *hurt*, dammit.

"Get off!"

"Make me," he counters.

Did I think he was beautiful before? I take it all back. He's an ugly bastard.

My legs kick, hips buck, but it does nothing. His knee digs in harder against my spine with every failed attempt to knock him away. I'm growing angrier and angrier with every panted breath, my body refusing to stop moving but too weak to break free.

"Stop holding back," Rip orders, tone suddenly stern. "You know what you need to do. If you want to get out of the circle, you have to actually put up a fight."

My cheek burns where it's pressed against the snow, but my anger burns hotter. "I'm trying!"

"No, you're not," he growls above me. "Listen to your instincts and *stop holding back*."

I go still beneath him, suddenly realizing what he wants. "I can't use my ribbons."

"Why not?"

Why? Because Midas wouldn't want me to. Because I have to keep them hidden. I have to keep *everything* hidden.

Like he heard my errant thought, Rip makes a noise of disgust. He releases me, the painful knee blessedly gone from my spine. I manage to get my hands and knees under me so that I can stand, snow stuck to my face and hair, my dress wet, my mood incensed.

He glares at me, making me feel so much smaller, so weak and insignificant. His breath is still slow and even, like knocking me down took absolutely no effort.

"Why do you keep hiding what you are?" he demands, anger shading his features, making the slash of gray scales over his cheeks seem darker.

"You know why," I say bitterly.

He, of all people, should understand. Maybe that's why he pisses me off so much. Some part of me feels like he should be an ally.

"No, I don't," he retorts. "Enlighten me."

I silently fume, daggers tossed between our glares. My ribbons start pinching my skin, little nips that tell me they don't appreciate being held back while Rip so openly provokes me.

"They're a secret," I finally say. "*My* secret."

But he shakes his head. "It's more than that. I already know about your ribbons—that they can move. You hold back because you're ashamed of them."

My eyes flare, spine going rigid. He struck a chord, a sour note that clangs through my ears and echoes in the hollow cavity of my chest.

"Shut up."

But he doesn't shut up, doesn't back down, doesn't stop. Of course he doesn't, because he's Rip, and for some damn reason, he's made it his mission to unravel me completely.

Starting with my ribbons.

Rip takes a step forward, gripping the space between us and tearing it to shreds. "You think of them as a weakness, but they are a *strength*, Auren. *Use them*."

I can't help the flash of fear that springs up in me like a pressed coil. For so long, I've taught myself to hide them, to keep them close, to not let anyone see.

Rip looms in front of me, blocking out the rest of the world, his presence all-consuming. "Stop thinking," he growls in my face. "Stop thinking about everyone else.

About *him*. About hiding."

I whirl, and my anger whirls with me. "Easy for you to say. You have *no* idea how things were for me, how they are."

There's a flash of something over his face, something scary, giving me the feeling that I went too far. "No?" he snaps back. "I have *no idea*?"

My throat bobs with dry fear that I can't swallow down. He has me on a ledge, finger pressed to chest, ready to push me over.

"What are you, Auren."

It's not a question. It's a demand, gnashed through teeth, pinched through the growl of his chest. It's a test that I'm sure to fail, because there is no winning, not for me.

I shake my head, squeezing my eyes closed tight. "Stop."

He refuses to let me escape him, though, because his aura presses in, just as demanding, just as unrelenting. Rip is tugging at my seams, trying to pull the bindings I've wrapped myself in, and my fingers are slipping around the knots.

"Say what you are."

My head pounds. My ribbons writhe. I open my eyes to glare at him. "No."

He's ink in the water. A black cloud in the sky. An abyss in the ground that I'll fall inside forever. I hate him for it. I hate him for every push, for every challenge he has no right to demand.

Fury flashes in his expression, jaw tightening around

his words. "Say it, Auren."

I try to walk away, but he prowls after me and matches my stride, not even giving me a second to think.

He cuts me off, gets in my space so I have nowhere to go. He shoves his demand down my throat until my entire body is shaking with anger and intimidation. The drum of my pulse slams in my skull as he looms over me like a thundercloud waiting to strike.

"*Fucking say it*!" he roars in my face, a yank to pull out my roots.

And I snap.

"I'M FAE!"

Fury rushes like a flood, so strong I can feel it sing down the length of my ribbons, flexing through them with a shudder as they come undone.

Spinning like golden tendrils of a cyclone, the edges of my ribbons fold like jaws ready to bite, lashing out in the blink of an eye.

My coat rips off my back from the force as they launch forward. They snap around his legs, pulling them out from under him, and then throw him across the circle with a vicious hurl.

Rip lands in a spray of snow, so hard that I feel his fall resonate up to my teeth. But I don't care, because he fractured something integral inside of me, and I'm not sure if I can put it back.

I stalk toward him, gratification oozing off of me, something feral taking over. Something that's intensely pleased that I've shoved *him* down into the snow, that it's him on his back and not me.

I raise a single ribbon, end hardened, edge sharp. I send it shooting toward his prone body, ready to slice him, ready to make him hurt.

But in a move that even now I'm impressed by, he leaps upright, planting both feet, facing me. He's ready, like he was waiting for me all along.

Right arm raising, Rip meets the sharpness of my attack, ribbon and spike clashing together like the blades of swords.

The clang reverberates up the silken length all the way back to my spine, vibrating my bones.

Rip moves so *fast*. Before I can tug my ribbon back, he curves his arm and twists the length around his sharp spikes. Trapping it, he pulls it so tightly that it pulls the base of my back, dragging me toward him like a dog on a leash.

With a screech of frustration, I send four more ribbons lashing out, but the bastard somehow catches them all. He crumples them in the ball of his fist, my ribbons thrashing against his fingers, like trapped fish in a net. His hold is so strong that I can't yank them away, a glimpse of his fae strength coming out to play.

He wrenches the ribbons hard, making me spin around, nearly toppling me over. Then he pulls me toward him, my feet skidding against the snow, heels digging in, until my back slams against his chest.

"Enough," he says.

I elbow him in the gut. The asshole doesn't even grunt, though, which pisses me off. His free hand traps the rest of my loose ribbons at my spine, cinching them off before they can even try to attack, trapping them between us.

His scratchy jaw scrapes against my ear, and all at once, I become aware of how our bodies are pressed together, how I can feel the heat of his chest sinking into my back.

"Enough, Auren."

His order is spoken deeply enough, calmly enough, that it seems to reach beneath my rage and lift me out.

Panting, I blink past the fury that had wholly consumed me. I glance down at his arm that's now banded around my middle, spikes gone, hand cupping my hip.

I can feel my ribbons pulled taut in his grip, but he's not hurting them. My heart is pounding so hard that it's just a war beat in my ears, thrumming through my veins and pulsing at my temples.

I don't know how long we stand like that or when exactly the fight flees me. But it does, slowly, like syrup dripping down through my feet, leaving my soles stuck to the ground.

My ribbons go limp in his hand, and as soon as they do, he lets go of them and peels his arm away from my body and steps away. I shiver from the loss of contact.

I'm suddenly exhausted.

He slowly walks around to face me while my ribbons

curl up, winding around me in retreat. I flick my gaze up to his face and brace myself.

I expect gloating. Or taunting.

Instead, he shocks the hell out of me when his face pulls into a smile. Not a cocky smirk or a patronizing grin. This smile is soft. It's *proud*.

"There it is, Goldfinch," he purrs, and that dark caress is back in his voice. "You've finally found your fight."

CHAPTER 25

AUREN

The fire has gone out.

It seems telling, that its flames were snuffed just as my own anger fizzled, just as my show of strength petered out.

I feel like those charred logs, aching with smolder, still smoking from the intensity of burning heat.

When I look up to watch the gray tendrils rise in the air, I see a rare star in the sky, poking out from the clouds like it's watching me, the Divine cracking open an eye.

I look back down to the ground.

"Why did you do that?"

Rip hasn't said a word for the last several minutes, maybe because he noticed that I needed time to think. Or maybe he's just silently gloating because he got what he wanted.

We're still in the fighting circle, but Osrik, Judd, and

Lu are gone, though I have no idea when they left. I don't even know if they saw, if they *heard*.

My ribbons tingle from the ghost of his grip, like I can still feel them caught in his hold. He picks up my torn feather coat from the ground and passes it to me, as if he can sense that I need something to hold onto. I'm certainly not holding onto myself. I quickly take it, folding it over my arms.

"You mean why did I push you," he guesses.

"Yes," I reply, eyes locked down on the feathers of my stolen coat, my ribbons wrapped around me, keeping me together.

"Because you needed me to."

I bristle at the conceit of that, as if he knows me so well. "You have no idea what I need," I reply evenly, raising my eyes to look at him. "You're doing this for *you*. I just can't figure out why."

"I admit, I am getting some personal satisfaction from it," Rip says without remorse.

"Is this still about Midas?" I ask, because I want to understand. I need to get a grasp on Rip's mind, his motivation.

He rolls his eyes. "Must we talk about him?"

"Why do you hate him so much?"

His gaze goes cold. "The real question is, why don't *you* hate him?"

I refuse to be baited. "Is it just because your king is his enemy, or is it something more personal?"

"King Ravinger has every right to wage war on

Midas. But I'll lead the fight gladly," Rip says, grabbing his tunic from the snow and pulling it over his head.

"Why? What's Midas ever done to you?" I press. "He's a good king."

Rip scoffs as he tugs on his black jerkin, securing the leather straps across his chest. "Oh, yes, King Midas with his famous golden touch, loved by all." He gives me a dry look. "Funny how his kingdom is rife with poverty, when he could simply touch a rock and save his people from cold and starvation. What a *great* king he is."

My stomach churns, the bitter taste of acid coating the back of my tongue. I open my mouth to defend Midas, to argue, but no words come out.

Because...Rip's right.

I saw it with my own eyes when I left Highbell. The ramshackle shanties crumbling to pieces in the shadow of the castle, his people as thin as the rags they wear.

Rip can probably tell from my face that I have no defense, but surprisingly, he doesn't rub it in. "You can see why I'd like to take him down a notch. Though I suspect my king has other plans."

My ears perk at that. "What do you mean?"

He shakes his head. "Nothing for you to know."

Frustration narrows my gaze. "What happened to tell a truth for a truth?"

"I've told you one from me. The truths of King Ravinger aren't part of the game."

"How convenient for you." I look away at the weak

smoke spilling from the logs still steaming in the snow. "Osrik and the others—did they see? Did they hear what I said?" I ask, not wanting to look at him.

"Yes."

I close my eyes, squeezing, squeezing—ribbons as tight as my lids. "You're ruining me," I whisper, cold air brushing against my face like a sorrowful kiss.

I don't hear him come closer, but I feel it. How could I not? There's something in him that keeps pressing against my skin, keeps demanding my every sense to awaken.

"Sometimes," he murmurs, "things need first to be ruined in order to then be remade."

A heartbeat pulses in that peeking star.

It takes a long moment for me to open my eyes, to take a steadying breath. "I want to see the guards."

Just as I knew he would be, he's so close that if I leaned in a few inches, I could press my ear to his chest.

Rip tips his chin. "Alright, Goldfinch. I'll take you to see the guards."

He leads me out of the circle, footsteps pressed into snow like a pockmarked ground.

I slip my torn coat over me, thankful that the damage is only at the back and I can still wear it, because I'm suddenly freezing. Anger has a way of burning enough to keep you warm, but when you let it drain away, the absence of that heat leaves you bleak with cold.

Rip keeps us to the edge of camp, not drawing us

in toward the tents. In the dark, with only scattered fire-light to illuminate us every once in a while, I don't feel so intimidated by him. Our shadows move together, crossing and melding with one another, like they recognize something familiar.

"How long have you been with King Ravinger?" I ask, voice quiet, though I know he hears my every word, my every breath. Maybe even the staccato of my heartbeat.

"Feels like forever."

I know the feeling.

"And does he know that you have me?"

Rip nods. "He's aware."

Dread becomes a hard block of ice in my gut. I don't really know why, since I've been Fourth's captive all this time. But having Rip in charge as my captor versus King Rot are two very different things. If the king knows about me, it's only a matter of time until he figures out how he wants to use me.

I've come to learn that's what men do. They use.

"If he orders you to kill me, would you do it?" I ask boldly, a curious glance cast his way.

He pauses, as if caught off guard by my question. "That won't happen."

My eyebrows jump up at his naivety. "You don't know that. I'm Midas's favored, and the two of them are enemies." I drop my voice down to a whisper, in case there are any wandering ears. "And if that isn't enough to condemn me, I just confessed to being a full-blooded fae, the most hated betrayers in Orea. Three of your soldiers heard me, and they could easily slip him that fact."

"They would never breathe a word to anyone unless I ordered them to. They're my Wrath."

I frown. "Your what?"

He gives me a sidelong look. "Lu came up with the name years ago. But the three of them, they're my hand-picked team. They help advise, they each lead their own regiment in my army, and if I have a sensitive mission, they're the ones who carry out what must be done when I can't do it myself."

I'm slightly taken aback. Not at the thought of Rip having a small team of soldiers that he trusts, but at the conviction of his words. He really does trust the three of them—I can hear it in the timbre of his voice.

Still, that doesn't mean that *I* trust them.

"They just heard me confess to being a *fae*. You really think they're not going to tell anyone? Not tell your king?"

"I don't *think*. I know."

He sounds so certain, and a creeping suspicion has me asking my next question. "They know that you're fae too, don't they?"

A single nod in the dark. "They do."

If we weren't walking, I'd have sat down for a moment to process that. My head spins as I shake it, lips parted with so many unasked questions. "But that's...it's... *How*?"

"As I said, they're my Wrath, and they've worked

alongside me for a very long time. I trust them more than I trust myself sometimes. They would never betray me."

"But you're *fae*. Oreans hate us. Even if your Wrath kept it a secret, how has no one guessed what you are? How has the truth not slipped out?"

Eyes flash over in the dark. "I could ask the same for you."

"I stay hidden," I counter. "Or I did before I left Highbell. But you, you've been notorious since King Ravinger made you his commander. How does no one see?"

His shoulder lifts. "People accept what they hear if it agrees with their predispositions. They believe I'm the made-monster of King Rot, and I let them because it suits my needs."

"Does your king know?"

The corners of his lips tilt up. "That's another question of the king, and like I said, we're not playing for those."

I chew on his words like a wad of meat, turning it over, trying to digest it all. "I hope you're right about your Wrath." If not, I'm screwed.

"I am. But you owe me a truth now."

Nervousness takes off like a flock of birds in my stomach. "What do you want to know?"

"Who is your family?"

The bones of my chest seem to fuse, my breath snapped into stillness, my surprise palpable. I wasn't expecting him to ask me that.

"My family is dead," I choke out.

He pauses. "A name, Goldfinch."

His question presses, demanding. I shouldn't have traded truths with him. I should've known the payment would be too steep.

"I don't remember my family's name." My confession hurts. It scrapes something inside, leaving me raw.

He gives me a second to settle in the silence, maybe to trick me into thinking he won't keep digging, but I know he will. All he does is challenge and poke and prod and cleave. Maybe that's why they call him Rip—because he tears through people, rips open their truths.

"Where are you from?"

"Why do you want to know?" I shoot back. "How are you going to use this against Midas?"

I see the dark outline of his hand curl into a fist. "Like I told you before, we're not talking about *him*."

All the quiet calmness that was between us is suddenly gone, no trace of it left behind. But it's better this way, I try to tell myself. It's better for us to be at odds, where we belong.

"Osrik told me when I first got here that you expected me to sing, to spill all Midas's secrets," I point out. "The least you could do is not deny it and make me feel stupid. Don't try to trick me."

He scoffs, a rough, malignant sound. "The only

person tricking you is your golden king. Tell me, when did you decide to trade your ruination for his?" he asks cruelly.

My lips press together in a firm line, but his viciousness reminds me what an asshole he is, reminds me of what he is to me. His anger sets me back on more familiar ground than whatever confusing misstep we took tonight. We're not friends. We're not allies. We're on opposing sides.

"I'll always choose him," I say, facing off against him in the dark.

"So you've said," he retorts scathingly. "I wonder, if the roles were reversed, if he'd so easily give up his truths for yours. What sacrifices has your king made for *you*?"

"He's done plenty," I retort.

His expression goes flat, as cold as the night air. "Right. Like taught you to be ashamed of everything you are."

My spine goes rigid and fuses with hurt. I feel tears prick the backs of my eyes, and I dash them away before they can fall, furious with myself. Why am I giving his words any leverage? How is it that he can always slash through me with a single swing of words?

Rip turns and points, and my eyes follow the direction of his hand. A few paces away, there's some kind of large walled cart—the kind where prisoners are kept. Beside it, there are several of Fourth's soldiers standing watch near a small campfire. Some of them are looking our way, nervous glances traded between them.

"Your guards are kept there. I'm sure they'll be good company for you. Go swap stories of Midas's greatness. I've got better things to do."

My chest twinges as he abruptly turns and stalks off, barking an order at the gathered soldiers to let me visit, but to *watch me*. Then he disappears into the camp without giving me a second glance, not staying to see the tear that freezes on its way down my cheek.

The ache in my chest doesn't go away, not even when I finally lay my eyes on the guards and reassure myself that they're okay. Because even though I'm glad to see them, to know they haven't been hurt or killed, I'm gutted, devastated.

Devastated, because who I was really looking for, who I really wanted to see, isn't there. The only person who gives me a sense of home when I'm around him, is absent.

The pain of not finding Digby's face in the group is a punch to the gut. It hurts. The last of my hope is cut, and it *hurts*.

Midas's guards are okay, but *my* guards are not.

Sail is drifting somewhere in a tomb of snow, and Digby is lost forever. And I have to face that now, alongside Rip's digging words that are scraping against my chest.

Crystal tears fall as I walk back to my tent alone.

Above me, that squinting star closes her eye and hides behind the clouds.

CHAPTER 26

QUEEN MALINA

D*ammit.*"

My hissed curse makes Jeo, the handsome male currently stretched out on my chaise, look over at me. "What's wrong?"

I glance up from the letter and sigh, tossing it on my desk. "Franca Tullidge can't meet with me because she isn't currently in Highbell. She's gone traveling for six months," I say with irritation.

"And this is bad?" Jeo asks.

I rub my temples before leaning back in my chair to give him my full attention. "Yes, it's bad. The Tullidge family has a private guard of seven hundred men. Men I might need, so it's important I get her loyalty settled."

Jeo springs to his feet, and I get momentarily distracted. Currently shirtless, the freckles on his skin are like flakes of cinnamon sprinkled over him, spice added to the muscled, decadent body they adorn.

He picks up the crystal pitcher on the table and fills two glasses of honeyed wine. I take a moment to enjoy his physique as he comes over with cups in hand, his walk like a panther, strong and graceful. The thick red hair on his head reminds me of the color of a fresh kill.

He places one glass in my hand before leaning against the edge of my desk. With his knee pressed against my thigh, I can feel the heat of his body even through the multiple layers of my skirt and his trousers.

"If it comes to that, if you need the noble houses to band with you, they'll do it," he says confidently, tipping the wine into his mouth as he swallows half the contents in one gulp.

I take a sip, amused. "Is that so?"

He nods. "It is so, my queen."

"You sound awfully confident."

Jeo downs the rest of it. "I am," he replies with a shrug, setting the glass down. "You are a Colier. Orea might be dazzled by Midas's gold, but it's *your* bloodline, your name that Sixth Kingdom trusts. If you put out the call to arms, they'll answer."

I tap my fingertip against the glass. "We'll see."

I hope it doesn't come to that, hope that I can get the pieces in place to force Midas's hand, but I have to plan for every contingency. Tyndall, while lacking as a husband, excelled as a ruler. Not because he was trained for it as I was, but like Jeo said, he knows how to dazzle.

That man knows how to leave an impression, how to spin a narrative, how to gain the people's awed fascination. He's made a lot of nobles rich—nobles that I'll never win over.

But, he's also made a lot of enemies. He's left a lot of people to complain at their lack. When King Midas turned Highbell Castle gold, he failed to realize exactly what kind of shadow it cast.

The commoners, the peasants, the laborers—those are the ones he neglected, the ones he deemed beneath him.

Once I'm finished going through the list of nobles I think I can sway, I'll go for those forgotten masses next. The ones who were left to wallow in envy, left to stare after the castle in its immeasurable wealth.

Yes, a lot of people hate the king. His wife just happens to be one of them.

A slow smirk crosses my wine-whetted lips. I'm going to utterly destroy his narrative, wreck his public platform, crush his shiny façade.

By the time I'm through with him, I will make the *Golden King* a thing to despise. I will be the queen, beloved.

Jeo's face morphs with a knowing grin. "I know that look," he murmurs, pointing at me. "You're plotting."

A small laugh escapes me. "Of course I am."

Plotting is what I'm best at. A good thing too, since I lack both of the traits that this world respects: power and a penis.

A shame that I lack the first, but the second? I've found that most of the people who have those are altogether disappointing.

My gaze shifts to Jeo's crotch. Well, except for the ones you can buy.

When a knock on the door sounds, I let out a little sigh. I shouldn't be surprised at the interruption. It's hard to go even a few hours without someone needing something. Although, it's a problem I embrace, because finally, *I'm* the one they come to. It's *my* order they wait for. As it should be.

"Come in."

My advisor, Wilcox, strides inside, his blue eyes skating straight to Jeo. His thin lips press together tightly, the only outward sign of dislike that he'll show in front of me. Though I know on the inside, he's ranting, just like he did when I first came down to dinner with Jeo on my arm.

Wilcox believes it's *unsavory* for me to keep a saddle of my own so publicly, an opinion he let known at the dinner table.

Funny, I doubt he ever said such a thing to my husband, who kept a harem of saddles at all times. Not to mention that golden bitch.

Jeo straightens up from my desk and turns with a

grin. He *loves* to rankle Wilcox now that he knows the older man disapproves so thoroughly.

My advisor stops in front of my desk, sweeping low with a bow. "Your Majesty, I hope I wasn't interrupting."

"Not yet," Jeo says with a salacious wink.

Wilcox's lips clamp down in irritation, though he likes to think the gesture is hidden behind the messy gray whiskers growing over his chin.

He ignores Jeo as my saddle walks around my chair to stand behind me. His large, strong hands come down to start kneading my shoulders. A display—to touch the queen so freely is a power play—and I allow it.

"Hmm, so tight, my queen," Jeo coos.

My advisor's face turns slightly mottled, while I try not to smirk. I can't figure out if he hates our display because it's a show of my blatant disloyalty to Tyndall or if it's simply because I'm a woman who has her own saddle.

Perhaps it's a bit of both.

"Did you need something, Wilcox?" I ask evenly, while Jeo's deft fingers continue to massage my skin in deliciously firm strokes.

Wilcox's gaze snaps back to me from where they'd drifted to Jeo's touch. "Pardon. This missive came for you," he says, stepping forward.

I reach my hand out, taking the rolled parchment from him. "Thank you." When my eyes fall to the red wax seal, my pulse jumps, though I don't let anything show on my face. "You're dismissed, Wilcox."

My advisor turns on his heel and leaves, apparently all too ready to be gone from my saddle's presence.

As soon as the door closes behind him, I release the breath that got caught in my chest.

"What's wrong? I'd say you're white as a ghost, but that's always true," Jeo teases.

I don't give him a dry laugh, though. I'm too busy staring down at the blank stamp pressed into the cracked wax, sigil absent—telling of exactly who this letter is from.

"It's the Red Raids."

Jeo's touch pauses on my neck. "The pirates answered?"

A hum is my only reply before I slip my finger beneath the curled flap and break the seal. Unfurling the small scrap of paper, I quickly read the letter, noting the smeared ink, the sloppy scrawl. Honestly, I should be glad the thieves can even write.

I read the message again, chest pounding. "Great Divine..."

"What is it?" Jeo asks, coming around, his beautiful face marred with a frown.

My eyes flick up at him as all the implications run through my mind. "They don't have her."

His blue eyes widen. "The golden bitch? Why the hell not?" he demands. "You gave them plenty of time to get their sorry asses to the Barrens in time."

Shaking my head, I drop the letter and stand up from my seat, pacing a few steps away.

"Malina..."

I spin to face him, and he blinks in dumbfounded surprise at the brilliant grin that's spreading over my face. "Fourth's army came to their ship," I whisper, awed. "They took the saddles, the guards, everyone."

His red brows shoot up. "The gilded cunt?"

My smile is so wide my cheeks hurt. "They have her too."

Jeo's lips pull back, cheeks moving to match my grin. He knows what a win this is for me. I thought the Red Raids would be a good place for her. But this? This is so much *better*. "Fuck, yes!" Jeo exclaims. "This calls for more wine."

While he pours himself another cup, laughter spills from my chest, husky and quiet, a sound I haven't uttered in years.

She's gone. She's finally *gone*.

I won't ever have to lay eyes on her again. Won't ever have to watch the way Tyndall looks at her, the way his gaze grows hungry every time she enters the room.

His precious little favored is gone, taken by his worst made-enemy, and there's not a damn thing he can do about it.

Victory is sweet.

I shake my head, almost unable to believe this turn of events. "They're going to rip her to shreds," I say, my tone tinged with thrill.

"Worse than the snow pirates," Jeo agrees, finishing off another half cup of wine before passing it to me.

I take it from him and swallow a hearty gulp while he picks up the letter, amused eyes skimming over it. "Ha, the whiny bastards are mad! Lost the saddles to Fourth *and* their captain jumped ship with their gold too. Bad luck."

"I'll have Uwen send them a crate of gold to make it up to them," I say. At Jeo's surprised look, I shrug. "They're glorified mercenaries. With enough coin to assuage them, I can keep them as allies."

My saddle walks over and slips a hand around my waist. "My queen is viciously brilliant."

I smile before taking another drink, then press the rim of the glass to his mouth. He watches me with heavy-lidded eyes as I tip it back, letting the rest of the drink slip into his mouth. As soon as it's drained, he puts the cup on the desk and tugs me close with his hands on my hips.

I tilt my head, welcoming the hungry look in his expression. With that being all the invitation he needs, Jeo presses his mouth against my neck and starts peppering kisses and nips over the sensitive skin.

My eyes flutter closed as he trails up to my jaw, and when his lips meet mine, I let out a little moan of satisfaction, a fire stoking low in my belly.

I like the idea of fucking him while knowing that I've taken all of Tyndall's favorite toys away. His favorite harem of saddles is gone, while mine cups my ass and grinds his length into me.

I slip my tongue against Jeo's, and all I taste is sweetly spiced wine and wicked victory.

"Mmm, delicious," he murmurs against my lips.

"The wine?" I ask with a coy smile.

"*You*," he replies. "I love it when you get devious, but when those plots of yours succeed and you get that look about you? Makes me hard as a rock."

To prove his point, he grinds his hips into my front, letting me feel the impressive length of him beneath the pleat of his pants. "I'm going to take you right now, my queen," he says, teeth running over the edge of my ear. "Going to fuck you on your desk with that nefarious, devilish smile on your face."

My stomach lurches with needy heat, with the thrill of his filthy words, with lust that was never mine before. I was always ignored, set aside.

No more.

"Make it good," I order with an imperious purr before I reach down and cup him. He groans into my ear, and the sound makes me shiver with feminine power.

Jeo reaches down and picks me up, walking a couple paces before setting me on my desk. His hands reach beneath my skirts, the many layers bunching as he shoves them to my waist.

When his fingers brush against the wet curls at the apex of my thighs, he grins and nips at my lip. "Such a naughty queen."

"Stop talking and fuck me."

He laughs as he undoes the tie at his trousers, dropping them around his ankles. "At your service, Your Majesty."

Jeo thrusts into me a second later, so hard that my body slides backwards against the wood. But it's *good*. It's what I want, what I ordered, and I shall have it.

He leans in, hands holding my hips in place as he moves in and out of me in powerful strokes. "Does this please my queen?" he asks, mouth pressing against my neck, nibbling at the sensitive skin.

It does, but I want more. I want all the things Midas never gave me.

I shove at Jeo's chest. "Down."

The side of his mouth quirks up, but he dutifully slips out of me before lying on the floor. The thrill of it, the power, the pleasure, it sings in my veins as I look down at him with hungry eyes.

Slipping off the desk, I stand over him, leg on either side, and I stare. Jeo groans when my sight lingers on his proud cock jutting up. "Please, my queen. Don't be so cruel."

I like when he begs.

Lifting my skirts, I bend my knees and lower myself slowly, sinking onto him just the way I like. A queen sitting on her throne.

Sweat beads on his brow, his hands tightening at my waist, but I continue to move unhurriedly, enjoying the friction of his hardness as it stretches me. I rise up and down with my head tilted back in bliss, grinding into him with decadence.

"*Fuck*, Your Majesty," he grits out.

My entire body is singing as I take what I want, as I get the pleasure I went so long without. Never again. Never again will I sit idly by.

I will take what I want, whenever I want.

"Yes, you will," Jeo says, letting me know that I spoke those thoughts aloud. "Take it fucking all, so long as you come on my cock."

My throaty laugh cuts off when he thrusts his hips up into me, making him go deeper, harder, hitting that hidden part of me that I never knew was there before—not until him.

I take and take, letting it feed the hunger inside of me, the hunger that's only satisfied with pleasure and power.

With a moan, he starts to relentlessly fuck me from beneath, while I ride my saddle for all he's worth, rising higher to that unspeakable peak.

My pleasure cracks like splintered ice, and a breathy sigh of release crawls out of my throat. Three more grinding thrusts, and then Jeo curses with his release, his spend coating my insides with a foreign, wet heat.

Sagging on top of him, I let my nails score over the muscles of his chest, leaving red scratches on his freckled skin.

"Well?" he asks with a satisfied grin as he breathes hard, hands moving to prop behind his head. "Did I make it good, my queen?"

After another moment of catching my breath, I stand

up, enjoying the groan he emits as I slip off him. "You did well enough," I say breezily as I walk toward the door that leads to my bedroom and washroom. "But I require you to wash me and clean up your mess."

A second later, I hear him get up, feet padding after me. Hot lips appear at my ear as he grabs my hips. "Only if I can do it with my tongue."

A smirk crosses my face. "You'll do whatever your queen orders you to."

I get rewarded with his laugh. "Yes, Your Majesty, I will."

And so will everyone else.

CHAPTER 27

AUREN

I waste hours lying on my pallet, tossing and turning,
unable to sleep.

The coals burn down darker and darker until the
black husks go from fuming red to sobered ash, the last of
the warmth gripped in the fist of the cold night air.

With the dimming burn, my thoughts coalesce.

Ever since Commander Rip took me from the Red
Raids, I've been waiting for him to do something horrible,
for his soldiers to tear me apart.

Except he hasn't, and they don't.

Instead, I've been treated with dignity. Friendly,
even. I've been allowed freedoms that not even Midas
would give me.

But loyalty, that single word and moral, that conviction I hold onto so tightly, that's what's at stake. I'm

terrified what will happen if I falter.

I know I can't fully trust Rip. I know this, but...

But.

Maybe, I can't fully trust Midas either.

The moment that traitorous thought slips out, I realize I've spoken it aloud. It's a whispered confession, a sorrowful revelation for only the waning warmth of the coals to hear.

I sit up in my pallet and pull on my dress, the thing loose and overly worn now, dirty no matter how many times I try to wash it by hand. I slip on my torn coat and pull on my boots, deciding to walk around since sleep is eluding me.

I haven't seen Rip since our argument last night.

I shouldn't care. It shouldn't matter. Except I feel like he's avoiding me, punishing me, and it's twisting me up inside.

Ducking out of the tent, I'm greeted by the crunch of my boots on fresh snow. We're camped beside a small frozen lake tonight, and it glistens beneath a crescent moon.

Without really meaning to, I find myself walking to the east side of camp, where the saddles are.

I stop outside of the tent, noting the same two guards who let me visit when Lu was with me. They look up from their game—cards this time.

The one nearest me with brown hair raises his brows in surprise. "My lady," he greets. "Haven't seen you for a few days."

"Yeah," I mumble, not giving an explanation. "Is it alright if I visit them?"

"It's late," the other one says. "But you can stay for a few minutes. I heard some of them whispering in there, so I know they're awake."

I nod and move toward the tent flaps, but before I can lift them, someone pushes out and blocks my path.

I flinch back at her sudden appearance. "Polly."

Her blonde hair is in two thick braids, though it's tangled and greasy, and she looks thinner than usual. No golden flecks of makeup to adorn her face, no fancy dress, no coy smile. She looks weary, yet there's a hardness in her eyes.

"Gild," she says back, crossing her arms. "What are you doing here?"

I shift on my feet at the tone of her voice. "Umm, I just wanted to visit. See how you guys are doing."

"We're fine," she snaps.

My eyes flick to the tent she's blocking and back to her face. "Is there something wrong?"

She shakes her head. "Everyone heard your voice out here, but they sent me out. You can't come in."

My brow falls into a frown. "Why not?"

Her blue eyes hold no warmth as she looks at me. "No one wants to see you."

I flinch at her embittered tone.

I feel the soldiers on my right shift on their stools,

like they're embarrassed for me, which only makes my cheeks burn in shame.

"You need to stop coming here," Polly says haughtily. "We don't like you, and we don't want you poking your nose in our business just for you to report back to your new Fourth army friends."

"*What?*"

Polly rolls her eyes. "Oh, please. Like we don't know? You get to walk around freely, Auren. We know you've turned into the commander's little whore."

My mouth drops open in shock, and for a moment, my brain stumbles, unable to process. "That's... I am *not* his whore."

The bored look on her face tells me she doesn't believe me at all. "The soldiers here talk, you know. You stay in his tent every night. We aren't stupid, and we won't let you use us to betray our king. Don't come back again, traitor."

She shoves me in the chest.

It's not a hard push, but it shocks me so much that I stumble back, mouth gaping wide. She *never* would have touched me before. She wouldn't have dared.

The guards are on their feet in an instant, stepping forward to intervene. "Enough of that," the man barks at her. "Get back inside."

Polly's eyes flash in vindication, like their reaction just solidified my treason. With a hateful smirk, she turns and pushes back into the tent, leaving me to stare at the place she just was.

I can't even look at the guards as I turn away, my shame and embarrassment battering me. It makes my shoulders slump and my head tilt down, a flower wilted, given up on the reach.

"Don't worry about them, my lady," one says.

Quickly nodding, I walk away before I do something stupid, like cry in front of them.

Bitter shame carries the weight of my footsteps as I go.

I hug the shadows while I walk, ears tuned to the quiet of the sleeping camp of soldiers, who apparently believe I'm Rip's whore.

Don't come back again, traitor.

Tears threaten to rise, but I shove them down; let them be swallowed in a well of anger instead. Polly's venomous words are my fears spoken aloud—of my loyalty slipping, of my mind being tainted.

I'm not a traitor.

I'm *not*.

Determination sweeps over me, fuels me. Like coals suddenly burning to life again.

The glowing white of the moon is now a fingernail behind a cloud, though two stars hover at her side like fireflies caught in the wax of her crescent.

I have just enough light to see, but not too much to take away the shadows. Perfect for searching without being seen. With sure steps and fierce eyes, with Polly's accusation burning my ears, I follow pure instinct, like I know exactly where to go. Or maybe it's the firefly goddesses directing my way.

Just as I pass a large group of huddled horses, heads bent, eyes dozing, I hear it.

A soft screech.

I jerk to a stop, head tilting, ear cocked. The noise comes again, quieter this time, but that's all I need to home in on its direction.

My feet turn, steps and pulse quickening. Despite how consumingly cold it is, a flush spreads over my body.

Just past the horses, nearly obscured by a cart full of hay bales, I see it.

Covered in sleek black wood, sides unadorned, I hear rustling within the small black carriage and nearly break out into a run. Instead, I force myself to walk the rest of the distance toward it.

I reach the transport, though instead of doors on the sides, it has a smaller opening at the back. I look around, but the only movements are the occasional huff or shift of the horses, their quiet breaths puffing from lowered noses.

Lifting a hand, my shaky fingers grasp the handle, and the door opens easily, without so much as a creak. It takes a moment for my eyes to adjust and see what's inside, but as soon as they do, triumph tosses me up into the air, making my stomach dip.

Staring back at me with reflective yellow eyes, with

talons gripping their perches, is what I've been searching for.

The army's messenger hawks.

CHAPTER 28

AUREN

It's dark inside the carriage, but the flash of eyes and the movement of their shadowy figures reveals the four hawks inside.

It's a testament to their training, because they don't startle or snap, they just look at me with boredom.

Even in the shadows, I can see that they're gorgeous birds, large for their breed. Their tawny feathers carry a sheen that extends to their sharp beaks and feet.

I note their perches built into the walls, the bones of dead rodents picked clean amongst the brush at the floor. Above, there's an open window cut into the wood, allowing the hawks to come and go, letting faint moonlight in.

Swallowing, I glance down at the flat surface in front of me, the wood extended out like a desk, perfect for mobile message writing. Everything I need is here, right down to rolled bits of blank parchment stuffed into holes, bottles of ink and feathered quills set into indentations at the front.

I look around me again, but all is still and quiet.

Turning back to the desk, I reach forward and grab a roll of parchment, tearing off a small strip. I flatten it out, using a bottle of ink to keep the edge down, and then lift the quill, dipping it in.

My hand is trembling so badly that I nearly overturn the bottle, but I manage to catch it before it can tip.

"Get it together, Auren," I whisper to myself.

Pressing the metal nib against the parchment, I write quickly, sloppily, my handwriting so much worse than its usual drawl. But it'll have to do, because I'm in too much of a rush, too shaken on adrenaline and fear. My message is overly simple and hasty, but it's the best I can do.

Fourth's army has captured me and the others.
They're marching on you. Prepare.
—Your Precious

I drop the quill back in its holder and find a box of fine sand in the desk. I pinch a bit of the powder between my fingers and toss it over the wet words to speed up the set of the ink.

As soon as it's dry enough not to smear, I start to roll up the paper, but freeze at the sound of approaching soldiers.

"You got any smokes left?" a gruff voice asks.

"Yeah. In my fuckin' pocket, and you're not gettin' any of them."

"Aw, fuck off. I need a smoke."

There's a sigh, and then the footsteps stop, and I hear the distinct sound of a match striking.

There are only the two of them from the sound of it, but they're several paces away, coming up the other side of the hawk's carriage. If they head for the horses, I'll be caught.

Biting my lip, I stare down at the rolled paper in my hand. I could flee right now, take the letter with me, and try to come back again.

But this might be my only chance.

Heart pounding, sweat collecting in beads at the back of my neck, I lean in and reach for the perch post inside the carriage.

The soldiers are talking, a few coughs to go with their smoke, but I focus, trying not to panic. Opening my hand, I show the hawk the parchment, hoping it's as well trained as it appears to be.

The largest hawk snaps its beak at the others, as if claiming the job, and then jumps down from its higher perch. Landing at the post near my hand, the bird immediately turns so I can reach its legs.

Thank the Divine.

I grasp the empty metal vial attached to its right leg and pop open the cap. Left for north and right for south.

The soldiers start walking again, and my eyes flare

with alarm, making me nearly drop the damn letter. I manage to keep hold of it and stuff it into the vial, and as soon as it's in, I snap the top back on with the pad of my thumb.

The hawk stretches its leg, as if noting which direction to fly, and then it expertly launches itself up, flying out through the open window cut into the ceiling and flapping into the sky.

I hear a curse, some shuffling in the snow. "What the Divine hell?" the man grumbles.

The other soldier chuckles. "You gonna shit your pants from a little hawk?"

I immediately back up and close the small door as quietly as I can, but I'm too nervous to latch it, in case it makes a noise.

"Why's that thing even going out right now? There's no damn messages."

I freeze, eyes widening. It feels like my heart might beat right out of my chest.

"The thing hunts at night, you idiot."

"Oh."

With a puff of relief exhaling out of me, I let go of the handle and carefully round the corner of the carriage, putting it between me and them. My boots scrape over the snow, and I know that I'm damn lucky the horses are right behind me, covering up the sound as I slowly back up.

"Damn, those fucking horses smell."

"You're a whiny bastard. Why do I always get stuck

on patrol with you?"

"Because I give you smokes," the man says dryly.

"Oh. Right," he chuckles.

I crouch down to peek beneath the carriage, seeing their black boots on the other side. Snow dampens my skirts as I silently crab walk backwards with the tangled fabric around my knees. I slink toward the front of the carriage, watching their steps reach the back.

But they stop, boots turning just as I round the front.

"Huh. Latch is open."

I feel the blood drain from my face. *Shit.*

I look around in a panic for somewhere to hide, but the nearest spot is a tent ten feet away, and it's right in their line of vision. Unless I want to risk going back toward the horses, but what if I startle them?

"You gonna stare at it all night? Close the fucking thing and let's go closer to the fire. It's cold enough to freeze my prick off out here."

A snort. "Must not be much to it, then."

"Fuck off."

I hear one of them close the back latch with a click, and the hawks inside make a quiet screech, either in appreciation or irritation. Still crouched down to watch, I see the soldiers walking away, heading back to the warmth of one of the low-burning campfires.

I'm so relieved that I fall back on my ass in the snow, not even caring that more wet cold is soaking through my dress. I sit there for a moment with a hand over my racing heart, trying to calm down.

After a minute or two, I pick myself up off the ground and start walking as quickly as I can, adrenaline still riding me. It's not until I make it all the way back to my empty, dark tent that it well and truly sinks in.

I did it.

I actually did it! I got a message to Midas. He'll have a warning now, a chance to prepare. The advantage of Fourth's element of surprise is gone.

A smile of victory pulls past frozen teeth, my lip cracking slightly from the chapped cold. My dress is wet, I'm freezing, and I was nearly caught, but I actually did it.

I'm not a traitor. I'm loyal to Midas, and I just proved it.

But my smile slowly drops, weighted down, like a hook pulling at my cheeks. All that victory, that pride, it sours in my gut before it even has the chance to settle.

In its place, an awful feeling rises up, like my impulsive act to prove Polly and the other saddles wrong was a mistake.

Regret. That's regret there, festering in my stomach.

My breath shakes as I look down at myself, eyes settling on my wet hem. I should be proud of myself for standing my ground, that I didn't waver in my convictions. That I didn't let Rip trick me into thinking he's my friend.

I should be gloating that Fourth's army underestimated me, that their manipulations, their false camaraderie didn't work. I should be thoroughly content that I just helped my king and solidified whose side I'm on, because that—staying loyal—it's right.

...*Right?*

I become a flustered mess in the span of a heartbeat, as a war erupts inside of me. I've always known where I stood, and I always stood with Midas. So why the hell do I feel like this?

Shaking my head, I tell myself to stop. What's done is done. I can't take it back now, no matter how much I may regret it.

I feel guilty just by thinking that.

With my mind acting like a turbulent, churning storm, I start going through the motions of getting undressed.

With only a thin bit of moonlight coming in the tent, I strip out of my coat, dress, boots, and wet leggings, hanging them up to dry. I try to stoke some life back into the coals, but they're thoroughly burned out, nothing left of them but cold crumbles. No more warmth or light to give.

It's because of this, and the lack of lantern light too, that I never noticed him until right now, when his voice jolts across the tent.

"Have a nice walk, Auren?"

A yelp of alarm flies out of my mouth as I whirl around, hand over chest. With wide eyes, I panic, until I notice the shape of the spikes along the shadow's back.

Funny how the silhouette of a monster seems to calm my racing heart.

"You scared me," I say shakily, dropping my hand.

"Did I?"

He sits on his pallet, unmoving, his voice strange, like he's using a different tone with me than he usually does.

Unease slithers over my body.

The sliver of moonlight pouring in across the floor is like a line drawn between us.

He just sits there in the dark, not speaking, not moving. The dim light shines on the scales of his cheekbone, his black eyes only visible from the iridescent gleam in them. A feral cat waiting in the rafters to pounce on the unsuspecting mice.

"Rip?" I question, and I hate that my voice sounds so small, so scared.

He doesn't reply. I'm thoroughly unnerved, and more than a little frightened of him right now—a contradiction to the relief I felt just moments ago.

Dressed in only my shift, my knees begin to shake, but I don't know if I'm shivering more because I'm cold or because I'm frightened.

I back away a step, and that's when he stands up fluidly, with more grace than a male like him should be able to move. I flinch, like a rabbit caught in a snare, but I know that the twine around my neck will only tighten quicker.

My heart thumps hard with palpable threat, my ribbons starting to unravel, as if they're anticipating attack.

Three steps, and then he's right in front of me, close

enough that I have to tip my head up to look him in the eye. My tongue is stuck to the roof of my mouth, too dry, too heavy.

This close, I can feel something brewing beneath his skin, feel it like a wicked coarseness that leaves a tangible sharpness in the air.

Maybe this is it. Maybe this is the moment where I'll finally reap that vicious cruelty that Rip is known to sow.

I can be done with this interlude and finally face the real him. I can hate him and not be confused anymore.

So I lock my knees and put my shoulders back, and I wait for the blow. Wait for the noose to tighten and leave me swinging.

But Rip never does what I think he will.

His hand comes up to grip my neck, like he's going to strangle me right here in his tent. I flinch when his fingers close around my throat, except he doesn't squeeze. His touch just rests there, burning into me like a brand.

"I wasn't supposed to find you on that pirate ship," he murmurs, voice like rippling water, the fluttering waves slicking against my ears.

I blink in the dark, trying to keep hold of his black eyes, trying not to notice the heat from his hand on my skin.

He's confused me once again, and I don't know what to say, don't know what to do. For a moment, I wonder if he's getting ready to snap my neck.

I should shove him off, use my ribbons to push him

away, remind him that I don't like to be touched...but I do none of those things, and I'm not entirely sure why.

"You didn't have to take me with you," I say, throat bobbing against his touch, defensiveness crawling through my tone.

He strokes a fingertip across my racing pulse. "Yes, I did, Goldfinch."

And then, Rip leans forward and brushes his lips against mine.

A gasp pulls between my lips, but that just makes me taste him. His air, breathing into me, like inhaling awe.

He doesn't press harder against my mouth, doesn't demand. Just that barest of strokes, lip against lip, and then he's pulling away.

I didn't realize I'd closed my eyes until my heavy lids are snapping open again. His hand moves from my throat to my jaw, a skimming touch just at the edge.

"You'll be pleased to know..." he begins quietly, eyes roaming over my face.

I look at him dazedly, trying to keep up with what he just did, trying not to touch my lips that are still tingling. "Know what?" I ask, a cracked voice through the dark.

He drops his hand, and my body sways toward him before I can catch myself, like I wanted to follow his touch, to get it back.

"We'll arrive in Fifth Kingdom soon."

His words are jarring. Ill-fitting inside this confusing,

intimate moment.

Something in me droops. "Oh."

He reaches up and moves a strand of hair off my shoulder, leaving air to brush against the skin like another feather-light kiss. His eyes flick up, but they're as hard as granite now. "I'm sure you'll be pleased to see your king," he says, face unreadable. "Especially so soon after sending your message to him."

I rear back, like his words are an open palm slapped across my face. I'm left gaping as Rip turns and walks out of the tent, leaving me in the dark, leaving me reeling.

He knows.

He kissed me.

He knows.

He kissed me.

He knows what I did, and yet...he still kissed me.

CHAPTER 29

AUREN

Winter winds howl outside my dark window.

I can hear it whipping the castle's flags, wailing through the cracks in the glass, hail pelting the stone walls.

It's strange to see such a brutal ice storm raging in the night, while I soak in the heat of my bath. Steam still rises in steady tendrils, filling my bathroom, making it hard to see. Sweat beads like drops of glitter on my skin, my every muscle warm and languid as I laze in the water.

But a shout pulls me from my dozing rest.

Jerking my head up from the rim of the tub, my brows pull together tight. I look through the steam, but it's thicker than before, and the noise of the storm outside is growing louder.

I hear something, someone, maybe a voice.

Looking left and right, I call out, "Midas?"

But I don't get a reply, and I can't see anything past the steam. It's hot, cloying, and I realize that the water I'm submerged in feels like it's heating up.

I look down as something coats my fingertips beneath the water, like the thick soap I poured in earlier to make bubbles. I lift my hand out of the tub, water dripping off, rippling around me where it lands.

Except when I hold my hand close to peer at it through the haze of the steam, I see that it's not soap clinging to my skin.

All four of my fingertips are coated with liquid gold.

"No..."

My other hand comes up quickly, grabbing hold of my leaking fingers, squeezing them as if I can staunch the metallic drip.

But my left hand is seeping gold, too.

There's a bright flare that makes me squint, and I turn to look up at the window. It's lit up with daylight now, like the night was somehow blown away by the force of the storm.

Panic fuses to my pulse.

I shake my hands violently, but all that does is send golden droplets flying, some of it landing across my face like a splatter of paint.

"Shit."

The gold starts to slip down my wrists, past my elbows, my shoulders, my breasts. I jerk upright, feet nearly slipping in the tub, my heart slamming against my chest like it's trying to get out.

"No!" I shout, but the gold doesn't listen.

More of it smears down my belly, slips down my legs, bleeds into the creases of my skin.

"Auren."

My head snaps up, and there's Midas, but he's pissed. Furious. Enraged. His brown eyes don't hold any comfort right now, and I know it's my fault.

"Help me," I cry.

Midas just watches as the gold spreads and spreads until it encases my body completely, like I'm mummified with it. I was gold before, but not like this. This is polluting me, like an infection spreading, taking over.

Nothing of me will be left.

A whimper escapes when I realize that the liquid is now hardening in place, gilding me into a solid statue.

"Midas!" I cry, a sob shaking the chords of my voice. "Midas, do something!"

But he shakes his head, eyes gleaming now, so clear that I can see the reflection of my body in them. He isn't mad any longer, but the new expression on his face holds no comfort. If anything, it makes my fear worse.

"Keep going, Precious. We need more," he says quietly, firmly.

I try to jerk my feet up, try to step out of the tub so I can run, but the gold has already hardened beneath the soles of my feet. It's locked my ankles and knees, weighed down my legs. And the bathwater…it's turned solid too.

I'm frozen in place.

With every frenzied breath I take, the gold that coats my skin becomes harder, thicker, stronger.

Tears began to fall from my eyes, but those are gold too. They spill over, dripping down like the melted wax of a candlestick, solidifying against my neck.

My ribbons are panicking, twitching behind me, but they're heavy, soaked-through. Ends bent and sharp, they try to scrape off the hard layer from my skin like a chisel to stone, but they can't. They can't, and as soon as they touch the insidious coating, they get stuck, like ants to sap.

Seeing my ribbons curled at odd angles, stuck, trying to jerk free to no avail, it makes fear lock around my heart with a cold, merciless grip.

My terror-filled eyes snap up to Midas. "Do something!" I plead, but it's a mistake.

As soon my mouth opens, gold slithers past my lips, coating my tongue and teeth. A strangled cry pops out of me, the sound like bursting bubbles of magma as the liquid clogs my throat.

It slinks down to my gut, rises up to my eyes, vision tinted, the sharp metallic scent filling my nose. It ensnares my bones, sheathes my heart, takes over my mind.

The next moment, I'm completely solid from the inside out.

Unable to breathe, or blink, or think. I'm like

Coin—the bird in the atrium, never again to sing, to fly, stuck in place on my perch.

Midas's hand comes up to cup my cheek, fingernails tapping against the metal. "You're so perfect, Precious," he says before leaning in, placing a whisper of a kiss against my lips that I can no longer feel. I want to cry, but I can't, because my tear ducts have solidified too.

The steam in the room is so thick now that I can't see anymore. The gold in my ears makes it so I can't hear either.

But I scream. I scream and scream and scream, though no one can hear me, because my throat is plugged with gold. I'm going to choke on it, be trapped in it for all eternity.

Something against my chest pinches, and my eyes fling open wide from the pain.

I come awake with a thrash, flailing arms and gasping breath like I've just broken through the surface of that solid gold sea.

Sweat has soaked through my shift and leggings, and my hair is plastered against my scalp in damp tangles.

Around me, my ribbons are flapping and snapping with unease, some of them wrapped around my body and constricting around me in a painful squeeze.

I jerk upright and halt their frenzied pulls, make them loosen around me. I start to tear them away from my limbs and torso, untangling myself with shaking hands, trying to escape the hold of the nightmare.

The way Midas had looked at me... My eyes burn

as I try to shove the vision away. *Not real,* I tell myself. *It wasn't real.*

It's not until I extricate myself from the last of my ribbons that I'm finally able to take in a full breath.

"Bad dream?"

I jerk on my pallet and look over, finding Rip getting dressed. I wonder if he's what woke me or if it was just the pinch of my ribbons.

A glance at the front of the tent shows me it's still dark, my internal clock telling me that dawn is still an hour or two away.

"Umm, yeah," I say with some embarrassment, my mind still trying to shove the dream away. "You're up early," I note, then feel immediately stupid for saying such an inane thing, considering what happened between us just a handful of hours ago.

I wonder when he came back to the tent to sleep after I passed out, or if he ever slept at all.

"I want to get the army moving," he says, strapping a belt around his waist. "We've been going the long way, but I'm anxious to get to Fifth Kingdom now."

Something that tastes like remorse sits on the back of my throat. My tongue is poised with an apology, but something holds me back. Pride? Embarrassment? An argument to defend what I did? I don't know.

I sit up, keeping the furs tucked around me as I look at him.

He kissed me, and I still don't think my mind has

fully processed it. My body, on the other hand, seems to have memorized every single moment.

But why did he do it?

Just like last night, before I managed to fall into a fitful sleep, my mind spins with warring emotions. I feel like every single thought I have argues with itself, and I don't know which side is right.

Because that kiss, that soft, somber kiss, it didn't feel like the machinations of an enemy commander.

It felt like deep-seated want.

"Rip..."

He cuts me off, tone cold, eyes not looking anywhere near me. "I suggest you get up and get ready. We move out as soon as dawn breaks."

I get no time to reply before he walks out. With a defeated sigh, I push up and get dressed, and by the time I step outside, there are already two soldiers waiting there to break down the tent.

I mutter an apology for keeping them waiting and head to the fires for food, only to find that those have been put out early too. I find Keg next to a cart, passing out dried rations, which sends the men grumbling. The porridge may not taste any better, but it's hot, and that does wonders for morale when you're stuck marching through frozen wastelands.

"Morning, Gildy," Keg says, passing me a hard roll and a dried strip of salted meat.

"Morning."

Keg's usual banter is cut short, since all the soldiers are in a rush, the tents being broken down, horses being drawn, impatience thick in the air. I take my cue and wander away to leave him to it, biting off bits of food so chewy it makes my jaw ache.

When I get to my carriage, I'm surprised to find Lu there helping my driver hitch up the horses.

Lu turns with a cocked brow when she sees me. "Gildy Locks," she says before turning to tighten the strap she's working on.

"Morning, Lu." I run a gloved hand over the horse's neck, admiring his sleek black hair.

Finishing, she pats the horse on the back and faces me. "Someone pissed in the commander's stew. You wouldn't happen to know anything about that, would you?"

My face grows hot. "No."

I must fail miserably at trying to keep an impassive expression, because she grunts. "Mm-hmm. Thought so."

I suddenly become very interested in the horse's mane, making sure to keep my eyes trained on it.

"Can I give you some advice, Gildy?"

I shift on my feet. "Umm...sure."

"Own your shit."

My gaze snaps over to her. "What?"

Lu sighs and glances over at the driver, who just climbed up into the carriage's seat. "Take a walk, Cormac."

Pausing in his almost-seated position, the man lets

out a sigh, but he turns and climbs down, walking away without argument. It's more than a little impressive that she can give an order and men will follow it.

When we're alone with the horses and a slowly lightening sky, Lu leans against the wall of the carriage to face me. She watches me for a moment, like she's studying me, reading something in my eyes. "We're women in a man's world. I'm sure you know how that is."

I dip my chin. "I do."

"Good," she says with a terse nod, the shaven blades in her scalp stabbing down with the movement. "Then you know that we have two options." She lifts a finger. "The first is, we can conform. Be what they want, act to please. It's the safe option."

I fidget on my feet. Every part of me is listening, attention rapt, though uneasiness mingles alongside my intrigue. "And option two?"

She holds up a second finger, but instead of doing it on the same hand, she raises her other. I don't know why that feels significant, but it does.

"Option two is harder. It's harder for us," she admits, looking me straight in the eye. "There will always be someone who will try to make us choose option one. But don't. Don't lie down to make it easier for the world to keep you under its thumb. Own your shit and choose yourself."

She drops her hands, and I know right then that she knows what I did—that I sent that letter. What I don't get is why I'm not shackled in chains, tossed in the prisoner's cart with the rest of Midas's guards.

"You and I are different, though," I tell her thickly. "You're a warrior, and I'm..." My sentence trails off because I don't even *know*.

I don't know what I am now.

I do know what I *was*. I was a little fae girl who got ripped from her world. I was sold to flesh traders. I was used as a beggar before I got old enough to be used in other ways.

I was hopeless.

Then with Midas, he changed that, and I got to be something else, something I'd always hoped to be.

Safe.

But is that enough? Is it enough now, to just be that?

"You're what you *choose* to be," Lu tells me, and for some reason, I feel like crying.

My throat bobs as I pull the hood over my head, the sky bringing a gray, overcast dawn with a prickling on my skin. "What does this have to do with Rip?" I ask quietly.

She lifts a shoulder. "Nothing. Everything. You'll have to decide that, too, Gildy."

Lu pats the horse again, slipping a hand into her pocket before pulling out a couple of sugar cubes that she feeds to them. "I will tell you one more thing, though."

"What?"

She smiles down at the nuzzled snout of the horse before turning that expression on me. "That fae female

I saw in the fight circle?" she begins, her voice just a murmur in the cresting dawn. "She was a warrior too. And in my professional opinion, she could be a great one."

Lu leaves, as light on her feet as always, a bird taking flight.

I get into the carriage silently, and my hand comes down to press against my waist, fingers tapping over my ribbons with a small smile at my lips.

Warrior.

Yes, I think I would like to be that.

CHAPTER 30

AUREN

*Y*ou *call that a block?* My three-year-old niece could get through that shitty stance!"

Sweat is pouring down my face as I drop my aching arms with a glare sent in Judd's direction. "I'm trying!"

He's been dancing circles around me, smacking me around with a wooden sword, while I've tried and failed to block him.

He made me a smaller version of a fight circle by dragging his foot through the snow around us, and I've been getting my ass handed to me inside of it for well over two hours.

"You're not trying hard enough," he counters, coming to stop in front of me. "Where are your instincts? Did you drop them back in Highbell?"

I grit my teeth, wishing I could pluck his mustard-plant hair right from the roots. He grins in my flustered face, like he knows it.

Lu and Osrik are on the sidelines, just the four of us for the second night in a row. After my talk with Lu, I thought long and hard all day in the carriage.

By the time we stopped for the night, I was practically bouncing with nervousness. I wasn't sure she'd go along with it, but when I asked if she'd help train me, she grinned and led the way, bringing Judd and Osrik along.

We're careful though, making sure to train far away from camp, away from watching eyes. Tonight, there are only a couple of torches and the glow of a weak moon to light up our space, but it's enough.

So far, only Judd has gotten into the fight circle with me. I have a feeling I couldn't handle Lu and Osrik.

Lu, because she's damn quick on her feet, and even though she's smaller than Judd, I can tell she's fierce. And Osrik...the man is a damn beast, and even though he seems to not hate me anymore, his scowl still scares me.

Right now, they're both drinking on a shared fur outside the circle, calling out the occasional piece of advice, like, "Stop getting hit."

Really helpful stuff.

"We're way out here, freezing our asses off so that you can use your ribbons without being seen," Judd points out with a shake of his head. "But you forget to use them *every time*."

I stop to put my hands on my hips, stretching my chest so I can better catch my breath. I didn't even know it was possible to be this overheated when I'm surrounded by ice.

"It's not that I *forget*," I explain. "I've just always taught myself to hide them and hold them back, ever since they sprouted when I was fifteen. It's been ingrained into me."

"Well, un-ingrain it!" Osrik barks out. See? Really helpful.

I shoot him a dry look. "Thanks, I'll try that."

Judd regains my attention by clapping his hands. He's shirtless again, but I'm not going to complain, because the sight almost makes up for me getting thoroughly walloped.

"They're your greatest asset, Gildy. You need to use them to your advantage."

Sighing, I look down at the ground, the feeling of failure winding around me like threads on a spool. "I know."

I hear heavy footsteps trod forward, and then Osrik is bearing down on me, scowl and all. "She just needs proper motivation."

Without warning, he cocks back his fist and sends it flying forward, landing a brutal punch against my shoulder like solid stone launched from a catapult.

I'm knocked off my feet with the contact and fall on my ass in the snow, teeth gritted from the hit. "Ouch!" I snarl.

Osrik looks down at me without remorse, huge arms crossed in front of him like he's bored. "That was my half-punch. You went down like a sack of rocks."

"You hit like a sack of rocks," I grumble.

I push up to my feet, my shoulder feeling like it nearly knocked right out of its socket. I roll it back tenderly with a wince on my face. "I'd hate to feel your full-punch."

"Too bad, 'cause that's next."

My eyes widen as he raises his fist again, but before he can land a hit on my other shoulder, three of my ribbons snap up in response. They shoot out, wrapping around his wrist and forearm, their satin lengths gone firm as steel.

He tries to jerk away, but my ribbons don't let his arm move an inch. His teeth gleam behind his bushy beard. "See? Motivated."

Lu claps. "There you go, Gildy!"

I release a smug-looking Osrik, but my own lips twitch with pride that I finally managed to stop a hit.

"Alright, let's stop for tonight," Judd says, grabbing his shirt from the ground and tugging it on. "It's freezing balls out here."

Lu rolls her eyes as she comes over. "And they say women are the weaker sex. Men are only as strong as those sensitive dangly bits between their legs."

I laugh, reaching down to scoop up a handful of untouched snow to stuff in my parched mouth. It feels heavenly, crunching through the flakes as they melt on my tongue, cooling my heated body.

"Interested in my dangly bits, are you?" Judd smirks at her.

"Only their whereabouts so I know where to aim my kick when you piss me off," she drawls.

Both Judd and Osrik grimace, like they're imagining her doing just that. She shoots me a wink.

The guys pick up the two torches they brought out here, while Lu plucks up the bottle of wine and fur before we all start the trek back to camp.

"Here you go, your ribbons earned it," Lu says, passing me the bottle of wine.

"My ribbons earned it? Not me?"

"Yep. Your ribbons take charge when you're threatened or pissed and you forget to hold them back. But *you* need to start taking charge of *them*. Have more control, learn how to use each one to your best advantage."

Nodding, I lift the bottle to my lips and tip it back, gulping down the last bit of wine left at the bottom.

"You essentially have two dozen more limbs. You could really fuck shit up if you learn how to use them," Judd says from my other side.

I feel my ribbons puff up slightly like they felt his ego stroke.

The last drop of wine lands on my tongue before I pull the bottle away and hold it at my side. "Isn't this a little counterproductive for you guys?"

Lu looks over. "What do you mean?"

"Well, I'm technically your enemy, and you're training me to fight."

Judd nudges me slightly, but I flinch because I'm already bruised up from all the hits I didn't block. He notices and grins. "You're not our enemy."

...*Yet.*

I hear the unsaid word from all three of them, an unspoken question that hovers in the frigid air, freezing into something solid but untouched.

"Why are you doing it, though?" I press. "If you know I'm going back?"

To him. Going back to him.

"I guess we're just waiting to see how this plays out, Gildy Locks," Lu says vaguely.

"You're not ready for us, anyway," Osrik says. "You can't even take a little tap to the shoulder."

I whip my head to the left to glare at him. "It was *not* a little tap."

He shrugs. "You need to toughen up."

No argument there.

"So, are you three the only members of Rip's Wrath?" I ask curiously.

"First the enemy talk, and now you're trying to suss out our secrets?" Judd asks with an arched brow.

I quickly shake my head. "Sorry. I was just curious. You don't have to answer."

He hums. "Enemies are usually much better at

espionage than this, aren't they?"

The other two nod in agreement.

My steps falter. "No, I swear, I'm not—"

All three of them laugh, cutting me off. "We're just fucking with you," Lu tells me.

I let out a breath of relief. "Oh."

They chuckle a bit more...but I notice that none of them actually answer my question.

The four of us crest a shallow slope and then cross into the camp, still noisy with soldiers carrying on around their fires, crude tavern songs being sung from deep bass voices.

"More training soon, Gildy," Judd calls.

"Yeah, and be better at it," Osrik says.

I see Lu elbow him in the gut, hard enough that the monolith actually grunts and rubs his stomach.

With a smile, I break away from the three Wraths, feeling oddly energized despite how badly I just got my ass handed to me. With an idea sparking in my head, I veer away from my original direction and go in search of Keg.

I find him at his fire of course, but he's done serving for the night and is propped up against a nearby tent with a harmonica at his mouth.

He's blowing out a tune I don't recognize—one that lilts, hard to keep up with his quick breaths. There are a dozen or so soldiers around him playing dice, but when Keg sees me, he pulls the instrument from his lips.

"Ho, Gildy!"

Smiling, I walk over to him. "You play really well."

He nods. "I don't *just* make amazing food."

Someone nearby snorts. Keg chooses to ignore him.

I look down at the harmonica, at its polished surface. "Did you make that yourself?"

"No, my gramps did. He's the one who taught me."

"It's beautiful," I say, noting the engravings that resemble grains of wheat.

"Wanna have a go?" he offers, holding it up to me.

I shake my head. "I only play harp."

A whistle shrills through his teeth. "Harp? Damn, that *is* fancy, castle girl."

I won't tell him that my harp was made of solid gold.

"Maybe one day I'll hear you play," he says, dropping his hand. "But if you're not here for food or music, then to what do I owe the pleasure?"

"I was actually wondering if you could help me with something."

His eyes grow curious. "Let's hear it."

"How hard would it be to scrounge up a makeshift bath?"

Keg's black brows lift up as he shoves his spun hair over his shoulder. "A bath? In a traveling army?"

I shrug. "You've got the biggest soup pot around, so I figured if anyone knew how to make it happen, it would be you."

He taps his finger to his lips in thought before

jumping to his feet. "Alright, I got it. Come on."

With an excited smile, I follow him through camp, and he leads me to the tent specifically set up to do laundry. Stepping beneath the tarp, I look around at the giant soaking trays, deep enough to fit a smaller person, long enough if they bend their knees. A smile curves my lips. "Keg, you're a genius."

"Cook, musician, genius," he ticks off. "My attributes just grow and grow."

A few of the soldiers using the space look over at us, and Keg snaps his fingers. "Ho there!" He points at a pair of them. "We need that tray."

The soldiers frown, but they pull out their dripping wet clothes, still soapy, and toss them into the next tray over.

"Good, now we're gonna need your help carrying it," Keg says.

The soldiers share a confused look. "Carry it where?"

Keg looks over to me.

"Oh, umm, I'll lead the way."

The soldiers hesitate, but with another snap from Keg, they tip the large tin basin of water over, dumping it right outside the tent. When it's empty, they lift it between them.

"Lead the way, Gildy," Keg says.

Smiling, I grab a handful of cubed soap pieces from the ground and stuff them into my pocket. Then I hurry out with Keg beside me, the two soldiers dutifully following after us.

I pick the quickest way, having long since memorized the path. Keg frowns beside me. "Aren't we going to your tent?" he asks.

Shaking my head, I say, "The bath isn't for me."

He shoots me a confused look but doesn't say anything else as I make our way through camp, only stopping once we reach the saddles' tent.

I point to the ground next to the crackling campfire. "You can set it there, please."

The soldiers guarding the saddles look up in surprise. "What's that for?"

My helpers set the tray down with a shrug and then walk away. The guards turn to me and Keg for an explanation.

"It's for the saddles. So they can have a proper bath, wash their clothes, their hair..." I say.

The guards shake their heads. "I don't think so."

"It's a bath," I argue. "They aren't criminals. Their only wrongdoing was being caught by the Red Raids, and then by you. They've been cooped up in that small tent and given only rags and snow to wash with," I go on, my tone unrelenting. "So you two are going to help me fill this thing with snow, let it melt by the fire, and then you're going to make it so those saddles can bathe in peace."

I don't know who's more stunned by my order—the guards, Keg, or myself.

The men just stare at me, but I don't waver. I look at

them steadily, not backing down.

Beside me, Keg leans down and scoops up a handful of snow before dumping it in the tub. "You heard the woman," he says to them with a smirk. "Get on with it before I kick my foot in your arses. And one of you build up that fire, or this is gonna take all night to melt."

Keg's voice jerks them into action, and soon, all four of us are dumping snow into the tub, scoop after scoop. Keg dumps a few fire-charred rocks into it too, making steam hiss into the air and speeding up the melting process.

By the time it's full, my hands are numb, gloves soaked through, but I'm pleased. I stuff my gloves into my coat pocket as the four of us look over our handiwork.

When movement catches my eye, I look over and find Polly and Rissa peeking out of their tent, watching me. I go straight over and dig into my pocket to pull out the soap, plopping the cubes in Rissa's hand. "Enough for everyone to have a turn," I say.

The girls just look down at the soap, look at the basin, the fire, the guards.

Polly's lips thin. "If you expect us to fall down and kiss your feet, you're stupider than you look."

"I don't expect anything," I tell her honestly, because I don't.

I don't expect gratitude from them. I don't even expect a truce. I just wanted to give them a tiny sliver of *something*, because none of this is their fault. None of this has been easy for them.

It's the least I can do to help ease them, just a little bit. I've had freedom and comforts, as strange as it seems. They deserve some of that too, and this is what I can get for them.

"Enjoy your baths," I say before I turn and leave.

Keg sidles up beside me as I walk back to my tent. "That was nice of you," he says.

"You sound surprised."

"This army is a bunch of gossips. I heard how those women turned you away."

The tips of my ears burn. "Oh." It was bad enough that those two guards witnessed it, but it's much worse to know that it's become army chatter.

"Some would say that they don't deserve your kindness," Keg points out.

I shake my head, watching the ground as we go. "Kindness shouldn't have to be earned. It should be freely given."

Keg laughs softly. "My ma used to say something like that," he replies, looking over at me. "And you know what?"

"What?"

"She is a damn smart woman."

CHAPTER 31

AUREN

After living in Sixth Kingdom for the past ten years, I thought I'd experienced every kind of cold there was. But when we cross into Fifth Kingdom, I realize that's not true at all.

The cold in Sixth Kingdom is frigid wind, sharp needles of sleet, blizzards brought on by the loud wailing of a grieving gale widow, and an endless shroud of clouds.

But Fifth Kingdom is different.

We cross into its territory during midday, with the view of an arctic sea on the horizon. Chunks of ice as clear as glass drift lazily around with the tide, sea birds resting on them between their dives for fish.

Further out, cerulean blue icebergs jut from the water like frozen sentinels shielding the harbor, the floating mountains proud and tall.

We set up camp there, right on the shore. When night falls, the ground seems to glow, while the bright blue water goes black as ink, waves crashing into the shore with a ballad sung by the tide.

No, I've never known cold to be like this before.

This wintry land of Fifth Kingdom is nothing like Highbell. It's not blustery or loud or punishing.

It's still. Quiet. The glacial calm of a land at peace with the cold, rather than at war with it.

It's not just the weather that's different. The army is too. They're more sedate tonight, as if crossing territories into the crisp, calm land sobered everyone's thoughts.

After eating dinner alone in my tent, I wander outside toward the shore that's speckled with bonfires, a mass of soldiers gathered around.

Reconsidering, I decide to turn, and instead of heading right for the crowded beach, I go toward the shadow of boulders off to the right.

Gray and pitted, the stones are gathered in a clump, like timeworn marbles left to scatter the ground on the icy beach.

I carefully make my way over the rocks in hopes of finding someplace more private, because a night like this seems to call for it.

It's slow progress over the slippery surfaces, but I manage it by the heel of my boots and the grip of my gloves. Once I get to the top of the stone pile, I breathe in, enjoying the view for a moment before I start making my way down the other side.

I'm almost to the bottom when the toe of my shoe hits an ice patch and I slip. I go falling forward with pinwheeling arms, but before I crack my head open on the rocks, a grip catches at the back of my coat.

My body jerks to a stop, awkwardly suspended midfall. I look over my shoulder to find Rip, and surprise makes my eyes go as wide as saucers.

"I slipped," I say stupidly. I'm both embarrassed that he saw me fall, and relieved that he caught me.

In the moonlight, I can see him arch a brow. "I noticed."

He tips his head, indicating that he wants me to walk. Feeling flustered, I straighten up and face forward, regaining my footing carefully before I start to pick my way down the rocks, all too aware of his presence, of his hold.

Rip keeps a grip on my coat the whole time, until we're back on the flat ground. As soon as my feet hit the snow, he releases me, like he couldn't do it fast enough, like he's bitter he had to catch me in the first place.

It shouldn't bother me, but it does.

I turn to him. "Thank you," I say quietly.

He nods at me, but he's stone-faced, colder than the bobbing ice. "You should've brought your ribbons out immediately to break your fall. You need to work on your instincts," he says in reprimand.

A small sigh escapes me. "So I've been told."

I brush down the feathers on my coat and look around, noting the small, empty beach. It's caught between another mound of stones about forty feet away, making this little notch feel secluded, secret. A clandestine coast along an icicle sea.

"What are you doing out here?" I ask, turning to face him.

"Waiting."

I tilt my head in curiosity. "For what?"

Rip watches me for a moment, like he's debating whether or not he wants to reply. When he stays silent, I have my answer.

Disappointment fills me, but it's nothing more than what I deserve. I deserve a lot worse, to be honest. I deserved for him to let me fall on those rocks instead of catching me. I deserved to be locked up, to be hated.

"I'm sorry," I whisper. And I'm not exactly sure *what* parts I'm apologizing for, but my words are sincere nevertheless.

His expression shutters, giving nothing away.

When I realize he's not going to respond to that either, I almost turn and walk away. *Almost.*

But something keeps me standing there, rooted with him.

As we watch each other beside the brine-breathed water, all I can think of is how his lips grazed against mine. How the feather-light touch was so contradictory to his rough reputation and sharp edges.

Even though I shouldn't care, I find that I don't want him to hate me. I don't want his cold indifference.

My body remembers that night. From the heat of his breath, to the feel of his fingertips skimming my jaw. Every time I close my eyes, my heart pounds with the thought of it, my mind spinning with what it meant, why he did it.

Why did he do it?

I've tried fighting him tooth and nail since I met him. I've tried hating him. Blaming him, but...

But.

That argument of him being my enemy, it doesn't feel true anymore.

Something changed. Something split off, and I can feel it, I can feel *me* drifting blindly in the water like one of those pieces of broken-off ice.

Maybe it was the barely-kiss that did it. Maybe it was the poke and prod, the proud smile I received when I unleashed my ribbons and admitted what I am.

Or maybe it was right from the start, when he saw me and he knew what I was and he did not balk. Maybe I was doomed from the beginning, the moment I walked off that ship.

I wrap my arms around myself and move my gaze to the ocean. It's easier, to face that than to look at him as I talk.

"You've never treated me like your prisoner, not really," I say quietly.

Hopefully he can hear me over the waves, because my voice doesn't have the courage to go louder.

"I thought it was a tactic. Maybe it was—is. I don't know. I never know with you, because you confuse me. This whole damn army confuses me," I admit with a small scoff as I shake my head at myself.

I'm breathing harder, exerted from carrying the weight of my confession.

This could be a mistake. But everyone keeps telling me to listen to my instincts, and my instincts keep telling me to *stop*. To stop my knee-jerk reactions and try to see things in a different light instead.

Because even though that kiss was the softest, lightest touch, I felt its weight all the way down to my bones. And *that* can't be a trick.

Right?

This quiet night is perfect for these timid thoughts. Perfect for looking at the shifting waves and feeling myself shifting too. My cheeks fight between a flush and the frost, heat and chill.

The clouds move overhead, like a curtain peeling back, finger to lips, an eavesdropping sky.

"But I just realized something," I go on with an almost-smile.

Beside us, the seawater crashes against the rocks with a clap and a rumble.

"And what's that?" Rip asks.

Our gazes stay locked on the thundercloud sea.

"That even if you are tricking me, I'm grateful. For all of it."

Rip doesn't reply, but he's tense beside me. I can't hear him breathe, don't see his chest rise.

"You saved me from the Red Raids, but I think you also saved me from myself. And even if it is a manipulation, a ploy, it's worth it, for what I learned."

A pause. Then, his voice in the dark. "What did you learn?"

"I've been in a cage of my own making."

I finally turn to him and look at the profile of his face, the scales that perfectly follow the line of his cheekbone. I see the hard set mouth, the drawn brows, the spikes raised along his back. The waves crash again, and the brined mist sprays up, kissing my face.

"I'm loyal, but...I feel guilty about the hawk."

I know that it was a test from the goddesses. I'm just not sure if I failed or if I passed. What I do know is I've been churned and tangled up inside ever since I sent that message.

Rip doesn't say anything for a moment, but I see the slight drop of his shoulders, his spikes in a bend, like they've let out a sigh. "It doesn't matter that you sent that letter. Not in the way you think."

My brows lift, caught off guard. "What do you mean?"

"He already knew. King Ravinger sent a missive to Midas when I first got you."

Inside my chest, my heart missteps, trips over a beat. *He knows. Midas already knows.*

The roar in my ears is louder than the crashing waves, and I have to shake my head to clear it. "Why would your king do that? I thought the plan was to shock Midas and leave him to scramble? Why get rid of the element of surprise?"

"Fourth's army doesn't need the element of surprise," he says, and even if it's arrogant, I don't disagree. "King Ravinger likes to intimidate and brag. I'm sure telling Midas that Fourth's army has his most prized possession pleased Ravinger immensely."

I let that truth settle as my thoughts whirl, but I don't want to swim neck-deep in games of kings. Not tonight.

So instead, I let out a long breath and change the subject. "When I asked you before what you were doing out here, you said you were waiting. What did you mean?" I ask, hoping that this time, he'll answer me.

He looks up and points. "I was waiting for that."

Following the direction of his finger, I notice that there's been a change in the sky. There's a blue tinge to the moon now, a melancholy sapphire veil. As I watch, I see a star drop beside it, streaking downward, before it disappears behind the horizon.

"Wow. I've never seen the sky look like that."

"It's a mourning moon," Rip says, voice low, almost...sad. "It happens every few years. The fae used to gather to watch it in this realm."

My throat bobs as I glimpse another star falling, fading out of sight, like it dove into the dark sea. I instantly understand why they call it a mourning moon. She looks so blue where she hangs in the sky, so somber. All around her, the night is crying tears of starlight.

"The goddesses make this night so that we can remember," Rip tells me, and chills sprinkle over my arms. "The fae watch so we can honor the ones that we mourn. To remember them."

It's on the tip of my tongue to ask him who he honors, who he mourns. But that's too personal, and I have no right. Instead, I watch the blue glow of the moon become deeper, its color painting the clouds.

His head drops down, turning, and we meet each other's eyes. I used to think that his were as black as a bottomless pit, but I was wrong. They aren't suffocating or soulless. Something swims in them when he looks at me.

I'm afraid that if I look too long, that same thing will swim in my eyes too. I look away again, using the sky as an excuse.

There's a tentative truce between us, and the relief of it releases something heavy that was weighing on my shoulders.

When another star drops, I think of how I can offer my gratitude to him, and I decide to settle on a truth, freely given.

"You asked me before where I was from, but I didn't answer."

I feel him look over at me, those black eyes soaking in like dew against a parched leaf.

"I've come from a lot of places. From Highbell of course, and before that, a few villages in Second Kingdom. One of them was called Carnith." My voice nearly splits in half at the name, but I manage to hold it together. "Before that, a shipping port along one of the coasts of Third."

That ocean was so much different from this one. I can remember the smell of that beach, the markets that teemed there, the shore that was littered with boats and noise and people.

"The ships always came full and left empty. It was busy. It always reeked of fish and iron. It rained a lot," I say, tone like a lull.

"And before that?" Rip asks carefully, and my chest is beating so hard, because it hurts to think of it, to remember it.

I haven't spoken it aloud in a long, long time. I only ever dared to murmur it in my head on the cusp of a dream.

"Annwyn," I whisper. "I was in Annwyn."

The realm of the fae.

I feel the ache of home crack inside of me like an eggshell star.

Twenty years. It's been twenty years since I've been home. Twenty years since I've breathed its fresh air, since I've walked on its sweet soil, since I've heard its sun's song.

Rip and I watch the mourning moon for a long time after that. We don't talk any more, but we do sit on the stones together, and it isn't tense or awkward. Maybe for both of us, it's a comfort. Each of us represents a little piece of home, and maybe that's what we mourn most.

When I start to shiver inside my coat and shift it around me, his eyes fall to it. I quickly gather the hood and lift it over my head as Rip rises from the stones. "Time to go, Goldfinch."

My heart squeezes from the nickname as I get to my feet. I'm going to miss this, when I'm back with Midas. I'm going to miss *him*.

That realization, this awakening awareness, it feels as if the world is moving beneath my feet. Like I'm going to look up and see the ground while I walk on the sky.

Even more shocking is that it somehow feels right.

I'm going to miss him, and I can't lie to myself about it anymore.

He helps me over the rock pile and then walks me back to camp. The moon's blue shade is already fading, the stars going still and clear again in the sky, like drying tears.

When we get to the tent, he stops just outside of it. "We'll reach Ranhold Castle tomorrow night."

My pulse jumps. "Already?"

Rip nods, watching me steadily, expression unreadable. "King Ravinger will be arriving so he can greet Midas."

I feel my eyes flare as fear suddenly thrums through my entire body. "Your king is coming?"

"You need to prepare yourself."

I want to ask him to clarify, to ask what I should be preparing myself for, but he's already walking away.

King Rot is coming.

And yet, I'm not sure who I'm more nervous to face—him or Midas.

CHAPTER 32

AUREN

If the army was somber yesterday, it's been replaced tonight with tension. And it has everything to do with the spired building looming in the distance.

Several hours ago, we crossed into Fifth Kingdom's capital city, coming face-to-face with Ranhold Castle. Directly behind it, there are mountains of bright ice that border glittering plains of unruffled snow.

Before night fell, there was a white shroud of thick mist in the air, like all the clouds gathered together to stitch a gown for the sky to wear, its skirts trailing down over the horizon.

Ranhold City is a ring around the castle, and from my vantage point on the overlooking hill, I can pick out the shops, the tenements, the larger estates.

I tried to sleep for a while, but I gave up. I've been

staring at Ranhold ever since. I stand with my back to the camp as I look down at the city, my eyes skimming over the burning lights in homes and on lantern-lit streets.

"What are you doing up here alone, Gildy?" Judd approaches with his usual swagger, his yellow hair nearly glowing.

"Couldn't sleep," I reply, turning back to face the palace.

Midas is somewhere in that castle. I wonder what he's doing, who he's with. I wonder if he knows I'm here.

Right now, he could be looking out the window of the castle, watching Fourth's army where we've set up camp on the edge of Ranhold's border. Maybe he's looking at me.

Judd makes a noise beside me, a grunt that wordlessly says he sees all of Ranhold and he's not impressed.

"Come on. I have a job for you."

He turns to start striding away, and I have to hurry to catch up. "What kind of job?"

Judd glances at me from the corner of his eye. "You'll see."

Instantly curious, I let him lead me through the camp. He doesn't strike up any conversation, so I focus on following him as he squeezes us between tents and passes by campfires.

The soldiers we see nod at Judd and raise a hand or tip their heads in greeting. It seems most of them decided to give up on sleep too. Dawn is fast approaching, and with it, maybe war.

"Are you going to tell me where we're going?" I finally ask when it feels like we've been walking for ages.

"Shh," he hisses back at me.

I open my mouth to ask him what the hell is going on, but like he can sense it, he gives me a pointed look.

I huff out a breath but keep quiet.

After another few minutes of walking, my ears perk with the sound of women's voices. I snap my gaze around, and sure enough, there are women soldiers gathered around a campfire—and Lu is one of them.

I open my mouth and raise my arm to call to her, but Judd yanks me behind a tent and obnoxiously presses his finger to his mouth. "Shh! Are you *trying* to get me caught?"

Blinking at him in surprise, I raise my hands in a silent question, which he doesn't answer. Instead, he starts walking again, motioning me to follow. We duck behind a tent, putting distance between us and the fire.

When we pass a small collection of horses, Judd halts in front of me so fast I nearly collide with his back. When I peer around him, I see why.

"What are you doing here?" the woman soldier asks with clear distrust in her tone. She has an unlit wooden pipe tucked behind her ear, nearly obscured by the frizz of short brown curls around her face.

"Inga, always a pleasure to see you," Judd says.

She narrows her eyes on him before sucking her

teeth, like she's trying to get a wayward crumb out. "Is it? Shouldn't you be off with the left flank? I heard they're stroking each other's egos like they do their pricks. In need of a little pep talk so they don't wet their pants on the eve of battle?" she says with a mocking tip of her lips.

Judd rolls his eyes. "Please. We all know that it's the *right flank* who piss their pants before a fight." His eyes drop to her waist. "Speaking of, new trousers?" he grins.

She glowers at him.

"Anyway, I'm just bringing Auren to find Lu." Judd raises a hand and presses it against the edge of his mouth to highlight a fake whisper. "She's in need. Having her *women* troubles, if you catch my drift."

My mouth drops open, and embarrassed heat floods my cheeks.

Inga glances over at me. "Oh," she says, "the red flag is flying, hmm?"

Completely mortified, I start to say no, but Judd steps on my toes. *Hard.*

"Nn...yep," I say with a wince.

She nods in understanding. "Well, if you can't find Lu, come back and I'll sort you out."

"We'll keep that in mind." Judd smiles before he cocks his head at me to follow him.

I can't even look at her, my face is burning so badly. "Thanks," I mumble.

As soon as I catch up to him, I shoot him a glare.

"What the hell?" I rasp.

He snickers, leading me between a couple of tents. His hazel eyes are scanning all around us, but he finds what he's looking for because his face breaks into a grin. "I knew it."

I stop as he rushes over to what looks like a pile of furs. But when he yanks a few off, I see it.

Exasperation fills me, coming out in a sigh. *"Really?"* I say dryly.

"Come on, help me lift."

Grumbling, I come forward. Just like Lu had me do, I'm lifting a damn barrel of wine again.

It feels heavier this time, but maybe that's just my sore arms from the training I've been doing.

"Can you hold it up higher than that?" Judd asks as he clutches the bottom end. "You're weaker than I thought."

I glare at him. "Maybe it's all the blood I'm losing from my *women's troubles.*"

Judd laughs. "I had to think quick on my feet. It was the best I could do."

I strain to hold the heavy ass barrel up as Judd zig-zags through the tents, the clandestine movements apparent as he makes us turn around or duck behind a tent any time we see someone.

He has us bring it all the way to the other side of camp, where a group of men are sitting around a fire, chewing on food rations.

When Judd sets it down, the men notice what it is and let out a cheer, their sullen mood instantly breaking.

It doesn't take long for one of them to pop the plug and start emptying the barrel, cup by cup.

I stand at the back, watching with amusement as Judd claps the men on their backs, trading a few words with them. He sees me watching and wanders over, passing me a drink.

"So this is a thing? Steal the wine barrel from each other?"

Judd grins. "Yep."

I smile and shake my head in amusement before taking an appreciative sip. The wine hits my tongue with sweet, decadent warmth. "Mmm."

"Exactly," he says with a nod. "Best wine in camp. The other stuff is basically watered-down horse piss."

I wrinkle my nose at that visual.

After finishing our cups, Judd walks me back, and I notice that the sky is starting to lighten with impending dawn. Even though I think my gloves might have splinters in them and my arms are sore from lugging that barrel half across the camp, I'm grateful that it distracted me, at least for a bit.

"Thanks for giving me a job," I tell Judd as we stop in front of my tent.

"Any time. You had that look about you."

"Which one?"

He sends me a smile, not the usual snarky one, but sympathetic. "The look of a person about to face a battle."

My brows pull together. "But I'm not going to be the

344

one in a battle."

Judd arches a knowing brow. "Aren't you?"

I know what he's implying, but I don't know what to say. It does feel a little bit like I'm readying myself for *something*. I just don't know what, because I have no idea what I'll be facing tomorrow. I only know that I *do* have to face it.

I fidget on my feet. "Do you think King Ravinger will declare war? Do you think it'll be *you* battling tomorrow?"

He shrugs. "Who knows? That's up to the kings. I'm just here for the wine."

A laugh bubbles out my throat, Judd successfully popping the unease that had started to boil in my stomach again.

Movement out of the corner of my eye grabs my attention, and I turn to see Rip standing just at the edge of the tent. His posture is stiff, his face stern with a line pulled between tense brows, mouth pressed in a tight line. His eyes are on me.

The smile on my face wipes away.

Seeing my expression, Judd turns to follow the direction of my gaze.

Rip's eyes flick to him for a split second. "Leave us."

Judd passes me an unreadable look before he slips his hands in his pockets and walks off, taking the last of my happy distraction with him.

Now alone, Rip tilts his head at the tent, and I walk

inside, warmth greeting me from the coal bank. Rip follows after me, bringing a chill with him.

Something is off. Something is wrong.

The tension is thick enough to slice, and he's too still, too shadowed. His aura, which I've grown so used to, is restless, churning with agitation.

My hands wring together. "What's wrong?"

He stays where he is, right at the entrance of the tent, with a foot of space between us that somehow feels both incredibly far, and much too close.

"King Ravinger will be here soon to meet with Midas."

A little lightning bolt strikes into my stomach. I shouldn't be so afraid. I've known this was coming. Yet now that it's here, I can't stop my heart from racing or my stomach from writhing in dread.

"What's going to happen?"

To me. To Midas. To him. To them.

Rip shakes his head once. "That remains to be seen."

I cross my arms like I can ward off the unease.

He watches me for a long moment, making me wind up so tight that I don't even feel my ribbons around me.

"I have a question for you," he finally says.

Something tells me I don't want to hear it. "What is it?"

His black eyes are locked on my face, and I don't know what he sees, I don't know what he thinks. It's like this every time I'm around him, but right now, it makes me want to scream.

"Do you want to stay?"

My lips pull downward as his question spins in my head. "Stay?" I repeat breathlessly.

Rip takes a single step forward. Just one, but it divides the space between us in half. He's like he was that night, after I sent the hawk. Quiet. Pensive. An intensity about him that takes up all the air, makes every single one of my senses go alert.

His voice drops. "You don't have to go back. I could make it so that you could stay."

The breath catches in my throat when I realize what he's saying. I'm stunned, confused, I don't know what the hell to say.

"I could make it happen. But you have to tell me now, before King Ravinger arrives."

Restless unease makes me start to pace in the small space. "Why are you offering this?" I ask, bewildered. "I'm your *prisoner*, Rip. Your king no doubt wants to use me for some kind of ransom, and you're the commander of his army that's probably going to declare war tomorrow. You can't ask me if I want to stay. You can't."

He stands as proud and as unyielding as a wall. "I can, and I am. You have a choice, Auren."

I'm so confused, so damn shocked. "Your king would never allow it. Not if he already has a ransom in mind. He plans to use me, and he will."

"Not if you tell me now."

I stop to gape at him. "What would happen to you, to your soldiers?"

"You don't have to worry about that."

A noise of derision slips out of me. "Don't have to worry? All there is to do is worry. I can't stay, Rip."

For the first time since he came in this tent, a flash of emotion crosses his face. Anger, dark and quick, thickens over his brow. "Why not?"

I press a hand to my forehead, trying to quell my thundering thoughts. "Because."

He shakes his head, jaw tight. "Not good enough. Give me a real answer."

"I don't even know what you're offering. To hide me? To make me disappear? I can't do that to Midas."

If I thought he was angry before, it's *nothing* to the anger that brews now. It's palpable, thickening in the air like a storm building to rage.

"*Midas*." The word is spit from his mouth like a curse, something to detest. "What about those things you said on the beach? You're just going to let him keep you again like a bird in a cage?"

"No," I say with a resolute shake of my head. "Things are going to be different now. *I'm* different now. I meant what I said."

Rip scoffs. The sound is ugly, distrustful. "If you think for a second that things will be different, then you're a fool."

My hands ball into fists at my sides. "I'm *not* a fool."

"He keeps you like a pet. Uses you. Manipulates

you. Takes advantage of whatever twisted love you think you have for him."

He flings the accusations at me like a dagger, meant to pierce me.

"He kept me safe."

"*Safe.*" He growls it like he's a wolf who'd like to devour it whole. "Always the same damn argument. Yes, how magnanimous of him to lock you behind bars all day and call you his favored whore."

I flinch from the slap of his words, a hit that makes anger and hurt blaze in my cheeks.

"You can think what you want, but *no one* else ever did that much," I say, and I hate that my throat squeezes with emotion, hate that I can't stay as emotionless as him.

"I wilted in the streets, starving, abused, hated. You think he uses me? It's *nothing* compared to what I've endured at the hand of others."

Rip goes lethally still. Fury radiates off of him and lifts the hairs on the back of my neck.

"What's wrong?" I taunt. "Don't like to hear that a fellow fae didn't rise up in this world like you? So sorry that I didn't sell myself to King Rot instead. Maybe if I had, I'd be commanding this army, and you'd be in Midas's cage for people to gawk at and prod at your spikes."

Those spikes stretch and tighten, like they're imagining it—him being trapped behind bars.

"Stop being complacent. Stop being okay with being

a pet in a cage."

My lips pull back into a snarl. "Go to hell!"

He shakes his head. "No, Auren. You're the one that needs to burn. You need to spark to life and *fight*. Stop letting him dull you, stop letting the whole fucking world trample you," he shouts, making me flinch from the vehement demand. "If you tried, you could shine brighter than the fucking sun. Instead, you've chosen to sit back and wither."

An angry tear floods past my eye and drips down my chin. "You want me to run like a coward, but I'm not afraid of him. Despite what you think, he loves me and he'll listen to me," I say, dashing the evidence of my hurt off my face. "Why are you even doing this? Why do you care?" I demand.

But what I'm really asking is, *what did your kiss mean? What does any of this push and pull between us mean?*

A tic appears in his jaw, like he's biting his words, deciding which ones to swallow down. "Everyone deserves a choice. I'm offering you one."

"I can't leave the *one person* who has ever protected me."

He makes a growled sound and runs a hand through his thick black hair, pulling it at the roots, revealing his frustration. "Look, we do what we have to in order to survive. I'm not judging you for it."

I let out a humorless laugh. The air is lightening even more, a dread dawn ready to crest. "That's all you've done since I met you. You've judged me for every decision I've made to hide myself, to survive. Don't pretend otherwise."

"Fine," he says, dropping his hand. "But you don't have to hide, not anymore."

My expression goes cold. I force my legs to lock to disguise my trembling knees. "I told you. I'm always going to choose him."

I see the pale outline of his throat bob, like he's taking in what I'm saying, getting a taste of the bitterness. His eyes, though, they're drenched in it, and so is his voice when it hardens in a reply.

"So be it."

CHAPTER 33

AUREN

King Ravinger arrives with a flock of timberwings. I've never seen the flying beasts before. Their numbers are small, their breed barely kept from extinction a century ago. They used to live wild in Orea in droves, but now, only the wealthiest own them. Kings, for instance.

Just a couple of hours after dawn, six of the giant birds appear in the sky. Although, *bird* is used lightly.

They have tree-bark-colored feathers on the tops of their wings, and snow white on the underside to match the rest of their bodies. It allows them to blend into the clouds when in flight, their wings spanning a good twenty feet.

Unlike birds though, they have no beak. Instead, there's a wide muzzle with razor sharp teeth, perfect for scooping up prey and carrying them into the air, never even having to land to get a meal.

That reason alone makes me not want to get too close.

Instead, I watch from a distance as the six timber-wings and riders drop down into the heart of Fourth army's camp and disappear from my view.

I wander around for a bit, but the camp feels eerie. Most of the soldiers have gone to greet their king and await orders, but it feels like a ghost town. It's too quiet, too still, like the breath before the scream. I wonder if the city of Ranhold feels the same, with Fourth's army looming on their border.

I can't stand how tense it is. I can't stand to watch the soldiers sharpen their blades or put on their black plated armor instead of just leathers.

When I become too anxious to walk around, I sit by one of the campfires and watch the flames, listening to the crackle of the logs.

"This her?"

I startle, not having heard the trio that just walked up behind me. Standing to turn, I find two unfamiliar soldiers stopping to face me, and Lu coming up beside them.

Lu is dressed in full armor too, a chainmail mesh visible at her neck. "Yeah, this is her," she tells them, her face grim.

Frowning, I look between them. "What's going on?"

"The king wants you guarded for protection," one of the soldiers says.

My lips press together. I'm smack in the middle of their

army's camp. No one can get to me here, not even Midas.

"You mean your king wants me watched," I say, and the look on Lu's face confirms it for me.

"Fine. I'm just sitting here, so make yourselves comfortable," I offer, pointing to the empty stools off to the side.

But the guard shakes his head. "The king wants you kept secure. Lead the way to your tent, my lady."

My eyes flash over to Lu. "Seriously?"

She gives me a shrug. "Sorry, Gildy. Those are the orders."

I shouldn't be surprised, but all this time being a prisoner without really being a *prisoner* has spoiled me.

"Was a deal struck?" I ask. "Am I being traded for something? Ransomed?"

Lu braces a hand on the hilt of her sword. "I don't know yet."

I give a quick nod, hating the not-knowing.

She looks me up and down, and I can tell she wants to say something, but for whatever reason, she seems to hold back.

"Ready to go, my lady?" the guard asks.

I nod, because it's a natural response for me to be compliant, to follow orders. What I really want to do is stay by this fire, to give Lu a hug and tell her that I'll miss her if I don't see her again. To thank her and the other Wraths for helping me.

Maybe Lu sees the struggle in my face, because she

steps forward and says, "Remember what I said, Gildy. Don't lie down for the thumbs, okay?"

I can't reply, because I think I might cry, and Lu doesn't seem like the kind of person who wants you to sob all over her. I nod instead.

I'm silent as I lead the guards to the tent, my mood brooding. When I slip inside, the two soldiers stay outside to keep watch, their shadows outlined through the sunlit leather.

I can't just do nothing in my tent though, because I'll go crazy. So instead, I make myself busy.

I wash, I plait my hair, I clean out the ash and replace the basin with new coals, even though I'm not sure Rip will even be back to use it. I roll up the furs on my side of the tent. Unroll them. Roll them again. Decide maybe I should try to take a nap, so I unroll them once more. Lie down. Can't sleep.

I find the trio of peonies Hojat gave me, effectively smashed and nearly disintegrated, but I take the one that's held up the best and snap off the flattened head of the blossom before slipping it into my pocket.

Looking around the tent, I realize that the small space somehow became a comfort to me, and I won't be back after today. This is it.

There's a choking feeling that settles in my throat, and I lift a gloved hand to it, as if that will ease it.

But instead, I feel the scar from when King Fulke held a blade there. With simmering fear rising in my gut, I remember that the last time I was caught between two kings, I nearly had my throat slit.

So what's going to happen to me this time?

I don't know how the hell I manage to fall asleep, but I do.

Something wakes me though, like a shift in the air. I sit up on my pallet and wipe the weariness from my eyes. Stretching, I straighten my dress as I stand and then go to the front of the tent and peek through the open strip.

My watch dogs are still sitting outside, talking quietly, voices muffled. I pull my coat on, careful to draw my hood overhead even though it's not snowing, and then check my gloves, sleeves, and collar. When all is secure, I duck outside.

Both guards immediately jump to their feet. "My lady, you aren't supposed to leave the tent."

"I have to use the latrine."

They share a look with each other, like they're about to forbid it. Irritation swarms inside me that shows in the tightening of my mouth. "Did your king say I wasn't allowed to go pee? Because things could get messy *very* quickly," I deadpan.

The guard on the left goes pink in the face, as if talking about pee embarrasses him.

"Pardon, my lady. Of course you may go. We'll escort you," the other man says.

With a nod, I let them lead me away from the camp

and behind an embankment, then into an outcropping of bare-branched trees.

Much to my embarrassment, the guards stay only a few paces away while I do my business. Bright side? Soon, I won't have to go in the snow anymore.

When I'm finished, I peer around the tree, glimpsing the backs of the guards where they're standing. They took a few more steps so that they're on top of the gentle slope instead of behind it. At first, I think they did it to give me a little more privacy, but when one of them points, I realize it's because they're looking at something.

Unease creeps up my spine as I walk forward to join them, snow coming up around my ankles with every step I take. When I reach the top beside them, a gasp comes from my parted lips.

The city is surrounded.

Perfect formations of Fourth's army are placed in the frozen valley around the entirety of Ranhold, like a dark horseshoe tossed down, ready to strike the stake of the castle.

From up here, the semi-circle of black-clad soldiers looks like a curled hand, ready to squeeze, to strangle the city. I feel that hand like it's on my stomach, holding me in a painful grasp.

Seeing the army like this...it's so different from the way I've come to know them—gathering around fires, evenings filled with camaraderie. But I saw a glimpse of the battle-ready men when I saw them in the fight circle. I knew what was coming, so it shouldn't surprise me.

"Fourth is attacking?" I breathe.

"Not yet," the guard to my left answers.

My eyes dart from left to right as I try to pick out familiar soldiers in the lineup. But from this far away, they're not much more than black ants ready to swarm, though it still doesn't stop my eyes from skimming.

I'm looking for a spot of mustard hair, a behemoth male, a quick-footed female.

Spikes on a spine.

But I can't pick anything out, not from this distance.

I don't know what I thought would happen when we arrived. The idea of battle was there, but it didn't feel real.

This...this feels real.

"Your army is going to decimate them."

The guards don't disagree with me, and my stomach hurts with misery for the innocent people of Ranhold.

"Serves them right," the other guard tells me without sympathy. "They did this. Fifth Kingdom attacked our borders. Killed some of our men."

I turn to look at him. "What's your name?"

"Pierce, my lady."

"Well, Pierce, I heard that your soldiers slaughtered Fifth's army pretty effectively at that battle," I tell him. "Isn't that enough?"

He shrugs. "Not to our king."

My fingers curl into my skirts, gripping them tight.

I know Midas tricked King Fulke into attacking

Fourth's borders. I know that this is essentially Midas's fault. But to wage war, to be ready to decimate a kingdom...it's like a lead weight in my chest that drags me down.

I hate the power plays of kings.

Ranhold Castle flies purple flags at half mast, a symbol of their dead king. The walls of the fortress glitter gray and white like marbled stone, proud spires pointing up to the Divines.

It would be pretty, if it weren't for Fourth looming around them.

"Come, my lady," Pierce tells me. "Time to get you safely in your tent."

"I don't want to go back to my tent," I reply.

The thought of being cooped up where I can't see, can't know what's going on, it makes me anxious.

Pierce gives me a sympathetic look. "Apologies. It's orders."

I press my lips into a firm line as they turn and lead me back. They let me walk along the line of the embankment though, like they're trying to give me extra time to see.

It's a testament to just how big Fourth's army is that the camp isn't completely deserted. There are still some guarding the perimeter, some on horseback, others on foot.

But no one jokes or drinks or plays dice by the fire, no one smiles. The soldiers are in battle mode, faces formidable and bodies tense, none of them familiar to me.

Then, just as we're about to descend the slope, I feel it.

A pulse.

The single beat strums, rippling along the ground with a strange, errant swell. I stop in my tracks, every single hair on the back of my neck rising to attention in crippling awareness.

"What *is* that?" I whisper, palms gone clammy, fear racing in my heart.

The guards turn to look at me with confusion marring their faces. "What's what, my lady?" Pierce asks.

I follow my instinct to turn, to look, and that's when I see him.

A lone figure in all black, standing at the back of the army.

Even from this distance, even though I've never seen him before, I know who it is, because I can *feel* it. Because power pours from him, like a deluge of tainted water from the falls.

King Rot.

His menacing silhouette starts to move, striding forward, and I watch as the pure, glittering white plains beneath his feet begin to change.

Die.

My eyes widen as brown tendrils streak through the snow, forming from every footstep he takes. His power is reaching out, clawed fingers scratching the ground and leaving behind wounds to fester.

Veins appear in the snow like poisoned blood, the color of dead bark. Those lines stretch out, a frozen lake cracking, ready to crumble.

I can feel it every time he takes a step. Because that pulse of power comes again and again, delivered through the ground and traveling up my feet.

It makes bile rise in the back of my throat. The power feels wrong, ugly, like a sickness ready to spread.

The farther King Ravinger walks, the more land he ruins. The cracked veins infect the snow around it, destroying its crystalline purity. The frozen-flaked ground churns and collapses, turning a sickly yellow-brown shade.

Fear has an iron grip around me, but I can't look away, and I can't take a full breath. I don't know how his army doesn't run from it, run from *him*. I don't know how they stay in formation, because even at my distance, my every instinct is telling me to flee.

He continues to walk forward, straight up an empty path between the organized lines of his readied army. Not an inch of power crosses beneath the soldiers' feet. Not a single rotted line touches them. The control of that makes me shiver with intimidation.

This man doesn't have power. He *is* power.

King Ravinger's gait is steady but sure. He doesn't stop walking until he's standing directly at the front, with the might of his army at his back and his power around him like a halo of decay.

All the rumors about him are true.

No wonder a fae male like Rip follows him. This is might. This is true unfettered strength.

With this display, I have no doubt in my mind that he's something to fear. Because King Ravinger just proved that he can rot the world and collapse it beneath the arrogance of his feet.

The question is, who is he going to walk all over?

CHAPTER 34

AUREN

itting in the tent, I stare and stare.

There's a pendulum swinging in my mind, in my chest. Back and forth it goes, with every heartbeat, every thought.

Past and present. Right and wrong. Truths and lies. Knowing and not knowing. Doubts and trust.

It's a constant tick in an unending tempo.

I'm not sure how much time passes that I sit here without moving. I just know that I'm still staring, that pendulum still going to and fro, when I hear voices outside.

My tent flap is lifted, like the invitation of an open door. I take a deep breath as I stand, pulling my hood over my head once again, checking my coat and gloves.

When I walk outside, the skin of my face tingles all

over. I probably would've had to squint from the daylight if Osrik hadn't been looming over me.

He nods to my guard dogs, making Pierce and the other man depart, until it's just Osrik and me.

Just like the first night I met him, he's a mass of intimidation, but even more so in full armor. I don't envy the blacksmith that had to fit him for a chest plate.

Today, his usually unkempt shoulder-length brown hair is pulled back and tied at the nape of his neck. His beard though, that's as wild as ever.

He looks down at me, a sword at either hip and a helmet under his arm. He's wearing his signature scowl, and his brown eyes are hard. He's the epitome of a Fourth army soldier, right down to the wood piercing in his lip and the gnarled branched hilts of his blades.

"What happened?" I ask, though I can barely talk with my heart in my throat. My ears strain to listen, but I hear no sounds of battle. Everything is still quiet. "Is it going to be war?"

"Don't know yet," he says. "King Ravinger requested a face-to-face meet. Midas sent an envoy."

My heart leaps. "So a negotiation, then? They might not fight?" Hope clings to my limbs like it wants to make sure it doesn't get dragged away.

"Possibly. But Midas made a request too."

I pause. "What request?"

"An offering to be made by us in *good faith*." He spits the term, like he doesn't think it's in good faith at all. "The bastard should be giving *us* something. We're the ones with the upper hand."

I already know what the request is.

"Midas wants me."

Osrik nods. "He does. The envoy had a very specific message from Midas. He told us, and I quote: 'Bring me my gold-touched favored, and I shall let your King Rot have an audience with me.'" Osrik's face twists in displeasure. "What a slimy, arrogant prick," he says.

I'm not surprised by Midas's message, just like I'm not surprised by Osrik's disdain.

"And your king actually agreed? He's handing me over, just like that?"

"Yep. Just like that."

Now that *does* surprise me, but I can't even try to guess the way King Ravinger thinks or what he may be planning, though it makes me feel uneasy. It can't be this simple, can it?

I let out a slow breath. "Well, it's a good sign, right? That the kings are willing to negotiate terms? Anything is worth it to stop a war from breaking out."

Osrik sighs at me, like I've just disappointed him. "I'll never get how you fucking stand it."

It. Midas. Being kept like a pet.

"I know," I reply, and I also know that my voice sounds numb, because that numbness surrounds me.

Osrik grunts. "Ready?"

Yes. No.

The pendulum swings.

He leads me away from the tent and the camp, his stride so long that I have to take two steps for every one of his. We go up to the same embankment I stood on earlier, where five horses wait at the top of the slope, three with soldiers on them, two without.

"Can you ride?" Osrik asks.

I tug my gloves up, heart pounding, palms going slick. "Yes, I can ride."

"Take the dappled one," he says, and I smile at the black horse, admiring the sprinkle of gray spots on her chest. My mare is much shorter than Osrik's horse. Honestly, I wouldn't even be able to get up in the saddle of his stallion without a stepping stool.

Stopping in front of her, I give the mare a stroke before leaning down to make sure my leggings are tucked into my socks. "Need a leg up?" Osrik offers.

I shake my head. "No, thanks."

He gives a terse nod and then seats himself on his horse, waiting for me to do the same. I carefully step into the stirrup and hoist my leg over, checking my skirts once I'm settled in the seat.

Maybe Osrik can tell how nervous I am by the look on my face or the way I grip the reins, but he brings his horse right next to mine. He gives me a hard look while the other Fourth soldiers position their horses to flare behind us.

"Well, you were right. You never did betray your

golden king. That takes guts," Osrik says, surprising me.

I wring the leather straps in my hands. "It's not like you guys were torturing me," I say with a small laugh. "As far as prisoners go, I think I might've been the best-treated one in all of Orea."

He snorts. "Probably. Except I did give a good threat at the beginning. What was it I told you?"

I wrinkle my nose in thought. "I think you said if I talked bad about King Ravinger, you were going to whip me."

Osrik grins. "That was it," he says, proud of himself. "Did it work? Were you properly threatened?"

"Are you kidding? I almost peed myself. You're a scary guy."

A bark of laughter erupts from his mouth. He doesn't look so scary when he does that. I don't know what happened to make him not loathe me anymore, but I'm grateful. We've come a long way from his whip threat and calling me Midas's symbol.

I tilt my head in curiosity. "Does it still piss you off to look at me?" I ask, remembering his previous words.

The amusement washes off his face, and Osrik studies me for a moment with a slight tilt of his head, gruff face solemn. "Yeah," he finally replies. "But for a different reason now."

He doesn't elaborate, and I don't ask him to. I'm not even really sure why I asked him that question anyway. It doesn't matter now. I won't see him again after this. Even if we do end up at war, I'll be on the other side.

That thought makes my stomach hurt. It's hard enough being loyal to one side, but what happens when you have loyalty to both? I don't want anyone to die. Not Fifth's men, not Midas's, and not Fourth's army either.

"Time to go."

Nodding, Osrik clicks his tongue, leading his black stallion down the slope. My horse follows, while the three guards keep space behind me, protecting the rear.

When we reach the flat snow plains and start making our way across, I notice that Osrik keeps us well away from the rotted path that the king cut into the land earlier. Even so, my eyes can't seem to stop drifting to it, to follow the lines of deterioration, to take in the sickly, jaundiced snow.

I don't know where the king is now, but I'm glad he's not around, because I don't think I could bear to be near that man's sickening power ever again.

Once was enough.

As we get closer, I notice that the army is still in formation, though no longer at attention. They're waiting now, waiting to see how kings will decide their fate.

When we ride through a line between the soldiers, I can feel the weight of hundreds of eyes watching me as we pass. We're a silent procession, me readying to be handed off as an offering between monarchs.

The gold-touched saddle returning to her king.

Despite the fact that I can sense them watching me, I

don't feel the weight of hate or enmity anymore. I wonder what Orea would think if people knew the truth about Fourth's army. If they knew that they weren't monsters, not bloodthirsty villains set on killing.

Formidable? Definitely. Deadly? Without a doubt.

But they were honorable. Not once did I fear for my life, not once was I abused or used. Instead, I was treated with respect, and I suspect there's one person in particular to thank for that.

An army is only as good as its commanding officer.

As if my thoughts conjured him, a spiked form on the back of a black stallion breaks away from a line of soldiers and heads toward us. My ribbons coil around my waist, breath hitching at the sight of him.

Right now, Rip looks every bit the imposing commander of Fourth's army. In full armor, missing only his helmet, he's a reckoning come to demand retribution. He wears a fierce expression bracketed with the brooding line of his spiked brows and the sharp angles of his jaw.

His black hair is swept back as his horse rides toward us, the pale skin of his face more prominent from the scruff of his jaw and the black of his eyes. With spikes glinting on his back, jutting from perfectly melded armor, he's making it clear that the sword at his hip isn't the real weapon. He is.

My horse slows to a stop as Rip approaches. He nods at Osrik in greeting before stopping his horse beside mine, instantly dwarfing me on my mare. His energy is tense, like the snapping teeth of a beast, aggravated and sharp, wanting to maim.

Beside him, my nerves flip and flounder, a fish tossed on the shore. He doesn't speak to me, offers no greeting. He simply dismisses the three guards behind us and then starts to lead Osrik and I toward Ranhold— toward a royal envoy flying a golden flag with Highbell's emblem proudly displayed on it.

With Osrik on my left and Rip on my right, I get herded toward the line of men I don't know, not a single familiar face in sight.

"What about the other saddles? The guards?" I ask.

"Their release is part of the negotiation. They'll be escorted to Ranhold tonight," Osrik answers.

I peer over at Rip, but his gaze is straight ahead, expression stone-faced. I see the muscle at his jaw tighten, like he's clenching his teeth.

There's definitely no pendulum swinging inside of *him*. He's not wavering, not contemplative. He's just pissed.

I know that it's directed at me. Even after I sent the messenger hawk, his anger wasn't like this. I don't think he'll ever forgive me for choosing Midas, even though I warned him time and time again that I would.

Osrik must feel the animosity too, because he keeps glancing over, as if he expects Rip to snap.

A sadness settles over me, like the soft silt of sand. It covers my skin, so many tiny particles that I know will continue to cling to me for a long time.

I hate how we're leaving things. Even though it's

only been a short time since I've been with him, and even though I was technically his prisoner, I never once felt that desolate, empty discontent here that I felt back in Highbell. I wish I could tell him that.

But Midas... They don't get it. I can't stay. Midas won't let me go, not ever.

I don't care how fierce Rip is, or how powerful King Rot is. Midas will stop at *nothing* to get me back, and I can't let anyone try to step between that. It wouldn't be fair—not to Rip, not to Midas.

I couldn't do that to Midas, either. He and I are connected. Not just through gold, but through time. Through love. I can't abandon that, can't abandon *him*. Not after everything we've been through together.

I open my mouth to try and explain, to try and say something, *anything*, to make Rip hate me less, but then we're suddenly there, stopping in front of the envoy, and I've lost my chance.

My ticking pendulum ran out of time.

"Your king's gold-touched saddle, as requested," Rip says, his voice hard as steel, his expression even harder.

The men in the envoy approach on their shaggy white horses, and I have to try not to frown at their golden armor. I never realized before just how garish it looks.

I once thought of it as elegant, but next to Osrik and Rip, it just seems silly. Unlike Fourth's, whose armor bears the marks of battle, their gold gleams without a single imperfection, like it's all just for show.

"Lady Auren." A man with white-blond hair jumps down from his horse and steps forward, the rest of the envoy stopping in a line behind him. "We are here to deliver you to King Midas." He looks up at me expectantly, though not daring to come any closer.

"Aren't you going to help her down?" Rip asks, and the tone of his voice could only be explained as a growl. It makes the man's face go pale, the others shifting on their feet.

The golden soldier clears his throat. "No one is allowed to touch the king's favored."

Rip's head turns slowly toward me. I can feel the judgment in it, and my cheeks burn beneath the cover of my hood. I don't have it in me to look at him.

"Of course. How could I forget the rules of your golden king?" Rip replies with open disparagement.

Feeling increasingly uncomfortable, I remove my right foot from the stirrup, preparing to jump off my horse. But just as I swing my leg over, Rip is there, hands gripping my waist.

A surprised gasp slips through my lips, and my gaze snaps to his face. He's so stern, so intense. His black eyes carry a thousand words, but without any light for me to read them.

There's a sound of hissed shock that comes from Midas's soldiers, but I don't look away. I'm too busy letting my eyes run over Rip's face, like I'm trying to memorize him.

"Commander, I must insist that you don't touch King Midas's favored."

"I must insist that you shut the fuck up," Osrik drawls.

Rip doesn't look away from me, doesn't pay them any attention at all. He simply lifts me off the horse as if I weigh nothing and helps me down.

Awareness surges through my body with every dragged inch as he slowly lowers me to the ground in front of him. My heart is pounding so hard that I know he can hear it. I can feel the firmness of his grasp and the heat of his palms. Even through the layers of his gloves and my clothes, it makes me warm all over.

But when he brings me down far enough that our faces only have an inch of separation, I lean away from him on instinct.

The instant I do that, Rip's expression snaps.

Face hard again, the intensity in his eyes goes shuttered. A shadow falls over his features like a fast approaching dusk, darkening the scales of his cheeks until he regards me with nothing more than cold apathy.

The second my feet hit the ground, he releases his hold on me like I've burned him. All the warmth I'd felt from his touch is gone, leaving me bereft. He turns without a word, already walking away, while guilt freezes in my gut.

I watch him go, one foot poised to walk after him, the other foot firmly on the ground. My mouth is dry, but my eyes are wet. I want to say everything, yet I say nothing.

And so, the pendulum swings again, ticking with my choices. Somehow, it sounds like the hooves of Rip's horse as he rides away from me.

CHAPTER 35

QUEEN MALINA

I've never liked taking the ride down the mountain.

It's winding and steep, dangerous even on clear days, the road always icy and littered with slick divots and rock. But when there's a winter storm—and there usually is—the road becomes even more treacherous.

I keep the curtain drawn tightly closed against the window, my teeth clenching every time the carriage jolts.

I suppose I'm lucky that it's only slightly windy and snowy right now. I refuse to return to the castle tonight if there's a storm, so all I can do is hope that the weather holds.

Jeo reaches forward, squeezing my thigh. "It's alright, my queen. Nearly there."

I give a terse nod, saying nothing, a hand pressed to my miserable stomach.

"Why take this trip into the city when you're so frightened of the carriage ride?" Jeo asks.

My eyes slice over to him where he sits beside me. "I'm not frightened. The *route* is frightening," I argue sharply. "There's a difference."

Jeo flashes a stunning smile. "Of course."

I narrow my gaze on him, unamused, but he just smiles wider. He's as relaxed as can be in my golden carriage, legs spread out as much as the space allows, head resting against the wall, a quiet whistle on his lips.

The fact that he's so unworried, worries me.

It seems like a weakness, if I'm honest. The intelligent are always considering the what-ifs, the could-happens. Our minds a constant spin of possibilities and outcomes.

If you don't worry, you're either a fool or you've *been* fooled.

I watch him from my peripheral. At least he's a pretty fool who knows how to use his cock.

Letting out a breath, I reach up and smooth back his blood-red hair. "I need to make an appearance. Under the right patronage, peasants can be a powerful group to utilize. I intend to use them to my advantage. There's dissent among the impoverished, and I want to ensure that dissent is pointed at Tyndall, not me."

Jeo winces a bit. "Word of advice? Perhaps don't call them peasants. Or talk about using them."

I wave him off, my fingers gripping the edge of the velvet seat when we hit another bump.

Jeo pinches the corner of the gold curtain at the window on his side and peers out. "We've made it all the way down," he tells me reassuringly. "We'll be on the bridge soon."

I'm finally able to sit back in my seat and let out a tight breath. Shoving my curtain aside, I watch as we roll along the ground, blessedly off the narrow road of the mountain.

Soon, the carriage wheels are clacking over cobblestones, the sound of a bustling Highbell making its way to my ears. When I normally visit the city, I only go to the affluent part to dine or to shop.

Today, I'll be going right into the middle of its haggard heart.

My guards ride in formation around us, horse hooves clopping. When the carriage stops and my footman opens the door to let me out, I already have the queenly mask covering my expression, posture perfect, my white gown pristine.

As I step into the market square, my opal crown diffracts the brittle daylight, the bottom of my dress sweeping the snow-littered ground, polishing it clear.

The guards have blocked off a part of the square, a long table set up ahead of time. A crowd has gathered already, since news seems to travel faster than royal carriages.

Behind the curious spectators, the square teems with vendors, shoppers, and beggars. In the distance, the

Pitching Pines loom over the city, the enormous trees casting shadows across the city's roofs.

As I walk forward, the crowd's surprised murmurs begin to ripple out at my presence. All three of my advisors—Wilcox, Barthal, and Uwen—are here already, waiting for me by the table. They're wearing matching white overcoats to set them apart as mine—not Midas's—just as my guards also wear new steel armor.

No gold anywhere. Exactly as I want it.

For the next hour, I sit at the middle of the long table, Jeo and my advisors on either side of me, as we pass out coin, food, bolts of fabric, even small handmade dolls to give to the peasant children.

One by one, I win their favor.

They call me their cold queen. They curtsy and cry and thank me. Chapped faces, work-worn backs, tattered clothing, heads covered with sprinkling snow, faces strained with the weight of their poverty. They may not look like much, but these are the ones Tyndall ignored—they're the ones who hate him most.

So I intend to stir that hate, to let it simmer, to make it into something I can use. All while I separate myself—make them love me with equal ferocity that they loathe him.

The crowd doubles, triples, quadruples as word spreads that I'm giving away gifts, and my guards work hard to keep everyone in line.

Soon, we're nearly out of things to give out, and I'm

relieved, because I don't want to sit here for much longer getting snowed on. Despite my furs, I'm cold, and want to be back in my castle next to a roaring fire before nightfall.

Another woman is led up, and I wear a serene smile on my face. She's huddled in a coat with patches at its elbows, and I'm not sure she's got anything to wear underneath. Her eyes are gaunt, her teeth rotted, and she has a babe on her hip and another one clinging to her leg.

I can't help the twinge of jealousy that surges through me at the sight. I should have born a strong son. A dutiful daughter. My castle should be full of my heirs, but instead, it's an empty gold tomb.

The woman approaches with jerky, stumbled movements, and I can tell that the guards picked her out of the crowd simply because she looks so bedraggled.

"Come forward," I call.

As she walks up, her eyes skitter over the table laden with diminishing piles of gifts.

"Coin and fabric for the woman, toys for her babes," I say, my voice clear enough to carry.

My advisors grab her offerings and pass them off to a guard, who approaches her with the pile. She looks at the armful, to the guard, and back to me, but she doesn't take them.

I tilt my head. Perhaps she's daft.

"Your queen has bestowed great gifts on you, miss," Barthal says, his dark brows drawing together in impatience. "Thank Her Majesty and take her offerings."

A slow-simmered flame seems to catch in her gaze as she looks back at me. "What does this do?" she demands, voice hoarse.

My white brows draw together. "Pardon me?"

The babe on her hip fusses, rooting around at her shoulder, its gummy mouth sucking a wet spot on her dirty coat.

"All of this," she says as she gestures to the table. "What does this *do*?"

"It's my gift to the people. To help ease any suffering," I answer.

The woman laughs. An ugly, crass sound, as if she spends her days steeped in smoke, or maybe the cold has frozen the chords of her voice.

"You think giving away a few coins and dolls is goin' to ease us? Our great Colier Queen blessin' us with a single coin. How *grand*. Must be such a sacrifice, when you're up there livin' in your gold palace."

"Shut your mouth, woman," the guard snaps, taking a threatening step forward.

I hold up a hand to stop him. My eyes dart around at the crowd, finding people watching her with interest, some of them nodding their heads.

I grind my teeth in frustration.

This isn't how it's supposed to go. I want them kneeling gratefully at my feet. The plan was for the people to see that I'm the one taking care of them, while Midas continues to ignore them.

This stupid woman is ruining everything.

"Where you been, year after year, while the shanties get ignored?" she asks.

I need to take back control of this situation, need to turn it back in my favor. "King Midas ignored you, but I—"

"You ignored us too," she says, making my advisors gasp that she dared to cut me off. The crowd seems to take a step forward, the energy in the air spiking with something ugly.

"While you're warm in your palace, do you know how we live? How we die from cold and hunger?" she demands. "No, you're just a snow bitch pretendin' to care. I don't want your flashy tricks. We want *real* help!" she cries.

She ends her rant by spitting on the ground, and even though it doesn't land anywhere near me, I feel as if she spat in my face.

My guards surround her in an instant and begin dragging her away, but she just gets louder, more belligerent, her children adding to her shouts with their own wails and screeches.

"Don't touch me!" she hollers before she turns her vehemence to the crowd. "Don't take the bribes of the Cold Queen so she can feel better when she sleeps in her gilded bed!"

Whatever else she says is drowned out by the crowd as she's yanked from the square.

Beneath the table, my fingers have curled into fists. I slice my gaze over to my advisors, feeling my anger simmer. "Bring the next person forward. I want to get this over with," I order.

Wilcox shoots me a look of concern, though I'm not sure if it's for me or the shifting crowd. Some of them are laughing and cursing at the woman as she's dragged away, but most are watching, thinking about what she said, flinging dubious expressions at me like spoiled fruit.

They're considering whose side to be on.

"Next!" a guard barks.

But no one steps forward.

The gatherers have gone guarded, angry. Watching me not with reverence or awe, but with hostility. Not one of the threadbare people comes up to take my offerings.

My mouth tightens.

"Time to leave, Your Majesty," Uwen murmurs beside me.

"I refuse to let this mob dictate what I do," I snap.

Jeo comes around to whisper in my ear. "Look at them, my queen. You've lost the crowd. They're looking at you like they want to rip you to shreds. We need to go."

My eyes dart around, and I realize the truth of his statement when I see the people moving in closer, ignoring the guards' shouts to back away. The energy has changed in the blink of an eye, as if they were just waiting for a reason. The air is brewing with threat, dirty hands fisting, cold cracked lips pulling into sneers.

"Fine," I bite out, conceding to retreat, though it irks me.

Foolish, ungrateful lot. How dare they snub their true queen!

I rise from my chair, refusing to look flustered. With Jeo at my side, I start to walk back to the carriage, but as soon as I do, the crowd begins to shout, heckle, hiss. As if my retreat broke the tentative speculation.

Eight guards surround Jeo and me as we walk to the carriage, and my saddle grips my arm, urging me to walk faster. My heartbeat races when people begin to hurl things at my guards, my own gifts being thrown back at us, items clanging against my soldiers' new armor.

My men close in while Jeo flings his arm protectively over my head, making sure that nothing hits me. I duck down, steps quick as we rush forward inside our wall of steel and strength. Soon, we're ushered inside the carriage, and the driver lurches forward the moment the door is shut.

The shouting is louder now, a dull roar emitted from hundreds of malcontent mouths. I flinch when things are thrown at the carriage, something hitting and nearly breaking the window.

Jeo is wound tight, his movements jerky as he yanks the curtains closed while he still holds an arm over me.

I shove him away, vexation filling me, anger piercing through like splintered ice at how quickly the tables turned.

"Are you okay?" he asks.

I cut him a look. "Of course not! All my efforts were just wasted," I hiss out of the corner of my mouth. "I spent the last hour handing all of that out, and now, these ungrateful rats think that they can rebel against *me*?"

My mind spins with what to do as the carriage rolls on, putting more and more distance between the angry mob and me.

I wanted open dissent against *him*. Not me.

I played my hand wrong, and that incenses me more than anything.

My father used to say that people are just an unlit wick ready to catch. I was supposed to get them to hold a candle *for* me, not burn me instead.

"What a bloody mess," I seethe to myself. "I want that woman punished."

Jeo says nothing, which is probably best for him, because my temper is an arctic bitterness ready to bite.

The carriage takes a sharp turn, making me nearly fling against the wall, and then it jolts to an abrupt halt.

Jeo frowns and looks out the window. "Seems we took a side street to get away from the crowd. There's some kind of cart in the way."

"I've had enough of this," I snap before I shove open the door.

"My queen!" Jeo calls, but I step out and slam the door in his face. I'm finished with this day. I want to get back into my castle and regain control.

Stalking forward, my guards jump from their horses to follow me, but I wave them off. "My queen," one of them says, rushing forward. "We're taking care of it. You can go back inside where it's warm."

I ignore him, getting to the front, ready to lay into whoever dares to block a royal carriage.

In front of me is a weathered cart hitched to two horses, their brown coloring letting me know they're not from Highbell. My driver and two guards are arguing with a man, urging him to move aside so we can pass.

"What is the meaning of this?" I demand.

All four heads turn to look at me, but my gaze hooks onto the man standing in the center. He's not a Highbell peasant, I can see that immediately.

He wears finely tailored blue clothing, his shoulders are straight instead of hunched, and he dons a clean-shaved face. His blond hair is cut short against his scalp, and his eyebrows are a shade darker than the hair on his head. They arch up dramatically, giving him a look of intrigue.

He's handsome, but there's something more than just that, something that makes me want to keep looking at him. He's *magnetic*.

"My queen..." one of the guards says.

"Why are you blocking the road?" I say, my attention on the man.

As I stop in front of him, I notice that his eyes are a peculiar color. Not blue, but gray and almost...reflective.

387

"Queen Malina." He bows with practiced ease.

"What is your name?"

"Loth Pruinn, Your Majesty," he replies smoothly.

I rack my mind to connect his family name, but for the life of me, I can't. Strange, considering I know every nobleman in Highbell. "Sir Pruinn, you're in our way."

He smiles, a dazzling display to appease me. "Apologies, my queen. My wheel broke, and I was only mending it. I'm finished now, so I'll make quick work of getting out of your path."

"Good. See that you do."

I turn to go back to the carriage, but he says, "Might I offer you a token? To show my appreciation for your patience."

Facing him again, I hesitate for a moment, while the sky above us blows down soft flakes of snow.

"Please, Your Majesty," he says, placing a hand over his chest in supplication. "It would greatly honor me."

I nod, his respect somewhat calming my anger. "Very well."

The guards and my driver move away while Pruinn beams and walks to his cart. It's built like a covered box with a latch at the back. He opens it with a flick of a hook, lifting up the back wall and sliding it into a notch at the roof.

Inside, there are shelves that reach all the way to the front from bottom to top, the space cramped and loaded with too many items to count.

My eyes skim over the shelves. There seems to be a little bit of everything. Glass vials filled with exotic perfumes, baubles, shiny gems, books, spices, teacups, honeycombs, and candlesticks. It's all a mishmash of odds and ends, my eyes unable to take in every piece.

"You have quite the collection. Are you a traveling merchant, then?" It would explain why I don't recognize his name and why he looks and behaves the way he does.

"Something like that, Your Majesty," he replies with an ambiguous curve of his lips. "I collect rare and priceless items."

"Is that so?" I muse, picking up a silver hair brush and testing its weight and shine. Real. I can't help but be intrigued. "What is the rarest and most priceless thing you have then, Sir Pruinn?" I challenge.

His magnet-gray eyes latch onto mine. "That would be my power, Your Majesty."

My brows rise up in surprise. "You have magic?"

He nods. "I do."

For the second time today, jealousy wells up inside of me. If only I'd been born with magic, then I wouldn't be here now, struggling to take control of my own damn kingdom.

"What kind of magic?" I ask, eyeing him in a new light.

A wry grin pulls at his cheeks. He leans an inch closer, and that sense of being pulled toward him returns. "I can show someone how to gain their greatest desire."

All of my interest fizzles out, and I pull back with a disinterested sigh. "I don't take kindly to charlatans," I tell him, my tone cross.

He shakes his head adamantly. "No tricks, Your Majesty, I swear it."

I arch a condescending brow. "I'm sure," I say sardonically.

"Please, let me prove it to you," he says, probably because he knows I'm quite close to calling my guards over and having him arrested for being a swindler.

"And how will you do that, Sir Pruinn? Have me close my eyes while you read a crystal ball?"

"Not at all. I only need to hold your hand."

"You won't be touching the queen," one of my guards intervenes.

Sir Pruinn ignores him, his attention staying on me. "No tricks, Your Majesty." He holds out his hand palm-up.

I don't take it. "If you think I'm going to fall for silly palm reading, then you are a very poor charlatan, sir."

"Again, not a charlatan," he vows. "And I won't be reading your palm. Like I said, I'll only be holding it."

I'm impatient now, but I can't deny that I'm also quite curious. My guards are watching warily, hands on the hilts of their swords, but they know that ultimately, they have no say whether he touches me or not.

I study the man, trying to get a read on him. "Alright, Sir Pruinn. Prove it to me."

I place my hand in his, his palm surprisingly smooth

for a traveler who'd be catching his own food and fixing his own wagon. The guards move closer.

Sir Pruinn gently curls my fingers into a loose fist and wraps his hand over mine.

The moment he does, there's a sensation—a static that pops on the surface of my palm and the back of my hand, the energy jumping between us.

My gaze shoots up to his face, but his gray eyes are closed, arched brows tucked down in concentration.

"My queen..." my antsy guard says nervously.

"Quiet."

I stare down at my hand in awe, because I can *feel* it. I can feel the magic coursing over it, coming from his touch. It crinkles and snaps, little bursts of magical bubbles that nearly sting, but not quite.

Inside my fist, my palm begins to heat. I feel something form, small at first, and then it grows, until my fingers are unfurling to accommodate the size of the object that just appeared in my grasp out of nowhere.

I wear the wide, unblinking eyes of shock.

Amazement, surprise, doubt, excitement, confusion—all of these conflicting emotions fly through me in a swarm that wants to get out.

I look at the piece of rolled parchment now held in my grasp, my lips parted with a dazed gasp. It looks innocuous, harmless, but my heart is pounding in my chest.

Sir Pruinn's hand falls away, taking the magnetic crackle with it. "There you are, Your Majesty. Open it."

"I'll open it, my queen," my guard offers, tone thick with distrust.

But Pruinn shakes his head. "It has to be you, or it won't work, Your Majesty."

I hesitate for a moment longer, and then I slip my fingers beneath the edge and unroll the paper. It's not too large, maybe three hand spans, my mind spinning with spurred curiosity. "What is this?"

He peers down as I straighten it out, humming in interest. "It would appear that your greatest desire is somewhere quite literal. This is a map."

I take in the elaborate lines with a narrowed gaze. Normally, I'd toss the map back at him and question what sleight of hand he used to get it in my grasp. But the magic was real, and something about this paper *feels* like me, though I don't know how to explain it.

After I study it for a moment longer, I frown, my excitement abruptly dimming. "This map is wrong."

Orea ends at the edge of Sixth Kingdom, but this shows boundaries into Seventh. Wrong. All that's there is nothing. Nothing at all—not since the fae came and disintegrated it into the gray abyss.

My ridiculous spark of intrigue and excitement disintegrates right along with it. I should've known better than to believe this con artist. He nearly fooled me with his crepitate touch, but I'm clearly having an off day.

"Obviously, this isn't where I can find my greatest

desire," I say with bored irritation. "It's a misdrawn map you're trying to pass off as one-of-a-kind."

He should look frightened. At the very least, uneasy, since his magical trick failed. I could have him whipped on the street for being a fraud.

I let the paper roll up on its own, crushing it in my fist before I gaze up at Pruinn with a cool, unimpressed look and try to hand the map back to him. "Seventh Kingdom doesn't exist anymore—hasn't for hundreds of years."

Pruinn doesn't look worried or rattled. Instead, a slow, mischievous smile crosses his face, gray eyes glittering as he leans in conspiratorially and says something that sends static chills over my entire body.

"Are you sure about that, Your Majesty?"

CHAPTER 36

AUREN

*R*anhold Castle is cold.

That's the first thing I notice after I'm put into a covered carriage and brought around to the side of the castle through a small set of doors. Six guards escort me—Midas's favorite number.

The walls in this hallway look like ice, but it's a trick of the eye, a triumph in architecture. When I tap a gloved finger against it, I can see it's made of smooth stone bricks, yet covered with a layer of blue blown glass.

We edge around what looks to be the main entryway, where purple flags hang from the rafters, a crisscross of white wood that arches up against a window laid into a ceiling that's shaped like a ten-pointed star.

Aside from my guards, the space is empty, quiet, while my nerves are nearly rabid, nipping at my skin, breathing down my neck. I don't even know how I'm able to walk so calmly, to not break out into a run or stop dead in my tracks as I'm led into a narrow hall.

There's no doubt that the palace is beautiful. The elaborate glass moldings, the trimmed windows, the curved sconces. Every flair is a celebration of ice, every purple tapestry an homage to Ranhold's monarch.

But the further inside I go, the colder I become. Maybe it's all in my mind, maybe the glacial-looking walls are tricking me into thinking that it's colder than it really is. Either way, goose bumps have risen across my skin, and I find my ribbons wrapping around me just a little bit tighter.

I'm about to be reunited with Midas.

He's here somewhere, waiting for me, and my heart leaps at the thought. I haven't seen him in weeks, the longest I've ever been apart from him in over a decade.

I long for his familiarity. To be able to tell him about Sail, about Digby, and have him understand because he knew them too. My life changed drastically since I've been away, and I can't wait to tell him everything.

The guards lead me to yet another narrow passage-way, and still, no one greets us, no one is around. The whole floor is empty, and I frown in confusion as to why I'm not being led through the main parts of the castle. But then it dawns on me.

I'm a secret.

Until this second, I didn't even remember that when

he traveled here, Midas used a gold-painted saddle as a decoy. A move that was supposed to protect me—one that didn't work out so well.

The silence of the guards, the lack of a welcome, and the clandestine routes of emptied servant's passageways solidifies my guess. It's probably not public knowledge that I was captured, or that I've been traded now, not if Midas has kept up the façade.

I don't know how I feel about that.

I'm led up a bare stone stairway and then led down a path with slits of windows at the high ceiling carrying a smear of light that dusts the narrow hallway.

Then we seem to exit the servant's walkways, because I'm herded into a hallway that's much more decorated. A straight runner of plush purple extends the length of the floor from one end to the next, and gleaming silver sconces hang from the walls, unlit. The windows are tall and wide, curtains pulled back, letting in both the sunlight and a wintry draft.

Another set of stairs, then a second, and then we finally reach a wing of the castle that isn't empty.

I recognize Midas's king's guards immediately— six standing against either wall. They eye us, saying nothing.

I don't feel my chest rise or fall with breath when one of them raps a knuckle against a set of double doors. I don't feel my eyes blink when that door is opened. I definitely don't feel the weight of my steps as the guards move aside, and I walk through the doorway.

But when I enter that room, when I lay eyes on my golden king for the first time in two months, I do feel my heart leap.

The door closes behind me as I stop, and then it's just us. Just him and me.

He stands in the very middle of a large private study, the entire room bathed in deep purples and blues, all except for him. He practically shines with the golden threads of his clothes, the slightly tanned skin, his honey-blond hair. And those eyes, those warm hickory eyes—they glint most of all.

He releases a breath, one that's ragged, short. Like he'd been holding it in his chest ever since he knew I was captured, and he's only just now able to let it out.

"Precious."

The single word is nothing but a murmur slipping out of his mouth, but the agony of his pent-up worry blares through it, loud enough that it cracks his expression as if it were made of glass. His handsome face shows overwhelming relief that's so stark, so palpable, I can almost taste it.

At the sight of him looking at me like that, at hearing him speak, my own face crumples. In the next instant, I'm racing forward to close the distance between us, because I can't bear to not be in his arms for a second longer.

But right before I fling my arms around his neck, his hands come out to stop me, grasping my upper arms to hold me still. I notice he's wearing gloves too, though his are pristine, while mine are filthy and worn.

"Precious," he says again, but this time, I can hear the shade of reprimand tinging it.

I shake my head at myself as I wipe the tears from my eyes. "I'm sorry. I didn't think."

"Are you alright?" he asks softly.

It's like his simple question throws open the gate that I had shut on everything that happened. The fear and grief of those terrible moments come flooding out. Digby's and Sail's faces immediately flash through my head, making a golden tear drip down my cheek.

His eyes widen slightly. "What's wrong?" he demands, shaking me a little. "Did anyone touch you? Tell me every single name of who dared to lay a finger on you, and I'll burn them all to their bones and crush their ashes beneath my boots."

Startled at the vehemency of his words, I just stare open-mouthed at him for a moment.

"Who, Precious?" he asks, shaking me again.

I immediately think of Captain Fane, but I'm not ready for that discussion. Not ready to tell him what I did. I still don't even know what I'm going to do about Rissa.

"No, it's not that. It's my guards." I say with a shake of my head. "Digby and—" I sniffle, trying to shore myself up, trying to get the words out. "After the attack, what the pirates did to Sail...it was horrible. I can't stop replaying it in my head, of him being murdered right in front of me."

My heart feels like someone is squeezing it in a punishing fist, fingers digging in, making it hurt, making it bleed. "I didn't do anything to stop it. I just let him die there in the snow."

My guilt is a writhing, pitiful beast, dragging its claws beneath my skin and ripping me to shreds.

. "They dragged him onboard and they—" The vision of the pirates tying Sail up to that pole makes my throat close up. I'm crying so hard now that I'm not even sure he can understand what I'm saying.

"Shh," Midas croons, his hands running up and down my arms in comforting strokes. "It's alright. You don't have to think about any of that anymore. You're here now. No one will ever take you from me again."

I nod, trying to get a hold of myself, trying to stop the flood of golden tears pouring from my eyes. "I missed you."

He squeezes me slightly, warm eyes looking at me like I'm his greatest treasure. "You know I would stop at nothing to get you back."

A small smile tilts up my lips. "I know."

We simply watch each other for a moment, and I feel his presence tethering me to the comfort he represents. It's that old, familiar warmth, that sense of security. It makes the beast inside of me settle, her claws drawing back, maw closing.

All of the uncertainty and anxiousness that I've felt

all of these weeks, it all slowly retreats until I'm standing on familiar footing again. It's a relief that I no longer have to be so alert, to be so careful. A quiet sigh slips out of me, and my shoulders lower slightly, losing the months of tension I've been carrying.

Midas's brown eyes go soft, cushioning soil to pillow the vulnerable seed. "You're here with me," he murmurs. "Everything is okay now."

I desperately want to reach up and brush a hand against his chest, to feel the beat of his heart, but I manage to hold back.

After a moment, Midas's gaze takes on a more assessing edge, sweeping over me from head to toe. "You look a mess. Did they not even allow you a bath? A brush?"

I cringe, suddenly feeling self-conscious, embarrassed. Here he is, looking just as handsome as always, while I probably look like something not even the dogs would drag in.

I try to give him a smirk, but it feels forced, my cheeks trembling slightly. "It's not like there were many bathhouses in the Barrens," I joke lamely. Midas just frowns.

Pulling away, I look down at my wrinkled dress, hem stained and fabric loose. The top of my torn bodice is still gaping from where Captain Fane tore it, and my coat is ripped too. My boots are scuffed, my socks worn with holes, and I don't even want to think about the state of my body and hair.

"I know, I look awful." I pull at the end of my braid,

thankful that I kept my hood on. Weeks and weeks of rag baths have not done me any favors.

"We'll get you right as rain in no time, Precious," he says with a warm smile. "Now that you're back, we have so much to discuss. So much to do."

I'm content to simply hear him talk. I've missed the sound of his voice, missed the way he lights up when he has plans and dreams to share with me.

"I won't ever make the mistake of separating from you again," he vows solemnly. "I'll make it up to you. I swear it."

"You couldn't know this would happen."

"No, but I'll ensure it doesn't ever happen again."

With his fierce promise, he moves and goes around the desk where there are a pile of rolled up messages. I wander closer. "Did you get my hawk?" I ask.

"What hawk?"

I blink for a moment. "You...I sent you a letter. I found the army's messenger hawks and managed to sneak out a message to you. To warn you that Fourth's army was coming. You didn't get it?"

He shakes his head and grabs a golden-fur monarch robe from the back of the chair. Slipping it on, he then picks up his crown that I hadn't noticed was sitting on the desk.

"I received a message from King Ravinger himself. The bastard was gloating that he had you, that he *rescued* you from the Red Raids," Midas scoffs angrily. "As if you were in any better company with his soldiers."

"Actually, they treated me well. Much better than the pirates," I explain, and I can't suppress the shudder just thinking about them. I don't even feel a lick of remorse for killing a man. The world is better off without Captain Fane.

Midas places the crown on his head and shoots me a dark look. "I will deal with the Red Raids," he says, the promise darkening his eyes. "I'll skewer their wretched bodies on solid gold spikes, letting their screams echo from the ramparts. If they so much as touched a hair on your head, I'll peel the fingertips from their hands. I'll cut out their eyes for even daring to look at what's *mine*."

The threat brings a chill to my skin.

"There's so much I want to tell you," I say, hoping to redirect his thoughts.

I don't want our reunion to be tainted with his fury. I want to hold on for a little bit longer, to just bask in his nearness. I'm also desperate to talk to him. To really *talk*, the way we used to, when we wandered from Second Kingdom to Sixth, traveling by day and talking by night, wrapped in each other's arms beneath the stars.

"Soon," he promises. "For now, I have to meet with that bastard, King Ravinger. But I have a gift for you first."

"A gift?"

He tilts his head. "Come."

Intrigued, I follow him as he leads me through two rooms—a sitting room of some kind and then a bedroom. I look around, briefly noting the coat flung over a chair, the fireplace, the large bed. Both rooms are built with black iron and gray bricks, lush whites and purples to decorate every inch.

"It's so nice in here," I muse, looking around. I start walking toward the balcony so that I can check the view while he grabs a candlestick from his bedside table.

Before I can reach the doors, he lights the candle and gestures to me. "This way."

I give a longing look at the balcony before I turn around and trail after him into the next room. I come to a stop just inside the doorway, immediately understanding the need for the candle. There aren't any windows in here—it's nearly pitch black except for a lantern flickering at the back of the room, but it's obscured slightly by something.

Midas strides confidently forward while I hover at the door, trying to get my eyes to adjust. "What's this?"

He stops by a spot at the wall to the left and fiddles with something with his lit candle, and I realize he's lighting a wall sconce. A soft orangish glow flares to life.

"This is technically my dressing room, but I've made some adjustments."

A fingertip of unease prickles on the back of my neck as Midas goes to the opposite end of the dark room and lights another sconce.

As soon as he does, my blood runs cold.

Because there, built into the middle of the room, is a beautiful wrought iron cage.

CHAPTER 37

AUREN

I t's strange how your body reacts to certain things.
For me, when I see the cage, there's a roaring in my
ears. It howls, gusting over my skin and whipping
against my bones.

I wasn't expecting to come face-to-face with a new
cage so soon.

Midas turns to face me with a smile. "I had this made
for you," he says, motioning over to it with clear approval.
"I know it's small. This one is temporary for now, and not
gold yet, of course," he adds with a wink in my direction.

That roaring wind starts blowing hard enough to
batter my lungs, making it hard to breathe.

When I see something inside of the cage move, I
startle. "What—" My words cut off when a person rises
from the small bed. From the faint light, I see her—my

decoy.

She has bed-mussed hair and paint-smeared skin. A quick glance to the blankets shows stains from where it's rubbed off. Metallic gleam left behind on the sheets like the damning evidence of a secret lover.

The woman rises and looks between us. "My king?"

Her hair hangs around her shoulders, a little shorter than mine by a couple inches. She has round, light brown eyes, and a similar face shape to me. Her lips are plush, and her body is an hourglass wrapped up in a gold dress.

My gold dress.

And even though the paint covering her body and hair isn't my exact shade, and even though I can see it creasing around her eyes and wiped off her palms, the sight of her sets me on edge.

Midas strolls over and places the candle on a table just outside of the cage door.

"Good news for you, my favored has arrived," he tells the woman.

She smiles, creasing dimples into her cheeks. I can tell from the relief in her eyes that she can't wait to get out. I wonder if she feels like a wing-clipped bird. I wonder if she can't wait to wash the gold from her skin.

This was temporary for her, when it never is for me.

When she notices that I'm still staring at her, the smile on her face falters. I know it's not her fault that she's in there, that she's painted and dressed to look like me, but emotions roil through me as erratic as a cyclone.

I'm shocked, embarrassed, hurt.

To see that I can so easily be replicated, to see *me*, from the outside looking in...

Osrik was right—the woman I'm looking at right now? She's nothing but a symbol for Midas. Not a person, not someone in charge of her own life, but a living and breathing image to showcase the Golden King's might.

The sight of her makes me sick.

"I'm sure you're relieved to be back where it's safe," Midas tells me. "Where no one can get to you."

My eyes drag away from the cage and settle on his face. I grasp my skirts to stop my trembling hands.

"Ready?" he asks me.

Too fast, this is happening far too fast.

"Midas..." I choke out.

He crosses the room to come back to me, and takes my gloved hands into his. "I know I let you down, Auren. I promised to always keep you safe, and I failed you. But I won't fail you again," he promises, his expression focused with determined intent.

I swallow, trying to stop the whirling emotions so that I can be intelligible enough to talk. "That's one of the things I wanted to talk to you about. I'm not afraid anymore. Not like I was," I begin, swallowing past the acid that keeps climbing up my throat.

Midas frowns at me, and I fumble with what to say. This isn't how I envisioned our reunion. Not at all.

He was supposed to hold me and not want to let me

go. Our separation was meant to make him open to hearing me. I imagined being wrapped in his arms for hours while he listened to me talk.

Disappointment is a roughhewn boulder settling in my stomach. It rolls and scrapes, making me go raw with the realization that none of that is going to happen.

We're picking right up where we left off.

I thought because *I've* changed, that he would change too. What a silly, naive thought.

The road that we were on has forked, and I went on a different path. I need to explain things to him now, need him to catch up to me.

"There's so much that's happened, Midas," I tell him, trying to move that deadweight boulder, pushing it like I can push *him* to meet me on that forked road. "I know I need to prove it to you so that you believe me, but...I don't need the cage. Not anymore. *We* don't need it."

He stares at me for a beat, his blond brows pulled together. "What in the world are you talking about?"

"This," I say, my head cocked toward the cage, though my eyes can't bear to look at it, can't bear to meet the eye of the woman inside. "We don't need it."

The confused frown morphs into a scowl, and his tone grows incredulous. "Of course we need it. That fact should be *blatantly* clear after what you just endured."

"But that's what I'm trying to tell you. It's *because* of what I endured that we don't," I hastily explain, tugging my hands from his. "I spent all that time with the army, and everything was okay. I know how to handle myself now. I proved it to myself, and I know that once I tell you everything, I'll prove it to you too."

I relied on the cage for too long. And then I resented it—resented *him*, resented myself. I don't want to go back to that. I've outgrown it, and I'm finally strong enough to admit it to him.

Midas lets out a long-suffering sigh and rubs his blond eyebrows with his thumb and forefinger. From my peripheral, I can see my decoy watching us with rapt attention.

"Auren, I know you just experienced some terrible things, but for now, I need to go meet with King Ravinger. Afterward, once it's dark out, I'll bring you out for a bath and a meal, and we'll talk, alright?"

I shake my head, hands held up in front of me. "No, it's not alright. Just listen for a minute—"

He cuts me off. "I don't have time for this. Get into the cage."

He's doing what he usually does—talking over me, making me feel like I'm always wrong and he's always right. If I could just get him to listen, to really *hear me*, then he would understand.

He's under a lot of pressure right now with Fourth Kingdom breathing down his neck, and I don't want to add more stress to him. I know that, at the heart of it, he craves this control because he was worried about me, so I understand the root of his reactions. But...I need him to understand mine too.

For once, I need him to see my side.

I don't want to be cowed by him. I want to set a different tone now than the way things were before. I want to start off on the right foot and have a fresh beginning. Show him how things can be, that I'm ready for it. That I need it.

I take a calming breath. "It doesn't have to be this way anymore." My tone is gentle, as if it can draw out that softer side of him too.

Silence stretches between us, and it's filled with the reactions that play over his face, a song with the rhythm of his disapproval and disagreement. I don't want to hear it.

"We don't need it. Trust me. Things are different now. *I'm* different now," I say, pointing at my chest. "Things don't have to be the way they were in Highbell." I tilt my chin up. "And I don't want them to be."

He stands so still, and he's looking at me like he's never seen me before, and maybe I'm looking at him like that too.

Midas blinks at me for another moment before he runs a frustrated hand down his face. He starts pacing the small dressing room, shoes scuffing over the purple rug on the floor.

"I'm trying to be patient with you right now, considering what you've been through, but you're making this very difficult," he says before turning back to me.

"You've never behaved this way before."

I bristle from his chastisement, but he's right. I haven't, not with him.

Two months ago, I would've backed down immediately. I would've never pushed him in the first place. But I'm changed now, and the worries, the dangers—we can work through those together.

But the thought of being shoved back in a cage, especially one so small…

Osrik's words blare in my ears.

I'll never get how you fucking stand it.

Right now, in this moment, I realize.

I can't.

CHAPTER 38

AUREN

M y traitorous eyes flick over to the cage.

I take in its thick, menacing iron, its six curled pieces looped around the top to add decorative flair, before I look back at Midas.

"I know you're in a rush, and I don't want to make you late, so I'll stay in your rooms while you go to the meeting, and then we'll talk after."

He pins me with a fiery glare. "I don't know what the hell is going on with you, but you're not in charge, Auren. I'm your king, remember? You will do as I say."

My heart pounds with the command, and I know I've lost any hope of rekindling old Midas. King Midas is firmly in place.

He jabs a finger to point in the direction of the cage. "I'm not going anywhere until you're in that cage, safe and secure, where no one can get to you. Do you want to get taken again? Do you *want* to be vulnerable?"

"Of course not."

He's agitated, cheeks reddened, eyes lit with that temper I tried to subdue. I've failed miserably in keeping him calm and open to what I have to say.

"Did you betray me?" he asks suddenly.

His question makes me pause. "What?"

"You heard me," he says flatly. "Did. You. Betray. Me?" Every word is a sentence, each one bitten off.

My mouth drops open, mind whirling. "What... How could you—of course I didn't betray you!"

"Did you let any of those filthy pirates touch you? Did you let Fourth's army touch you?"

"Let?" My question stretches like a string ready to snap.

I know he can hear the hurt in my voice, because I hear it too. That hurt is stitched from my words to my face, woven through my features.

"Fine," Midas replies, but his voice is still hard, still cruel, the voice of a king who expects to be followed. "But if you didn't betray me, then prove it. Get into the cage."

I feel tears prick the backs of my eyes, and my shoulders stiffen. He's not going to listen. Even though I'm right here, standing in front of him, trying to tell him, he won't listen.

My chin drops to my chest, as if it feels the burden

of a forlorn weight pressing down. "Don't do this, Midas. Not now. Not after everything. *Please*."

His stony exterior isn't touched by my plea. "This is the way it has to be, and you know why. You agreed."

My eyes flick up. "I changed my mind."

Midas levels a flat look at me. "I didn't give you permission to change your mind."

I rear back like he's hit me. For the pain that's emanating through my body, he might as well have.

His mouth is tight, shoulders tense, crown still proudly sitting on his head. "Last chance," he tells me, a viciousness in his tone. "Get into the cage, or I'll put you in it."

It's like I've been pierced directly in the heart.

I haven't seen him for two months. I thought I was going to be killed multiple times. All I wanted was for him to tell me that he's proud of me, that he loves me.

I wanted him to hold me. To *really* hold me, head to chest, so I could hear his heart singing just for me again. But he didn't. He didn't hold me in his arms—*he held me at arm's length*.

"I'm trying to talk to you, Midas. *Really talk*," I say, voice bruised with the hurt he's pressed into my chest. "I always trust you. I always listen to you. Just this once, can't you listen to *me*?"

The look on his face is acidic enough that I'm surprised it doesn't burn straight through me. "Listen to *you*?" he spits. "Because you're *so* successful at living in the outside world, is that it?" he asks mockingly. "When I found you, everything was *okay*?"

My lips press into a thin line. "You know it wasn't."

"Exactly."

"But that was then," I argue. "I was just a girl, Midas. I've—"

"Proved it to yourself all of a sudden?" he says, cutting me off, throwing my previous words back in my face.

I cross my arms around me, eyes meeting his in defiance. "Yes."

He scoffs, a humorless laugh to shove against my confidence and try to topple it over like he's done so many times before. "What about Carnith Village?" he says, and the blood drains from my face. "You thought you were okay then too, didn't you, Auren? And look what happened."

The bruises in my heart seem to spread and discolor with mottled grief of blues and sickening greens. "That was an accident," I whisper, feeling my eyes well up, my vision blurring.

How could he bring that up? How could he say that to me, when he knows how badly it destroyed me?

He sneers. "Tell me, did you have any *accidents* while you were gone?"

"Stop it," I say, squeezing my eyes shut tight. I don't want to see him, don't want to hear him. "I've done everything you ever asked me to. I've been devoted to you for over ten years of my life, overlooked every flaw, shoved aside every hurt. I've done it all because I trusted you. Because I loved you."

I'm crying freely now, and the tears wound as they fall, as if they were plucked directly from the ache of my heart and sent to scratch down my walls.

He sighs, shaking his head as he looks at the floor for a moment. "Alright. You're tired and hysterical. You just need to go lie down. This isn't you, Auren."

"This *is* me!" I yell.

Midas is so shocked I dared to raise my voice against him that his eyes go wide.

"I am finally, after all this time, starting to be *me*," I cry, pressing a hand to my chest. "I'm finally starting to say what I think, and I'm not going to lie down again to make it easier for you to keep me beneath your thumb."

Midas may have put me on a pedestal, but I put him on one too. The height of those foundations made it impossible for us to look each other in the eye.

But we're looking now. *I'm* looking, not my romanticized fifteen-year-old self. I don't like what I see.

"I gave you everything, and yet you still want to take. You told me to lie, said it was the best way to keep me safe, but that wasn't really it, was it? You didn't do it for *me*. You did it for *you*." My words are an accusation spoken from the deepest parts of me—the ones I've long ignored. "I won't live like this anymore, Midas."

"You're *mine*," he roars, taking a threatening step

forward.

My eyes flash, but I don't flinch. "No, Midas. I belong to me."

He shakes his head, the glint of his crown catching like fire. "You gave yourself to me a long time ago, Precious. It's time to remember your place."

My place. The one in a cage. The one beneath his thumb.

I keep my expression unyielding. "No."

A sharp silence sticks between us, like a skewer ready to impale. And then in a blink, Midas moves so fast that I can't even gasp before he's on me.

He spins me around, gripping me around my middle, and I let out a surprised shout.

He wouldn't hold me for comfort, but he'll hold me for control.

My mind blares that realization in my head, and with it, everything, every single tattered pain, ignored doubt, shoved aside feeling, they all come barreling out.

I let him put me in a prison.

He rescued me when I was at my lowest, and because of that, I thought staying with him would keep me at my highest. But really, he's trapped me in place and forced me to accept it all.

He dragged me into a foreign, frozen kingdom.

He married a cold queen who hated me.

He fucked saddles in front of me.

He made me into a spectacle.

He kept me in that cage, day in and day out.

He used me.

There are so many things that he's told me to adjust to, to adapt to, because this is the way it has to be, the way it was expected to be.

I kept taking it and taking it, convincing myself that this was the way it needed to be. Lying to myself because I loved him, because he *manipulated* me.

I've been bending over backwards for so long that I forgot I even had a spine.

What a fool I've been. What a stupid, stupid fool. I learned not to trust people, but I thought I could trust *him*. I was wrong.

Fury and surprise send my legs kicking, fists hitting, but he doesn't drop me, doesn't let go.

"Auren, stop!" he barks in my ear.

"Let me go!"

Midas ignores me, ignores every hit I rain down as I try to break free. He slows my thrashing by squeezing me so hard that he cuts off my air. With jilted steps, he walks us backwards toward the cage, hand struggling to dig for the key in his pocket.

I tear at his arms, his face. His cheek presses hard into the back of my head, trying to stop me from whipping left and right, not letting my hood fall off.

"You—need—to—behave!" he grits out, a hiss against my ear.

But I don't. I don't, because I can't do this. I can't go

back in a cage. I can't, I can't, I—

I hear the key being tossed on the floor. "Unlock the door. Now!" he snaps at the woman. I'd forgotten about her until now.

"No!" The sound is choked off, but me begging doesn't stop her.

I hear her scramble to pick up the flung key, hear her fitting it in the lock, hear it turning. It turns inside of me too. Like the key is opening a door that I shut on every repressed emotion, every pent-up thought.

Midas pushes me.

One second, his arms are like steel bands around my waist, and the next, my body is crashing into the cold metal floor of the cage.

He did it. He actually tossed me in here without my consent. Without so much as a thought or care for what *I* want.

That's when I start to scream.

The scream goes on and on and on. It crawls up the walls, clings to my skin, digs into the canals of my ears to add to the drum, to feed the fire.

I'm completely rabid, frenzied, a sense of panic like never before.

"Out!" he barks at the woman.

I leap up faster than I knew I was capable of. Rushing forward, hands outstretched, I reach for the cage door.

The woman scrambles to get out first, but I know as soon as she does, Midas will slam the door shut on me.

I can't let that happen.

My ribbons unravel, like fury unfurling. Strips of angry satin strips poised at either side of my body, suspended in air.

In an instant, all of them shoot toward the door to keep it open, their long lengths wrapping around the bars in a vise grip.

But the woman is two steps in front of me, running fast, so I reach forward and shove her with a hand to her shoulder.

My palm burns.

Her body flies back, hitting the barred wall with a thud, but I concentrate on my ribbons as they push at the door, making my back strain.

Midas's mouth opens to shout something as he struggles against me, trying to slam the door shut, but my ribbons are stronger. The iron door makes a groan under the strength of them, and in the next second, my ribbons tear it clear off its hinges, snapping the iron like splinters. With a flick, they toss the useless door directly into Midas, hitting him in the chest and knocking him to the ground on his back.

My ribbons go limp, back screaming from the effort and strength that just took. My momentum nearly sends me careening forward, but I manage to lift a hand and catch myself on the bars of the cage before I fall flat on my face.

But that's when it sinks in.

The burn.

My head snaps up, gaze landing on the bar, on my hand that's grasping it. My *bare* hand.

Sometime during my struggle, my glove came off.

I quickly snatch my hand away and start to back away, but it's too late, of course.

Gold streamed from my palm the moment I touched it, like blood pouring from a wound. I was too frenzied to control it, too panicked to direct it.

The gold leaks down the bar and then puddles at my feet. It moves, spreading across the cage floor like it has a mind of its own, crawling up every bar, reaching toward the domed ceiling of the ironwork, coating every inch of the iron cage.

I whirl around with a warning poised on my tongue, but instead, it becomes a strangled cry.

No.

No, no, no.

Running forward, I trip over my ribbons as I go, but getting closer doesn't do anything to confirm what I already know. My palm burned when I shoved her, but I was too distracted to pay attention to it.

I stare in horror at the woman's solid gold body, her mouth still open in a soundless scream. Her body is at an odd angle, stuck in the same position from when I shoved her into the bars, her neck snapped forward with whiplash.

But her eyes—her eyes are squeezed shut, like she felt every agonizing inch as the gold consumed her.

"No..."

My legs give out, and I fall to my knees, a desperate sound bursting from my throat.

"Look what you did, Auren!"

I flinch at his angry accusation as I look behind me, finding Midas shoving off the heavy door from his chest and rolling up to his feet. He looks from me to the woman with a bitterly disappointed look on his face—one that's laced with condescension.

He shakes his head. "Do you see?" he demands, pointing at her. "Do you see why you need to stay in your cage?"

Sobs crush themselves in my chest, pummel up my throat, pinch at the back of my tongue.

I killed another innocent. This poor woman did *nothing* except be forced to act as my stand-in, and I murdered her.

Horrible guilt rings through my hollowed chest, rattles my entire body until I'm trembling with the resonance of agonized regret.

"I didn't mean to..." My pathetic response makes me hate myself even more.

Why did I push her aside? Why didn't I notice my glove had fallen off?

I hear the sound of Midas's shoes as he walks forward to stand over me, the lantern light causing a long shadow to cast from him.

He clicks his tongue in reprimand, shaking his head as his eyes skim over the woman's statue. "Do you see,

Auren? This is why you need the cage," he says again, his voice grating against my ears like metal against stone. "Not just to protect you, but to protect everyone *from* you."

My tears drip.

My spine aches.

I called Rip a monster, but really, I am.

As I continue to kneel there, staring at the woman's tortured face, Midas lifts my hood and places it back over my head and then lets out a long, heavy sigh. "It's alright, Precious," he tells me, tone softer. "I'll fix this. You don't need to worry about a thing."

He's being kind now, his voice no longer hard or accusatory as his hand comes down to pat me. His fingers graze adoringly over my head, a heeled pet to be stroked. And right then, I wonder how the hell I fooled myself into thinking this was love.

How did I look into his eyes every day and not see that when he looked back, he was devoted to the gleam of my skin rather than the love of my heart? How did I miss the blinding truth that's been there all along? How did I mistake an *owner* for a *lover*?

"You've probably exhausted your power with this little tantrum," he muses. "It's a shame, because I have a list of things I need you to make gold for me, but no matter. I can wait a bit, and in the meantime, you can regain your strength."

Midas talks and plans and goes along on his path,

while I lie battered and bloody on mine. Bile floods my mouth until I'm choking on the acidity of heartbreak.

"I'm sorry I lost my temper with you, but you see now why I'm right. Why this is so important," he tells me. "You'll get used to this again, Precious, and everything will be as it was. Don't worry, I'm not angry at you." Something feral in me wants to growl and bite off his petting hand. "Now, be a good girl and roll up your ribbons. Stay put while I go to my meeting. I'll have to get the cage door repaired tomorrow."

All I can hear past my thudding anger is the cracking glass as it shatters between us.

Midas starts to leave, stepping over the door as he goes, but I turn, my voice stopping him just before he gets to the doorway of the room. "If you walk out now, I'm done. I will never forgive you. For any of it." My voice is hard, enraged, pushed past the brink.

He hesitates a moment and then says, "I love you, but I don't need your forgiveness, Precious. I just need your power."

CHAPTER 39

KING MIDAS

I n the corridor, I straighten my robe. It's thick, but so is the draft in this ice castle. It doesn't matter that the weather isn't battered with blizzards here. The cold seeps inside in a different way.

I look back at the closed door once. The wood is thick, the walls thicker, so I can't hear if Auren is still shouting, but I sent an entire contingency in there to guard her.

My shoulders are tense, jaw sore from how hard I clenched my teeth. I do not enjoy handling her by force. Not at all.

She has always been compliant, trusting. It's one of the things I admired about her. That she had the capability of being soft and malleable, despite her circumstances.

Auren has never looked at me the way she looked at me just now, and I don't like it.

I shouldn't have lost my temper with her, but she caught me off guard. I expected to get her back broken and afraid, ready to crawl behind her bars where it's safe.

Instead, she's...changed.

But that's a worry for later. I'll fix things with her, resettle her. She just needs time. I failed her, and I need to prove to her that she's still safe with me. She'll be her old self again, and then we can get to work on this drab, icy castle.

Not a moment too soon either, because the nobles of Ranhold are becoming impatient.

I subdued them with the promises of gold, but promises are the debts of demands, and demands can quickly become the clamor of unmet discontent.

They want wealth lining their pockets and filling their coffers. I want to sit on the throne uncontested and merge the borders of Fifth and Sixth.

It's all within reach, and when she understands that, she'll come to heel. I'll be the ruler of not one kingdom, but two.

But first...

I start making my way down the corridor and across the castle to where I'll be meeting that bastard King Slade Ravinger.

I had the servants prepare the throne room rather than the meeting room or even the war chamber. A calculated move, of course. He'll be forced to speak with me while I sit on a seat of power.

I'm giving him a message. That I am not cowering from the shadow that his army has cast or trembling from this display of power. I rule here as acting monarch, and his intimidation tactics will not work on me.

After years of plotting, everything is falling into place.

But first, I have to purge the rot.

As I walk, guards follow behind me, a golden procession in a castle of glass and iron and stone. It will be so much better once it's gilded. It will take Auren weeks, if not months of constantly draining her power every day, but it will be worth it.

Gold is *always* worth it. No matter the cost.

I enter the throne room expecting for Ravinger and his men to be waiting for me. Instead, the only people inside are a mix of Fulke's guards and mine standing against the walls.

With a scowl, I make my way across the giant space.

Blue crystals from the chandeliers cast rivers of light along the floor where I walk. There are frosted windows along the back wall behind the throne. Probably a calculated consideration when it was built. A vision of light spilling in to shine on the Divine-blessed monarch. Or to force people to squint at the king's seated splendor.

Once across the room and up the white marbled dais, I turn and take a seat on the throne. Made of pewter and iron, there's an amethyst stone set into the center of it—only one, but I've already spoken to a blacksmith for him to add five more.

Six is the superior number out of all the kingdoms.

At the back of the room, my main advisor, Odo, comes bustling in. Several others follow, about half of them my own, the other half having served under Fulke.

A few of them are loyalists, so they haven't fully joined my cause yet. Especially since they have Fulke's son, Niven, to consider. They're priming the boy to take over when he comes of age.

Unfortunately for him, that's not going to happen. Taking over *or* coming of age. A mercy, really. I can already tell that the boy isn't cut out to rule.

While I sit on the throne, eyes straight ahead, I tap my finger against the pewter armrest six times. Then a break. Then six more taps.

With every minute that passes, my impatience turns to offense, and offense is my cornerstone for anger.

My advisors settle on the bench seats to the left, behind the banister built to separate nobles from commoners. Ravinger's people though, they'll be kept standing in the common galley.

Another calculated move.

Minutes go by. Then those minutes are doubled.

All the while, I wait, tapping. My irritation rises with the temperature of my temper.

My guards are too well-trained to shuffle on their

feet, but my advisors are growing impatient, muttering amongst each other, sniffling, coughing, moving in their seats. The noises make my teeth grind.

Still, I sit and wait, enough that the light reflected off the blue chandeliers has moved a few inches across the marble—a re-routed river flowing through the floor.

"Where is he?" I bite off, the words as hard and dry as jerky.

Odo jumps to his feet, scrolls and quills sticking from the wide pockets of his coat—for note-taking. If the bastard king ever shows up.

"I'll go inquire, my king."

"Hurry up."

He nods quickly, balding head rimmed with a halo of gray hair curling around like a topless hat. As Odo departs through the back door, my foot bounces, knee jumping.

He's playing mind games, of course. For every move I make, so will he. Still, I could be in my rooms right now, comforting Auren, helping her to settle.

My mind flashes to the flare in her golden eyes as she spewed anger at me like dragon's fire. Never. I've never seen her look like that.

I don't like that, either.

I'm not sure what happened to her out there, unprotected. But I *will* find out. I will get every possible detail from the guards, the saddles, everyone. And then I will extract vengeance.

I'll start with the Red Raids. They only had her for

hours, but I'll make them pay for each one, right down to the second.

King Ravinger, though. His army had her for days and days. No wonder she's so out of sorts.

My finger taps six times.

Good faith. He returned her back to me out of *good faith*. I didn't actually believe he would do it. It was a test. The result of which tells me the most important thing of all—he doesn't know what she is. What she can do.

Once I knew that, I was able to breathe for the first time in weeks.

So long as that secret is secure, the rest can be managed.

I feel my lips curl with a self-satisfied smirk. What a fool he is. He gave away the most valuable treasure in the entire realm, for *free*.

I'd laugh in his face if I could, just to rub it in.

But the secret is much more valuable than my ability to gloat. It's why I've learned to do so in private. Every time Auren turns something gold under my direction, I gloat. Every time someone else marvels at *my* power, or calls me the Golden King, I gloat.

I've fooled the entire world of Orea.

And now, I've claimed two kingdoms for my own. I just need to ensure that I keep them both, which is why this meeting is so important.

If the meeting ever actually happens. The tapping starts up again.

Six more minutes. I'll give the bastard six more

minutes, and then I'll go down there to his encampment and drag him out myself.

No one keeps me waiting.

My fingertip counts the seconds. One minute. Two. Three minutes. Four. Five. When I hit six, anger is thick in my chest, like viscous mucus I'm unable to clear.

I get to my feet, shoulders set with vexation, the corners of my eyes creasing with stress.

"I'll go after the bastard myself," I bark out.

Just as I'm about to take my first step, the door to the throne room is tossed open like a wayward wind tore through the wood as it slams against the wall.

Three sets of footsteps echo in—no, four. One of them has a tread too light to hear. All of them are in full black armor and helmets, but even without being able to see their faces, I can sense their arrogance.

The one who walks quietly is small, both in height and in stature. But the next one is massive, a brute no doubt chosen as guard for his size alone.

The third one on the end appears of average size, with the same black armor and leathers as the other two, same crude tree branch sword hilt.

The emblems of Fourth Kingdom are displayed on their chest plates—a bare, crooked tree with four craggy branches and its roots full of sharp thorns.

Yet my brows pull together as I watch the fourth member of the quad walk toward the dais. This one, I've heard of.

The commander of the army.

It seems the sharp points depicted on their armor's emblem have been brought to life in him, because black thorns jut from the armor along his arms and back like sinister barbs yanked from the soils of hell.

He's a walking message made by Ravinger himself, if some of the rumors are to be believed. The king corrupted his commander into something to be feared and reviled.

He is the vicious thorns that root the wicked tree.

The quad stops in front of the dais with identical postures. Feet spread, arms loose, helmets facing straight ahead. None of them say a single thing. So silent you could hear a pin drop.

Instead, I hear an easy, unrushed gait.

My eyes lift to the doorway just as King Ravinger himself walks inside. Despite myself, I find my body going rigid. He seems to step with the same rhythm as my tapping fingers.

Calm and collected, he comes forward as though *he* were the one to win this kingdom, rather than me.

My eyes track his every movement as I take in the infamous King Rot for the very first time.

No kingly robe for him—he wears the black and brown leathers of his army men, only missing the armor and helmet. But coming up from his neck and extending over his jaw and cheeks are some kind of lined tattoos.

No. Not tattoos.

As he gets closer, I realize these are *under* the skin, not on top. Something like veins, though they're as dark as crow feathers. A quick glimpse down confirms that the smooth, reaching lengths even wrap down his hands like coiled stems embedded into his skin.

I look between him and his commander.

Between the roots and the thorns.

It's not until the king reaches his guards that I realize I'm still standing. I drop down into the throne, but it's moot, because the bastard strides *up* the dais without pause, only stopping once he stands directly in front of me.

My soldiers stiffen, but his are still relaxed, not bothered at all. I, on the other hand, am seething.

Instead of me looking down on him, the opposite is true now.

Green eyes and a sickly-gray pallor bear down on me, and yet somehow, he's a vision of strength. "King Midas, I'd say it was a pleasure if I wanted to lie, but it seems I can't be bothered today."

I stand again so that I don't have to keep looking up, but the move only makes the prick smirk.

His crown is slightly tilted on his head, like he's put it on without a care. It's a ring of tangled branches, thorns like spires at the top. There's nothing regal or handsome about it. It's raw and rough and twisted, so much like his tainted power.

My eyes are flat, my tone even more so as I regard him. "You're late."

He glances around lazily. "Am I? Pity I kept you waiting."

The way he says it lets me know he doesn't think it's a pity at all.

"Shall we get started?" he asks, as if he has the right to take control and direct this meeting.

Without waiting for me to answer, he turns and strides confidently off the dais, toward the door at the back. All four of his guards follow him, while I blink, stupefied.

Odo appears in front of me, panting, like he ran all the way back here. "It seems King Ravinger has arrived and proceeded to the meeting room, Sire."

"Obviously," I snap.

Stalking for the door, I then cross the threshold while my advisors and guards quickly follow after me. One look around the space has my blood ready to boil.

Ravinger sits patiently at the head of the long table, his guards a wall of silent menace behind him.

It takes all of my practiced mannerisms not to snap at the audacity of this man. The tic in my jaw is the only slip-up that reveals my irritation.

Even so, somehow, the bastard sees it. As he relaxes back into his chair, a smirk curls his lips. It's a look that says, *your move*.

My advisors share a glance between them, but I move around to sit at the far end, the *other* head of the table. Damn it all to the Divines, I don't care if it does put twenty-four feet between us. I refuse to sit at his side like I'm lesser.

After I take a seat opposite him, my soldiers stand at the wall behind me, backs against the plum-colored wallpaper. The light is dimmer here, only a single window at my left, the panes covered with starburst frost.

As soon as I take my seat, I begin to speak, cutting off his chance to do so first. "It appears we have a problem, King Ravinger."

He dips his head. "On that, we can agree."

He's right—because we aren't likely to agree on much else.

"You sent rotted corpses to my borders."

That smirk comes back. "And which borders would those be? You seem to have accumulated more since last I knew."

I tap my finger on the armrest of my chair to keep myself calm.

"*My* borders at Sixth Kingdom, as you well know. I am simply acting monarch here until Fulke's heir can come of age."

His green eyes gleam. "Indeed."

I bristle at his tone, at his very lackadaisical demeanor.

Ravinger leans forward, the markings on his neck and face unnerving. For a moment, I think I see them move, just as the rotted fissures outside slithered across the ground when he was showing off his magic.

"If you're looking for a formal apology, you won't get one," he tells me. "They weren't even *your* soldiers, they were Fifth's. Yet I thought it best to deliver them, considering your alliance with this kingdom has been so vocal. I wouldn't want you to get the wrong idea, King Midas."

"And what idea would that be?"

"That I am someone you can cross." His statement lands bluntly, a strike of strength without even moving.

"And I'll remind you that I haven't crossed you. Sixth Kingdom has no qualms with Fourth."

Ravinger lifts a hand and glances around the room. "And yet, here we are, in Fifth, right at the center of a *qualm.*"

If I could only reach across the table and choke off his miserable throat, rot-filled veins be damned.

"King Fulke was dealt with," I say, not letting him ruffle me. "Unless you want to murder an innocent boy for his father's sins, Fifth Kingdom is no longer your enemy. It was a last-minute attack from an eccentric king who's now dead. I had nothing to do with it."

"I have reports that say otherwise."

All previous amusement is gone from his face in a blink. In its place, there's something dark. Deadly. I'm reminded in an instant of how powerful he really is, which is exactly what he wants.

Despite myself, I feel a chill raise the hairs at the back of my neck.

"Your reports are inaccurate," I reply steadily. I don't dare look away from his eyes, no matter how much I want to.

One mustn't look away from a predator.

"Are they."

Not a question. A demand. To prove it.

I hold my arms out, the calm gesture of a benevolent king. "Surely we can come to an agreement. I want no battle from you, King Ravinger."

"That's unfortunate, since my army is already poised and at the ready, and as you said, *you're* the acting ruler here." The unnatural lines on his face remind me of war paint, marks of aggression created from his malignant magic. "The fact is, Fifth's army attacked my border, and I do not let such offenses go unpunished."

My rising worry is sharp. I feel it like rigid corners that dig beneath my skin, threatening to pierce through.

I'm close. So close to securing my hold here. I can't afford this battle, because we would *lose*.

"Some would point out that there have been reports indicating you have been encroaching upon territories that are not your own. Perhaps that's why Fulke attacked. He was protecting his borders," I put in carefully.

Ravinger grins, but it's not a smile, not even close. It's a baring of teeth, and all that's missing is the snarl.

He leans forward. "Prove it."

I can tell his four soldiers are watching me, though I can't see their eyes through the slits in their helmets. I look at the thorned one, my eyes flicking over the sharp points on his armor. He looms, as dark and heavy as the rest, his presence meant to remind me of the army outside.

My eyes drag back to the king. "As I said, I want no battle with you."

"Then it seems we are at an impasse," Ravinger replies with a shrug, as if deciding to wage a battle is of little consequence.

But really...it *is* of little consequence to him. I've observed Fifth's soldiers. Ravinger's army will obliterate this kingdom. He wouldn't even have to use his power to do it.

"Surely we can think of something else, in order to spare innocent lives," I offer with a placating smile. "Reparation for the attack on your border, for instance."

Ravinger steeples his fingers together, watching me over the top. "I'm listening."

Finally.

I pretend to contemplate for a moment and then say, "Move your army back to your kingdom without attack, and I'll pay your reparation in gold."

Nothing.

I get nothing in return. No reaction, no excited glint in his eye. It doesn't even seem as if he's heard me.

Desperation crawls down my back. "Name the weight, Ravinger, and then we can be done with this business of war and you can return to your kingdom."

Still, he looks. Says nothing. Letting me sweat.

He is toying with me, intimidating me. Flaunting. Has been ever since he arrived.

He flaunted his army by bringing its might to Fifth Kingdom's doorstep. They don't even appear to be disgruntled or weakened, and they just marched across the Divine-damned Barrens.

And they went the *long* way. Came right up to the palace and bypassed the mountain pass where I'd had a contingent to head them off. Not to mention the fact that the soldiers I sent to infiltrate their camp and grab Auren never returned. I have a feeling they won't.

Ravinger didn't stop there. He then flaunted his magic in front of the city, letting rot spread through the ground as a warning, a threat to intimidate.

And again, since the moment he walked in the throne room and stepped up on the dais, and then chose the seat at the head of this table.

Flaunting. Because he can. Because he's an arrogant bastard.

My impatience plucks at my tongue. "Well? How much, Ravinger?"

"None."

I lean back against the chair in shock. "What do you mean, *none*?"

Surely, I misheard him. Gold is what everyone wants. It's the *only* thing that everyone wants.

"I mean what I said," he replies evenly. "I don't want your gold."

I'm at a loss, and I have a creeping suspicion that he's steered this whole conversation from the very start.

"What do you want then." It's my turn to demand now, my tone unable to pretend otherwise. He's frayed my countenance like splitting hairs.

"I want Deadwell."

My brows pull together a second later as my mind creates a map in my head. "Deadwell? The strip of land at the edge of Fifth?"

He tips his chin. "The very one."

I look at him suspiciously. "Why?"

"As you said, there have been rumors that I have... encroached on territories outside of my own," he says, shoulders back and proud, tone unwavering. "To appease such rumors and to pay restitution for Fifth's unprovoked attack on my border, I will now *take* that border, which, as acting ruler, you will give me as *your* sign of good faith."

A pause.

Ravinger leans in, and an ominous feeling leans with him, like a brittle tree being blown by the wind. "Otherwise, my army attacks by nightfall."

I regard him. He regards me.

Thoughts and questions come up one after another.

He wants Deadwell.

But *why* does he want Deadwell? I rack my mind, trying to recollect what's there, but I'm not as familiar with Fifth Kingdom as I am Sixth. Still...I'm fairly certain that it's just a strip of land between his kingdom and this one, with nothing there except ice.

He'd rather have *that* than his weight in gold? I can't make heads or tails of it, because I know there's a catch. There must be.

It's on the tip of my tongue to ask him why he wants it, but that's not how these games are played. We say what we want, without saying what we *actually* want.

"Deadwell," I repeat, an edge of question in my tone.

Ravinger inclines his head again. "Sign Deadwell over to me, King Midas, and my army leaves."

I narrow my eyes. "Just like that?"

He gives me a benign look. "My army has been traveling for weeks. Surely, you'll extend an invitation to me and my soldiers in your newly acquired city so that they may rest and celebrate the avoidance of a war."

My mouth presses into a firm line. Like hell do I want them in Ranhold. "I do not think—"

He cuts me off. "Of course, you'll already be hosting another kingdom in a few weeks' time, won't you? I'm sure you can see the advantages of having not just one kingdom, but two, to join in your celebrations."

I go still.

Behind me, I feel my advisors tense, no further scratch of quill against paper.

How the *hell* did he find out about Third Kingdom's traveling party?

I grin through gritted teeth. "Of course. You and

your army are more than welcome to rest and replenish yourselves."

Ravinger grins, the polished teeth of an animal used to chewing on those he defeats.

The chill down my spine is all the confirmation I need. I may have prevented his army from attacking Ranhold, but while I bent to his whim to get them to stay *out*, I think I may have invited the true threat *in*.

CHAPTER 40

AUREN

G *old.*

Such a heavy, heavy word.

Some people hear it and think of wealth. Others, a color. Someone else, perfection.

But for me, gold is my identity. Has been, ever since I took my first breath.

I remember my parents saying I shone with the warmth of light. I remember them calling me their little sun.

I wonder what they would think of me now— locked in a windowless room and surrounded by ice, stuck in a world that seems determined to keep me from rising.

As I pace in the room, I keep seeing the statue from the corner of my eye—the woman who's now stuck in an agonized wince. Her mouth doesn't need to emit any sound for me to hear her screaming.

Will that be me one day? Will the gold consume me, suffocate me, just as it did in my dream?

My eyes prickle, like the barbed edge of a leaf. I wonder how different things would've been, only *if*.

If my body had never glimmered with the shine of a little sun.

If gold-touch magic had never dripped from my hands.

If ribbons had never sprouted from my back.

If I'd never met Midas.

But all of those things *did* happen, and here I am. In the dark space of an ex-dressing room, now-cage room. My ribbons drag on the floor behind me with every step I take, and outside the door, guards are standing watch.

Bright side? I don't fucking know.

My eyes fall to my bare palm, to the gold that's caked to it like dried blood. It still drips, a spigot left to dribble. I hold the weight of wealth in my hands, and it's so damn heavy to carry.

This power—this magic that the goddesses bestowed upon me, it has cost me everything. And apparently, it wasn't enough that I was born gold to be gawked at, because then, when I turned fifteen, it started to stream from my fingers and turn me into a murderer, while ribbons sprouted from my back like a monster.

I wish there was a window so I could rage. Rage at the stars hiding behind the light of the sun.

Instead, I rage at the heavy locked door.

Storming over to it, my fists pummel the wood, making splotches of gold drip into the grains before it begins to spread.

"Let me out!" I yell, teeth bared and ready to bite.

He will *not* trap me in here like an animal. I won't let him do this to me. I will not spend the rest of my days waiting for scraps to be tossed my way.

My gold-touch magic, my ribbons, my own damn *thoughts*, I've tried to hide them all. Been ashamed of them. Been ashamed of *me*, and he nurtured that shame, though I was too blind to see it.

I sat and I smiled, withering beneath the gild. Played pretty music as I stayed locked in my birdcage and accepted when I should have fought.

And Midas...

He gave me feathered kisses and spoke sweet words, and it isn't enough. Who I've allowed myself to become isn't enough.

Rip was right.

A veil has been lifted—a veil I put there, over my own eyes. Now it's ripped away, and I can see everything more clearly.

I've made many choices in my life, and for the last decade, all of them have been for Midas. But like Lu said, it's time to own my shit.

It's time to start choosing *me*.

I had one chance, one person who could've helped me, but I fumbled that when I turned Rip down. So I need a plan. I need to figure out what I'm going to do. No more hiding from the world while I stand on Midas's pedestal.

I grip the handle of the door in my bare hand, my magic swallowing it until it gleams. I yank hard, as if I can get the lock to come free, but of course it doesn't.

"Let me out!" I scream again, but Midas's guards ignore me.

My ribbons snap up like snakes rising in a pose to strike. With fury taking over, I send them lashing at the door as I continue to pound my fists against it.

Some of the strips wrap around the handle, some start slicing into the hinges, while the rest hack at the door like an axe to kindling, because I can't give up, can't give in.

My ribbons are tired though, overwrought. They aren't acclimated to being used so much. But I push them, ignoring my screaming muscles and the mental effort it takes to control them.

They broke the door to my cage, and they can break down the door to this room too. They *have* to.

Panic makes a sob tear from my throat as I scream at the door for not budging, scream at me for not being stronger.

I hear the voices of the guards as my efforts grow louder and louder, but I stupidly didn't put a stopper on my gold-touch. With my rage too consuming, I've gilded the whole damn door, and the exclamations of surprise tell me that it's gleaming on the guards' side too.

I slap my palm against it, fuming.

My ribbons could probably hack through wood, but not through solid gold.

"Shit," I curse, furious at myself, at Midas for locking me in here in the first place.

"Stay inside and back away from the door, miss," one of the guards orders.

My head snaps up. "Fuck you!" I shout back.

In a moment of clarity, I send a ribbon squeezing beneath the small slit at the bottom of the door. I crouch down to give it plenty of length, and I hear a guard shout in surprise.

I close my eyes in concentration while my ribbon reaches for the handle on the other side, searching for a flip lock. But my hopes are dashed when all I find is a keyhole too small for my ribbon to squeeze into.

Someone tries to grab hold of it, so I yank my ribbon back beneath the door and onto my side again for fear of them trying to pin it in place.

Chest heaving, I glare at the door as if it's my nemesis.

My ribbons quiver like overworked muscles, and I yell out another curse of frustration as I whirl around and search for something, anything, to help me get the hell *out*.

I stalk into the cage, determined to look through it to see if my dead decoy had anything in there that might help. I have no idea what that might be, but I can't just do nothing. I have to try.

Because I meant what I said. I won't live like this anymore.

I start searching the cage with manic desperation, while gold continues to drop from my bare palm like a steadily bleeding vein.

Just as I'm tossing aside the mattress to see if the woman hid anything beneath it, I feel it—the change in the sky. I don't need a window to know that night has just fallen, because my prickling skin is proof.

The sun flees, and my gold-touch magic flees with it.

"Dammit!" I shout, kicking at a tray of food at my feet. My power is gone, sapped, the last of the gold curdling against my palm as the incessant drip goes suddenly dry. I curl my hand, not wanting to watch the metallic sheen soak into my skin.

At least with my gold-touch, I'm a walking weapon. But now, I'm just an irate woman with strength-sapped ribbons and no way out.

I really, really hate the goddesses.

My legs threaten to give out, either from the weight of my fury or because of my depleting strength as my power gets stripped out of me, dormant for the night.

My ribbons manage to catch me, but they're struggling too. I stumble forward, clutching the bars of the cage. I'm a mess of tangled hair and shaking ribbons, but my fury for Midas's betrayal keeps me standing.

Just as I'm about to force myself to bang on the

door again, something else changes in the air. Something heavier, darker, more ominous than night.

It's subtle at first, like an inhale, a hum. The fluttering of lashes against a cold cheek, the strike of a match right before it catches.

Then, there's a sudden shout outside my door.

I hear more exclamations of surprise, cursing, yelling, the guards sounding confused and authoritative at first—but it changes into something more like desperate begging. There's the unmistakable noise of swords being yanked from their hilts and running footsteps, but it's all followed by a series of ominous *thumps*.

And then...nothing.

No sounds at all.

My heart races and my stomach roils, while fear squeezes me in its nefarious grasp.

Then, the doorknob jiggles. Just once. Like someone tested to see if it was locked. A second later, I see the handle fall away completely, disintegrated into grains of golden sand.

I tense as the door swings open, and a silhouette appears in the threshold like a demon stepping out of hell.

The dim light of the room shouldn't be enough for me to recognize who it is, but I know. I think even in the pitch black, I'd know.

Because I can feel it.

Just like when I was on that hill, his power seems to travel from the ground and soak into my feet. Another wave of nausea roils through me, making my fingers curl tighter around the bars as King Ravinger himself steps into the room.

All the air in my lungs dissolves like that doorknob did, and my body freezes in fear. He steps in almost boredly, without even squinting in the dim light, as if his eyes don't need to adjust to the dark.

Maybe that's because darkness lurks within him already.

Walking forward, he scans the room methodically. He's wearing neat black leathers with a high collar shirt, and a barbed crown of branches sits proudly on his head. They look withered, petrified, like they died long ago and then hardened in a molded polish.

He stops in the shadows, a few feet away from my cage, but I don't need him closer to see how his gaze hooks onto me.

His are deep green eyes, like rich moss right before it's about to turn brown. Life, right before death. Richness, right before rot.

But it's the markings on his face that I can't stop staring at. They rise out of his collar, trailing up his neck, curling over his jaw, like roots searching for soil. Like veins come loose from a poisoned heart.

As I watch, they move, curling and writhing, like something sinister is contained in those insidious markings.

He stands there, and my eyes warily look at the door-way, but no guards are gathered there. It's as silent and heavy as death.

"Did you kill them?" I ask through labored breaths.

He gives me a shrug of his proud, unbothered shoulder. "They were in my way."

My heart falls in fear. He killed all of them within *seconds*.

"Do you know who I am?" he asks, his voice a low rumble that makes me shake.

I swallow hard. "King Ravinger."

He hums, and my mind races with why he's here, why he's come. I thought I'd escaped him, but I should've known that trade-off was too simple, too easy.

He doesn't seem at all nervous that King Midas might find him here. In fact, I suspect he'd welcome an excuse for the confrontation.

The firelight bathes his crown in vibrant orange, like autumn to a leaf. His black hair is somewhat creased, while a shadow clings to the jaw of his slightly gray-toned face. He's younger than I thought he would be, but no less terrifying.

"So, this is where King Midas keeps his famous gold-touched favored." Even with the dark distance between us, I see him studying me from bottom to top. "You really do look like a caged Goldfinch. Shame. You don't belong in there at all."

Eyes widening, my heart pounds in my chest, thrumming with a sharp hurt. Rip told him. Rip told his king his nickname for me. And the way Ravinger repeated it makes it sound crude, almost mocking.

Is that what Rip did? Mock me when he spoke to his king?

Too much emotion rises up inside of me, making me want to scream again.

I find myself straightening up and tearing off my feather coat in a blink. I step out of the cage and throw it at him through the broken doorway. "There. You can give that to Rip," I say with a sneer as soon as his hand shoots out to catch it. "Tell him I'm not his little Goldfinch that he can mock behind my back."

His eyes look down at the feathers, and just then, I realize my mistake.

Shit.

I freeze, hoping maybe he won't notice.

After a moment, his hands still, and then Ravinger lifts the coat up with the pinch of his fingers. The light of the lantern makes it shimmer, and my hope plummets right through my toes.

"Now, *this* is interesting, isn't it?" he purrs.

I feel the blood drain from my face as he turns the coat inside out, revealing the truth within.

Lined throughout the inside, a gold glint shines.

A nefarious smile spreads over his face as he looks back at me, but then he laughs, and that's so much worse. His haunting, gravelly chuckle boasts from his lips and seems to rope around me, holding me captive.

"I must admit, I'm not often surprised," he muses,

rubbing the hidden gold fabric. "But *this* surprises me."

His fingertips brush over the wayward feathers along the wrists and hood where I'd accidentally gilded them with my skin. It was incredibly difficult to stop the spread, but at least I managed that much. Though, what good is that now when I've just tossed my secret at his face?

Ravinger's attention flickers over the room again, as if he's seeing it in a new light. He lingers on the woman's statue behind me. "Midas is far more devious than I suspected. And so are you."

It sounds like that actually excites him.

"What do you want?" I ask as I edge for the door. I don't care if his power can kill me in seconds, I'll try to make a run for it anyway.

He grins at me from the shadows as I step sideways, but he can mock me all he wants, I know better than to turn my back on him.

"Now *that's* the question, isn't it?" he asks, and his *voice*...

His attention flicks down to my wayward ribbons and skims over their crumpled, tired lengths. Just his look makes them shiver, a timid tremble that I feel against the skin of my back.

"It all makes so much more sense now. Why he keeps you. Why your skin is truly gold. Why you're trapped with him." Ravinger glances down at the broken cage door lying on the floor. "But perhaps...not as trapped as one might believe."

His power becomes cloying again all of a sudden, like it's reaching out in invisible tendrils and trying to latch onto my own, trying to get a feel of what lurks inside of me. Sweat breaks out against my brow, my stomach flipping, and I take another two steps toward the door.

If I can just get there. If I can just get through—

Another wave of sickness makes me nearly stumble. "Stop," I pant. I feel like I'm a second from vomiting all over the floor.

Immediately, his power recedes, and with it, those dark lines on his face grow, like a flash flood of rivers unleashing, nearly reaching the sharp planes of his cheeks.

"You should probably get used to that," he says, amusement evident in the deep timbre of his voice as he watches me sweat and shake. "Can't have you getting sick every time I come into the room."

"Why?" I ask nervously, squinting toward his dark shrouded body. I don't know what would be scarier, for him to stay hidden in the shadows as he is, or if he were to step into the light so I could see him more clearly.

"We're going to be around each other for a while."

Chills rush down both arms, and I stop my retreat. Is he stealing me? Is he going to use me worse than Midas did?

"What are you talking about?" I ask, fear breaking

my voice. I take the last few steps to the threshold, feeling a surge of victory when my fingers close around the doorframe. I turn, keeping my back to Midas's room and my eyes on him, the predator who can pounce at any moment.

"Oh, Midas hasn't told you yet?" he says smoothly, not moving from his place. "We've negotiated peace, and he's also hosting a celebration. Fourth has been invited to stay and attend."

All at once, a dozen thoughts hit me.

I swallow down a lump of hope in my throat as I shove damp hair off my face. "Your commander? Is he staying?" I blurt, though I immediately want to kick myself for letting my interest slip.

If there's no war, if Rip is staying here...

I need an ally if I have any hope of getting away.

Ravinger chuckles, and the rasp abrades my ears, like the splintered wood of a rotten log. "Oh Goldfinch, I asked you before if you knew who I was."

My foot hesitates from its move to back up, my brows pulling together in a frown of confusion even as my heart pounds, warning me to flee. "What?"

Without warning, his power suddenly pulses out again and tightens like a fist, yanking a noose around my stomach. This time, it's different, a surge instead of a reach.

I gulp out strangled air and double over, a cold sweat immediately drenching my skin as I breathe through my nose, trying not to be sick, trying not to fall.

My shaky hands grip the doorframe hard as I try to stay upright. My tired ribbons wince, curling up behind me and diving beneath my dress like they can hide from his magic.

Dizziness overtakes me with a hot flush as I lean against the wall, but right before I'm about to be sick, the power suddenly dissolves, like salt in a sea.

Panting, I look up, and right before my eyes, the reaching roots over Ravinger's face recede.

He walks toward me, no longer half-hidden in the shadows.

As the veins fade away, his green eyes shutter, like his irises are soaking up all that black, putrid power.

His entire body shudders, and my eyes go wide with shock as his face changes, sharpens.

I'm stuck in place, unable to breathe, unable to even *blink* as the bones of his face taper like the edge of a blade. His ears pinch to a point at the top just as scales appear on chiseled cheeks.

"Great Divine..." Shock is infused with my tone, holding it under, suffocating me with the weight of realization.

Spikes stab through his arms and shoot from his spine. He unfurls, the wild, wicked fae, transitioning until all that's left of his horrible power is the viscid press of a very familiar dark aura.

"You're...you're..." My tongue goes thick, catching

up with the sheen in my eyes while the betrayal, heavy and solid, sinks into the depths of my soul.

Rip rolls his shoulders, as if his metamorphosis from rotted king to monstrous fae was painful. Though I can guarantee it wasn't nearly as painful to him as it was to me.

The blacks of his irises that seem to have swallowed the power are the only indication of the foul magic lurking within.

That *voice*. Deeper, crueler than usual, but with a timbre of familiarity. I should've known. I should have damn well figured it out.

He takes one more step, and then he's so close that I can feel the fiery temperature of his blackened soul, taste the press of spiced air as it passes from his lips.

He's Rip and he's Rot. He's the fae and the king.

I swear, I feel a knife to my back all over again. But this time, it's from a different betrayal, from a different man.

And I *do* feel betrayed. He tricked me. Confused me with a kiss and lied about who he really is. Maybe that's unfair, considering I've lied too, but I can't help feeling like he played me.

"You're King Ravinger," I breathe in hurt accusation, because it's the only thought clanging through my bones and shrieking in my skull.

Rip's mouth slowly pulls into a grin, and he speaks with the dark, sensual stroke of a villainous purr that matches the glint in his eye. "Yes, Goldfinch, I am. But you can call me Slade."

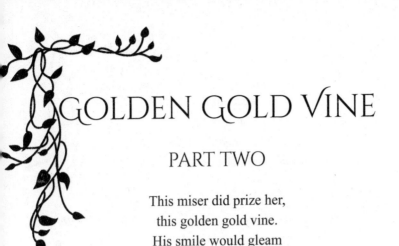

GOLDEN GOLD VINE

PART TWO

This miser did prize her,
this golden gold vine.
His smile would gleam
at all of her shine.

He gave her his all,
so she'd answer his call.
Rejoiced every inch
that her length grew up tall.

But soon she outgrew
his garden, until,
she then made her way
into his house on the hill.

She twisted and curled
in every inch.
No room to move,
he was prodded and pinched.

He shoved out his furniture
to be left in the rain,
abandoned front door,
knocked out window panes.

Every offering he made,
she grew larger still.
Her metallic glint covered
each floorboard and sill.

This miser hoarded
every petal and thorn.
Skin marred with scratches
where sharp barbs had torn.

When his hair was all gone,
but he still wanted more,
he gave up his nails,
taking them, peel from core.
He presented them all,
onto stems he did pour.
Not once did he ask,
what's it all for?

Her flowers, so pretty,
grew heavy with gold.
Though his fingers too sore
to take them to hold.
So he split them away
by the work of his teeth.
Bit them from vine
and hid them in sheaths.

All gathered, so heavy,
hundreds of blooms.
All golden, these flowers,
but he ran out of room.

The old miser didn't dare
ever take some to town.
If they knew of his treasure,
they'd surely come 'round.
So spend them he never,
and stayed home forever.
Loved ones he severed,
(he thought himself clever.)

He murmured and pet,
each golden rosette.
Her vine he let twine,
all while whispering, "mine."

But without reparation,
she'd quickly go dim,
so frantic, he'd cut,
blade into limb.
When his nails were all gone,
from ten fingers and toes,
he had to give up
his ears and his nose.

The blood that he spilt,
he staunched with petals of guilt.
But the drips of his red
made the vine rightly fed.

This miser bled freely
so his wealth may yet grow.
He let veins collapse,
let his heartbeat go slow.

Her vine slurped his life
like nectar to birds,
and he lay in the room,
his body submerged.

While she grew out of the house
and over the hill,
a contagion that caught
every space up to fill.

But he wanted still,
he had to have more,
so out plucked his eyes,
sockets empty and sore.

He had no room to sleep,
and no eyes to weep,
but from this golden gold vine,
ever more would he seek.

TO BE CONTINUED...

Acknowledgments

This is my dream job. After two years, I still can't believe I get to do this and that people actually read my books. But even dreams can become heavy, and I absolutely would not be able to continue doing this if it weren't for the people who help me carry the load.

So, to my family, thank you forever. Your love and support is the core of my drive, and I'm grateful to you all. You're also just the best people on the planet, and I'm blessed to have you in my life. Whether we're squished together on the couch or states apart, just know that I love you.

To my book family, this can be such a lonely business sometimes, and I'm lucky to have found my squad. I'm forever indebted to your help and I'm damn thankful that I know such funny, kind, and gracious people. Ivy Asher, Ann Denton, S.A. Parker, C.R. Jane, Helayna Trask, and my favorite sister, thank you for helping me with this book and for all your insight. You make me better.

To the readers, my heart is so full. This series means a lot to me and it's probably my favorite thing I've ever written to date. So the fact that you've taken a chance on it means a lot to me. And, as an indie author without the support of a publishing house, all of my success comes down to you. Every time you write a review, recommend me, post about my books, every damn page you read of mine…it matters. Thank you so much.

—RK

Raven Kennedy

About The Author

Raven Kennedy is a California girl born and raised, whose love for books pushed her into creating her own worlds.

Her debut series was a romcom fantasy about a cupid looking for love. She has since gone on to write in a range of genres, including the adult dark fantasy romance: *The Plated Prisoner Series*, which has become a #1 international bestseller with over two million books sold worldwide.

Whether she makes you laugh or cry, or whether the series is about a cupid or a gold-touched woman in a castle, she hopes to create characters that readers can root for.

When Raven isn't writing, she's reading or spending time with her husband and daughters.

You can connect with Raven on her social media, and visit her website: ravenkennedybooks.com